Scorn of the Sky Goddess
Keepers of the Stones, Book Three
Tara West

Scorn of the Sky Goddess

With the balance of power shifting, the young witch Dianna must destroy the Sky Goddess, Madhea, before the world turns into a frozen tomb. First, she'll need to convince the Ice People to give her their goddess stones, making them vulnerable to Madhea's wrath. Next, she must confront an army of dwarves and giants to retrieve the final and most powerful stone. Only then will her magic be strong enough to take on the Sky Goddess. But even with all the stones, she can't fight Madhea alone. Forced to rely on the two men competing for her love, she has to convince her rivals to work together while ignoring her pining heart.

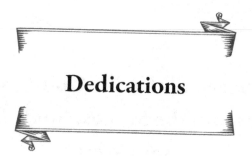

Dedications

Theo, God of Grammar, blessed by the Elements with the magic of the red pen, you rock!

Ginelle and Suanne, thanks so much for your valuable feedback. You've helped make this book so much better.

Bob, another amazing cover! You've captured Dianna and Tan'yi'na perfectly!

To my husband, thanks for reading my books, giving me archery feedback, and having faith in me. Your support means more than anything.

Foreword

"Wise and beautiful goddess, thank you for sparing my life." Kneeling before the Sky Goddess, Rowlen couldn't believe he'd ascended to the top of Madhea's impenetrable Ice Mountain, which would've been an impossible task if it hadn't been for the pixies. He'd briefly wondered why the reclusive goddess had sent them to help him. Was it compassion or curiosity? Either way, he thanked the Elements for this opportunity.

The deity's wings fluttered as she leaned forward on her throne carved of jagged ice columns that resembled menacing dragon fangs. Steepling her fingers, she regarded Rowlen for a long moment, a cascade of pale hair falling over her shoulder, her green eyes shining like twin gems against skin as white as snow.

Rowlen couldn't help but be captivated by her beauty. She was far prettier than any human woman he'd ever seen, even more so than his fair wife. Thoughts of her sweet smile and red-rimmed eyes just before he'd set out on his quest filled his heart with shame, that he would admire the beauty of another.

Madhea's wings slapped the back of her throne as she crossed one leg over the other. "What is your name?"

Keeping his head bent, he peered up at her. "Rowlen, My Deity. Rowlen Jägerrson." He felt like a thick strip of venison as her gaze raked his body. Why was she looking at him so?

"You are bigger than most mortals." The deity shifted again, licking her bottom lip. "Why did you try to scale my mountain? Did my sister send you to kill me?"

"Nay, My Deity." He vehemently shook his head, shifting weight from one sore knee to the other. "I have come to plead for your help. My son is very ill."

She stiffened, her eyes narrowing. "You have a wife?"

"Aye, and a young son. He can scarcely draw breath." He fought to keep the pleading note out of his voice, knowing from tales of old that the goddess had little compassion for human weakness.

She leaned back, carefully examining her smooth fingernails. "And what do you expect me to do about it?"

"You are our only hope. Please show my child mercy. He is barely two winters old and such a sweet boy." His voice cracked as the memory of Alec's pitiful whimpers resonated in his mind. He cursed his foolish emotions, biting down on his knuckles to keep from crying out.

"So you want me to heal him?"

"Please, My Deity," he begged, a tremor involuntarily rattling his chest. He sucked in a sharp breath as he awaited her answer, feeling like a hapless climber in that space between the crack of the mountain and the avalanche that ensued.

She regarded him with eyes as cold as a serpent's. "And what will you do for me in return?"

"I will build a shrine in your honor and pay homage to you the rest of my life." Though he meant what he said, he feared this wouldn't be enough.

"You should be honoring me anyway." She waved with a disinterested flick and draped one leg over the armrest of her throne. "If I save your boy, every mortal with a sick child will be clawing at my mountain."

He wanted to tell the cold-hearted ice shrew that as the people's goddess, she should be helping them, but he bit his tongue, forcing back words he knew would bring Madhea's wrath upon his head.

"I will tell no one. You have my word." He placed a hand on his heart. "What would you have me do, My Deity? I will do anything for my boy."

One pale brow arched, and her lip curled up in a feral smile. "Anything?"

Rowlen's heart hit his stomach when he realized he'd just placed his fate in the hands of a madwoman. Elements save him.

ROWLEN HURRIED ACROSS the thick rugs of Madhea's bedchamber, pulling his tunic over his head. As he slipped on a vest, he cringed at the shrill scream that echoed off the walls, the sound licking at his heels like dragon flames.

The Sky Goddess advanced behind him, her toenails scraping the ice floor as she wrapped a white robe around her lithe body. "Must I beg you to stay, Rowlen? Is that what you wish? To bring a goddess to her knees?"

"Nay." He spun around, heat flaming his face when he recalled the feel of Madhea's cool flesh beneath him. Though he purposely avoided making eye contact, he saw that her once smooth hair resembled a bird's nest, unkempt and wild. He hated himself even more. How he wished he could take back that night. The memory of his adultery would haunt him forever. "I wish you to let me go." He still had a wife and child, though he deserved neither of them.

She crossed her arms, pouting like a child, her wings angrily buzzing like a swarm of hornets. "What does your mortal wife have that I do not?"

He stifled a groan, doing his best to keep a straight face. "I have already broken one vow to my wife. I will not break another. I have honored our agreement. You had me for one night." He held out a shaky hand. "Now please honor your blood oath and give me the potion."

The goddess's cheeks colored to a deep crimson as she fell upon an ivory dresser covered with glass bottles. With a roar, she swept all but one of them to the floor. They shattered in a cacophony of light and smoke. She grabbed the remaining bottle and flew at Rowlen with such speed, he braced for impact.

"Take it!" She threw it at him, laughing when it bounced off his chest. She screeched when he caught it and deftly slipped the delicate vial in his pocket.

He didn't wait for the ice shrew's next action. He grabbed his fur cape off a nearby chair and hurried out the door.

He didn't know if he should have felt relief or worry when he saw one of Madhea's magical daughters waiting for him.

She held out a hand, her eyes wide with fright. "The Elementals are waiting. Come. You must hurry."

He took her hand and raced alongside her as she fluttered through a maze of ice halls. He was nearly out of breath by the time they'd reached the coven of sisters. They stood along the cavern's ledge, a swarm of pixies flying above them. He saw nothing of the outside, for a thick mist of clouds obscured his vision. An icy wind blew into the cave, burning his face and neck. He pulled his fur hat tightly over his head, steeling himself for the descent. He felt the vial in his pocket, relieved to find it still intact.

"I'm afraid this potion will not heal my son. I fear your mother has gone back on her word," he said to the girls, not knowing who was who, for they all looked too much like Madhea.

One of the sisters fluttered forward. "She can't. She made a blood oath, but that doesn't mean she won't seek revenge. You should never have come."

He shrank back when Madhea's violent scream echoed through the cavern. "What was I to do? Let my son die?"

"Yes," the girl said. "The Elements would have been far more merciful than my mother."

Fear numbed his limbs, and his heart thudded heavily against his ribs. "What do you mean? What will she do to him?"

Another sister cast a furtive glance over her shoulder. "Do not worry about your son. It is your own soul you must fear for."

He stiffened. He already knew his soul had been lost the moment Madhea had tumbled into his arms. "She can do her worst. I care not for myself so long as my son is safe."

Madhea swooped toward him. "You may live to regret those words."

Rowlen sucked in a hiss. Before he could shield himself, she struck him hard in the chest with a bolt of green light.

The air around him electrified as he struggled against an invisible bond that squeezed his chest like a vice. He pounded on a translucent barrier that resembled frosted glass. Madhea hovered above him, laughing and ignoring her daughters' cries for mercy.

Her shrill voice echoed around him and through him, penetrating the very marrow of his bones. When she pierced him with cold green eyes, he was paralyzed with terror. She spun around him like a cyclone.

"Elements of flame and fury
Show this man no mercy
Crush his heart to dust
Wither his soul to bones and rust
Elements of ice and fire

Grant me this desire

That Rowlen may only know hatred and pain

When he looks upon his son again"

The barrier disappeared in a puff of smoke. He reached for his boning knife. Before he could plunge it into Madhea's chest, the pixies swarmed him, their little claws digging into his clothes and exposed flesh. He tried swatting them away, but they only dug deeper. They lifted him off his feet and carried him down the mountain so fast, he thought he was falling. The goddess's ugly cries punctured the thick air around them.

As he spiraled faster, the echo of Madhea's screams faded. When the clouds broke, he saw the smoke from his family's hearth, rising beneath his feet. What would he say to his wife? A hard shell formed around his heart. Why had he risked his soul and sanity for one sick child? Damn the boy for ruining his life!

"MOTHER, DO YOU WISH to hold your daughter?" Kia sat beside Madhea on her bed of soft furs, cradling the crimson-faced infant in her arms. The child fussed and squealed, waving her arms like an impatient pixie.

Madhea scowled at the babe before turning up her nose. "No."

Why had her Elemental daughters brought her Rowlen's child, other than to taunt her? Despite being born of a goddess, the infant had absolutely no magic. Even worse, she had thick black curls, too reminiscent of Rowlen.

"Well, will you at least pick a name for her?" Ariette sat beside Kia, cooing at the babe and stroking her chin.

"I already told you her name," Madhea said curtly, her patience wearing thin.

"But Jae is a cruel name." Ariette's hand flew to her throat, her dazzling green eyes muting to a soft heather. "It means 'without light' in Elemental tongue."

"I know perfectly well what it means. Why do you think I picked it?" Madhea turned up her nose at her daughters, despising them for their beautiful, youthful faces, like hers had been before she'd used dark magic to curse Rowlen. Now her skin was wrinkled and her hair a scraggly gray, like that of an old woman. No wonder her babe had come out lacking magic. Madhea felt her magic slowly slipping away, too, flowing from her fingertips like melting ice.

"Come, Mother." Kia tried to thrust the babe into Madhea's arms. "You can't deny your child."

"She has no magic." Madhea pushed the offending infant away.

"No." Kia frowned. "But my sister will be special in her own way."

Special? Was that what her daughters called weak and infirm mortals? Though Madhea's Elemental daughters looked like her and had powerful magic, that was where their similarities ended, for their hearts were as soft as runny porridge. They were weak and useless goddesses, and Madhea wondered more than once why she'd kept their Council.

"She will die a mortal death." Madhea scooted away from the child. "She will leave me, just like her father." How she hated herself for sending her pixies after Rowlen. She should have let him perish trying to reach her, but she'd been so taken by his broad shoulders and dark eyes.

Ariette's wings drooped. "What should we do with her then?"

The censure in their eyes made her chest swell with fury. "Feed her to the pixies for all I care." She waved them away.

The babe's cries intensified.

"Mother! We're not feeding an innocent to the pixies." Kia clutched the babe to her chest.

"Come, sister." Ariette placed a hand on Kia's arm. "We will take care of her. Do not cry. I'm sure Mother's heart will change."

Kia and Ariette quickly fluttered out of the bedchamber, and Madhea heard Kia whisper to her sister, "Our mother has no heart."

Their censure shouldn't have bothered her. After all, she had heard worse from her children. Still, she couldn't help but resent her daughters for thrusting a mortal babe upon her bosom. Most of all, she resented the babe for being born.

"GIRLS, GIRLS, COME quick!" Madhea's cries echoed through the icy cavern. Eighteen long years it had been since the birth of the child she'd conceived with Rowlen. Far too long for her to have been fooled by her deceptive Elemental daughters. Now they would pay for their treachery.

Her six daughters fluttered into the cavern, not knowing they were flying into a trap. Once they were in the center of the stone circle, Madhea blasted the seventh stone into place, sealing their prison. She hit the pyres with a bolt, lighting the tops of the stones with a ring of impenetrable fire. She fluttered to the top of the cavern, smiling.

"Mother," Ariette screeched, jumping into the air only to be struck down by the invisible magic barrier. "What have you done?"

Madhea's lips twisted as she repressed the emotion that welled in her throat. She would not take pity on them, not after their betrayal. "No, deceitful daughters, what have *you* done?"

Kia jumped next, her head smacking against the magical barrier. She fluttered to the ground like an ember cast from the fire, landing in her sisters' arms with a groan.

"We're trapped!" Ariette said to her sisters. "This is a heptacircle."

Madhea's wings angrily buzzed as she jutted a finger at her daughters. "Do you know what my swirling mists revealed to me? The missing ice dragon you said was still buried under an avalanche was flying across the ocean with a witch girl on her back. Who is this witch, daughters, for she looks far too familiar?"

Ariette turned up her chin, her shoulders and wings stiffening like blocks of ice. "She is Dianna, our sister."

Magic crackled in her palms as she fought the urge to strike her daughters down. "And Jae was—"

"The mortal child we traded Dianna with at birth." Ariette didn't even blink. Her sisters cowered behind her like whimpering mongrels. Ariette had always been the most powerful and persuasive of her daughters.

Madhea suspected they were secretly plotting to overthrow her and install Ariette as the new goddess. "Why?"

Ariette crossed her arms, leveling Madhea with a challenging glare. "Because we knew you'd use Dianna's powers for evil."

The insolent shrews! How dare they trick her with a weak mortal babe and deny Madhea the right to raise her child! "Why has she taken my dragon?"

Lydra's disappearance was most troubling. Her ice dragon had served her for over a thousand years. Not even the Elementals could control the beast, and yet this half-mortal girl was able to ride astride the dragon's back?

Ariette shared a knowing look with her sisters before turning back to Madhea. "To stop you from setting Lydra on innocents."

Madhea could perish, thanks to them. Red hot anger blurred her vision. "The swirling mists showed me Dianna has defeated my sister. How do you suppose a half-mortal witch defeated Eris, a powerful goddess?"

Though her other daughters averted their gazes, Ariette looked her in the eye. "She must have a goddess stone."

After the boy hunter had deflected her bolt, nearly killing her, Madhea knew he had to have used a stone. Had he given it to his sister? Her wings faltered, then angrily buzzed. "Indeed. The stone her brother used to deflect my magic—unless, of course, they have discovered more than one stone."

When Ariette broke eye contact for a half a breath, Madhea knew Dianna had more than one stone. What other secrets were they keeping from her?

She floated down, impatiently tapping her foot on the invisible barrier above their heads. "Who do you think she'll destroy next?"

"You, Mother," Ariette snapped.

"That's right. Me." She fought to keep emotion out of her voice, the sting of her children's betrayal burning her all over. "All because her deceitful sisters turned her against me."

"Mother." Ariette splayed her arms wide, trembling as she craned her neck toward Madhea. "We can negotiate a truce with Dianna."

Her heart lurched when a tear slipped down Ariette's face. Her sisters sank down behind her, softly sobbing into each other's arms. Madhea suspected they weren't crying because they felt remorse at betraying their mother. No, they cried because they feared a slow and painful death.

"And why should I trust you now?" she taunted in a sing-song voice.

Ariette fell to her knees, clasping her hands in prayer. "Please, Mother," she sobbed. "Dianna will listen to us."

Madhea flapped backward, scowling at them one last time. "Such a pity you'll all be dead by the time she gets here."

Ariette jumped to her feet, rushing the barrier. "Mother, no!" She pounded the stone wall while her sisters wailed.

Madhea covered her ears as she flew away, blasting the entrance behind her. She couldn't bear listening to their cries another moment. Though they deserved nothing less than death for betraying her, her mother's heart ached to free them. Her life had been empty and dull until the Elements had pollinated her womb, and she'd birthed six beautiful daughters, all created in her image. Her life would be dull once more unless... no, 'twas a fool's hope that Dianna would harbor anything but animosity toward her mother. She'd already proven her disloyalty by stealing away with Lydra. Though Madhea was loath to destroy the spawn of her memorable night with Rowlen, she had no choice. Dianna must die.

Chapter One

A Mother's Blessing

Dianna stood beside Simeon in their small fishing vessel, holding tightly to his muscular arm and doing her best to ignore her growing attraction to the dark-skinned sand dweller. Shielding her eyes against the glare of the rising sun, she gaped at the monolith before her, illuminated with prisms of bright light. The dwarf Grim had told her about the great wall his kinsmen had erected around their village by the sea. It was made of thick tree trunks as tall as the giant Gorpat, if she were to stand on her toes and stretch her fingertips to the sky. The wall ran along a rocky cliff that jutted out over the sea like the stern of a ship. Under it, waves crashed against the cliff face with violent force. Beside the cliff was a sandy beach and a shallow lagoon. Steps were carved into the embankment leading from the beach to the fortress.

Their arrival was heralded by the sound of a powerful horn, low and deep like a dragon's roar, shaking Dianna to the marrow of her bones. The rest of her party grumbled, sitting up and wiping sleep from their eyes. Her brother Alec had been tucked in the corner of the vessel with the pretty young islander, Mari, sleeping in his arms. No doubt they'd been startled by the horn. Mari gasped and Alec grabbed his blade, stumbling to his knees. Their blue friend Ryne, who'd been stretched out beside them, jumped to his feet with the alacrity of a mountain cat.

Dianna turned her attention to the wall. Several armed dwarves stood on top of it. Fortunately, their arrows weren't aimed at Dianna's party. Hopefully the army had recognized them as friends, not foes. The dragons Lydra and Tan'yi'na dove for fish farther down the shore, out of reach of arrows or cannons, giving Grim time to prepare his kinsmen for their arrival.

"Magnificent, isn't it?" Grim called down from his giant daughter's shoulder. His gray beard blew in the breeze, eyes twinkling like stardust as he

out the food and wine, which flowed in abundance. A good thing, be-
over the years the dwarves had also adopted over a dozen giants, raising
onsters as if they were kin.

Grim and Gorpat Hogbottom!" King Furbald called as he and his giant
d beside them. "We thought you'd become siren food."

yne chuckled. "Hogbottom!"

lec froze, then shook his head. "Quiet, Ryne."

Aye," Grim snapped, glaring at Ryne. "'Tis an old family name, one I'm
 proud of."

rim turned back to the king, bowing low. "You can't get rid of me that
, my sovereign." He waved to Dianna's boat. "King Furbald, these are my
ls. They helped us escape the sea witch's den." The dwarf puffed up his
, pointing at Dianna. "This is Dianna, a powerful witch who destroyed

he king gawked at them a long moment. "Eris is dead?"

ye," Grim answered, "and her island reduced to rubble."

he king stroked his beard, eyeing Dianna. "And what of Naamaku?"

illed by Dianna's dragons." Grim pointed to them in the distance, frol-
 along the shoreline.

he king jerked back, nearly stumbling off the giant's shoulders. "The
 dragon—is he the same who served the benevolent Goddess Kyan?"

le is," Dianna answered. "His name is Tan'yi'na." Dianna cupped her
 around her mouth and whistled. Though it wasn't nearly as loud as the
's bone-jarring horn, her ice dragon's sensitive ears were attuned to her
ure enough, Lydra looked up, then let out a playful roar and skipped
 the water toward her, Tan'yi'na following in her wake.

ne and Alec swore when Lydra landed beside them, splashing them
 wave of water and almost capsizing the boat.

org wike dwagons." The giant giggled like a toddler, clapping his
 "Dwagons pway wif Borg."

lence," the king roared, smacking the side of Borg's neck with his silver
 he staff made strange hollow sounds, vibrating in the king's grip as a
 ed welt appeared on the giant's flesh.

neon swore beneath his breath, pressing closer to Dianna.

smiled up at the fortress and waved to his kinsmen. Gorp
eight to ten men in height, waded chest-deep in the water,
pool for her.

"I wasn't expecting the wall to be so high," Dianna ca
The glow from his ruddy cheeks warmed her heart. He w
home. How she longed for that hut she and her brother, D
the shadow of Ice Mountain, though she knew she could n
as Madhea lived.

Grim nodded. "Tall enough to repel Eris's mightiest w

"The dwarves need not worry about that now," Dia
she'd destroyed the evil Sea Goddess with help from her th
She patted her heavy pocket, inwardly smiling when w
hand. Her companions had been quiet most of the trip.
the stones, which possessed the spirits of her cousins, w
other in a secret language.

"As long as the other bitch still lives," Grim grumbled,
"we will always worry." His red cheeks flushed crimson. "
frowned. "I didn't mean to speak ill of your mother."

She shrugged, an uncomfortable ache lancing throu
no mother to me."

As they drifted closer to shore, Alec and Ryne grabb
backward to keep the vessel from slamming into the wall.

The horn sounded again, and a giant emerged from b
stomped down the beach. With a few long strides, he
them. A boy, from what Dianna could tell, slightly talle
a much rounder belly, a cleft lip that receded into a flat
eyebrow that stretched across the width of his forehead.
ant's shoulder was a dwarf. He appeared to be at least a he
with a trimmed beard of solid white, bushy brows to m
gray nose. A crown made of polished silver and glowing g
his head. He clutched a gnarled silver staff in one hand a
ant's ear in the other. This had to be King Furbald; Grim
of his sovereign during their journey across the ocean.

The dwarf had spoken often of the dwarf kingdom c
by the sea. He'd told Dianna about his wife and cousins,

Her heart twisted when the giant hung his head, lip hanging down in a pout. "Yah, Dada." He sniffled, wiping a trail of snot on the back of his hand.

Gorpat fidgeted while her father whispered soothing words in her ear.

Dianna was relieved to see not all giants were treated with such abuse. When she looked at the king's scowling face, she was reminded of her late father Rowlen, back when Madhea's curse had made him mistreat Alec. She looked at her brother, who was glaring at the king, eyes narrowed to slits and hand on the hilt of his dagger, ignoring Ryne's warning look as he settled a hand on Alec's shoulder.

Oh, this wasn't good. Though she'd no wish to condone the king's behavior, the giant was big enough to defend himself against a dwarf, and she had other pressing matters that needed her focus. Namely, she needed food and shelter while she and her friends plotted Madhea's demise. She wouldn't want to jeopardize her mission by angering the dwarf king.

Tan'yi'na landed gracefully behind Lydra, like a swan following a duckling. He ruffled his wings, two giant plumes of smoke rising from his nostrils as he settled in the water.

The king clutched his staff, bowing stiffly to the golden dragon. "It is an honor to meet you, oh wise one. We have heard many a legend about you."

Tan'yi'na answered with raised brows and a turned-up snout. Though he couldn't speak aloud, he was able to project his thoughts. He remained silent. Dianna knew the dragon well enough to see he wasn't impressed with King Furbald.

Grim cleared his throat and ran a hand through his scraggly beard. "You may recognize the ice dragon, Lydra. You need not fear. She no longer serves Madhea. She follows Dianna now." He flashed her a shaky smile, a bead of sweat dripping down his brow.

The king puffed up his chest, leveling her with a look so dark and puzzling, she was unsure if he was displeased with her or simply had a disagreeable visage. "I have heard of Dianna and Lydra from young Des."

Dianna swallowed hard, apprehension pounding a wild staccato against her chest. "My brother is safe?"

The king's thin lips turned up in the slightest of smiles. "Safe and well."

Her hand flew to her throat as relief swept through her. "Thank the Elements, and thank you, sir, for giving him safe haven."

"Sir?" The king's bushy brows drew together, his forehead wrinkles collapsing into one another like sliding layers of sediment. "No need for formalities. You may call me King Furbald or Your Highness."

Dianna's breath hitched as she waited for the king to break into laughter. When none came, she simply nodded. "Yes, King Furbald."

Tan'yi'na let out a low chuckle, then jumped into the sky without so much as a nod of recognition at the dwarf king. Lydra followed, and the pair rained cold droplets on her head before flying off behind the trees.

Grim cleared his throat again, so loudly she feared he was choking.

"My sovereign," he said, his cheeks turning as red as the lava that spewed from Eris's volcano. "Will you let my friends seek shelter in Aya-Shay? You have my word they mean us no harm."

This time the king did laugh, a deep, hearty bellow that elicited a chuckle from the giant Borg. When the king's laughter abruptly stopped, Borg followed suit, hanging his head when the king glared at him.

"Why would you ask such a question," Furbald bellowed, "when you are well aware of the law, Grimley Hogbottom?"

Grim looked like he'd been struck dumb. He gaped at the king. "But Eris is dead, and—"

The king shot a fist into the air. "Her sister is not!" His words erupted like they'd been fired from a cannon. He cleared his throat and plastered on a smile, one that didn't mask the coldness in his eyes. "You may take our guests to the hold. I will have food and refreshments sent straight away." When he banged on Borg's head with his staff, the giant flinched before marching back into the forest.

What an odd and unpleasant king. Poor Borg, to have such a brute for a father.

Alec looked up at Grim, shielding his eyes against the sun. "The hold?"

Grim scrubbed a hand down his face before sharing a look with his daughter. "An area set up for visitors outside the village walls."

Simeon flinched as if he'd been slapped, the look of indignation in his eyes so serious, it was comical. "We are not allowed inside the village?"

Gorpat stuck a thumb in her chest. "Only we dwarves allowed inside."

Grim let out a heavy sigh. "I had hoped the king would make an exception."

After such a cold welcome, Dianna suspected their time with the dwarves would be brief, which was fine with her. She'd no wish to remain the guest of such an unpleasant ruler.

MADHEA SQUEEZED HER hands into fists, surprised at the strength of the magic that flowed into her palms. She had not felt such power since before her fateful night with Rowlen. Could it be that with Eris's demise, her sister's Elemental magic was transferring to her? Madhea sent a silent prayer to the Elements that her beauty would return with her magic. She fluttered into her bedchamber and landed in front of her looking glass. Her skin appeared slightly less sallow. Her brittle gray hair, that she'd been forced to braid ere it became too unkempt and wild, had a touch of softness. Perhaps Dianna's betrayal had served one useful purpose.

She flew into her throne room, landing beside her swirling mists, spinning a hole in the circle with the tip of her finger.

"Reveal to me Dianna," she whispered.

But her stubborn mists only showed blackness. With a curse, she swatted them away and flew past her throne room to the cell where her guest was being held. She threw a bolt at the thick ice wall barring the prisoner's escape and entered the frigid chamber. A man was curled into a ball on a stone slab, shivering under a thin fur.

Madhea hovered above him, nudging him with the tip of her toe. "Sit up, blue man."

He pushed the fur off his shoulders. Madhea was dismayed at the sight of his skeletal appearance. Such a prisoner would do her no good if he perished in her care. She made a note to feed the man more, as her plan to starve him into submission clearly wasn't working. Perhaps if she showed him a bit of kindness, he would give her the information she sought.

He slowly sat up, piercing her with eyes set in hollow sockets. The rust-colored streak running through the top of his silvery hair had faded, along with his skin. Once a vibrant blue, it was now the color of water beneath the glare of the noonday sun.

"You look famished." Madhea forced a pout. "Have my daughters not been feeding you well?"

"Very little." He ran a hand down his gaunt face, a look of derision in his beady eyes. "They said on your orders."

"Lying witches." She waved off his words with a shrill laugh. "Do not fret. They have been punished for their neglect. I shall fetch you food, then we shall talk."

He turned his gaze to his lap. "I have nothing to say."

"Of course you do, my dear." Her buzzing wings came to a halt, and she dropped down beside him, placing a hand on his knee, ignoring him when he flinched under her touch. "You have much to tell me about your people, about your magnificent blue skin." She stroked a hollow cheek, licking her lips when he flushed beneath her touch. Could her charms be returning? Perhaps she could seduce this man into obedience.

His face flushed brighter as he leaned away. "I will not betray my people again."

"Such loyalty to those who care nothing for you." She stroked one narrow arm, dismayed by his lack of muscle. This man had the bones of a bird, whereas Rowlen had been built like an ox. "Where were they when you were in great peril? If my pixies hadn't flown down to save you, that snow bear would have eaten you alive."

He leaned farther away, but she was not to be deterred. "Come to my chamber." She got to her feet and held a hand down to him, forcing a smile. "I will bring food and wine. Would you like that?"

When he did not answer, anger welled in her chest, sparks crackling in her palms. She forced herself to swallow her ire, for she suspected this young man had information about the villagers who'd once lived under her mountain, then betrayed her and mysteriously disappeared 300 years ago. Wherever these people were, Dianna's brother Markus had been with them, too. Why else had his skin been tinted blue that fateful day he'd snuck into her tower?

"Don't be afraid." She forced a smile so wide, her skin cracked under the strain. "Take my hand. I shall not bite."

She inwardly cackled with joy when he placed a hand in hers. She would get this man to reveal the hiding place of the blue people. Then she'd strike them all down, save for one. She'd take Markus back to her tower and use him as bait to lure Dianna into her trap.

"EXCELLENT SHOT."

Markus couldn't have been more proud of Ura. After only a few weeks with her new bow, she'd become quite proficient, striking the targets in the lungs almost every time.

"Not as good as you." Ura lowered her bow, leaning it on her hip, her pale curtain of hair tied behind her slender neck, her blue-tinted cheeks flushed with crimson after exerting herself for over an hour.

"Good enough to slow your target, and that's what matters." Markus had fashioned a few targets of old slog skins and one worn gnull hide. Each target had several holes in the kill zones.

She arched a fine brow, looking at him with silvery eyes that sparkled like diamond dust in the reflection from the massive icy tusks that loomed overhead. "When do you think I'll ever need to shoot someone?"

"You never know, Ura." Markus took the bow from her, cleaning it with a slick serpent-skin cloth until the wood shone once more. "It's best to be prepared. You're a fast learner."

Elements forbid Ura ever find herself in a position where she'd need to use her bow, but at least she'd stand a chance against her enemy. He was glad he'd been able to bring enough materials from above to make it. Ura had been the envy of every ice dweller when he'd presented her with a bow, arrows, and quiver as an engagement present.

After Markus slid it back into the buckskin quiver, she leaned into him, toying with the leather fringe on his vest.

"Thank you for my bow." She bit her bottom lip. "It's the most beautiful gift I've ever received. I know it took you days to carve."

"Weeks," he said with a wink, "but you are worth it."

He was rewarded with a kiss. Not a long one, like he preferred—for there were climbers practicing on the gnull tusks—and he didn't want to set their tongues wagging. They'd had enough to talk about after he'd returned without the stone. Chieftain Ingred Johan even wanted to out him, but after

Ura's father, Jon, and the old prophet, Odu, intervened, they'd convinced the Council to let Markus stay. For that, he would be eternally grateful. He'd have lost his mind if he'd been forced from Ura for good, even though he was reminded almost daily he was no longer welcome among the ice dwellers. He put up with their scowls and grumblings to wake each morning to the sight of Ura's smile and the sweet sound of her laughter.

"Are you nervous about tonight?" she asked as they bundled up, preparing to travel through the dark, frigid tunnel known as the icy lung.

"I'd be lying if I said I wasn't." He pulled her fur hat tightly over her ears. She was accustomed to the cold, but he didn't want her getting sick. "Are you?"

"A little, but the ice has stopped melting. I think that's a good omen." She linked her arm through his, leaning into him as they walked.

Scowling blue faces passed in a blur; Markus only had eyes for Ura. "Is it?"

"Of course it is." She motioned to the bright dome above them as they passed through a row of plants almost as tall as Markus. "Our ice walls and ceilings are stronger, and the river is receding."

An uneasy feeling settled in the pit of Markus's stomach. "But we still don't know why."

"I don't care why. Our kingdom is safe once again, and soon I will be your bride." She squeezed his arm. "Nothing else matters."

If only Markus were as hopeful as his bride-to-be, but he couldn't help but worry that the strengthening ice walls and receding river were bad omens. Signs that Madhea was gaining power.

Chapter Two

Dianna and her companions trudged up the sandy incline, wringing water from their clothes. Two dogs shot out from the foliage at the edge of the beach, racing toward them. Ryne fell to his knees, holding his arms wide. The larger hound knocked him back in the sand.

She smiled, admiring the blue man's love for his companion. He heartily laughed while the mutt coated his face with slobbery kisses.

"That's disgusting." Simeon stood beside her, scowling at Ryne.

She shrugged. "I don't think so. I'm rather fond of dogs."

"Elements only know where that mutt's tongue has been," he grumbled.

She laughed. "I could say the same of the girls who fawn over you. I'm sure more than one has greeted you the same way." She stole a sideways glance at him, pleased to see his cheeks flush with color.

"Someone wants to say hello to you." Alec placed a squirming Brendle in her arms.

She held the little mutt to her chest as he yapped and licked her nose. "Hello, Brendle." She giggled. "I'm pleased to see you, too. Have you been keeping a good eye on my little brother?"

As if on cue, Des sprang from the canopy of leaves, racing down the beach. "Dianna!" He wildly waved his arms.

She set down the dog, who raced in circles around her. She was amazed at the boy's strength when he plowed into her, nearly knocking her to the ground. Tears welled in her eyes, and her chest ached, then expanded, as if her heart had suddenly grown three sizes. She held her sobbing brother to her bosom. Until that moment, she hadn't realized how terribly she'd missed him.

"Oh, Des." She ran her fingers through his dark hair, which had been cut short. She missed his untamed curls. "I've missed you so." She choked with emotion and was unable to say more. She kissed the top of his head, surprised his hair smelled like fresh lavender and not sweat and grime.

He pulled back, wiping his eyes. "I've missed you, too."

She inspected him for any signs of injury or malnourishment. What she saw both pleased and surprised her. He must have gained a stone since she'd last seen him, especially around the middle, which was soft and round, like when he'd been a baby.

Alec tapped her shoulder. "May I join the hug?"

"Of course." She and Des welcomed Alec into an embrace, but Dianna inwardly cringed when she realized she hadn't yet told Des of her relation to Alec. She didn't know how her little brother would react when he discovered Dianna wasn't his blood sister.

Alec broke free first, patting Des's back. "Zier took good care of you."

Des turned up his chin, jutting a finger in his chest. "I'm big enough to look after myself."

Alec's smile faded, and he plastered on a look so severe, it was comical. "Of course you are, but there is no shame in relying on friends for help." He gestured at the group behind them, who were surrounded by at least a dozen dwarf women, plying them with fruit and drinks. "Dianna and I wouldn't have escaped Eris without help from our friends."

Des's mouth fell open. "You escaped Eris!"

"Yes, and the sea witch is no more. It's a long story. I'll tell you after supper," Alec said with a wink before returning to Mari, who was sitting beneath a tall, shady tree. Two dwarf women hovered over the lovely Mari, insisting she take their offering of *palma* fruit.

Des looked at Dianna with watery eyes the color of rich mahogany. "Can we go home now?"

Dianna's relief at finding her brother unharmed turned to sadness. How she wanted to take him back to their hut and return to their simple life, but she feared her future would be anything but simple. Even if she were to defeat Madhea, how could she return to her old life when people would be looking to her to take her mother's place?

"Not now, I'm afraid." Dianna wiped a tear from his lashes, wanting to tell him they might never return to their home, but she was too much of a coward to risk disappointing him.

"I'm bored." Des heaved a dramatic sigh, going boneless as he leaned against her. "The dwarves won't let me inside their walls, and I have nothing to do."

She sensed King Furbald was prejudiced against humankind, but to deny even children safe haven showed an unreasonable level of prejudice.

"But you have a beautiful beach and a lagoon."

He crossed his arms. "Missus Zelda says the water's dangerous."

She squinted. "Zelda?"

He nodded emphatically. "Zier's wife. She's been watching me. She makes me take baths every day, and she forces me to eat with a fork." He stuck out his tongue, as if eating with a utensil was akin to slurping down slugs.

"Oh my." She covered her mouth to hide a smile. "Sounds like you've been through quite an ordeal."

"It wasn't all bad." Des licked his lips and rubbed his belly. "The dwarves make the best pies."

She couldn't help but laugh. When two smiling dwarf women approached her with food and drink, her growling stomach reminded her she had a dragon-sized hunger that needed to be sated. Today she'd toss all cares aside and feast, celebrating Eris's demise and bonding with Des. Tomorrow she'd wake up to the stark reality that one more evil goddess needed to be vanquished before her brother and the rest of the world would be safe.

DESPITE THE BONE-JARRING chill deep in the bowels of Ice Mountain, sweat beaded on Markus's brow and his hands were clammy. The only parts of his body remotely cold were his feet, so mayhap there was truth in that saying. Still, he wouldn't flee, though the last time he'd been so terrified was the day Madhea's ice dragon pursued him. After today, he was going to be a married man.

He shifted from foot to foot, trying to avoid eye contact with the few dozen invited guests who sat upon fur rugs lining the prophet's chamber, anxiously whispering while they awaited Ura's arrival.

"You okay, son?" Odu was bent like a broken arrow, his long white beard nearly scraping the dull gray ice floor. He leaned forward on a gnarled cane, resting his backside against the raised pool of swirling mists, the fog pouring from the pool shrouding the old man's feet.

"Aye. Just worried." He turned his gaze to the serpent-skin flap that covered the entryway. Every time it moved, his breath caught in his throat, and his limbs seized with panic. Any moment Ura would walk in.

"Nothing to fear." The old man chuckled. "Ura loves you, and you love her."

He wasn't afraid of pledging himself to one woman for eternity; he was terrified of failing her. If Madhea's wrath came down on their heads, he wouldn't be able to shield his bride from the witch's magic. Or worse, their children would be cursed by the Sky Goddess.

He expelled a shaky breath, homing in on that doorway as if his life depended on it. "'Tis not our love I fear, but what the ice witch could do to that love should she ever find us."

The many lines framing Odu's eyes crinkled like crumpled parchment.

"Then let us pray she doesn't."

Markus fought the urge to curse, fearing it would bring bad omens on his wedding day. "Believe me, Odu." He rolled his eyes. "I have sent a thousand prayers to the Elements." Indeed he had: every morning when he awoke, before he broke his fast, at every meal throughout the day, and finally before he crawled under his furs each night.

The door flap pulled back again, and Markus thought he'd pass out from fright when he saw Ura's father, Jon, emerge dressed in his finest white furs. Jon winked at Markus as he held the flap open. Markus sucked in a sharp breath when a beautiful young woman with skin the color of the summer sky and a curtain of translucent hair stepped into the room, a crown made of dried flowers on her head. She wore a long pale gown that fell around her fur boots like a waterfall spilling into a pool. When she smiled at Markus, she reminded him of a frosted *cotulla* flower preserved in full bloom. And this beautiful, fair maiden was to be his bride? What had Markus done to deserve her? Not enough, of that he was certain, which was why he was so terrified. Surely fate would find a way to take her from him.

Jon walked Ura to the center of the room and placed her delicate fingers in Markus's meaty, sweaty hand before he had time to wipe his palm on his tunic. He flashed Ura an apologetic grimace, but she simply smiled and squeezed his hand tight, amazing him with a firm grip for such a small woman. Markus was vaguely aware of Jon stepping back and Odu clearing his throat as he held an ancient parchment before him.

"People of Ice Kingdom, we are gathered here today to witness the binding between two souls whose hearts are already entwined. The lovely Ura from the house of Nordlund and the land dweller Markus Jägerrson of the town of Adolan. These two souls seek a union blessed by the Elements." The old prophet steadied himself against the side of the pool and held out his hands. "Markus and Ura, take my hands."

Markus hesitantly joined hands with the old man, and Ura did the same. Holding the old man's bony, brittle fingers felt like cradling an injured bird wing, and he hoped he wouldn't forget himself and hold too hard.

The prophet turned his milky gaze on him. "Markus, do you take Ura to be your beloved bride, to cherish, love, and protect from this day forward?"

"I will," he blurted, hating how his voice snapped like a broken bow-string.

"And do you promise to faithfully return Ura's love and put no other woman before her?"

He blinked hard at the prophet. He wasn't sure, but he thought he heard accusation in the old man's words. He had to have been mistaken. Surely Odu could see how deeply he cared for his bride. He would never, ever love another woman but Ura. "Of course I will."

"Very well." The prophet solemnly nodded before turning to Markus's bride. "Ura, do you promise to faithfully return Markus's love and put no other man before him?"

She flashed a dazzling smile. "Absolutely."

"And do you take Markus as your gallant groom," the prophet continued, "to cherish, love, and nurture from this day until the end of time?"

She turned up her chin, her gray eyes shining like silver gems in the soft glow of the overhead lights. "I will, and I will also protect."

The prophet released their hands, thoughtfully scratching his beard. "That's not part of the woman's vows."

She pulled back her shoulders. "It's part of *my* vows."

"Ura," Markus warned when Odu flinched as if he'd been slapped.

"Markus?" She arched a brow, issuing him a challenging look that weakened his knees.

He knew not what to do. Jon had warned him Ura was headstrong. That was one of the things that attracted Markus to her. Still, to challenge the prophet and her new husband during their wedding ceremony set an unfavorable precedent. He could tell he was not going to win this argument, so he did the only thing he could do—swept her up in his arms and kissed her so hard, the breath expelled from her lungs. She punched his chest at first, then surrendered to his kiss, turning as soft as clay in his arms.

A loud, hacking cough brought him back to his senses. They pulled apart, chests heaving and breathless.

Odu waved a finger in their faces. "It's not time to kiss yet."

"Sorry." He shrugged, flashing Ura a sideways smile, pleased when her cheeks flushed a bright crimson.

Odu lifted his hands.

"Oh, heavenly Elements,

Let your will be done.

Bind their souls as one.

Bless their union with soil, seeds, and light from above.

Grant them peace, health, laughter, and love.

Keep them safe from ill will and strife.

Gift their love with eternal life,

So when their candles no longer bear flame,

Their souls may rise together again."

He reached into his pocket and withdrew a frayed rope, grimy from centuries of ceremonial use. "With this rope, I do bind your two souls as one."

When the old man held out his hand, waggling his fingers, Ura placed her hand in his, and Markus followed suit.

Odu slowly wound the rope around their wrists.

"Markus Jägerrson." The prophet flashed a knowing grin. "*Now* you may kiss your bride."

Before he could sweep her into his embrace, she threw her arms around his neck and pulled his head down to hers, pressing her lips so hard against his, he winced at the blunt pain. He wrapped his arms around her waist, lifted her off the ground and deepened the kiss, trying to wrestle control from her.

She broke the kiss, then laughed, swatting his chest. "I think you've proved your point."

Odu banged his staff on the ground, the sharp sound ricocheting off the walls and causing the spikes above them to rattle. The crowd gasped and dove for cover, and Markus instinctively tucked Ura under his arms, hovering over her like a hen protecting its egg. When the spikes stopped rattling, he glowered at Odu, who had the nerve to smile.

"People of Ice Kingdom," the prophet said, seemingly oblivious to their grumblings as they helped each other up. "I present to you Markus and Ura Jägerrson."

The crowd broke into cheers and hollers, then the room went eerily silent when the spikes rattled again.

"And now for the conclusion to our ceremony." Odu leaned on his staff and turned to the raised pool shrouded in fog. "Your first challenge as a wedded couple is to look upon your fate in the swirling mists."

Markus felt as helpless as a deer caught in a hunter's crosshairs. He'd almost forgotten about this part of the ceremony.

"Nervous?" She held his hand, smiling.

He wiped a bead of sweat off his brow with a trembling hand. "That's an understatement."

"Do not fear." She stepped forward, tugging, while the fog swallowed her feet. "The mists almost always show favorable prospects."

He dug his heels into the floor, refusing to yield. "Unfortunately, my life has *almost always* been ruled by *un*favorable prospects."

"Don't be silly." She tossed her silky curtain of hair over her shoulder with a wink. "You got to marry me."

He knew not what act of madness compelled him to follow his bride to the pool of mists. Fool that he was, he followed her like an elk chasing after a cow's scent. He stared at the pool as she stirred the mists with the tip of her finger, spinning the clouds so fast, they created a turbulent vortex before breaking apart and revealing a smooth pool of water. At first he saw only their reflections, Ura smiling and clinging to his arm, his face once the color of the fine grains of sand found at the bottom of an hourglass now a pale blue, like the other ice dwellers. Even his broad shoulders were narrower, and his dark mop of hair had a translucent, silvery sheen.

He let out a sigh of relief when the mists revealed nothing more than a young couple in love. But then the image faded, and a new one appeared. A screaming winged witch shot bolts out of her hands, ice splintered while people ran for shelter, and Markus was crumpled on the ground at the witch's feet. He barely had time to catch Ura when she fell into his arms, a scream dying in her throat.

Oh, heavenly Elements, Madhea was coming to Ice Kingdom.

Chapter Three

Dianna's group got off to a rough start. The dwarves denied entrance to Alec's blue friend until he'd asked the dwarves for forgiveness for wrongly accusing them of theft shortly before he'd been captured by Eris's soldiers. Ryne was a proud man, holding his head high and walking with confidence. The dwarves had made him kneel, apologizing to at least thirty of them individually before they'd let him pass into the hold. For such a man to have been brought so low was quite shocking. Even more shocking was that Ryne endured the humiliation without so much as a sneer. In the short time she'd gotten to know him, she'd discovered he seemed to prefer giving dark looks to smiles.

The hold was a veritable town, with several thatched cottages offering fresh rushes, cozy beds, and warm blankets. Clean cobblestone paths lined with flowers of every color wound between the cottages. There was even a well in the center of town, the water tasting as fresh as if it had come straight from the Danae River. These temporary shelters were far better maintained than Dianna's modest home. Given such furnishings, she wondered how lavishly the dwarves must live within the walls of Aya-Shay. What she wouldn't give for a peek.

The king may have been inhospitable and unwelcoming at their first meeting, but he sent servants with enough food for an army of giants, including pies of every flavor. Though King Furbald only stayed long enough to bark orders at a cluster of young dwarf servants, many of the dwarves and a few more giants came to the hold to celebrate Eris's demise. After the sun dipped behind the horizon, everyone gathered at a campfire near the well in the center of the town surrounded by carved wooden chairs and benches. They listened attentively while Grim regaled them with tales of their adventure, starting with their imprisonment on Eris's ship. With each new development, dwarves hooted and hollered and drank in honor of "the heroes who vanquished the sea witch." They drank not the wine given to the guests but something much stronger, for their bulbous noses and cheeks turned a brighter crimson with each swallow. By the time Grim ended his story with Eris's island volcano exploding in a maelstrom of ash and smoke, the dwarves were so tipsy, many had fallen over on their sides or were draped across their giant children's feet.

Dianna stared incredulously at one dwarf who vomited into the fire, then took a swallow of his drink before vomiting again. As he stumbled back to his bench, his black beard peppered with angry embers, he let out a hearty belch, and flames engulfed his beard. He ran in circles, yelping like a wounded dog, before a giant doused him with a tub of water.

A cluster of staggering dwarves gathered enough wits to pick up their instruments and play lively music. They danced circles around the fire with Grim leading them. When the giants sitting outside the perimeter tapped their feet to the music, the ground shook, and the dwarves laughed, stumbling into each other.

As the wine flowed, it went straight to Dianna's head, and she leaned against Simeon's side for support, hating herself for loving the warmth radiating off his body. She didn't remember when, but sometime during the night, his arm found its way around her shoulders. She hadn't realized he'd been holding her until she caught Ryne scowling at them from across the campfire. She thought about shrugging Simeon off, but fool that she was, she didn't want him to let go.

Alec sat on the bench beside her, helping Des steady a stick with an impaled sausage above the campfire. After being overcome with exhaustion from practicing using her new legs all afternoon, Alec's love interest, Mari, had already retired to bed. Dianna inwardly smiled, watching her two brothers' heads bent toward one another. Alec's patience with Des made her love her half-brother even more. Then joy turned to sadness when she realized Alec and Des would be dead within a blink of her immortal eye, and she'd be forced to live out her long life without family. She did her best to push back the rising tide of melancholy. This night wasn't the time for sadness. It was meant for celebration.

Throughout the night, she caught herself calling Alec her brother. Des didn't seem to notice. Perhaps he was too young to understand the nature of their relationship. She was thankful for that, for she dreaded having to tell Des that she was not his sister, that his true sister had been murdered by Madhea.

She stumbled to her feet, balance impaired.

"Are you all right?" Simeon stood, steadying her by the elbow.

"I'm fine." She shook her head, trying to clear the fog that permeated her mind. "I just need to relieve myself." She smiled at Simeon, shrugging out of his grip, then staggered toward the bushes.

"You don't need to use the bushes, my dear." Zier's wife, Zelda, stopped her at the edge of the forest. "We dwarves are better hosts than that." The older woman led her to a long log hut.

Inside was a humid room lit with wall sconces and a pleasing glow from a stone hearth. Three deep, round wooden barrels must have been baths, for each one had a narrow table beside it offering linens, soaps, and more candles. Along one side of the room was a long table with basins and jugs of water. Three pretty looking glasses hung above each basin. Opposite were four stalls with wooden doors intricately carved with cotulla flowers. Zelda nodded to the nearest stall, and Dianna stumbled inside. She'd rather wished she hadn't looked inside the hole, for she realized too late she was in an outhouse. How odd that it was located in the bathing room. Mayhap that was the reason for all of the candles, which put off the pleasant scents of lavender and sage.

When she finished, she washed up in the basins, watching Zelda's reflection in the looking glass. The dwarf woman gazed at her with a look that Dianna hoped was one of interest and not suspicion. The older woman was somewhat smaller than the male dwarves and had long auburn braids peppered with white and gray streaks, striking vivid blue eyes, a button nose, and a pleasant, dimpled smile. In fact, her face was so fair and sweet, she imagined that many men had once competed for her hand. Her countenance was serene as she leaned beside a wall sconce, candle wax dripping precariously close to her feet. Dianna hardly knew Zelda, but the woman had such a pleasant personality, it was hard not to quickly become fond of her.

"I want to thank you for looking after Des in my absence." Dianna dried her hands on the linen beside the basin. "I know children his age can sometimes be challenging, and I am more grateful to you than words can express."

"It was no trouble at all." The woman waved away Dianna's concern. "I miss caring for children now that my twin daughters are grown and have moved so far away."

"That's right." Dianna remembered Zier speaking fondly of his girls when he visited her parents. He'd always brought lace for them and toys for their children. "They live in Kicelin now, don't they?"

"Yes." The old woman's gaze dropped to the wood plank floor. "They fell in love with human twin brothers while accompanying their father on a trade mission. It has been five years since they left home." She released a heavy sigh. "But it feels like a lifetime."

She sympathized with Zelda, for she knew the pain of missing a loved one. When she'd first left Des to fly to the Shifting Sands, she felt as if she'd been forced to carve out a piece of her heart, leaving it behind with Des while the dull blade remained lodged in her chest.

"How often do you see them?"

"Not often enough." She frowned. "They have babies of their own, and the trek up to Kicelin is much too arduous for me. What I wouldn't give to have them live here, to watch my grandchildren grow, but King—" Zelda's eyes widened as she bit down on her knuckles, then turned her back.

Dianna wondered why Zelda was afraid to speak her mind about the king. Did she hold her tongue out of respect, or did she fear retaliation? She surmised the king wouldn't allow the women's families to live within the walls of Aya-Shay because their husbands were humans. But why?

"Would it be so bad to have a few humans living within your walls? Couldn't the king make some exceptions?"

"He has his reasons." Zelda wiped her cheeks, a glint of defiance in her eyes as she pulled back her shoulders. "'Tis a sad tale that I do not wish to repeat."

Heat flamed Dianna's face. She felt ten times a fool for asking Zelda such an insensitive question. "I'm sorry."

The older woman patted her hand. "No worries, dear."

She followed Zelda out of the hut, not surprised when she bolted for Zier, no doubt wanting to put distance between herself and Dianna's questions.

Though night had fallen, the grounds were alight with bright torches. Dianna's head was still swimming, her world slightly off kilter. When she spied the long buffet table laden with food, her stomach instantly roiled, then calmed. Great Goddess, she was hungry enough to eat a full stag! When she'd first arrived at the hold, she'd only had a few bites of fruit and one meat pie, for she'd been too eager to spend time with her little brother. She'd wrapped him in furs, taking him for a ride on Lydra's back, soaking up his squeals and laughter as Lydra chased Tan'yi'na through the clouds and across the ocean. They'd only recently returned to the celebration, where the dwarves toasted in her honor, refilling her goblet so many times, she'd lost count.

She piled a platter with berry and meat pies, strange pickled vegetables of every color, roasted meats, and fruits with cream and biscuits. She hadn't even made it halfway down the table, and already her platter overflowed with food.

She sat at a table away from the others, behind a copse of trees, not wanting Simeon to see her devour her meal. She feared she'd look more like a siren picking a mortal's bones clean than the delicate Shifting Sand's girls with the painted toenails, who nibbled their palma fruits like rabbits eating corn while shooting him coy looks.

She ate so fast, she hardly tasted it. She just knew it was all delicious. The pickled vegetables had a sweet and salty taste, so pleasing that once her platter was clean, she loaded her plate with more, sucking vinegar off her fingers after she'd finished. She belched into her fist, doing her best to muffle the sound. Had it been just she and Des, they would have made a competition out of it, one in which Dianna would let her brother win but not without a good fight. But that was before she'd discovered she was the daughter of a goddess. She feared her days of living carefree were over.

"Why do you call Alec your brother when he is not your brother?"

Her heart caught in her throat when Des emerged from the shadows. "Oh, I-I—"

"I heard Zelda and Zier talking when they thought I was asleep." He gazed at her with innocent, dark eyes. "Zier said he believes our parents weren't your parents, and that you were Madhea's daughter."

She swallowed a lump of apprehension when she realized she'd no choice but to tell her brother the truth. She prayed to the Elements he'd be understanding and their bond wouldn't be diminished. "I'm sorry you had to hear that." She beckoned him to sit on the bench beside her. She rubbed his shorn hair, kissing the top of his head. "But 'tis true. The Elementals switched me with your true sister at birth, something I only just learned." She arched back with bated breath, fearing his response.

He swallowed, a visible knot working its way down his throat. "So you are not my sister then?"

She placed a palm across her chest. "In my heart I will always be your sister, and you will always be my little brother. I was there the night you were born. Papa was hunting when Mama birthed you. She'd said you came too early. She was in so much pain, I feared I'd lose you both." She stopped to regain her composure, close to breaking down at the thought of her sweet mama and brave papa, both lost to her and Des in an avalanche two winters past. What she wouldn't give to have them back with her. "'Twas when my magic had begun to bloom. I laid my hands on Mama's womb to ease the pain and delivered you myself. I was the first person to hold you. You were a perfect little mite with chubby cheeks and a cry that could shatter ice. You had thick, dark hair even then." Though tears streamed down her face, she smiled, rubbing her brother's hair again. "I'd never known love like the moment I first held you. Don't you see? My soul knows no difference. You were my brother then, and you will always be my brother."

He stared at her a long moment, his face scrunched up so tight, she feared he'd forgotten how to breathe. Then he let out a wail, launching himself into her arms. "Oh, Dianna, I love you so."

She sobbed as she rocked him, singing a song their mama had sung to them each night.

"Hush baby mite,
Sleep tonight.
Tomorrow cotullas will bloom anew, anew.
Rest little fawn,
And after dawn,
The flowers will be ripe with dew, with dew.
Close your eyes.

When you rise,
Mama will pick them for you, for you."

His sobbing subsided, and she thought he'd fallen asleep. But then he jerked with a start, looking at her with a trembling lip. "What happened to my other sister?"

Siren's teeth! She'd feared he'd ask that question. She willed her limbs to stop shaking. "Madhea killed her."

He let out a strangled cry, his hand flying to his mouth. "Oh, no!"

"Des, I'm so sorry."

His face turned as red as the lava that flowed from Eris's volcano. "The ice witch is evil."

She let out a slow breath, willing the tears to subside. "I agree, which is why she needs to be stopped."

"But she's powerful." Des jumped to his feet, clenching his hands. "She'll destroy you, and then I won't have any sisters."

"I am not without power, and I have three magical stones." She patted her pocket. Though they had been silent since she'd arrived at the dwarf village, they were also warmer than before, buzzing with magic. No doubt the sisters were getting reacquainted in their silent language. "Hopefully, I'll have three more soon." If she could persuade the Ice People to relinquish them, though Ryne had told her she'd have better luck stealing a rib bone from a siren's mouth.

"Come." Dianna stood, brushing crumbs off her breeches, shocked at the mess she'd made. "Let us return to the merriment. Alec is probably looking for you."

He slipped his warm, sticky hand into hers. "If he's your brother, can I call him my brother, too?"

Warmth flooded her heart. "I'm sure he'd like that."

The music came to a screeching stop. She feared she'd somehow offended the dwarves with her long absence until she heard a commotion behind Gorpat. The giant stood with lifted foot, revealing a party of ragtag dwarves and humans huddling in the shadows behind her.

Zier pushed his way through the crowd like the prow of a ship, his brows drawn together. "Who goes there?"

"It is your daughter Sofla, Papa." One of the dwarves stepped forward, a fair young woman cradling a babe in her arms. "And your other daughter Sogred." She nodded to a woman who was without a doubt her identical twin, for she had the same button nose, alabaster skin, and thick, fiery curls. The only thing that made it possible to tell them apart was that one wore a brown dress, the other a mossy green. "And our families." She nodded to two human men, twins as well, with blond hair and wiry frames. The men were short for humans, only about two heads taller than their wives. One of the men had two flame-haired tots in tattered trews clinging to his leg.

"Sofla! Sogred!" Zelda raced through the dwarves, who parted to let her through. "Oh, my grandchildren!" She pulled the women, who each carried an identical infant, to her ample bosom. "What has happened?" She kissed each infant on the forehead. "Why have you left your homes?"

When the toddlers left their father's knees and held their hands up to Zelda, she swooped them into her arms, kissing their grimy faces.

"Mama," Sofla said. "We barely escaped with our lives."

Sogred nodded, tears streaming down her dirt-stained face. "All of Kicelin has turned to ice. Everything is coated with frost, and we cannot make fires to melt it."

Sofla shivered, pulling a threadbare shawl tightly around her shoulders. "I've never known such bone-numbing cold."

"Mama," Sogred added, "we've come with nothing but the clothes on our backs."

Zelda gasped, rocking the toddlers on her hips. "You must be famished."

"We are." Sofla heaved a sigh before passing the infant in her arms to her father. "And tired."

"Your families can come live with us," Zier said as he took the other infant from Sogred. "We have plenty of room. I will appeal to the king."

"You need not appeal to your sovereign," a deep voice bellowed. "You know the rules, Zier Wanderson."

Dianna squinted as the king came into view, perched on the shoulder of his giant son, regally holding his chin up high and clutching his staff in a white-knuckled grip.

"King Furbald," Zier pleaded, his voice cracking, "these are my children. They are dwarves, and by right deserve to live within the walls of Aya-Shay."

"Aye, your daughters have that right." The king glared at the crowd of refugees. "But their husbands and half-breeds do not."

Though Dianna wasn't shocked by the king's decision, she was disappointed. What had made the king hate humans so?

Zier's cheeks and nose turned bright red, like three over-ripe, bulbous apples. "I don't understand why giants can live within the walls but my son-in-laws and grandchildren cannot."

The king snarled. "A giant's angry fist cuts a smaller path of destruction than the cunning of man."

Such an interesting metaphor. She wondered if 'twas true. If man had wreaked so much destruction. Perhaps some human catastrophe had turned the king against them.

"Not all men are like Eris's and Madhea's soldiers!" Zier's booming voice made the infants cry, making his daughters quickly scoop the babies from their father's embrace.

"Enough!" the king hollered, shaking his staff at Zier. "I will not abide you challenging our laws. Your offspring are welcome to stay in the hold, but if you continue to argue, they may stay elsewhere."

"Papa, it's okay." Sofla led him away from the shadow of the king's large son.

Zier frowned, swiping tears. "It's not right."

"We don't mind staying in the hold." Sogred grabbed his other elbow while deftly burping her infant on her shoulder.

When Borg set King Furbald on the ground, the dwarf ruler marched toward Dianna with purpose in his stride, his tall staff striking the cobblestones, creating sparks like flint striking tinder. "Dianna of Adolan. I've come to ask how long you and your party will be staying."

She could tell by the king's tone he did not relish playing their host. She met his direct gaze with one of her own. "We will not impose on your hospitality another day. We leave on the morrow."

"Impose!" Zier threw up his hands, stomping a foot. "You're not imposing. You killed Eris, for Elements' sake! Surely you're entitled to a few days' food and rest."

"I'm sorry, but I cannot dally a moment longer." She offered Zier a weary smile. "If the cold is as your daughters say, then Adolan will succumb next, and it will continue to spread as Madhea gains power. She must be stopped."

King Furbald's bushy brows dipped low over his eyes like angry white caterpillars. "And you think you are the witch who can stop her?"

"I know she is," a familiar voice boomed. "She's defeated one goddess. She can defeat another."

Simeon stood behind her, legs braced, arms folded, his golden eyes as un-wavering as stone.

"Aye," the king answered, mistrust showing in his drawn mouth as he leaned against his staff. "But Eris wasn't her mother."

She flinched, then stiffened, regretting that the king witnessed how much his words stung. "Madhea is no mother to me. She is a danger to civilization and must be defeated." Would she forever be compared to that curse of a mother?

"So you say." The king chuckled. "But you are young and not familiar with Madhea's persuasive powers."

"For the love of my family and friends, I will not let her persuade me." Her gaze swept the throng before settling on the king. "I swear on all that is sacred."

He flashed a sideways scowl. "Let us hope that is true, for the future of humanity depends on it."

Chapter Four

Markus held tightly to Ura's hand, willing his pounding heart to slow as Chieftain Ingred Johan glared at them over her beak nose. Rather than feasting with friends and celebrating their nuptials, Markus and Ura had gone before the Council to warn them of Madhea's impending attack. He fought a shudder as he looked over his shoulder at Jon, who was standing stoically behind him, along with Odu and the rest of the wedding guests, come to offer their moral support. The Council chamber was especially frigid today, if for no other reason than the cold reception they'd received from the members, who'd glared at them when Jon requested they grant his children an emergency hearing.

"Ura and Markus?" The chieftain drummed long, bony fingers on the armrest of her chair carved of gnull bones. "What are you doing here? I thought 'twas your wedding day."

Ura cleared her throat. "It is, Chieftain, but we wanted to tell you of a disturbing vision we saw in the mists."

"Disturbing vision?" She slowly sat up, her neck elongating like a slog trying to reach a pocket of mites. "During the ceremony?"

Ura and Markus shared a look and then Markus nodded. "Aye."

The chieftain assessed them for a long moment. "But the mists only reveal favorable outcomes to wedded couples."

Ura stiffened beside him. "The mists showed us Madhea in Ice Kingdom."

The crowd behind them gasped, and the Council members flanking the chieftain erupted into hushed whispers, sounding like hornets buzzing a nest.

Ingred leaned forward, her thin brows dipping low over her eyes. "Surely you're mistaken."

When Ura swore under her breath, he knew he had to act before his new bride said something they'd both regret. He forced back the knot of panic that welled in his throat. "We know what we saw."

He found himself caught in the crosshairs of Ingred's beady-eyed glare. "And we are supposed to trust you, land dweller," she spat, "after you claim to have survived a battle with Madhea and then lost our sacred stone?"

He fought back the urge to match his wife's colorful words with a few of his own. From the moment he'd returned to Ice Kingdom, the Council and their chieftain had been after him about the stone, summoning him to their chamber no less than seven times, asking him to answer the same accusations. *Why would you give your sister our stone? How can you be sure it had a goddess inside? What if your sister uses the stone for evil? When has she promised to return it?*

"I didn't lose it." He groaned. "I have already told you my sister is borrowing it."

"Ah, yes." Ingred tossed back her head and laughed, a grating sound punctuated with whistles from her wide nostrils. "The sister you say flew off with the ice dragon and our warming stone."

He bit down hard on his lip, trying to rein in his temper. Ura leaned into him, holding his hand, the only source of comfort.

"Again, 'tis more than a warming stone," he growled.

Ingred tossed up her hands, her voice turning shrill. "Even more reason you should have brought it back."

"That stone belonged to my family." Ura turned up her chin. "The argument has already been settled between Markus and my father."

Ingred narrowed her eyes at Ura before nodding to Jon standing behind them. "And yet your father was fool enough to allow you to marry this land dweller after he discarded our heritage's greatest treasure."

"Chieftain," Jon boomed so loudly, Markus nearly jumped out of his boots. "About the vision."

"What about it?" Ingred's thin lips twisted in a scowl.

"The Elements have warned my daughter and son-in-law." Jon's voice dropped to a normal volume. "Why would the Elements lie?"

"I didn't say the *Elements* lied." Ingred shot up from her chair, wagging a finger at Jon. "Your family has a history of deceit. Your son convinced my son and our other young men to travel on a dangerous quest in search of the melting ice. Where is this melting ice now?" She motioned to the frozen cavern around them. "The river drops daily while the ice hardens."

What kind of a fool was the chieftain to have forgotten that just a fortnight ago, the ice had been melting at an alarming rate?

"Your ignorance will be the death of the Ice People."

Ura's warning came before a growl so low, Markus thought he'd imagined it, but when he saw she was brimming with fury, he knew she'd spoken the words aloud.

Ingred's blue skin had turned an alarming shade of fuchsia. "Insolent child! I ought to have you outed for speaking to me that way!"

Markus held his bride's hand and took a step back. "Ura, please," he whispered. "Don't anger her."

"Go ahead." Ura said, heedless of Markus's pleas. "I'll be safer on the surface than down here."

Shadows fell across the chieftain's eyes as she looked down at Markus, reminding him of a predatory bird preparing to strike a rodent. "Land dweller, it would serve you well to keep your wife in line."

"Ura," he said through clenched teeth. "There is no use arguing." He remembered too well the way the chieftain had easily outed her own nephew Bane Eryll, and he'd no wish to have his young wife forced to the surface. With no goddess stone to shield them from Madhea's eye, they were sure to be caught.

Ura looked at him. "But everyone will die."

Determination hardened his spine, and he pulled her through the throng and out of the chamber. "Not if I can help it."

EVEN THOUGH DIANNA was to bed with Mari, she'd followed the men into their hut. With distended bellies full of scraps, the dogs curled up by the fire, snuggled together like best friends. Dianna, Ryne, and Alec sat around the hearth on oversized comfy benches padded with downy feathers and covered with smooth leather, swapping stories about their journey.

She was painfully aware of Simeon quietly sitting beside her, sipping his tea and observing the others. She wondered what made him so reticent and realized he probably wasn't used to camaraderie with men. He most likely spent his evenings in the company of women. The thought made her heart twist with jealousy, though she did her best to put it out of her mind. Instead, she focused on Des, who had fallen asleep with his head in her lap. She ran her fingers over his scalp, loving his sweet smile as he softly snored.

They shared a good laugh when Alec recounted the tale of Gorpat sneezing and coating them with layers of snot, but then everyone hung their heads as they recalled Ryne's three fallen companions, two of whom had been eaten by sirens and the other mortally wounded in battle. Dianna sensed Ryne wasn't looking forward to returning to Ice Kingdom with the news that their three sons had perished.

After a long and awkward silence, Alec pulled a scroll from his pack, flattening it on the floor beside the hearth. "We need to plan our days ahead."

She slipped off the bench and knelt in front of the map, amazed at the details, from the Werewood Forest, which took up most of the bottom third of the map, to Aloa-Shay, a few smaller villages at the southeast tip, and even the giant colony northwest of the woods. Toward the top of the map was Adolan, which was northeast of the forest and south of Madhea's mountain, and then Kicelin, now a tomb of ice, situated almost at the base of the mountain. Even more impressive, the dwarves had labeled a variety of routes, from the fastest to the most dangerous.

"Where did you get this map?" she asked her brother.

"Zier gave it to me," Alec said with a smile. "Ryne and I have plotted our route from here to Aloa-Shay, where we will leave Mari and Des. Then we will travel directly through Werewood Forest. This straight route is the fastest." He pointed to the lines that were labeled the most dangerous, with skulls and crossbones. "'Tis the route the dwarves take, with a wide path carved by the giants, so the dragons can take off and land as they please. Because we will have two dragons with us, we need not fear any woodland creatures."

Though she didn't wish to take the most dangerous route, with the freeze approaching, they'd have little choice. They had to make it to Ice Kingdom before the path was impassable, if it wasn't already. The dragons had gone hunting in the Werewood Forest and were to return on the morrow. If Tan'yi'na felt it was too dangerous, certainly he'd tell her.

She sat back on her heels, contemplating their journey. She was impervious to the Elements, and years ago her father had taught her how to scale ice. Though it had been a while since she last wielded a pick and rope, she'd remember fast enough. But what about Simeon and Alec? Would they be able to keep up with her and Ryne? She feared they would impede their journey.

"It appears you've thought of everything," she said, forcing a smile as realization hit her. She must leave Alec and Simeon with Des and Mari in Aloa-Shay. She didn't know which was more unsettling, telling her brother and Simeon they must stay behind or traveling alone with Ryne. Though he was hard-headed and not particularly pleasant, she couldn't deny he was attractive, tall and lean with a square jaw, full lips, and piercing silver eyes. She'd be more comfortable traveling alone with Simeon. He was flirtatious and sometimes crass, but he had an ease of manner that made her feel comfortable. Ryne was as cold and aloof as he was blue. Though he was only a few years her senior, he gave the impression that he was far older. He was a natural born leader. She didn't know whether she should admire or resent him for that.

When Ryne knelt beside her, and Simeon flanked her other side, she felt trapped by the tension radiating off them. She stole a sideways glance at Simeon, who was like his own personal sun, melting Ryne with hot looks. A quick look at Ryne revealed a block of ice, reflecting that sun with frigid glares. Mayhap it was best she traveled alone with Ryne, for she didn't know if she could stand the two rivals together much longer. She looked over at Alec, who flashed an impish grin. Good thing someone thought this was amusing.

Ryne pointed to the edge of the forest that bordered on expansive grasslands. "We shall leave the dragons in the forest with instructions for them to wait for our return."

She stared at Ryne a long moment, waiting for him to ask her opinion. Did he just think to leave the dragons in the forest without her consent? When he said nothing, she cleared her throat. "We haven't discussed the option of leaving the dragons."

Ryne frowned. "That's because there is no other option."

She fought to remain impassive, though inside she was seething. Last she'd checked, nobody had elected Ryne the leader of their quest, yet he'd assumed the position.

Before she could respond, Simeon placed a hand on her knee, giving her a knowing wink. "We need to let Dianna decide what to do with the dragons."

She appreciated Simeon's support, but she didn't know why he thought she needed him to speak for her—or for the dragons, for that matter. She was sure Tan'yi'na would have plenty to say on the matter.

Ryne chuckled softly, a low dark sound that matched the look he shot Simeon. "And risk Madhea spotting us, or worse, risk her reclaiming Lydra?"

Curse the Elements! He was right. One look at Alec confirmed Dianna had no option other than to trust Ryne.

"No, Simeon." Dianna heaved a frustrated groan. "We must leave the dragons behind, though loath I am to do it."

Rather than agree with her, Simeon engaged in a stare-down with Ryne. The tension between them was as thick as churned butter. She suspected they were competing for her favor, which was ridiculous. She didn't want any man's favor. All she had to do was recall images of Feira spoon-feeding her corpse husband to know what lay in store for her should she ever allow a man to steal her heart.

"Back to the map," she said, hoping to break through the fog of male ego. Her gaze shot to a big *X* through an area marked Empire of Shadows in the center of the grasslands. "What is this?"

Alec shrugged, and Simeon held up his hands.

Ryne carefully studied the spot on the map. "We will pass it on our route. It's a haunted place. It's best we skirt around it."

"You've been there?" Alec asked.

"I've seen it, but only from a distance." Ryne shivered as if recalling a nightmare. "'Tis not a place I'd wish to enter."

She wasn't so sure she liked the idea of passing a haunted place, especially as the dragons wouldn't be accompanying them on that portion of the journey.

"Once we reach Ice Kingdom," Ryne continued, "we must persuade my people to flee before you battle Madhea. If her mountain were to fall, as did Eris's volcano, my people would be crushed under it."

Dianna agreed. "I cannot possibly battle Madhea with the Ice People living below her." Besides, she wanted the Ice People's three other stones before she engaged in a fight with the Sky Goddess. If 'twas true that Madhea's powers were strengthening, then Dianna would need more than three goddess stones to battle her mother.

"What about the people of Adolan?" Alec asked, pointing to a spot by the Danae River that was near Alec's home, or what was left of it.

"The cold will drive them away soon enough, just as it did the people of Kicelin," Ryne answered.

Adolan wasn't much more than a day's journey from Kicelin. She worried for the people of Adolan, her people. Had they already fled their homes in search of warmer weather?

"How do we know the Ice People haven't left already?" Simeon asked.

"We are called Ice People for a reason," he said to Simeon, clearly not bothering to mask the derision in his voice. "We thrive in the cold."

"Do you think they will want to leave their kingdom?" Alec asked.

Ryne shrugged, dark lines tugging at his angular features. "They won't have a choice, will they?"

Suddenly it hit Dianna that she was about to displace an entire race of people. She had no idea their number, but Markus had said they were in the thousands. Mayhap it was wise if Ryne led their mission, for he would be the best person to be responsible for their safety. No wonder he was always so severe. He had the weight of his people's survival on his shoulders.

A feeling of hopelessness washed over her. How would the Ice People react when they were told they must relinquish their stones and their kingdom?

"Where will they go?" she asked Ryne, hoping he'd already thought of a plan.

"I'm not sure yet," he answered plainly.

Her heart sank like a stone.

"Mayhap we can convince King Furbald to allow them in the hold," Alec suggested.

Ryne frowned at the map. "The hold isn't big enough for everyone."

She noted how Ryne answered Alec without venom in his voice, as opposed to when he addressed Simeon. If Ryne and Simeon were truly at odds over her, they were in for a sore disappointment.

Simeon pointed to a patch of unmarked land across the ocean. "What about Kyanu?"

"In the Shifting Sands?" Her hand flew to her throat. Relocating the ice dwellers to a new land seemed like such a daunting task.

"Yes." A wide grin split Simeon's face in two, reminding her of Des after he'd taught Brendle a new trick.

"You want to take my people from the ice to the desert sun?" Ryne snapped. "They will perish in the heat."

Simeon responded with a smile so smug and patronizing, she feared the two would soon come to blows. "Do you have a better suggestion?"

Ryne and Simeon locked gazes like two rutting elk fighting over cows. Stupid, stubborn slogs!

"Simeon has a point," she interjected, hoping to diffuse the mounting tension. "The Shifting Sands will be safest and farthest from Madhea's wrath."

She refused to cower when Ryne turned his icy glare on her.

"And how do you propose we get them all there?" he spat.

"I don't know. Mayhap we can think of a way."

"Does Aloa-Shay have enough ships for us to buy passage?" Simeon asked.

Ryne shook his head. "Doubtful."

"If needed, I can be very persuasive." Simeon flashed Dianna a seductive smile.

She felt heat creep into her cheeks as she thought about the kiss they'd almost shared. Her hand tingled at the memory of her handprint on his mahogany skin after she'd smacked his face. Yes, he could be very persuasive, but she was no man's fool.

"Why didn't you persuade King Furbald to let us inside his kingdom?" Ryne's tone was laced with accusation as he narrowed his eyes at Simeon.

Simeon arched back, sneering. "I didn't know it was urgent we see inside."

"I want to see what he's hiding." Ryne pouted, stabbing the map with a finger.

She looked at Ryne, carefully considering his words. Shadows from the hearth's fire danced across his blue-tinted skin, making the angles of his face more severe.

"How do you know he's hiding anything?" she asked, glad to know she wasn't the only one who didn't trust the king, especially after he'd turned away Zier's family.

He stabbed the map again, this time puncturing it with the tip of his finger. "Why else won't they let anyone in?"

Alec snatched the map from Ryne and rolled it up with a scowl. "What could they be hiding?"

"Weapons?" Ryne shrugged. "Gold? A goddess stone?"

"Surely, if they were hiding a goddess stone, Grim would have told us." Alec slid the map back into his sack.

"Whatever they are hiding is a treasure indeed." Ryne stood and stretched before grabbing a wine goblet off a nearby table. "Why else would they adopt so many giants? And how did they acquire them? I can't imagine giants would give up their young so easily." Ryne took a sip of wine before wiping his mouth with his hand. "I counted at least a dozen giants coming and going from the hold to Aya-Shay today."

"That is a lot of giants." Dianna, too, had wondered where they'd come from and how the dwarves kept them fed. "It makes no sense."

Simeon shot to his feet, hands clenched. "Are you always this mistrustful, Ryne?"

"No." Ryne jutted a foot forward, his hand coming to rest on the blade hanging on his belt. "Not always."

Simeon tossed up his hands, snickering. "They feed us, shelter us, even give us warm furs, and you thank them with suspicion?"

A muscle twitched above Ryne's mouth as he tapped the hilt of his blade. "I am merely making an observation."

"Maybe it's not your job to observe." The lines on the sides of Simeon's neck swelled as he raised his fists. "Maybe you should just be quiet and not concern yourself with the dwarves."

"Everything is my concern when I'm trying to save my people from Madhea's wrath!" Ryne bellowed, sticking another foot forward and grasping his blade with white knuckles.

"Like you saved your last three companions?" Simeon laughed, exposing a cynical side Dianna hadn't seen before. "You falsely accused the dwarves of theft, which lead to your imprisonment and their deaths."

Boar's blood! She shared wary looks with Alec, then glared back at the stupid slogs, who were going to kill each other before the night was through.

"You son of a siren!" Ryne hollered, flying toward Simeon, a flash of steel in his grip.

"Enough!" Dianna cried as she stood, throwing her arms wide. A loud crack rent the air. Both men were flung back, their backs slamming into the stone walls. They slid to the ground, groaning and clutching their sides.

She rushed to Alec, who'd been toppled by the force of her magic, and helped him stand. She spun around at the sound of Des crying, and her heart hit the floor. He'd rolled off the bench onto a bearskin rug.

The startled boy continued crying as she helped him up.

"See what you made me do!" She scowled at Ryne and then Simeon, who were still sitting on their arses, eyes wide with shock.

She helped Des to a nearby bunk, tucking him under the furs and whispering, "It's okay, brother. I'm sorry. I didn't mean to hurt you." She kissed his forehead, then wiped his eyes.

By the time she'd gotten Des back to sleep, Ryne and Simeon had stood and were returning to the hearth, their eyes downcast like mongrels caught stealing scraps.

When a loud knock sounded at the door, Dianna feared she'd accidentally flattened the entire campsite.

Alec shot her a worried look before reaching the heavy wooden door in a few long strides.

Zier rushed inside, clutching his woolen cap in his hands. "I'm sorry, Mistress Dianna, could you spare a moment?"

"Of course." She wiped her wet fingers on her breeches. "What is it?"

"The children are sick with fever."

She remembered the two sniffling, flame-haired tots hanging onto their father's leg when Zier's family had first arrived at the hold. She should've realized the children were sick, especially as Sofla had said they'd nearly frozen to death.

"Oh no," she cried, snatching her leather boots from beside the bench. "Take me to them."

The little man let out a shuddering sigh. "Thank you."

She scowled at Simeon and Ryne, who were sitting opposite each other, heads in their hands as if they'd imbibed too much. "There is to be no fighting while I'm gone." She wagged her finger at one man and then the other. "Do I make myself clear?"

Simeon nodded, but Ryne answered with a scowl.

"Don't worry, sister." Alec placed a comforting hand on her shoulder. "I will make sure they behave."

Ryne snorted before leaning back and crossing his arms.

"Do as he says, Ryne," she scolded, "or next time I'll make sure you land so hard on your bollocks, your eyes will be crossed for a week."

That seemed to achieve the desired result. Ryne shot up, his shoulders stiffening while he pressed his knees together and cupped his crotch. He looked at Dianna with wide-eyed horror before nodding his understanding.

She left in a huff, cursing all men as foolish *broots*. Still, she couldn't help but smile after asserting her dominance over Ryne. Mahap next time he'd consult with her before deciding her destiny.

DIANNA FOLLOWED ZIER into the hut, her eyes adjusting to the dim candlelight, and spied two small children bundled up in furs on a cot along the wall. Sitting beside them was their mother, cradling their hands. The other adults were gathered beside the fire, the men staring into their cups with lines of worry etched into their faces, and Zelda and Sogred rocking the infants in a long cradle.

"There, there, Sofla." Zier patted his daughter on the back. "Do not cry, darling. I have brought your sons a great healer."

Sofla looked up at her father with a trembling lip. "Their fevers are so strong."

Dianna nodded to the others, feeling as if she was intruding on family privacy as she crossed the room to the children. "Let me see them." She sat beside Sofla, looking down at two sleeping cherubic faces whose flushed faces matched their flame-colored hair. "Oh, they are cute little mites."

She stroked one little boy on the cheek, as she'd done so many times with her brother, alarmed when he didn't so much as twitch. Only his chest moved, heaving up and down as he strained for ragged breaths. Dianna felt the flushed face of his twin brother, who gave the exact same reaction.

"Aletha," she whispered, rubbing her stone. "I need you." Aletha's stone was easy to recognize, for it was rounder than the others, with a small dent in one side.

I know, her cousin's answer reverberated in her mind.

"Can you help me heal them?" she whispered.

I shall do my best, Aletha answered. *These babes will die by morning if their sickness progresses.*

She swallowed hard. "We cannot let that happen." She hated how her voice shook and hoped Sofla could not detect her fear, though something in the way Sofla gaped at her made her think the dwarf could not just sense her panic but see into her very soul.

Hold me in your hand, Aletha commanded, *and press it against their hearts.*

She withdrew the stone from her vest and cradled it against the nearest twin's heart. She allowed her magic to carry her to that place between this world and the next and warm pulses poured from her fingers.

Good. Now the other, Aletha said.

Her eyes shot open, and she smiled at the little boy with the porcelain cheeks who blinked up at her. She placed the stone on the other child, closed her eyes, and let her magic flow through her.

Wonderful. Look, they are feeling better already.

Dianna opened her eyes again, amazed that both children were smiling at her. She'd hardly used her magic to heal them. Were her powers getting stronger or had Aletha done most of the work? She pocketed the stone, whispering her thanks to her cousin.

"My sweet Hamily and Finlay!" Sofla flung herself on top of her children, alternating between weeping and showering them with kisses.

Her husband came to stand beside her, his eyes overflowing as he ran a hand across his children's foreheads.

Sofla turned to Dianna, hands clasped. "Oh, my dear, most benevolent goddess, with all my heart, thank you."

Heat flamed Dianna's face. "I am no goddess." How odd that the dwarf would call her that. She'd never felt like one. Nay, she was Dianna, reluctant witch and sister to three brave brothers, nothing more.

"You are to me." Sofla sniffled and pulled one of her tots into her lap, kissing him and then handing him to her husband. She picked up the other child, smoothing his wet hair out of his eyes. "A compassionate, kind deity like the fallen goddess Kyan."

She wasn't so sure she liked being compared to Kyan, for she could never measure up to that goddess.

"I thank you." She slipped Aletha's stone out of her pocket, showing it to Sofla before pocketing it again. "But I had help. I'm only doing what any woman with my powers would have done."

Sofla's husband chuckled and returned to the hearth, rocking the toddler in his arms. She wondered what was so amusing.

"My dear deity." Sofla patted her hand. "The town of Kicelin has been directly under Madhea's mountain for centuries. Every winter we lose many children to plague and disease. Madhea has never once flown down to help."

She cringed. How ashamed she was to have such a mother. "I'm sorry for that."

And truly she was. She felt the weight of Madhea's sins as if they were her own. It was silly, but she feared other people would feel the same way, that she was somehow responsible for her mother's cruel behavior.

Sofla shifted the restless child in her arms. "I can hardly believe you are Madhea's daughter."

"Neither can I," she blurted.

"But we do not hold your parentage against you." Sogred sat down on the other side of the cot, patting Dianna's knee as if comforting a child. "Our father has told us how kind you are, how you saved the people of Adolan by stealing away the ice dragon."

She released a pent-up breath of air, not even realizing she'd been holding it. "Thank you."

Sofla's face, blotchy and red from crying, turned ashen as her smile faded. "I hope you are able to defeat her, not just for your sake, but for all our sakes, for if you should fail, she will freeze the world, and we will all perish." She ended on a sob, then gently rocked the child in her arms.

Dianna fought to swallow the knot of emotion in her throat. "I promise I will do everything in my power to prevent that from happening." She only prayed her efforts would be good enough.

Chapter Five

Madhea buzzed into Ariette's chamber, an opulent room lined with white furs on the walls and floors, and a wide bed with posts made of polished ivory gnull tusks. This bed was a remnant of when her kingdom had been great, back when she'd had an army with thousands of strong, virile men and magic flowed freely from her fingers. After her army's last battle with Eris's soldiers, Madhea's great force had been vanquished, and the Elementals had forced her to sign yet another truce with her sister. Madhea had neither the patience nor desire to rebuild again, so she'd signed, allowing Eris to take even more land, including prime seaside villages. With Eris dead, all that land belonged to Madhea once again, and she wasn't about to risk losing it to Dianna, which was why she needed a plan. Madhea knew not how many stones Dianna had in her possession, but she suspected the girl's half-brother, Markus, had helped her acquire them. Madhea had thought all night of the man/boy who looked too much like his father. She wondered how close he was to Dianna, if they'd yet formed a sibling bond. If so, Madhea could use that to her advantage.

She fluttered toward her daughter's bed, now occupied by the blue man from the dungeon. He was sleeping soundly under the furs, no doubt his first good rest since he'd been released from his cell. Madhea landed softly beside him, grabbing a bony shoulder and shaking him. "Wake up."

The blue man's eyes shot open, his pupils as dazzling as frosted glass. He sucked in a hiss and scooted back against the fur-lined wall. "W-what do you want?"

She released an impatient sigh. She'd no time for coddling. She needed answers. "What is your name, blue man?"

"Bane." He jerked a fur higher, covering a skeletal ribcage. "Bane Eryll."

Madhea's gaze narrowed on the man, his hollow cheeks appearing to recede into his skull as he shrank from her. "Bane Eryll." She pointed an accusatory finger at him. "Why were you wandering my mountain alone?"

He gaped at her like a dumbstruck pixie moments after flying into a reflective wall of ice.

She gritted her teeth, leaning forward. "Tell me, Bane."

He clutched the fur with white knuckles, his cheeks flushing as he turned his gaze to his lap. "I'd been outed."

She arched a brow. "Outed?"

He slowly nodded. "Cast out."

Madhea crossed one long leg over the other, eying him intently. Whatever he'd done, she was certain he'd deserved it. "By whom?"

He averted his eyes, his face turning bright with crimson splotches. "My people."

Oh, yes, he'd deserved it. Still, she didn't care about his crime, especially as she planned on outing him as well as soon as she got what she wanted. Only Bane Eryll wouldn't survive her outing, for discarded mortals were pushed off the ledge, a narrow strip of ice with an unfathomable drop beneath.

She traced his bony knee under the furs. "Are they all blue like you?"

He jerked his knee away. "Yes."

Madhea ran a hand over the knots in her braid. This man in a boy's body was nothing like Rowlen. He reminded her of a fragile flower preserved within in a block of ice. "Where do these blue people live?"

His gaze shot to hers before he again looked away. "In Ice Kingdom."

She forced a smile, stretching her lips so tight, her skin cracked like old leather. "And where is Ice Kingdom?"

"I cannot tell."

Madhea bit back a curse. "Why not?" she snapped, wincing at the sharp edge in her tone.

He scooted farther away from her. "I-I cannot betray my people."

"You mean the people who abandoned you for snowbear bait?" she said on a hiss, her patience wearing thin.

"I broke their laws." His lip turned down, his lashes glistening with tears, making him look more baby than man.

Perhaps, she thought, she needed to treat him like a child. This man had obviously been used to coddling, which would explain his pathetic cowardice. Rowlen wouldn't have shied away and cried. Rowlen would have looked her in the eyes and faced her fury. If only Bane was more like Rowlen.

"Whatever you have done," she cooed, stroking his arm and forcing another smile, "surely, this outing was too harsh a punishment. Have the Ice People no compassion?"

The man-boy shrugged, pressing his back against the wall.

"I came across a blue man not long ago," she continued. "He was from the town of Adolan, but he'd been living with your people. He goes by the name of Markus."

Bane stiffened, his wide, innocent eyes narrowing, twin fires burning within their depths.

Finally! The reaction she had been seeking. "You've heard of him?"

He nodded, his mouth hardening into a firm line. "Yes."

She fought the urge to cackle with joy. She'd managed to stoke Bane's ire. Good. She'd use his hatred of Markus to her advantage. "He had something quite interesting in his possession." She flashed a sideways grin. "A magical stone."

His jaw dropped. "A warming stone?"

She shrugged indifferently, pretending the stone mattered nothing to her. "Is that what you call it?"

His face colored a deep crimson. "Those belong to the Ice People."

She fought the urge to jump out of her skin. "There are more?" she asked evenly. Oh, heavenly Elements! How many stones had been given to Dianna?

"We have five," Bane said, lifting his chin in proud defiance. "They belong to the most affluent families of Ice Kingdom, mine included."

She thoughtfully rubbed her jaw, forcing a note of calm into her voice, though her heart was pounding like a hammer in her ears. "Five stones?"

"Yes." He crossed his arms. "They are used to warm our hearths. They are very valuable to my people. The land dweller should *not* have had one."

Oh, what simpletons the Ice People were! Warming stones! Each stone had the power of a goddess inside. Madhea knew this because it was she who'd cursed Kyan and her six daughters over a thousand years ago. The Elements had taken the stones from Madhea and given them to Kyan's two fool-ish sons, who'd lost their minds and misplaced them. She had thought the magical stones were lost to her forever.

"Perhaps he stole it. My mists revealed to me that he gave the stone to a pretty witch named Dianna."

His cheeks colored such a deep purple, she thought he might explode, like Eris's volcano. "I knew he wasn't to be trusted." He kicked the furs off his body, revealing two skeletal legs. "And Ura was foolish enough to fall in love with him."

Her brows rose. "Ura?"

He paled.

This girl Ura meant something to Bane. Perhaps Markus, too, for she'd sent her pixies to retrieve the boy hunter, and they'd come back empty-hand-ed. Markus had most likely returned to the Ice People, especially if he had inherited his father's penchant for passion. Her eyes shut as she remembered the feel of Rowlen's thick fingers running through her hair.

She struggled to push thoughts of Rowlen out of her mind.

Once she'd regained her composure, she continued. "Indeed, he is not to be trusted. He was a cruel hunter, who brought the curse of the ice dragon upon his people. I'm not surprised to learn he stole your people's warming stone." She paused, gnawing her lower lip while eyeing Bane through slitted lids. "My mists no longer reveal him to me. I believe he's back with your peo-ple, no doubt to steal the rest of the stones."

Bane shot to his knees, thrusting a fist in the air. "That land-dwelling son of a gnull!"

Her heart leapt with joy. She'd found his weakness, and she'd use it against him to get the information she needed. "If I could but find him, I'd punish him for his crimes."

He gave her a dumbstruck look. "But what would you do to the Ice Peo-ple?"

She dropped her voice to a sultry whisper. "What would you have me do to them, Bane?"

"Nothing." He arched back, a look of terror flashing in his eyes. "They simply want to live their lives in peace."

"And that is what I want for them." She forced herself not to blink as she looked directly into his eyes. "What I want for all my people. But how can they know peace when such a wolf lives among them, preying on their generosity and then stealing their sacred stones when their backs are turned? If you help me find Markus, perhaps the Ice People will welcome you back once we expose the boy hunter's thieving ways." She inwardly smiled as her beautiful lie easily slid off her tongue.

The look of mistrust in Bane's eyes filled her chest with dread, then ire. He pulled back his narrow shoulders, his attempt at bravery belied by his trembling limbs. "My grandfather told me the Ice People have been hiding from you for 300 years. That you sent your dragon to destroy our people after a great plague had killed half the village, and they were too sick and weak to hold a festival in your honor."

She remembered all too well how the people of the fallen town once known as Shadolan, named for the Ice Mountain's shadow that permanently shrouded the town in gloom, had used the excuse of the plague and failed to honor her. 'Twas their own fault. Madhea had sent the plague to them once she realized they were harboring the enemy.

"Is that what your grandfather told you?" She twisted the hem of her gown, focusing on the soft silk and trying to repress the rage that threatened to split her skull in two.

He eagerly nodded like an obedient pup. "And his grandfather told him. The story has been passed down for generations."

"Did your grandfather also mention how the plague came to their village?" She fought to keep ire from her voice but 'twas no use. Slivers of ice sliced the air between them. "That they'd opened up their homes to Eris's soldiers, my sworn enemies, after they were bribed with palma fruits and gold? Eris's soldiers also brought them ill health and bad omens. Still, I was able to forgive them their treachery, but my Elementals overruled me and sent my ice dragon to mete out punishment." She paused, watching his eyes narrow, then widen, as her lie sank in. "That was 300 years ago. My Elementals are now locked away. They can no longer hurt the Ice People, and I do not believe in harboring old grudges." She ended with a smile, pleased with herself for her mastery of deception. Bane gaped at her, hanging on her words like an ice climber dangling from a ledge. Surely, he'd fallen for her ruse.

His mouth snapped shut. "How can I believe you?"

Curse the stupid slog! "Why would I lie?" She forced another smile so wide, her facial muscles ached. "What could I possibly gain from a village of blue people and their old stones? A better question you should be asking yourself is how can your people trust Markus, a cruel hunter who's used your sanctuary to evade justice while stealing from those who risked their lives to help him?" She leaned into him, so close her whisper was hardly more than a cool breath in his ear. "What I can't understand is why they have outed you, Bane, when they should have outed the deceptive land dweller." She lazily dragged her fingers down his thigh.

The blue man's narrow features screwed up tight, like the gnarled wood of a frosted tree. "He has them fooled."

She tossed a braid over her shoulder with a laugh. "Of course he has. So what are you going to do about it?"

THOUGH THE DWARF BEDS were warm and soft, Dianna had had anything but a peaceful slumber, for she'd dreamt of her mother. Not the sweet soul who'd raised her, but the malevolent bitch who threatened all of humanity. Madhea's cackling laughter echoed off the stone walls while she hovered over six sobbing women, trapped in a familiar-looking circle.

She had woken with a start, perspiration on her face and lungs heaving. Had it been merely a nightmare, or had Madhea truly trapped the Elementals, her own children, in a heptacircle?

"Cousins," she whispered, rubbing the stones in her vest. "I had a nightmare."

What was it? Sindri's familiar voice echoed in her skull.

"Madhea trapped her Elementals in a heptacircle." She was unable to keep the fear out of her voice. The dream had felt so real.

I would not put it past your mother to do such a thing, Sindri replied.

All three stones buzzed in Dianna's pocket. Were her cousins conferring? She prayed they could come up with a solution. Though she did not know the Elementals, they were still her sisters. From what her brother Markus had told her, they were kind, unlike Madhea, and their primary focus had been to prevent Madhea from unleashing her wrath on the world. If they'd been imprisoned, who would stop the evil goddess from destroying all of humanity?

"What do I do?"

There is nothing you can do for now, came Nerephine's stoic reply. *A battle with Madhea would put the Ice People at risk.*

She bit down on her knuckles, stifling a sob, for dawn had not yet broken, and Mari was still sleeping in the cot beside her. "But my sisters will die."

Whose lives are more valuable? Aletha asked. *Thousands of innocent mortals or six Elemental witches who've failed for centuries to contain their mother's wrath?*

Though she was right, her cousin's honesty pierced Dianna's heart like a thousand serpent stings. "They will die by the time I am ready to battle Madhea."

Then let us hope it was just a nightmare, Sindri whispered, *or that your mother has a change of heart before then.*

But she feared this had been no ordinary nightmare, and she knew to the marrow of her bones her mother had no heart.

DIANNA COULD HAVE WASHED her face a thousand times, and it wouldn't have erased the memories of her nightmare. She submerged her face in the bowl of water, hoping to push dark thoughts to the back of her mind. She straightened with a gasp, staring at a pair of haunted eyes in the looking glass's reflection. Despite yesternight's hearty supper, she looked gaunt, her eyes hollow.

When the bathing room door creaked open, she forced a smile as Sofla and Sogred entered, the candlelight flickering across their smiling faces.

"We are here to see you off." Though Sogred's spine was not as bent as Zier's, the dwarf mother reminded Dianna too much of the trader, only with a sleeping infant rather than a pack of goods strapped to her back.

Dianna reached for a cloth to dry her face. "Shall I finish up first?" For she still needed to clean her teeth.

Sofla twisted her fingers together, sharing a wary look with her sister. "Actually, we were wondering if we could trouble you for a few moments before you go."

She set the cloth down and leaned against the dresser, giving them her full attention. "Of course."

Another look was shared before Sofla cleared her throat. "There are some who say we are witches."

Dianna arched a brow, completely taken by surprise at Sofla's admission. She had believed herself to be the only witch who lived beneath Madhea's Ice Mountain. There was the old prophet, Dafuar, but Dianna wasn't sure what powers he had left, for he acted more like a madman than a witch.

Sogred added, "We never let the rumor spread beyond our families, for our villagers would've been forced to sacrifice us to Madhea."

She nodded her understanding. Her family, too, had had to conceal Dianna's magical gifts, for Madhea wanted no witches challenging her authority and would strike down entire families if they were found to have been harboring one. Dafuar was the exception. Dianna's father once told her the villagers had offered him as a sacrifice decades ago, but Madhea had flown down and spared his life. Why he'd been spared, she had no idea.

Because Madhea was hoping he'd lead her to the stones, Sindri answered.

That made sense, though she doubted the stones would've worked for Madhea if she'd found them.

We'd rather be cast to the Elements than obey your mother, Neriphene said, *but she still wanted us, if for no other reason than to prevent other witches from finding us and challenging her rule.*

Too late, Dianna thought wryly, turning her attention back to the twins.

Sofla splayed her hands. "But we have only minor gifts compared to you."

"We are empaths." Sogred placed a hand on her heart.

"Empaths?" She had heard of them. They had the ability to see into souls, and some could even predict the future. She suspected Dafuar was an empath, for there were days she thought he was looking into her soul when he turned his milky gaze on her.

Sofla frowned and took her hand. "We sensed a great chasm in your soul yesternight at the mention of your mother."

"And who could blame you after all you've been through?" There was no masking the pity in Sogred's voice.

"Our mother is also an empath," Sofla said. "She taught us a blessing that we would like to do on you."

"A blessing?" She shifted from one foot to the other, warily eyeing the dwarf sisters. She did not believe in blessings, not since the tragic death of her foster parents, and not since discovering her real mother was a cursed bitch. If the Elements had truly wished to bless humanity, they wouldn't have created Eris and Madhea.

Sogred clasped her hands together, starbursts in her mossy eyes. "The mother's blessing, since we know your own probably never blessed you, as ours did."

Dianna flinched. "I was raised by a wonderful mother. I'm sure she did the blessing."

Sofla leaned forward, patting Dianna's arm as if she was comforting a child. "But did she have magic? The blessing is stronger if it comes from a witch."

"No, she did not have magic." Her heart ached as she recalled her mother's sweet smile, the same gentle smile Des had. What her mother lacked in magic, she'd made up for with a love for her children that knew no bounds.

"Like we said, our magic isn't much, but we would like to try it." Sogred slipped the babe off her back, laying the pack on a nearby cot while the infant slept like a caterpillar wrapped in a cocoon. "We think it will help ease your heart."

Sofla eagerly nodded. "And it may just bring you good luck on your journey."

"All right." She shrugged. "If you think it will work." After all, who was she to turn away luck? She needed it if she was to battle a goddess, not that she expected the spell to work. Still, mayhap there was a slim chance it would.

She cringed when Sofla grabbed her hand, surprised by the smaller woman's strong grip as she pulled Dianna to her knees. She slipped a necklace around Dianna's neck. The sisters laid their hands on her head, humming softly before their melodious words flowed, making her flesh tingle with a strange yet familiar feeling.

"Elements of land and sea,

Hear this mother's plea.
Bless this child's mind
With wisdom, strength, and sight.
Bless this child's heart
With laughter, love, and light.
"Elements of spirit and sky,
Here this mother's cry.
If she wanders from me,
Or should she slip from my arms,
Shield her with my love,
That none may do her harm."

She felt odd when they pulled away, like the world had tipped and then righted itself. She looked at her arms, which tingled as if thousands of tiny mites were burrowing beneath her skin. The tingling spread outward, replaced with a soothing warmth, as if she'd just downed several gulps of the dwarves' special brew.

Sofla clasped her hands. "Well, how do you feel?"

She looked at one hand, then the other, turning her palms over to examine fingers which felt detached from the rest of her body. The feeling, though unusual, wasn't bad. In fact, it was oddly pleasant, infusing her with a combination of tranquility and energy, so much energy, she was eager to scale Ice Mountain.

"Strangely at peace," she breathed, amazed how it felt as if someone else was speaking for her. She clutched the emblem hanging around her neck, a seven-pointed star. It was silver on a leather cord, and so beautiful it sparkled like frost under moonlight.

"We're so glad," they said in unison, their warm, sweet smiles reminding Dianna of her departed foster mother.

"Thank you." She jumped to her feet, taking them both in strong hugs. "Thank you so much."

"It is our honor," they squeaked.

As they held onto each other, the ache in her heart subsided. Her origins were something she couldn't change or control, and 'twas her destiny that mattered.

THE DWARVES WHO'D GATHERED to say goodbye to Dianna's party complained that the morning was unusually cool. Dianna, who was impervious to the Elements, enjoyed the feel of the brisk ocean air. More so, she loved the pungent smell of the seaweed that washed up on the shore. Simeon didn't appear as impressed. Though he was wrapped in warm furs given to him by the dwarves, he shivered beside her, shielding his eyes from the sun that peeked over the horizon. 'Twas then Dianna knew she would certainly have to leave the sand dweller in Aloa-Shay, for the climate would only get colder the farther they ascended the mountain.

Dianna thought the entire kingdom of Aya-Shay had gathered on the beach to see them off. Well, the entire kingdom minus King Furbald and his giant son, Borg. She wasn't too disappointed by the king's absence, though. The little sovereign made her uncomfortable with his condescending looks and words, and she especially hated the way he treated poor Borg. She felt relief, rather than the bitter sting of rejection, when he refused to make an appearance.

The dragons had already gone into the forest, where they were to stay until the party left Aloa-Shay. That had been Ryne's idea. Curse him for his common sense. He had said the dragons would frighten the villagers, who would most likely fill their wings full of arrows. So it was to be Dianna, Alec, Des, Simeon, Ryne, and Mari the first leg of the trip. Dianna feared Mari and Des would slow them down, but she had little choice but to follow them. She would have preferred them to have remained at the hold, but Mari had to return to her crippled cousin Tung, who'd been left all alone after Eris's soldiers had taken Mari and her father hostage. Dianna prayed Tung had survived their absence. She did not wish to deliver her brothers to a gruesome scene.

"This is taking too long," Ryne grumbled, the usual scowl marring his features.

"I know," she said with a sigh.

Simeon chuckled. It seemed the more Ryne grumbled, the more Simeon laughed. She couldn't wait to leave Simeon in Aloa-Shay, for this foolish rivalry was driving her mad.

Though she hated to agree with Ryne, she wished her brothers would make haste in their goodbyes with the giant, Gorpat. Dianna kept her distance, for the giant was crying so profusely, long bands of snot hung from her nose like twin pendulums. She cringed when one band broke, splattering close to Des's feet. Fortunately the boy had quick reflexes and jumped out of the way. She gasped when Des tripped over his dog, Brendle, then smiled when Alec caught him before he landed on his arse. Alec was a fine brother to Des. She knew he would be well cared for when she left them together.

She had to blink hard when she saw a tall contraption wobbling toward them. The creature was Zier, laden with pots, pans, and other goods that stretched far above his head, as if he moved his own personal mountain. The pack was so heavy, his footprints in the sand were deep indentations that immediately filled with water. He had donned a new leather vest, his hair was freshly washed and combed, and his crimson beard had been neatly trimmed. Wherever he was headed, he seemed determined to make a good impression.

The dwarf came to a halt in front of her, his goods jangling for a few heartbeats. "I hope you don't mind if I accompany you on your journey."

She stepped away from a bear trap dangling precariously at the top of the heap. "You want to come with us?"

He nodded ever so slightly, but enough to set off the clanking and rattling of pots and pans. He looked at Ryne. "If you think the Ice People will be up for trade."

Ryne eyed the trader with a smirk. "I'm sure they will welcome many of your tools, but it's a dangerous journey."

"I'm aware, lad." Zier stuck a thumb in his chest. "You think this old trader hasn't seen his share of danger?"

"And you are a skilled climber?" Ryne asked.

The trader straightened with a groan. The veins on his leathery neck popped out like raging torrents beneath the strain of the heavy weight on his shoulders. "Skilled enough and strong as a boar."

Behind Zier was his wife and daughters, standing stoically with red-rimmed eyes. Zelda's hands trembled like leaves in an autumn breeze as she dabbed her nose with a handkerchief.

Dianna shook her head, the weight of Zelda's sorrow striking her like a hammer. "Your family doesn't look happy to see you go."

Zier's shoulders dropped. "They never are."

Dianna braced herself when her brothers joined her, the ground shaking as Gorpat followed them.

"No want friends go to danger," the giant cried.

"Never fear, my friend." Alec patted the giant's grimy toe, smiling up at her. "I will have my sister and two mighty dragons as companions."

Grim huffed and puffed as he chased his daughter. "Come along, my pearl. We must let them go." He marched up to Alec, holding out a hand. "I bid you safe travels, my son. Please be careful."

When Alec took Grim's hand, the smaller man jerked him down for a hug, sniffling as if Alec was his son.

"I will," Alec said with a wheeze before pulling out of the embrace. "For I have much to live for." He nodded to Mari, who was feeding fruit to a donkey under the shade of a palma tree. Mari had only recently gained the use of her legs after Eris had banished the girl's spirit after holding her body captive for fifteen years. Because Mari was not accustomed to walking, she could only stand for short periods of time, so the donkey was a welcome necessity for their journey.

When Grim had brought them the animal as a gift from King Furbald, Dianna wasn't sure if 'twas an act of generosity or if the king wanted to ensure they'd leave. Either way, she was grateful, for that meant the men wouldn't have to take turns carrying her. After she caught Simeon with Mari in his arms, she'd no wish to witness such a spectacle again. Not that she was jealous, as she and Simeon were never meant to be, but she did not wish to upset Alec, who'd so obviously surrendered his heart to Mari.

This morning Dianna had come upon Alec helping Mari walk with all the patience and tenderness of a mother assisting her toddler. She suspected the two would be wed by the time she returned from Ice Kingdom.

Dianna gave Zelda a sympathetic look when she approached, taking Dianna's hand in hers. "This is for you." The sweet matronly dwarf placed a soft, thick scarf with bright purple bands in her hands. "Something to keep your neck warm."

"Thank you. It's beautiful." Dianna didn't wish to offend Zelda by telling her she was impervious to the Elements.

"My sister doesn't feel the cold," Des blurted.

Zelda raised a thick brow. "Oh, she doesn't?"

Dianna instinctively reached for his shoulder, hoping he'd take the hint and be quiet.

"Ow!" He jerked out of her grasp and dashed off, Brendle yapping at his feet.

Dianna stroked the scarf, enjoying the feel of its soft fabric caressing her fingertips. "It's beautiful nonetheless, which is enough reason to wear it." She wrapped it around her neck.

When Zelda crooked a finger at Dianna, she bent toward the smaller woman.

"Slip it off. I will show you the other usage."

Zelda flipped the scarf inside out, revealing several hidden pockets sewn inside the material. "You may hide things here."

She noted seven pockets, seven hiding spots for her stones, should she find them all.

"Oh, Zelda," Dianna breathed. "How clever of you to think of this."

"Nay, not clever." The older woman twisted the frayed hem of her frock and squinted at Dianna. "Mayhap my daughters told you we were empaths."

She took the woman's hand in hers. "Yes, they did."

"A little voice told me you will be needing this." Zelda frowned, scratching the back of her head. "Don't know if 'twas the Elements or my own mind telling me. I'd originally made this for my girls, only it had four pockets. I sewed three more last night."

"I'm so very grateful, but I hope your daughters don't mind." Dianna warily eyed the dwarf sisters, wondering if they knew Dianna had taken their scarf.

"No bother." Zelda shrugged. "I shall make them another."

"'Tis a wonderful gift. Thank you." She wrapped it around her neck as the dwarf sisters approached.

"Here." Sofla held out a sack.

She pulled a smooth, round stone from it, amazed at how much it looked like her goddess stones, only smaller. She peered into the bag and counted six more.

"They look very much like my stones." And they would come in handy should she need decoys.

Sogred turned up her chin, triumphantly smiling. "We polished them all night."

"You never know when you may need them," Sofla said with a wink.

"Thank you."

After she exchanged hugs with Zelda and the twins, Grim stepped up, holding out his hand.

"I bid you a safe journey and thank you again, Dianna, for saving my pearl," the dwarf father ended on a rasp.

"Tell your king we thank him for his hospitality." Dianna nodded at Alec and Des as they helped Mari onto the donkey.

"Aye, lass," Grim said with a wink, "but you and I both know he was anything but hospitable."

She hid a smirk behind her hand while Simeon laughed outright. "The dwarves have been so very kind and generous." She swept a hand toward her traveling companions, who wore new warm furs and boots, and wielded shiny weapons. "One day I hope to reciprocate."

Grim's face hardened into a mask of stone. "Just kill the bitch. That will be reciprocation enough."

Chapter Six

Though Markus knew little about building boats, he did know how to construct a bow and he'd helped his father build a wagon and repair their family hut. What he didn't know, he was eager to learn from the small assembly of builders who'd agreed to help him.

They'd come to the Danae River, which ran through a tunnel deep within the bowels of the glacier, bringing tools and material—enough gnull hides and bones to assemble four boats. Each boat would carry twelve people, which was a start. Hopefully, as other ice dwellers learned of Markus's plan, they'd contribute as well.

The plan was to escape along the river that ran under the glacier when Madhea came, for she would come. Markus was certain of it. Why else would the Elements show her attack in the mists? Markus didn't want to think about the vision he'd seen. He'd been crumpled at the ice witch's feet, which meant he'd not survive the encounter. Still, he needed to ensure his bride and her father made it out alive.

Ura had not mentioned the vision again after they'd spoken to the Council, though she'd spent most of yesternight alternating between trembling in his arms like a frightened mouse and sobbing into his chest.

This morning, when he'd told her of his plans to assemble an escape party, she'd not objected, stoically agreeing to help organize a crew. And she'd done just that. Though they were mostly comprised of Odu's loyal followers, who spent their days taking turns with Odu's pipe and staring into the mists, Markus couldn't afford to be picky. Despite the pipe they passed around, they were determined and focused on their jobs, which was what mattered most.

Ura quietly worked with the other women, wrapping bones together with her stiffened back to him, and he suspected silent tears streamed down her face. He feared that when the time came, she would not flee with the others, that she'd stay with his broken body and perish when Madhea reduced their kingdom to rubble. He'd tried to coax a promise out of her that she'd go with her father, but she'd simply cried. He'd pressure her until she relented, enlisting her father if necessary.

He oversaw the men as they prepared the hides, stretching them across the rocks beside the riverbank and coating them in a thick wax that hardened them like a shell. When the wax was almost dry, they would wrap the hides around the bones, molding them like skin to a skeleton until they formed the hulls.

Markus turned at a commotion coming from the mouth of the cave leading to the Danae River. He cringed when he saw Chieftain Ingred Johan and her Council pushed their way through the crowd.

"What is all this?" Ingred demanded, her voice a thunderous boom above the noisy din of the rushing water, her stony-eyed glare settling on Markus.

"What does it look like, Chieftain?" he grumbled, in no mood to argue. "We are building boats."

The woman, who was nearly his height, glared at him, her thin lips pressed together. "I didn't authorize you to build a fleet."

"I didn't know we needed your authorization," a familiar voice boomed behind Markus.

His father-in-law, Jon Nordlund, winked and settled a hand on his shoulder.

"Where do you plan on going in these boats?" Ingred snapped.

"Downriver," Jon said.

"Are you mad?" Her hand flew to her throat, a comical look of horror on her face. "The gnulls nest downriver."

Markus braced his feet and crossed his arms, refusing to be intimidated. "I'd rather face a nest of hungry gnulls than one mad goddess."

She laughed, a loud cackling sound that echoed off the walls of the tunnel, causing a few of the ice dwellers to throw down their tools and cover their ears. "So, all of this is based on one land-dweller's claim to have seen Madhea in the mists?"

"This land dweller is my son-in-law," Jon said in a surprisingly calm and collected tone, "and my daughter saw Madhea in the mists as well."

"You are all fools." She sneered. "And soon you will be gnull-bait."

Markus had had enough of her rebukes. They had work to do before Madhea arrived, and he refused to let one thick-headed chieftain delay their progress. "If you don't mind stepping out of the way." He shooed her away, as if she was Ryne's mutt, Tar. "You are impeding our work."

She turned up her nose, releasing an indignant huff. "The Council will have a say about this."

Great Goddess! If Madhea didn't drive Markus mad, surely this ignorant chieftain would.

"Oh, I've no doubt they will," he said on a low growl, barely able to contain his growing rage, "and just as they have refused to listen to us, we, too, shall refuse to listen to them." He pushed past her, stomping toward a boat that was almost finished. "Good day, Chieftain."

THEY'D TRAVELED ALONG a path through the forest, close enough to the beach that Dianna could hear the waves hitting the shore, but far enough away that they wouldn't be spotted by any sun-bathing sirens. They walked at a slog's pace, constantly having to coax the temperamental donkey to move. It seemed he wasn't fond of carrying Mari, no matter how light she may have been.

She had to bite her tongue several times while sitting by the campfire, forced to endure her companions' complaints. Des's feet hurt, Mari was tired, Simeon was cold, and Ryne had too many grievances to list. At the rate they were forced to travel, they wouldn't make it to Aloa-Shay for two more days. How she wished she, Ryne, and Zier could send the others to Aloa-Shay while they cut through the forest to Ice Mountain, but she'd already given Mari her promise she'd heal her cousin, Tung, and she needed to ensure her little brother arrived safely and was provided with a warm bed.

To make matters worse, she was trapped between Simeon and Ryne again, and the others in her party weren't providing much company. Alec and Mari sat opposite them, heads bent together, acting as if they were the only two souls in the forest. Zier was off to the side with Des, teaching him how to whittle animal figures out of discarded wood chunks. The dogs sat at the dwarf's feet. They'd been his constant companions after realizing he carried an abundance of jerky strips and bones.

Despite the raging fire that put off plenty of heat and light, Simeon shivered in his furs while palming a cup of tea, sloshing it all over the ground every time he tried to take a shaky sip.

Finally he gave up and set the mug down with a sigh. "Zier, do you happen to have any warm furs?"

Zier set aside his dragon carving. "Why of course." He hobbled over to his pack, which was leaning against a tree.

Ryne leaned forward, scowling at Simeon. "You are bundled up already."

"It is not enough." Simeon pouted. "This place is cold."

Ryne rolled his eyes. "If you think it's cold here, you will not survive Ice Mountain."

Firelight danced in Simeon's golden eyes. "My comfort is not your concern." He took a fur from Zier, thanking him as he draped it across his legs.

"It *is* my concern if you slow us down," Ryne grumbled.

"That's it!" Simeon kicked the fur to the ground, jumped to his feet, and drew back his fists.

Ryne got to his feet, too, and his big furry canine rushed to his master's side, baring sharp fangs.

Dianna stifled a curse as she stood, holding out her hands. She'd no wish to flatten them all like hotcakes, but she'd have no choice if they continued to act like toddlers.

"Enough! Ryne is right, Simeon." She turned to him, hating the look of hurt in his big golden eyes. "The mountain climate is too harsh for you. You will stay in Aloa-Shay with Alec and Des."

Alec gaped at her from across the campfire. "I'm coming with you, sister."

"No," she said firmly, in no mood to argue. "I need you to look after Des."

Alec threw his hands in the air. "And send you off into danger alone?"

"I will have Ryne and Zier." She turned from Simeon when he swore and kicked the sand like a temperamental child. "The smaller the party, the less chance we have of being seen by Madhea."

"And the more chance you have getting eaten by snow bears," Alec argued. "I'm skilled with a bow."

"But you are not a skilled climber." Ryne glared coolly at Alec, as if waiting for Alec to challenge him.

"And who will help Zier carry his goods up the mountain?"

"I can carry my own pack," Zier said. "It will be much lighter after we leave Aloa-Shay."

"Brother," Dianna pleaded, "it would ease my mind and my heart if you were to stay with Des."

"But—" Alec's protest died when Mari tugged on his tunic.

"Alec, I think Dianna is right," Mari said. "You should stay with me."

Dianna recognized Mari's smile, for she'd seen it enough times whenever one of Simeon's admirers was trying to coax him into her arms. Though she should've been grateful for Mari's help, she wasn't sure how she felt about seeing her brother manipulated. At least Mari wasn't trying to seduce Simeon. Not that she cared. At least she tried not to care.

"You need to stay, Alec." A mischievous grin split Ryne's face in two, reminding Dianna of Lydra before she bit an evil mage in half. "Unless you think it's a good idea leaving Simeon alone with Mari."

Simeon stepped around Dianna, facing down Ryne like a snowbear staking his territory. "What's that supposed to mean?"

"I hadn't thought of that," Alec grumbled.

Simeon spun toward Alec. "Do you all think me a baseless worm?"

Dianna swore beneath her breath when Ryne answered with a deep chuckle. Simeon whipped back around, his fist connecting with Ryne's jaw so fast, Dianna didn't have time to stop him.

Ryne stumbled over the log behind him, falling flat on his arse, blinking up at Simeon in shock. "You son of a siren!" He rubbed his jaw.

Simeon jumped back when Tar snapped at him.

Growling, the dog advanced.

"Enough!" Dianna yelled. "We cannot possibly hope to defeat Madhea if we are fighting among ourselves."

"Quiet," Zier spat. "I hear something."

Everyone froze. There were thunderous sounds in the distance. Was a storm approaching? She thought not, for she didn't feel a shift in the weather.

No, those booms meant a monster was approaching. She only hoped it was friendly.

"The fire!" she whispered, nodding at the bright flames.

The men threw dirt into it.

The tree branches swayed, pine needles raining down on the ground as the booms drew nearer. The braying donkey jerked free from his rope and ran off into the forest. Alec dove for it, but he wasn't fast enough. She'd had no idea the donkey could move so fast. If only he'd put that much effort into carrying Mari, they might not be in danger now.

The ground under Dianna's feet shook with earthquake force. She stepped back, the stones in her pocket warming with magical energy as she braced for an attack. Tar jumped in front of her, the hair on his neck standing on end as he faced the thunder. Alec stood beside her with his bow and arrow, Zier with his hatchet. Simeon wielded a spear, and Ryne drew a sword while Des led Mari and Brendle behind them.

The booms were so close now, Dianna could feel her brain jarring against her skull. Imagine her relief when a familiar giant head poked from between two pines, his meaty fists bending the trees like twigs.

Borg flashed a lopsided grin. "Hi, fwiends."

"Borg!" Zier's shoulders slumped as he threw down his hatchet. "Thank the Elements."

"Da says I go wif you." Spittle flew out of the giant's mouth, raining down on their heads.

Ryne and Simeon sheathed their swords, grumbling while swiping slime off their arms.

"Go with us, Borg?" Dianna asked as she threw kindling on the fire pit's embers. "To Ice Kingdom?"

"That big gnull can't go with us to Ice Kingdom." Ryne sneered at Borg as the giant sat down, flattening a patch of weeds and brush under his wide arse.

"Borg, are you just to accompany us to Aloa-Shay?" Dianna thought mayhap this would work to their advantage. If Borg carried Mari and Des, they could reach Aloa-Shay in under a day.

The giant scratched the back of his head, his eyes nearly crossing. "Borg no remember."

"You can accompany us to Aloa-Shay," she said, "but then you must turn back. Okay?"

The folds of his forehead sagged over his long eyebrow. "Da will be mad."

"Da will have to get over it," Ryne grumbled. "You will be spotted by Madhea if you travel with us past Adolan."

"Besides," Dianna added with a forced smile, hoping her soothing tone made up for Ryne's dark mood, "you are not dressed for cooler weather, so surely your father meant for you only to accompany us to Aloa-Shay." The giant wore breeches, a vest, a short-sleeve tunic, and no socks or shoes to protect his big, grimy feet. His toes would freeze before they reached Ice Mountain.

The giant frowned, shaking his head. "Borg no want Da to be angry."

Ugh. Poor Borg. She could only imagine the beating the giant would get if he returned too soon. Why had the king sent him? Was he a protector or a spy? She feared the latter, though she suspected Borg wouldn't remember enough to report.

She scanned the camp as the men rebuilt the fire. "I'm afraid we haven't brought enough food for you, Borg."

"That okay." He reached into the pack that was slung over his shoulders and withdrew the biggest fish she had ever seen. It was larger than Mari's donkey, its skin slick and gray with feline-like whiskers and a large, gaping mouth.

"Do you need help cooking it?" Zier asked.

"No fanks, cousin." Borg smiled before tipping back his head and dropping the fish into his mouth. He smacked his lips loudly while he chewed, the bones making sickening crunching sounds. When one large fin slipped from between his teeth, landing on the ground with a *thud*, Tar swiped it, then dove into the forest, Brendle chasing after him.

Borg burped and then softly hummed to himself, staring up at the starry sky.

The others returned to their places. Unfortunately, Simeon and Ryne sat even closer to Dianna than before.

"He can't come with us," Ryne whispered in Dianna's ear.

"I know." She repressed a shudder at the feel of him so near her. She didn't know why, but his arm pressing against hers made her uncomfortable, very uncomfortable. Yet if she was being honest with herself, she didn't know if the discomfort was because she abhorred his touch or enjoyed it.

"We need to get rid of him," he whispered again.

She cast her gaze at Borg, who was still staring up at the stars, a goofy grin on his face. "We will."

"How?" Ryne pressed.

"We'll think of something." She spoke out of the side of her mouth, hoping Borg wasn't listening, though not sure he'd understand the conversation if he was. "I'm sure his Da didn't mean for him to follow us up the mountain. We will try reasoning with him first."

Ryne shook his head, snickering. "I don't think reason will work on him."

"We'll have to try." She wasn't sure if she was more aggravated with Borg's intrusion or Ryne's complaints.

"And if it doesn't work?"

She had to fight to unclench her jaw. Ryne truly was annoying. "Then we'll sneak away."

"He can run faster than us."

"Okay, Ryne. I get it." She groaned, raking a hand down her face. Curse her brothers for befriending this annoying ice dweller. "Let's just worry about getting to Aloa-Shay. We'll take care of the rest later."

Borg would present a real danger if he followed them up the mountain, which made her wonder at King Furbald's true purpose for sending the giant. He had to know Borg would endanger their mission. Mayhap that's why the king had sent him.

"HELLO, MY HANDSOME blue friend." Madhea giggled as she floated into her guest's chamber. "How are you feeling?"

Bane Eryll was sitting up in bed, his complexion a deeper shade of blue, but his face was still gaunt, his mouth twisted in an unpleasant snarl.

She was beginning to realize his outward appearance was a reflection of his character, an insignificant man who'd been rejected by his people, probably for cowardice or theft, unlike Rowlen who'd been admired for his looks and bravery.

"Slightly better," he answered, focusing on her with beady serpentine eyes.

"Good, good." She sat beside him, hiking up the sheer fabric of her gown while crossing her legs. Though they were still wrinkled and spotty, they were looking smoother every day. Soon she'd regain her youthful beauty. "You are looking heartier." She trailed a finger down his scrawny arm, imagining he had Rowlen's strong biceps. "Have you given our discussion any thought?"

He turned his gaze to his hands, fisted in his lap. "I couldn't show you how to reach the Ice People even if I wanted to. Your mountain is so vast, I could never find my way back."

Liar. She forced a smile. "What if I had my pixies bring you to the spot where they found you?"

He blinked at her. "I was lost when they found me."

She did her best to maintain a calm, kind demeanor, though it was hard not to scratch his ugly face to shreds. "But you couldn't have wandered that far from your home."

"I have no idea." His gaze shifted to the wall behind her. "I was caught in a blizzard." He shivered, wrapping his arms around himself. "It's a wonder I didn't freeze to death."

"You know what I think?" she purred, smoothing a finger down his thigh. She did her best to ignore it when he flinched and then scooted away, looking at her as if she was infected with the plague. "I think you don't want to tell me where they are. I think you're still afraid I'll try to harm them. What can I do to make you trust me?" She licked her lips and scooted closer, reaching for his leg again, her internal temperature soaring with rage when he continued to retreat. This time the horror on his face was so pronounced, it was almost comical. Too bad for him, she didn't find his rejection funny.

She'd have to work more magic before he was willing to tell her, and tell her he would, for she was almost out of patience. If Bane didn't relent soon, she'd mark his final days with misery and torture, making him wish she'd left him at the mercy of that snowbear.

Chapter Seven

A Gathering of Ghosts

Thanks to Borg, who carried Des, Mari, Zier, and Zier's pack, they arrived at Aloa-Shay by mid-afternoon. After trying to match stride with a giant, Dianna was breathless by the time they reached a small patch of farmland carved out of the lush landscape. Tall pines had given way to shorter, leafier trees and thick flowered bushes. The air was warmer here, too. So warm that even Simeon had discarded his furs and vest, running through the jungle with his bare chest gleaming with sweat.

She tried not to gape at his tattoos or his glistening bronze muscles. He was definitely better sculpted than Ryne—or most men for that matter. No wonder so many women threw themselves at him. Fortunately for her, she wasn't like most women, and Simeon's muscles held little appeal. She repeated that to herself several times while sneaking peeks at his broad shoulders.

Mari's home, if that's what one called it, was a wreck. The hut's roof had caved on one side, the door was in shreds, and the barn and chicken coop were blackened from fire. The place smelled of burn and decay, and Dianna feared they'd find the corpse of Mari's cousin inside what was left of her house.

Alec sat Mari on a tree stump, insisting she wait while they search the grounds. Dianna instructed Borg to sit behind the house, hoping he'd be quiet and not frighten Mari's cousin—if they found him alive.

"Tung!" Alec called, rushing through the house.

"Tung, come out!" Mari yelled.

When Tar and Brendle raced into the burned shell of the barn, sniffing and barking, Ryne followed them.

"In here!" he called.

Mari tried to stand on shaky legs. Dianna rushed to her side, letting Mari lean on her for support.

Alec emerged from the house and raced past them. "Stay there," he said to Mari.

She leaned into Dianna, clutching her vest with trembling hands. "Please let him be alive," she whispered.

Dianna's heart ached for her. Mari had only recently lost her father. She'd hate to have to bury the girl's cousin, too.

"Let me go!" A man screamed, thrashing as Alec and Ryne carried him out of the barn.

"Tung!" Mari's hands flew to her face. "You're alive!"

The man went still, craning his neck toward Mari as Ryne and Alec laid him on the ground by her feet.

"Mari?" the man rasped.

Dianna stepped back, overwhelmed by a rotten stench that rose up from the man whose face and arms were blackened with filth. His clothes, or what was left of them, were in tatters, and his face was so gaunt, he looked like a skeleton draped with a sock.

"Tung, these are my friends." Mari gestured to Alec and Ryne. "They're here to help."

"Mari!" Tung pointed at her with a shaky finger. "Your body!"

She smiled, running a hand down her side. "I got it back."

He blinked hard at her, then broke into a wide grin. "Eris gave it back to you?"

She frowned. "No. Long story."

"Uncle Khashka?"

Mari's face fell, and she vehemently shook her head. "Carnivus."

Tung let out a low wail, so pitiful and heartbreaking, he sounded like a dying animal. He covered his face with his hands, sobbing.

Alec and Dianna helped Mari kneel by her cousin.

"Tung, listen to me." Mari grabbed her cousin's shoulder. "Eris is dead."

He peered at her between a crack in his grimy fingers. "Dead?"

"Yes. Dianna killed her." Mari smiled up at her. "She is a powerful witch. A good witch."

A vortex of emotions swirled in Tung's eyes. "The sea witch is dead?"

"Yes." Mari smiled, smoothing a lock of Tung's matted hair.

"So she can't harm you again?"

"She can't harm anyone ever again." Mari's voice shook with emotion. "Tung, listen. Dianna can restore your legs."

She backed up a step when Mari nodded to her.

Tung gaped at Dianna. "You can do that?"

She shrugged. "I will try." Though she'd healed many injuries since she'd come into her powers, she had never had to heal a paralyzed man. She hoped she was up to the challenge. "Aletha, I need your help," she whispered to her cousin, and the stone warmed inside her vest pocket. She knelt beside him, breathing through pinched nostrils; his odor was strong, a combination of mold and feces and Elements only knew what else.

She splayed a hand across his bony knees, so frail and withered, they looked like twigs. Then she shut her eyes, letting her spirit drift between this world and the next, summoning her healing magic.

She woke in Alec's arms. She didn't know how long she was out. "Did it work?"

"See for yourself." Alec nodded to Tung, who was being held up by Simeon and Ryne, both men scowling while turning up their noses.

"I can feel my legs. I can feel them!" Tung's bony legs shook like feeble, bare sapling branches in a blizzard. "I-I can't walk. I don't think my legs are strong enough."

"It's okay," Mari said as she patted the ground beside her. "I imagine you'll be like me at first and have to learn how to use your legs again, but you *will* walk, Tung."

Ryne and Simeon deposited Tung beside Mari, releasing him and shaking their hands as if his stench had scalded their fingers.

"I will walk again! I will." Tung clasped his hands together, his bright, wet eyes standing out against his grimy skin. "Thank you, Dianna."

She couldn't help but smile. "You're very welcome." She turned to Alec, patting his arm. "I'm okay now."

Alec released her and went to Mari, kneeling beside her with a hand on her shoulder.

"Tung, this is Alec, Dianna's brother." Mari looked at Alec with a look of pure adoration, as if the sun and moon revolved around him. "He's the most amazing man I've ever met. He and his friends are going to stay and help us for a while."

At that moment, Dianna realized she'd been a jealous fool to be envious of the connection Alec and Mari shared. To have a woman look upon her brother like that made her heart swell with joy.

"I would be most grateful for the help." Tung motioned to his grimy legs.

Ryne and Simeon exchanged wary looks. 'Twas then Dianna realized they would probably rather fight to the death than share the task of bathing Tung.

"I'm not staying," Dianna said, "but I would be indebted to you if my brothers had a place live until my return."

"They are welcome here." Tung thumbed at the crumbling home behind him. "Unfortunately, our home isn't as comfortable as it once was. I've salvaged what I could and brought it to the barn. You are welcome to stay there with me."

She scowled at the barn, which didn't appear to be in any better shape than the hut. Des and Alec wouldn't be safe sleeping there. She thought they could make it back to the hold by nightfall if they hurried, but after King Furbald's cold welcome, she didn't think her family would be safe there either.

Simeon walked a wide circle around Tung and held a hand down to Dianna. "Did you know my grandmother, Feira, could heal objects like she could heal people?" he said as he pulled her to her feet.

"Really?" she asked, quickly stepping away from him and hating herself for acting like a spooked deer during a full moon. She had to keep her distance from Simeon if she wanted to retain her sanity.

He nodded. "I once watched her fuse a broken table together with just one touch."

"Do you think I could do the same?"

"Ask the stones."

She smiled when the stones instantly warmed her chest. Today she'd heal Mari's home. Tomorrow, she'd journey to Ice Mountain.

"DON'T EAT IT." ARIETTE scowled at the basket of breads and cheeses and the bladders of water, delicious food Madhea could have kept for herself. "It may be poisoned."

Ungrateful child. She made Madhea's decision to imprison her and her sisters all the more bearable. Children should honor and respect their mothers. Most of all, they must obey. Had the Elementals been good daughters, they would not be imprisoned now.

Madhea's wings angrily buzzed as she hovered above them. "Why would I need to poison you when I could simply starve you? I've decided I may need you to stay alive a bit longer."

Unable to withstand the censure in her daughters' eyes, Madhea turned her attention to her painted fingernails, pleased by how much smoother and stronger they were today. Her magic was strengthening, and with it, her beauty was returning.

Oh, Rowlen, I wish you'd survived to see me return to glory.

"We will no longer do your bidding, Mother."

She scowled at Ariette, deciding for her sisters as if she was their goddess. "Not even if I agreed to spare your lives? Surely you do not speak for everyone, Ariette." She scanned the faces of her other pretty children, disappointed and angry when they looked away.

"What do you want of us?" Ariette snapped.

"What did Markus tell you of the Ice People when he was here?"

"Nothing," Ariette answered flatly.

She arched a brow. "Nothing? He did not tell you where they were hiding or how to reach them?"

Ariette's face hardened. "No."

Lying bitch. "Did he tell you how many stones they kept?"

"No, and even if he did, I wouldn't tell you." Ariette folded her arms, tapping her foot while her wings buzzed like a swarm of angry hornets. "Perhaps you shouldn't have murdered Jae. I'm sure Markus would've told her."

She narrowed her eyes at Ariette, heat flaming her face and chest as she spun and flew away, her daughters' laughter echoing off the ice cave walls and burrowing into her heart like a thousand tiny needles. How dare they make a mockery of her! How dare they treat her so cruelly after she'd been kind enough to offer them food! Perhaps she *should* have poisoned her offering. Her daughters wouldn't be laughing for long if they were clutching their throats and gasping for breath.

A thought struck her. Perhaps she would poison them and leave them squirming on their backs until they agreed to sign a blood oath. If they did that, they could not defy her. Their magic would be hers to wield. Sparks crackled in her palms at the thought. She laughed all the way to her chamber.

"WE'VE MADE GREAT PROGRESS today, don't you think?" Markus dropped his hammer on the frozen ground and held a hand down to Jon, helping the older man to his feet.

Jon stood with a groan, nodding to Ura, who was silently packing up her tools. "You should be enjoying your honeymoon, not building boats."

Markus looked away from Ura, unable to stare at his bride for too long. Every time he gazed at her, he was overwhelmed by the despair in her haunted expression, as if she knew she was looking at a dead man.

He cursed. "How can I enjoy my honeymoon when a vindictive goddess threatens my family?"

"What did you see in the mists, son?"

Jon's question sounded more like an accusation, startling Markus.

"I-I told you," he faltered, breaking eye contact. "Madhea in Ice Kingdom."

"What *else* did you see?" The older man grabbed Markus's shoulder, desperately searching his face. "I fear you're not telling me all of it. My daughter will not stop crying. She can't even look at me when I speak to her."

He hung his head, a feeling of hopelessness washing over him. "I was at Madhea's feet. I appeared dead."

"Oh," Jon breathed, a strangled sob dying in his throat.

He jerked his head up. Jon couldn't break. He needed his father-in-law to stay strong for Ura's sake. "Whatever happens, you need to make sure Ura gets on a boat." He grasped the man, shaking hard. "Do you understand?"

"She is strong-willed." Jon flashed a watery smile. "Just like her mother was."

"I know." Markus dropped his arms. He was determined to see his plan through, though it pained him to imagine Ura living a life without him. "One of the reasons I love her so. Don't let that bitch kill her. Get her on a boat."

"I will, son." Jon stepped back, casting one more forlorn look at Ura. "I will."

"Thank you." He barely choked out the words before brushing past Jon to kneel beside Ura.

They finished packing her things, then Markus slung the bag over his shoulder and held her hand while they trudged toward the tunnel that would lead them home. They followed Jon, who held the party's lone torch. The only sound in the dark, winding tunnel was of boot spikes crunching ice. A shiver coursed down Markus's spine, and it wasn't due to the cold. It was because of the overwhelming feeling that they might one day be nothing more than a gathering of ghosts.

DIANNA WOKE SLOWLY, stretching after a much-needed nap. She'd been tired after spending all afternoon restoring Mari's broken home, but now the task was finished, and Mari was left with a comfortable three-room hut, a barn, and a chicken coop. She even had ten hens, thanks to Zier, who'd generously traded his goods for the birds after a visit to Aloa-Shay. He'd also given her pots, pans, and other household goods that had gone missing, no doubt stolen by Eris's soldiers when they'd first raided the farm.

The room was dark, save for a candle beside her narrow cot. Looking out the window, she spied a bright moon and a smoky campfire. Zier and Ryne sat beside the fire, bent over a map, while Simeon hovered nearby. A pang of guilt stabbed her chest when she thought about leaving Simeon behind, but he'd left her no choice. He would not survive the frigid weather.

We were warming stones for three hundred years, Dianna, Sindri's voice echoed in her head. *We can warm your mate for a few weeks.*

She stepped away from the window. "Simeon is not my mate."

Not yet, Aletha said and giggled.

"You want me to let him hold the goddess stones for the journey?" What if they encountered dangerous monsters, and she needed the stones to fight them off?

He only needs one of us, Neriphene said.

"Which one of you will do it?"

He can rotate us, Sindri answered. *Make sure he hangs us on that broad chest of his,* she said wryly.

Heat infused her face. The stones had been listening to her thoughts earlier, when she was admiring his shirtless chest. How embarrassing. "Stay out of my head, will you?"

I'm sorry, cousin. Sindri laughed. *The life of a stone is a boring one. We must have something to gossip about.*

She refrained from rolling her eyes and looked out the window again. "Simeon can't come. I'm not putting up with him and Ryne fighting the whole way."

Simeon has powerful charms, Aletha admonished. *You never know when you may need him.*

She quickly shut the curtain when Simeon caught her watching him. He homed in on her like a wolf, stalking its prey. "That's what I'm most afraid of."

ONCE AGAIN, DIANNA found herself crowded by Ryne and Simeon as she studied the map with Zier. She couldn't have a moment's peace without them swarming her.

"If we cut through this way, the route is faster." Zier stabbed the map with a stubby finger. "It may be more dangerous though."

"I don't care. We're running out of time." Ryne rubbed his chin, the fire highlighting the lines around his eyes and making him look far older. Though he'd told Dianna he was only two and twenty winters, she could hardly believe it.

"Borg carry fwiends. Borg make us go faster."

She looked up at Borg, who sat with his legs wrapped around Mari's hut. He was so close to the thatched roof, she feared he'd fall over and crush it and the occupants inside. Des and the dogs had already gone to bed, and she didn't feel comfortable with a giant hanging over her brother.

Alec must have felt unease as well, because he'd already asked Borg several times to move back. "Borg." Alec cleared his throat, then waved at the giant as if shooing a dog. "Your legs."

Borg frowned down at the hut. "Oh, sorry, fwiend."

When he scooted back, she cringed as he pulled off a few wooden planks with the heel of one foot.

"Over there, Borg." She nodded to the other side of the yard, where Tung had planted a modest garden. She'd rather have crushed roots than crushed skulls.

Once the giant was settled, flattening a section of wooden fence with his behind, she knew it was time to make sure Borg knew he couldn't follow them to Adolan. "Borg," she said with a frozen smile, doing her best to keep her composure, "I've already explained that you can't come with us."

He frowned, stabbing the earth with a broken piece of fence. "But Da will be mad."

"No, he won't," she said. "I'm confident he only wanted you to follow us to Aloa-Shay."

"Da no say only Oh-Shay." The giant crossed his arms, the folds of his forehead meshing in an angry *V*. "Da say follow. Borg follow."

"Well, I guess that settles it." She shared knowing looks with Ryne and Zier. "Don't sleep too soundly."

"Believe me." Ryne scowled at Borg. "I won't."

When Borg had gone to relieve himself, they'd conferred privately. If the giant refused to stay behind, they'd sneak away from camp in the middle of the night, while he was asleep.

"Tung." Dianna decided to change the subject so as not to arouse Borg's suspicion. "You never told us how you survived all this time."

He stretched beside the campfire, one scrawny leg pressed against the other. "I've been subsisting on riverweed and berries I could reach, plus the roots in the garden."

"Now that Zier has given us a net," Alec said, puffing up his chest, "we shall feast on salamin."

"I can hardly believe our good fortune, cousin." Tung leaned into Mari, covering her small hand with his. "I wish Uncle Khashka was here to see it."

Mari turned her hand over in Tung's grip. "He may be watching us even now, Tung. You never know."

"Borg no wike ghost talk." The giant wrapped his arms around his waist and scanned the dark jungle with wide eyes. "Borg scared of ghosts."

Ironic, because Borg was probably the scariest thing south of Werewood Forest.

Mari shook her head. "My father would never hurt you, Borg."

The giant's lip hung down, making him look like a temperamental toddler. "Da hurt Borg." Borg's hand flew to the welt by his ear. "Da hit Borg many time."

Alec narrowed his eyes at the giant. "Why do you let your father treat you that way? You're bigger than him."

Dianna sucked in a sharp breath. The last thing she needed was to spawn a revolt among the giants. The dwarves would never forgive her.

Zier cleared his throat, issuing Alec a challenging look. "Methinks we need to change the subject."

"I agree," Dianna added.

Borg leaned over and grabbed a palma pod hanging in a nearby tree. She hoped he was careful with the fruit. One pod was as heavy as three men and could easily be a weapon in a giant's hands.

He snapped the trunk in half as he jerked the pod from its branches. "You no understand what having mean da like."

"My father beat me almost every single day, from the time I was a toddler until the day he died." Alec struck his chest like he was pounding a drum. "So don't tell me I don't understand."

Borg's eyes widened. "You da beat you?"

"Your flesh was always covered in cuts and bruises," she admitted, knowing they needed to change the subject even as demons from the past threatened to resurface. "Always." She frowned. "You hid beneath your cloak."

Alec chuckled softly. "I thought I was hiding it well until the night you confronted him."

Oh how she wished she could forget that night. When she'd pulled back Alec's cloak, she'd expected to find a new cut or bruise, but he looked like he had the plague. Alec's father, whom she later realized was also her father, had been cursed by Madhea, forced to hate his son through dark magic.

"You confronted him?" Simeon asked. "What happened?"

"She called him a monster," Alec answered. "The whole village witnessed it and they turned against him."

"He sounds like a monster," Ryne said as he poked the fire with a stick. "No wonder your brother was so troubled when he came to us."

"He didn't mean to." She stared into the fire, feeling shame for hating her father so. They'd never exchanged kind words, and now he was dead. "He was cursed by Madhea." One more reason why the Sky Goddess needed to be killed. She'd destroyed too many lives with her vindictiveness.

"My da no cursed." Borg crushed the palma pod between his meaty fingers, splattering juice all over his arm. "My da just mean."

She cringed. "I'm sorry, Borg." So much for the fruit. It would have sustained her brothers for weeks.

"How you da die?" Borg asked Alec.

She glared at Alec. *Don't give him any ideas*, she thought, hoping her look conveyed the message.

"A knife to the back," Alec answered evenly.

Ugh. Dianna wanted to reach across the fire and smack her brother upside the head.

Borg's mouth dropped open. "Who stab you da in back?"

"Me." Alec hung his head, a solitary tear slipping down his face.

"Oh, Alec," she whispered, "you shouldn't have told him that." But when she saw realization dawn in the giant's eyes, like clouds parting after a storm, she feared it was already too late.

Chapter Eight

Dianna sat up, tossing her legs over the narrow bed she'd shared with Mari. She was still fast asleep, so Dianna quietly tiptoed out of the hut, and relieved and cleaned herself by a narrow stream that ran close to the property. Though the day had been warm in Aloa-Shay, the night was cool. She wondered if that was typical for the seaside village or if Madhea's frost had reached them.

When she returned, she was glad to see Zier and Ryne awake and dressed for travel. The sky was still dark, and the moon hung low in the sky. It would be several hours until dawn. By then they should be far enough away from Borg if they made haste.

Dianna scowled at Simeon when he came out of the hut wearing furs and carrying his pack. Before she could argue, he held a finger to his full lips, then nodded to Borg, who was lying on his back, loudly snoring.

The tricky broot. She knew what he was about. As quietly as she could, she stormed back inside, jarring Simeon's shoulder on the way.

Alec and Des were curled up together with the mutt Brendle on a pallet beside the hearth. It was no soft bed, but it would have to do. She shook them awake, ignoring the dog's whimpers, then placed a finger to her lips as her brothers opened their eyes.

Des let out a groggy yawn and stretched, looking at her with innocent, wide eyes. "Are you leaving me, sister?"

"Yes." She kissed his forehead. "But I shall return, sweet brother."

Fear shone in his wide eyes. "You promise?"

She cupped his cheek. "I will do everything in my power to come back to you."

"What if everything isn't enough?" His voice trembled with watery emotion.

"Look into your heart." She placed a hand on his chest, feeling the strong pounding beneath. "What does your heart tell you?"

His mouth hitched up in an impish grin. "That you will return to me."

"Then I shall. Be good for Alec." She kissed him again, nuzzling his cheek and wishing she could pack his scent—a mixture of dirt, sweat, and sticky palma fruit—with her. "I love you."

She turned to her other brother. "Thank you for staying."

Alec scowled. "I didn't have much choice, did I?"

"Please be safe," she begged, reaching for his hand.

Their fingers entwined. "I will, sister."

She sucked in a steadying breath, jumped to her feet, and strode out before the tears that pricked the backs of her eyes escaped. She would miss her brothers, but she had to leave for their sakes.

She passed Simeon, who was warming his hands by the fire, and found Ryne with his tail-wagging dog and Zier, standing in the shadow of the barn's thatched roof. "Let's go."

Ryne looked over her shoulder. "He's not coming."

She didn't need to turn around to know Simeon had followed. She could practically feel his warm, broad shoulders hogging up her personal space.

She looked at him pleadingly. "Simeon, please don't make this any harder on me."

"I won't," he answered with little inflection in his deep voice. "I'm coming with you, and there's to be no argument."

His golden eyes shone beneath the starlight, dazzling her like twin suns. When she leaned into him like a reed bending in the breeze, fighting the urge to place a hand on his heart, she knew he was using his persuasive magic on her.

"Damn you, Simeon," she hissed, then spun on her heel and marched toward the jungle.

She followed Zier who'd already started down the path at a fast pace for one without long legs. His pots and pans, which had been wrapped in furs, made no sound. He looked like an upright bear from behind.

"I can't believe you capitulated so easily," Ryne scolded at her back.

"Shut up," she growled over her shoulder, in no mood to argue.

"I'm not carrying him when his toes freeze off," he grumbled.

She whipped around so fast, Ryne backed up with a start, holding up his hands in a defensive gesture. She slipped a stone out of her pocket, marched up to Simeon, and slapped it in his palms. "If you lose this, you will not be able to charm your way out of me whipping your arse."

Simeon pocketed the stone with a wink. "Thanks. It's warming me already."

Ryne scowled. "Usually you have to ask the stones to warm you."

"Girls don't wait for Simeon to ask when he needs a favor," she grumbled, then turned and hurried to catch up with Zier, ignoring the irritating laughter of her two remaining stones.

"DAUGHTER. WHAT ARE you doing here? It is late, and you should be honeymooning with your husband."

Ura looked at her father through a foggy gaze. "I couldn't sleep." She wished she could enjoy a peaceful slumber in her husband's arms. Instead, she found herself in a dark *kraehn* cavern, staring bleakly into a hole carved in the ice, watching the demon fishes' fanged, gaping maws as they sucked at the air, waiting for Ura to throw them her waste.

"You look tired." He father laid a soothing hand on her shoulder. "You should not be around kraehn. It is dangerous."

She turned into her father, wishing so much his strong embrace would bring her comfort, as it had done so many times when she was a child. "I know."

He rocked her, kissing the top of her head. "Do you have a death wish, child?"

She stifled a sob, resting her forehead against the soft furs of his vest. "Not yet." But if what she saw in the mists came to pass, she'd no wish to live on this earth without her husband.

Her father coursed a hand through her hair, just like he used to do when she woke from a nightmare. "Markus asked me to make sure you get on a boat when the time comes."

"I'm not leaving without him." Her heartbeat quickened. How could they expect her to abandon her husband?

"I was afraid of that. And what of me? What of Ryne?" His eyes shone in the darkness like two iridescent pools. "Have you not thought of our broken hearts if something were to happen to you?"

She had to bite down on her knuckles to keep from crying out. "I think of nothing else but our broken hearts."

Unable to stand the sadness in his eyes, she jerked out of his embrace. She needed to flee but didn't know where to go. She shrieked when she slipped and almost fell face-first into a kraehn hole, then gasped when she was rescued by her father.

"Careful, daughter." He deposited her on a bench beside the cavern wall. "You were almost kraehn bait."

She sat down, head in her hands. He stroked her back as she struggled to breathe. Her mind had been so muddled with grief, she hadn't realized she'd almost fallen into a trap.

An idea struck her. *A trap!*

"That's it!" She shot up from her seat, thrusting a fist in the air.

Jon quickly stood, placing a firm hand on her shoulder. No doubt he didn't trust her not to slip again. "What is it, daughter?"

"All this time we've waited for Madhea's attack, like bait caught in a kraehn hole," she said, words eagerly tripping off her tongue. "What if we were to bait *her*? What if in the vision I saw of Markus, he wasn't dead but bait for a trap?"

One of his silvery brows arched. "You think you can ensnare a powerful goddess?"

"Yes, yes." Ura rubbed her hands together as the wheels in her mind turned. "I think we can."

"How will you go about doing that?"

"Markus is a mighty hunter," she said. "I think I know of a way. Come, Father!" She raced out of the cavern toward the small ice cave she and her husband shared with him. Though she knew he was sound asleep, she had to wake him. They needed to put their plan in motion before the ice witch found them.

DIANNA'S FEET WERE sore and her legs were cramping, but she dared not slow down. Dawn was breaking, and they had to put more distance between themselves and Borg. They decided to take an alternate route, one that was slightly longer and more treacherous, with too many overgrown bushes and loose rocks along the old path. The trees were so tall and thick in some spots, they could hardly see where they were stepping. Dianna hoped the overgrown vegetation would throw Borg off their trail.

Thank goodness for Zier and his big blade. He led the line, deftly clearing a path so that most of the branches didn't slash Dianna's arms. Still, enough of them got her that her clothes had several tears, as if she'd been beaten by a slaver's whip. Simeon's arms were even worse. He scraped most of the limbs with his wide shoulders, cutting his protective furs to shreds. Ryne also had his fair share of cuts. Their furs and arms would be in tatters by the time they left the forest. Even Tar yelped a time or two.

Even more alarming was Simeon's ragged breathing as he trudged ahead of her, so loud at times, she feared he'd keel over.

She scanned the forest, amazed at how huge the trees had become. Some were as thick as her childhood home and taller than Borg, with branches that hung almost to the ground, weighted with leaves that were larger than her. She imagined these were the trees the dwarves had used to build the fortress around Aya-Shay.

"We've been running long enough," Ryne said at her back. "We need to take a break." He had the unfortunate position of bringing up the rear, a hand on the hilt of his sword should some ghoul or beast decide to trail them.

"No stopping." Dianna grunted, though she wished they could rest for just a few moments. "We can't take the chance."

"Very well." Ryne chucked. "Don't blame me when your sand dweller collapses."

"Don't—*gasp*—concern yourself—*gasp*—with me—*gasp*." Simeon's chest heaved between each word. Odd that someone with such a muscular chest would have so little endurance.

Oh, I won the bet! Sindri squealed. *I told my sisters you'd be thinking about Simeon's chest again before daybreak.*

You are like a trio of old hens, Dianna chided. *Not happy unless you are pecking dirt.* Heat flushed her cheeks, a new warmth that wasn't from exertion. Not even Dianna's most private thoughts were safe around the nosy stones.

"We will rest tonight," she said, annoyed as Ryne's laughter intensified. Even though they followed Zier's lead, she did slow their brisk walk ever so slightly when the loose gravel had become more treacherous.

"Tonight?" Ryne chuckled. "You think your sand dweller will last that long?"

"I'm growing even more tired of your jests than of the run, ice dweller," Simeon grumbled.

"And I'm growing tired of listening to you breathe like a dying snowbear," Ryne said, far too much humor in his tone.

Simeon stopped long enough to scowl at Ryne. "And I'm growing tired of your ugly blue face."

Dianna slapped Simeon's back, urging him forward. "Enough."

"Just wait until we halt for the night," Ryne said. "Then you can stare at my ugly blue fist."

Tar whimpered. Dianna knew the dog hoped for peace, just as she did. She was just about to box Simeon and Ryne's stubborn heads when a booming in the distance made her suck in a sharp breath.

"Quiet." She turned to Ryne, holding out a staying hand.

Zier stopped, too, his heavily laden back stiff as a pole.

The booms grew louder, shaking the ground beneath their feet.

"What is that?" Simeon breathed.

Ryne swallowed hard, a knot working its way down his throat. "Maybe it's one of the dragons."

"They wouldn't be running through the forest. They'd be flying overhead," Dianna whispered. "It has to be Borg." She looked up, cursing under her breath when she saw the branches shaking and leaves falling to the ground.

"What do we do?" Simeon asked.

"Quick." Ryne pointed to a massive trunk off the path, the brush cleared around it as if it were intentional. "There's a hole inside that tree."

It looked almost like a small door. Could it be a dwelling for a sprite or a lone dwarf? Simeon grabbed her hand, and they raced for the tree, with Ryne trailing. As they neared the tree, Dianna realized it was indeed a door, covered with a crude flap. If someone lived inside, she hoped they didn't mind guests.

"Wait," Zier called, chest heaving as he raced to catch up. "You don't know what's in there."

She placed a hand on Simeon's arm. "He's right."

The booms were so close now, an avalanche of leaves rained down on them.

Simeon cast a glance over his shoulder. "I'm willing to take that chance." He pushed his way inside, taking Dianna with him. Ryne followed, pulling the top end of Zier's pack, followed by Zier pushing the other end. Tar scurried in, with his tail between his legs. She heard the thud of Zier's pack as he dropped it against the wall, but otherwise, everyone remained quiet.

The air in the cramped room was heavy with mold and dirt, and it was so dark, she could only make out Simeon's gold eyes looking anxiously at her.

Pull me out, Sindri whispered.

Dianna slipped her hand into her vest pocket and pulled out the stone. Panic iced her limbs when the stone's light illuminated their small abode. Whoever had once lived here had died long ago, though he was still sitting at a table with a mug in his bony grip. Spiders crawled out of his skeletal orifices and scattered across the table. She sucked in a scream when she saw more spiders scattered across a dusty rug and stone hearth.

"Great goddess!" Simeon yelped, clutching Dianna's arm. "This place is infested!"

Tar whimpered, alternately lifting his paws, looking up at Ryne with large, pleading eyes.

"Easy, buddy," Ryne said to his companion. "It will be over soon."

The booms were closer now and much slower.

"Fwiends," a familiar deep voice said outside. "Where fwiends go?"

She swore under her breath while Zier swatted spiders off his pack.

"Dianna," Simeon said, his voice breaking into a high-pitched, girly squeal. "I'd rather take my chances with Borg." He jumped when a spider ran between his legs.

"No." She spoke through clenched teeth. "We can leave when he passes."

"Fwiends!" Borg called again. "Borg smell you."

"Curse the Elements!" Ryne hissed, elbowing Zier. "You didn't tell us giants had a good sense of smell."

Zier shot Ryne a menacing look. "Not all do."

"Well this one does," Ryne grumbled.

"Quiet, both of you." Dianna shined the light in their faces. "Before we're caught."

They stood there quietly, waiting for Borg to pass. She sucked in shallow breaths, trying not to gag on the musty air. Tar pressed against his master, whistling through his nose while Ryne held the dog's jaw shut.

After several interminable heartbeats, the echo of the giant's footfalls receded.

"He's gone," Simeon said. "Let's get out of here."

Dianna placed a steadying hand on his arm. "Just a little longer." A spider as wide as her palm climbed down Simeon's braid. She did her best not to alarm him, forcing a note of calmness into her voice. "Hold still."

His eyes bulged. "Wh-what?"

She unsheathed a boning knife from her belt. Carefully she leaned up and swatted the spider to the ground. It ran across the floor with a screech.

"Dragon balls," Simeon mumbled, his eyes rolling to the back of his head before he fell against her.

"Don't you dare faint on me, Simeon," she hissed, struggling to hold him up even as her knees buckled. "A little help," she said to the others.

He was lifted off her so fast, the displaced air ruffled her loose braid. She gaped at Ryne and Zier, who gawped back at her, then at the empty space in front of her where Simeon had been.

"Simeon?" Her mind raced, fear pumping out a wild rhythm in her chest. Where had he gone?

She shone the stone's light up, screaming when she saw a dark, hairy creature dragging Simeon up a network of vines. "Let him go!" She hit the shadow with a blast. The force of her magic ricocheted inside their musty space, knocking Zier, Ryne, and Tar on their backs. The tree groaned like a thatched cottage roof on the verge of buckling beneath the weight of heavy snow. The shadow faltered, nearly dropping Simeon, but then it swung to the next vine, latching on with feet that had long, curled finger-like toes. The beast clutched Simeon by the waist in one meaty arm as it slowly made its way up the rope.

"I said to let him go!" Magic balled in Dianna's fist as she prepared to strike again.

"Wait!" Ryne cried, stumbling to his knees. "One more blast and this whole tree will come down."

The creature swung up and into a hole, disappearing.

"Simeon! No!" Dianna shrieked.

"It's gone outside." Zier waved them out the door. "Hurry!"

She stumbled out of the tree, followed by Ryne and Tar, as the structure groaned and slowly rocked to one side. The ground beneath them buckled.

"The roots!" Zier hollered. "Run!"

She flew over roots as they burst through the ground and jutted into the air like geysers. Zier wasn't fast enough to dodge a massive root. It swatted him like a bug as it broke from the soil, flinging him into the forest.

"Ahhh!" Zier cried, disappearing into a mass of hanging vines.

"You go after Zier," Dianna said to Ryne. "I'll find Simeon."

Ryne and his dog broke off, racing after Zier.

The tree groaned again, roots snapping. The tree fell faster. She raced beside it, shining a light at the overhead branches. A dark figure swung from limb to limb, barely outpacing the tumbling tree. Dianna tried to center her aim, but the creature moved too fast, and she didn't want to collapse the entire forest on their heads.

Her chest ached, and her legs screamed in pain, but she ran faster, dodging roots and debris. She cast a glance over her shoulder, surprised to see Ryne, Tar, and Zier behind her. How had they caught up?

The creature landed on a branch with a thud, faltering for a heartbeat as it readjusted Simeon's limp body under its arm. Dianna seized the opportunity, centering her magic on the monster's backside, releasing a ball of energy with a grunt. The beast jumped to a higher limb with surprising strength, as if its legs were made of springs. The magic struck beneath the beast, slicing the tree in half. The creature squealed when the top half of the tree tumbled toward the ground. It struck a nearby tree, whose trunk was as wide as a giant. The larger tree caught the half-tree in its thick branches. It hung suspended horizontally above the ground.

Dianna ran under the creature while it dangled above her. Tar barked wildly. The beast hissed at the dog, holding on to a flimsy limb with one hand, Simeon tucked under the other arm. Struggling to gain purchase, its gruesome, demonic face that looked part bear and part human, contorted as it clawed at the branch, but it continued to slide. Dianna's heart came to a grinding halt when the thing released Simeon, his limp body hurtling to the forest floor. A large hand shot out from behind the tree, capturing Simeon before he struck the ground, and her shoulders slumped in relief.

Borg stepped into view, plucking the creature from the branch. The giant frowned at the beast as it squealed and clawed at his fingers. When Borg set Simeon down beside Dianna, she raced up to him, cradling his head in her hands. She shook him hard. "Simeon! Wake up!"

His eyes had rolled to the back of his head, and he did not wake. Tar licked Simeon's face, then snuffled as he sniffed his hair.

Dianna gasped when she pulled her hand away; it was covered in sticky blood. He was injured! No wonder he couldn't wake! She turned to the others. "Help me!" Desperation rang in her words.

Zier and Ryne helped drag Simeon behind a tree. She clutched the massive trunk while Borg shook the monster like a child angry with his toy.

"Owie!" the giant screamed before throwing the creature to the ground.

The beast rolled onto its side, its face made even uglier with anguish when it cradled its wide ribs with long arms.

Tar shot out like a bolt of lightning, racing straight for the creature.

"Tar, get back here!" Ryne yelled.

The dog circled the beast, jumping when it rolled into a sitting position and spit at the dog.

"No, Tar!" Ryne hollered again.

Panic turned Dianna's limbs to ice. That thing could easily kill Tar.

"Be careful!" Zier cupped his hands around his mouth, calling up to Borg. "Trolls spit venom."

A troll? That's what that creature was? As a child, she'd had nightmares after her father warned her about the monsters, about how they were as strong as ten mortals and feasted on human flesh. She'd thought her father had only told her fables to ensure her good behavior. Now she knew. They were indeed real, and they were creatures of nightmares.

The troll let out an ear-piercing howl when Borg lifted his mighty foot. Dianna had to look away when the giant's foot came crashing down. She heard the distinct splatter and crushing of bone.

That was enough to send Tar yelping back to Ryne, his tail between his legs.

Dianna cringed when Borg stomped up to them. She didn't fear he would squish them next, but she sensed they were about to be assaulted by a giant-sized guilt trip.

"Fwiends not nice." He jutted a red, swollen finger at them. "Fwiends leave Borg."

She cleared her throat, struggling for the right words. "Borg, we were being nice and saving you from freezing to death. You are not dressed for cold weather."

Borg crossed his arms, the many folds of his brow furrowing like collapsing drifts of snow. "Da says Borg follow."

She let out a shuddering breath. There was no convincing him. Mayhap when the weather turned colder, he'd change his mind. In the meantime, she had to heal Simeon before he succumbed to his wounds.

She choked back a sob as the realization struck her that she'd almost lost Simeon to that monster. How could she have lived with herself if Simeon had been killed? Curse the flirtatious sand dweller! He was beginning to mean too much to her. She didn't know what made her heart ache more, the prospect of losing Simeon or loving him forever. Of one thing she was certain, either outcome would break her heart.

Chapter Nine

Madhea admired her reflection in the looking glass. Most of her wrinkles had faded, and color was returning to her once brittle and dull hair. She no longer looked like a decrepit old crone, but perhaps a woman at the end of her middle years. The magic in her veins was stronger than ever before. All of Eris's power was flowing to her. Soon, no one would be able to overpower her, especially not that foolish witch, Dianna. Unless, of course, she had collected all the stones. In that case, Madhea would need another kind of leverage to ensure she defeated Dianna. She'd need to set a trap to force her to bend to her will.

And Madhea knew the perfect man to use as bait for that trap. All she needed to do was find out how to reach him. She and her pixies had flown up and down the mountain, looking for caves and tunnels—anything that would lead her to the Ice People—but the mountain was vast, and every search had been fruitless. She had no hope of finding this blue race without help from her prisoner. As she stared at her reflection once more, she thought she would soon be pretty enough to seduce him. Though the thought of being held by such feeble arms repulsed her, she had no choice. She would do what she must, then discard him after winning her true prize.

"URA, I CAN'T BELIEVE we are contemplating theft." Markus raked a hand over his face with a groan. His wife had gone mad, totally mad, and he feared 'twas he who'd corrupted her.

"Not theft." She snuggled next to him in their narrow bed. "We're merely borrowing a stone, and they don't rightfully belong to the Ice People anyway."

"Do you think the Erylls will look upon it as borrowing?" He'd a feeling they'd be none too pleased if they discovered Ura rummaging through their possessions in an attempt to steal their precious stone.

"I don't care what they think." Her voice rose to a feverish pitch. "We could've borrowed Odu's stone if the Council hadn't stolen it."

Markus still felt terrible about their acquisition of Odu's stone. After the old prophet had defended Markus's decision to let Dianna borrow Ura's family stone, they had taken it upon themselves to punish the prophet by "borrowing" his stone as well. "Yes, but the difference is they have the law on their side, and we don't."

"*Pffft.*" She slapped the furs on the bed. "Don't speak to me of laws. Chieftain Ingred has been making up new laws ever since she came to power. She's getting as greedy as Madhea. And speaking of her, the Ice People will thank us when we defeat the evil goddess." Her cool breath tickled the nape of his neck, and he feared she was distracting him to get her way. "You need a stone to deflect her magic. You're the only one who can bring her down."

"I hope you're right." He heaved a weary sigh.

"Of course I am." She sat up, hovering over him, her soft curtain of hair tickling his chest. "Don't you know the first rule of marriage?" She giggled. "The wife is always right."

"Lass, I don't like putting you in danger." He ran his fingers through her hair. Of all the physical features he loved about his wife, 'twas her hair he loved the most, smoother than the soft grasses that grew under any lake and finer than the most expensive threads imported from the Shifting Sands. But more than her hair, he loved her mind and spirit. He didn't wish to risk her life. He couldn't bear the burden of causing her brightly burning flame to be extinguished.

She frowned. "There will be no danger."

She clearly hadn't contemplated the severity of the consequences should they get caught. "They will out you if you're caught."

Her eyes lit with determination. "And you and Father will come with me, and the Ice People will be forced to battle Madhea without our help."

A shudder coursed through him. Truthfully, he didn't relish the idea of having to face the vengeful goddess again. He'd only survived the last encounter with her due to pure luck and the stone around his neck. "Elements forbid it should come to that."

BESIDES BEING A STRONG protector, Dianna was grateful for another thing about Borg. The giant had cut their journey through the woods in half by carrying them all, giving her sore legs a much-needed rest. She and Simeon sat on Borg's head, ropes around their waists tied to his hair, should he accidentally tip his head, which he'd done a few times after forgetting he was carrying his "fwiends." Ryne had complained that Borg's head smelled worse than his feet, so he perched with his dog on one shoulder while Zier sat on the other. Borg had stuffed Zier's pack and everyone's sacks in a pocket. She had to admit he was handy.

Dianna had never laughed so hard as these last two days with Simeon. He'd told her wild stories about the people of Kyanu and his sisters, endearing himself to her. There was a fondness in his voice when he spoke of them, especially of Jae, his non-magical twin.

When she first met him, she'd thought him incapable of feelings, only interested in luring women into his arms. But then he'd risked his life for his sister, and here he was, following her on a dangerous quest. Mayhap she'd been wrong about him. If only... she cleared her head of such foolish thoughts. She'd not allow herself to fall for any man, for she'd no wish to be spoon-feeding him three-hundred years later, too selfish to let him pass to the Elements.

"What are you thinking?" Simeon asked, toying with the stems of the cotulla flowers he'd picked to ward off the musty smell of Borg's scalp. She was relieved that after her healing magic, Simeon showed no signs of his earlier head injury from the troll's poison, though it had burned a fist-sized hole through his skull. Trolls were nasty creatures.

"Many things," she answered plainly, leaving it at that, for she'd no desire to tell him she was thinking how they could never be together.

He plucked a long petal from the lavender flower, eyeing her from under thick lashes. "Is that why you frown so much?"

She tried not to flinch at his words, but they made her uneasy. She hadn't realized she was always frowning. Still, it was unkind of him to point it out. She was on a mission to destroy the woman who'd birthed her or watch the world perish. Hadn't she a reason to frown? "I carry the weight of the world on my shoulders," she snapped.

When he placed a gentle hand on her arm, she flinched.

He blinked at her with large, golden eyes, looking far too innocent and sincere. "When will you let me share in your burden?"

She looked away. "I can't." Why was he being so kind? She liked him better when he was an obnoxious flirt. At least then she could slap him without feeling remorse.

"Why?" He squeezed her arm. "Haven't I already proven my loyalty to you, that I do not have eyes for another?"

When he scooted so close their knees touched, she jerked her leg away and shook off his grip. The feel of his warm skin on hers was too much. *He* was too much. Too much longing. Too much heartbreak.

"It's getting dark." She stood, turning her back to him while dusting debris off her pants and trying not to think of where it had come from. "I must tell Borg to find a place to camp." She cupped her hands around her mouth and stomped a foot. "Borg! We need to stop for the night."

The giant stopped so suddenly, they both lurched forward. Simeon tumbled into Dianna, smashing his face into her buttocks. She landed on her knees with a grunt, then unwrapped his arms from her waist. Thank the Elements for her willpower, because she'd been sorely tempted to turn into his embrace.

"Okay, fwiends," Borg boomed.

"I know you have feelings for me," Simeon whispered at her back. "You can't hide from your heart forever."

"You are too sure of yourself." She stiffened, then slowly turned, unclenching her fists. "Just because every other woman falls at your feet doesn't mean I will."

"I'm sorry." He dropped his gaze to his lap, his shoulders falling as if they were burdened by the weight of Zier's pack. "I thought you—never mind."

An arrow of regret shot straight to her heart. Damn Simeon for making her care about his feelings.

When Borg dropped them off in a narrow clearing beside a shallow stream, the first thing she noticed was a fire pit, still warm with embers.

Ryne held his hands over it. "It looks as if someone has already camped here."

She knelt beside an indentation in the ground, then reached for a pile of wet tea leaves. "The villagers of Adolan."

"How can you tell?"

"The markings on the ground." There were triangular indentations all over the clearing. "Left by their hunting tents and these." She held out the leaves.

"Thyme tea is a favorite drink among the villagers," Zier added as he leaned his pack against a stump. "I've sold it to 'em often enough."

She feared Madhea's icy winds would soon encompass the whole world. "The cold must have driven them out."

Zier frowned, thoughtfully rubbing his bearded chin. "I fear Aya-Shay will soon be overburdened."

She cringed, worried for her people—not just for the displaced, but those who couldn't escape the cold. What about the sick and infirm? Had the townspeople helped them get to safety? "Will your king turn them all away?" she asked Zier, fearing his response.

"I'm not sure." He slid onto a thick boulder and pulled out a bladder of his dwarf brew.

She worried the king would not accept the villagers from Adolan, which meant they'd overrun the town of Aloa-Shay and the smaller villages, most likely already full to capacity with the villagers from Kicelin. What would happen when the cold spread to the shoreline villages? Where would every-one go?

She meant to ask Zier, but he looked in no mood to speak, sitting by himself, drinking his brew. She'd no idea how the dwarves could stomach such swill, for it was so strong, it tasted like poison. She knew this because Zier had sold a small jug to her father once, and she had boldly taken a sip when nobody was watching. After coughing so hard she thought she would die, she'd found relief after drinking an entire pitcher of water.

She looked over at Simeon and Ryne, surprised they were working to-gether to rekindle the fire.

"Borg." She turned to the giant. "Could you please get us some fire-wood?"

"Okay, but fwiends stay here."

Dianna heaved a weary groan. "We're not going anywhere."

Without another word, the giant stomped into the forest, heedless of the trees he flattened. Dianna wondered why he didn't just break those up, but she didn't feel like arguing.

She wanted to run away when Ryne stalked toward her, determination in the firm set of his mouth. "We should reach the edge of the forest by tomorrow evening. Then it will not be long before we reach what is left of Adolan." He nodded toward the forest where Borg had disappeared. "That giant slog will put us at risk."

Her heart fell. "I know, but I don't know how to get rid of him, and he has been helpful."

"Simeon," Ryne called. "Use your persuasion."

He nodded to Ryne as the giant returned to camp, carrying a small pine, roots and all.

Simeon faced Borg. "Go home, Borg. You can't come with us." His voice wasn't firm and powerful like before. Dianna wondered if Simeon was even trying.

"Borg no go." He dropped the tree, then stomped a foot like a toddler on the verge of a tantrum. "Da says Borg follow."

"I thought you had the power to persuade," Ryne snapped.

"I do." He shrugged. "It just doesn't seem to work on giants. If you'll excuse me." He turned on his heel, marching into the forest without even so much as looking at her.

"What's wrong with him?" Ryne asked Dianna, his tone mocking, not concerned.

"I don't know," she lied, averting her eyes. Could he still be upset by what she'd said? Simeon had many admirers in Kyanu. Why should he be miffed over one rejection? She wanted to go after him, but she had no idea what to say. Besides, she had more pressing matters, namely getting rid of the giant before they cleared the forest and were spotted by humans with spears or even worse, Madhea could see them from Ice Mountain. That is, if she hadn't already spotted them in her mists.

"But, Borg." She stood, clasping her hands in a prayer pose. "You have no shoes, no winter coat. You will freeze to death."

"Da be mad if Borg no follow." When a tear slipped down his wide nose, her heart fell. She wanted to despise this giant for jeopardizing their journey, but she felt only pity. What kind of control did that king have over Borg, that he'd risk freezing to death rather than displeasing him?

"Owie." Borg fell on his rump with a boom, causing Dianna and Ryne to tumble to the ground.

Ryne swore as he sat up, wiping dirt off his breeches.

She looked at Borg, who was scratching the bottom of his foot. She was surprised to see a wide hole on his sole that looked like the flaming pit of Eris's volcano.

She struggled to her feet and cautiously walked up to the giant. "Let me see your foot, Borg." As she got closer, she nearly gagged on the horrifying stench radiating from his heel. "It's infected." She waved a hand in front of her face, though it did little good. The wretched smell was as thick as soup. "Why didn't you tell me?"

"Borg no want to bother fwiends."

"But you know I'm a healer." She plugged her nose. "I healed your finger after the troll spit on you. The troll venom must have got you when you stomped on it. I can't believe you've been walking on that foot all this time." She pointed to a flat patch of moss behind him. "Lie all the way down, so I can get a good look at it."

"Dianna, a word," Ryne grumbled in her ear.

"Hold on."

He dragged her away from Borg, surprising her. "Hey!" she protested, but he kept pulling until they were standing behind a copse of tall pines.

"Are you mad?" he spat, his normal scowl deepening. "Why would you heal him?"

She blinked. Was he in earnest? "Because he's in pain, and if I don't do something, the infection will spread. He could die, Ryne."

He laughed. "Don't you see? This is how we get rid of him."

She stepped back, eyeing him with disgust. "By letting him die?"

He rolled his eyes to the sky. "If that's what it takes."

Dianna waited for him to tell her 'twas only a joke. She had always thought the ice dweller a bit harsh, but she was beginning to realize he was more than that—he was downright awful. "Have you no heart?"

He made an exasperated sound. "This beast puts our lives in danger with his presence. He jeopardizes our chance of saving an entire race of people. If having no heart means I'd rather see him die than thousands of my people perish, then yes," he hissed, "I have no heart. But at least you can't accuse me of having no sense, which is more than I can say for you."

She was stunned, for her parents had taught her that the highest virtues were kindness and understanding, and she was feeling neither of those things at the moment.

Zier hobbled up to them. "Borg is getting impatient. Is something the matter?"

"Do you agree, Zier?" she asked, suddenly choked with emotion. "That I should let Borg die?"

"Nay, lass. I cannot agree." The dwarf turned a disapproving frown on Ryne, his graying bushy brows drawn together. "He means us no harm. He is only following his father's orders."

Ryne surrendered. "If you heal him now, he will die in the frigid weather, or Madhea will kill him when she kills us. Either way he will die."

Zier grabbed her elbow, looking at her with soulful eyes. "Heal him. We still have time to throw him off our trail. He can save us time by carrying us one more day through the forest. Not to mention, you will not find a better protector."

"She can summon her dragons," Ryne argued.

Her neck stiffened at the mention of the dragons. "No, I can't."

"Why not?"

"I don't know. I've tried to reach out to Lydra, but I can't sense her. It's as if she's disappeared." She'd tried to call Lydra numerous times since they'd entered Werewood Forest, and her dragon had yet to answer. Were Lydra and Tan'yi'na okay, or had some creature harmed them?

Ryne scratched the back of his head, looking lost in contemplation. "That can't be good."

She forced a smile. No sense in worrying the others. "I'm sure it will be fine. Perhaps she and Tan'yi'na are deep in the forest. I doubt there's anything that could harm them."

"Then we need Borg," Zier said. "We don't want another incident like what happened with the troll. I promise, once we reach the end of the forest, I will come up with a way to lose him."

Relief swept through her. She didn't want to let the giant die a slow and cruel death, especially as he'd gotten the injury by protecting them. "All right." She was relieved when he didn't break eye contact. "I'm relying on your promise."

The dwarf placed a hand over his heart. "Lass, when a dwarf gives his word, he keeps it."

Chapter Ten

U ra felt a momentary pang of guilt for attempting to steal Dame Eryll's stone. The matronly widow had nearly died from heartbreak after so recently losing most of her family. Still, it was not to be helped. The Ice People had greater need of that stone than Dame Eryll.

Ura was familiar with the layout of the Eryll clan's cavernous dwelling. Her father had forced her to dine there during the early stage of Bane's failed courtship. The Eryll cavern was thrice the size of her father's modest dwelling, though the former chieftain only had three children. Well, one child, now that one had been eaten by a gnull and the other outed for cowardice, presumably eaten as well.

She was fortunate she had not married into the Eryll clan and had a brave, strong husband. All she had to do was ensure his survival by stealing the Eryll's stone. Markus and Ura had spent the last few days alternating between finishing up the boats and planning their theft. The plan was simple. She would sneak into the Eryll cavern and take their stone while the rest of the Ice People celebrated the Festival of Lost Souls. Markus would stand watch outside, whistling if he suspected someone was coming.

The Festival of Lost Souls was an important day of celebration and remembrance. On this day over three hundred years ago, Madhea had struck down their small mountain town, killing over half the villagers and forcing the survivors to flee beneath the surface. Fortunately for the Ice People, the wanderer Odu had been staying with them the night Madhea attacked. It was he who led them to their new homes and provided the most affluent families with the warming stones, which she now knew to have far greater capabilities than just boiling water. Markus had told her each stone possessed the spirit of the fallen goddesses Kyan and her daughters.

She found it bewildering that the Ice People had used these stones to warm their cooking pots for three hundred years, not realizing goddesses resided inside. Because of that, she didn't feel guilty in the slightest for stealing the Eryll clan stone. It had a far greater purpose than keeping their toes warm at night.

She rummaged through the kitchen first, opening each drawer, then checking the shelves and finally the oven. She smiled when she saw the innocuous-looking stone lying at the bottom of the greasy oven, its smooth, pale surface covered in grime and food. She clucked her tongue as she wiped the stains off on her vest. The Eryll clan didn't deserve such a treasure.

"Ura?"

She spun around, quickly pocketing the stone. "Dame Eryll, you frightened me." Curse the Elements! What was she doing at home?

The older woman, who looked too much like her son Bane, with a gaunt face and a concave chest, eyed her with suspicion. "What are you doing here?"

"J-just come to see why you aren't at the festival."

"My son is ill." She looked at Ura's hip pocket. "What did you take from my oven?"

She backed up a step, willing her racing heart to slow. "'Tis nothing."

Dame Eryll lurched forward, shoved Ura aside, and opening the worn oven door. Flames brewed in her beady gaze. "'Tis my stone. Thief!" Her scream was so shrill and deafening, Ura feared the ice walls around them would crumble. "Thief! Thief!"

Dame Eryll lurched forward, latching onto Ura's arm. "Let's see what the Council has to say about this."

"Let me go!" she pleaded, struggling to break the woman's surprisingly firm grip. "We were only borrowing it. Markus needs it to defeat Madhea and save the Ice People."

"I don't care if that bloody land dweller needed the stone to save the entire world." Her thin mouth pulled back in a snarl. "It's my stone, and you'll not be having it!"

She froze at the sound of heavy footsteps.

Dame Eryll's snarl morphed into a wicked grin. "Now you're in trouble."

Her heart lurched when Markus's broad shoulders filled the doorway. "Let. Her. Go." His deep bellow shook the room like the roar of a snowbear.

Dame Eryll gasped, dropping Ura's arm.

"We will return the stone to its rightful owner as soon as we are able." Shadows fell over his face. "You are not to say a word, or you will have to contend with me. Do you understand?"

The woman silently nodded, lower lip quivering.

He pulled Ura out of the Eryll dwelling.

"I'm afraid she'll tell," Ura cried.

He remained silent as they continued toward the dwelling they shared with her father.

"Markus," she pleaded, tugging on his arm. "What are we going to do?"

He stared straight ahead, his features as solid as a block of ice. "We're leaving."

"Now?" she gasped.

"Now." He left her at the entry to their dwelling, placing a quick kiss on her cheek. "Pack our things. I'll go to the festival and alert the others."

Her mind raced, fear clogging her veins like a river of icy slush. Without thinking, she flung herself into his arms. "What about Madhea?"

"She's not my concern." He cupped her cheek in his large, calloused hand. "Your safety is what matters most. Those who are left will have to deal with her. Meet us at the boats." He kissed her once more, a hard, desperate kiss that nearly stole her breath. And then he was off, racing to the great hall like fanged Krahen were snapping at his heels.

She fell against the wall, paralyzed, for she feared neither of them would make it to the boats, and that kiss would be their last.

FROM HER VANTAGE POINT atop Borg's head, Dianna could see they'd reached the edge of the forest. There was a break in the trees up ahead, the rise of Ice Mountain to the north, and the ruins of an abandoned kingdom to the west. They would camp one final night in the forest and emerge onto the expansive grassy slope leading to Ice Mountain on the morrow.

Then what? Madhea would surely spot them with a giant among their party who was easily the height of ten men.

The trees were much smaller on the edge of the forest, the tallest ones barely coming to Borg's head. Their trunks were not wide enough to carve out dwellings, and bushes and weeds were more plentiful, making the area look more like an overgrown garden than a woods. They made camp by a shallow stream in stoic silence, Ryne casting Zier accusatory looks while the dwarf leaned against a tree, downing his strong brew like 'twas medicine.

Camp was set up by the time he corked his bottle, slipping it back inside his vest. He stood, wobbling a bit before finally standing still, bent over as if he still carried that pack on his back.

"Come with me, lad." He waved to Ryne. "I need to find some herbs. Dianna, you, too."

Borg's eyes widened as he stumbled to his knees. "Where fwiends go?"

"We'll be right back, my boy." Zier patted the giant's grimy toe. "Simeon, stay with him."

Simeon answered with a nod, turning his back to them. She cast a wary look at Simeon before following Zier, Ryne, and Tar, aggravated by the happy tune the dwarf whistled and the dog's constantly wagging tail when there was strife all around them. She hated when Simeon pouted, something he'd been doing a lot recently. He'd refused to ride with her atop Borg's head and wouldn't even look her in the eyes when she spoke to him. At first she'd felt sorry for him, but soon pity turned to resentment. He had the attention and admiration of every other woman on the planet save for her. Why couldn't he ease his heartbreak with someone else?

Is that what you want? Sindri's voice echoed in her head. *For Simeon to run into another woman's arms?*

She balled her hands, tension radiating down her spine as she followed behind Ryne through a thicket of bushes. Nosy stones were always spying on her thoughts. "Maybe," she grumbled.

Sindri gasped. *Truly?*

She shrugged. "Maybe not." She inwardly smiled at Sindri's audible sigh.

Perhaps he wouldn't be so glum if I told him you cared for him, Neriphene interrupted.

She stopped as if she'd run into a wall. "Don't you dare!"

Tar nudged her hand with his cold snout.

Ryne spun on his heel, giving her a questioning look. "What was that?"

"Nothing." She pushed forward, wincing as barbs in a thick patch of weeds cut her leg.

"We are almost to the end of the forest, Zier," Ryne called as he hacked at the brush with a thick blade. "You said you'd come up with a plan."

"Aye." The dwarf stopped whistling long enough to agree. "I did."

"Well," Ryne huffed, "have you?"

Judging by Ryne's tone, he wasn't assured the dwarf had figured out a way to rid their party of the giant. Time was up, and they had yet to hear of Zier's solution.

"I think I know something that will work," Zier said in a sing-song voice as he hacked away at large dead bush. Then he stopped, eyeing a patch of blossoming flowers. The flowers were of different variety and color, nature's wild garden in full bloom. "These might do."

Little glowing winged creatures no bigger than Dianna's thumb sprang from the flowers, hissing and buzzing about Zier's head. He swatted them like flies, sending a few careening through the air with terrified screeches. "Be gone, fairies!"

The creatures hissed once more before flying off.

Ryne leaned against a pine, impatiently tapping his foot while his dog sat beside him, slapping the ground with his bushy tail. "What are you doing?"

"I told you, lad, searching for herbs." Zier plucked flowers from one bush and then another. "There's a particular herb that grows aplenty this time of year." He lurched forward, grabbing the roots of a bush with blooms so deeply purple, they were almost black. "A-ha! Methinks this is the one." He waved Ryne over. "Help me pull it up."

Ryne's face turned from blue to almost the same deep purple as the flower as he helped Zier pull the entire bush from the ground. "What's it used for?"

"It's an herbal medicine." He crossed to a small clearing of snake moss, dropping the bush at his feet and turning up his chin as if he was proudly displaying a prized pig. "It gives you a sense of joy, hence the name, euphoria root." He plucked a dark petal from its stem, handing it to Ryne. "Try it."

"Euphoria root?" Dianna wrinkled her nose. "I've never heard of it." Her mother had taught her much about herbs and home remedies, and this was something she'd never run across.

"What's the matter?" Ryne took the petal from Zier, then scowled at her. "Are you afraid of being happy, Dianna?" He flashed an impish grin and shoved the petal in his mouth. He chewed once, then swallowed with a triumphant grin. His eyes rolled back into his head, and he fell like a falling timber into a patch of bushes.

Tar barked, frantically licking his master.

"Zier!" She climbed over the shrubberies and knelt beside Ryne. "What have you done?" He still had a pulse. He let out a blubbery snort, a smile on his face, before rolling onto his side, snuggling the thorny bushes as if they were made of the softest wool.

"No worries." Zier chuckled, rocking on his heels. "He's only sleeping. It will wear off by morning."

Ryne stuck a thumb in his mouth, suckling it like a newborn babe before letting out another loud snort. Tar showered his face with more slobbery kisses.

"Why would you do that?"

The dwarf chuckled. "Don't tell me you haven't wanted to knock this blue broot on his arse a time or two."

She was unable to repress a smile. "A time or two."

His smile faded. "I owed him a turn after he tried to convince you to let Borg die. We dwarves don't forget slights to our kin, and he's slighted us many times."

She plucked a purple petal from its stem, examining it before sniffing. The smell was overpowering, almost enough to knock her out. She threw the petal down.

"So euphoria root is a sleeping shade?" she asked.

"'Tis no such thing as euphoria root." Zier hefted the bushel into his stout arms. "This is Sirensong. It's a sleeping herb. At least I wasn't sure if it was until Ryne tried it." He flashed a devilish grin. "Now I'm sure. There's a whole bushel of it. Enough to put a giant to sleep for at least a day."

Ah, now she saw where he was going with this, but there was just one problem. "What good will that do?" she asked as she stood, brushing pollen and dirt off her breeches. "He will catch us like last time."

"This flower I hold in my other hand is the source of fairy dust." The dwarf flashed a bright yellow flower that resembled a cross between a tulip and a rose. When he turned it upside-down, sparkling specks of pollen rained down on his leather boots.

"Fairy dust?" Sparkles tickled her nose. Fortunately, it didn't make her sneeze. She was overwhelmed by an odd smell, unpleasantly strong at first, but then the scent morphed into something so sweet that it made her crave one of her mother's berry pies. "Oh, it smells quite lovely."

"Lovely enough to mask our scent," Zier said with a wink.

She smiled. "I knew I liked you for a reason, Zier. Thank you."

"No need to thank me now." He pocketed several fairy dust flowers and then hefted the Sirensong bush over one shoulder. "Just remember how much you like me when you're a goddess."

"What do we do with Ryne?" A trail of ants marched over his boot. She hoped for Ryne's sake, they didn't take up residence in his sock. Fortunately, his mongrel was keeping watch over him, so he was safe from bigger dangers.

Zier moved toward camp, saying over his shoulder, "Simeon can carry him."

She raced up to the dwarf, grabbing his shoulder. "I'm not sure he'll like that."

"That boy would lick your feet clean if you asked him to," Zier said with a snort.

She grimaced as Zier left, whistling some awful happy tune. She'd no wish for Simeon to lick her feet. Not only was it humiliating, but it was too personal. She was already bothered by his touch; she couldn't imagine how much she'd be bothered by his tongue between her toes. "Well, I won't ask him to," she mumbled.

But you wish you could, don't you? Sindri giggled.

"Shut up," she hissed, annoyed when both stones broke into nauseating laughter. If Simeon didn't drive her mad on this journey, her cousins surely would.

MARKUS BERATED HIMSELF for wasting time, for none of their crew were at the festival, which meant they were all at the river, finishing up the boats. He could have gone with Ura, and they'd be sailing downriver. The festival was held in the largest of the dining caverns, a wintery hall with thousands of glowing spikes hanging from the ceiling. The fur rugs that normally lined the floor had been used to transform makeshift cottages made to represent the fallen town of Shadolan. There was music, merriment, and roasted fish, which he was sure was contrary to the atmosphere of the fateful day Lydra had attacked their descendants.

He pushed his way through the crowd as they prepared to reenact the gruesome scene when Madhea sent Lydra down to terrorize the village. They had created a smaller version of the dragon out of painted gnull hides, and every year they picked a village matron to play Madhea. Ura had explained that in this celebration, the reenactment ended differently. Instead of the villagers fleeing the dragon's wrath, the beast turned on her mistress, imprisoning her in a curtain of ice. Markus thought it odd how the Ice People were so determined to rewrite their past while paying such little heed to their future, for Madhea would descend upon them soon—he could feel it in the marrow of his bones.

"Thief! Thief! Stop him! He has my stone!"

Markus froze, then bolted through the crowd at the sound of Dame Eryll's shrill voice. Before he could reach the only exit, a dark tunnel at the far end of the cavern, the music came to a screeching halt and the crowd closed in on him.

"Stop that land-dwelling scum!" someone bellowed.

His breaths came in shallow gasps, his heart a dull hammer in his ears as he fought off the men who'd latched onto his arms, but 'twas no use. The crush was too powerful, a wave of people suffocating him as they pushed him to the ground. He cried out when more weight pressed upon his back, and he felt the agonizing snap of a rib.

"Release him!" a woman screamed.

He rolled onto his side, clutching the broken rib, a silent scream on his lips and his eyes watering.

Chieftain Ingred pressed a boot on his chest, knocking him flat against the ground. He gasped, pain lancing through him like venomous barbs of fire.

"Land dweller?" She folded her long arms as she looked down at him, her hawkish eyes narrowing like a predator homing in on its prey. "Why does this not surprise me?"

Chapter Eleven

"Father!" Ura called over the din of the rushing water as she barreled into the cavern where the underground river flowed and dropped her heavy packs to the ground.

She stopped to catch her breath, chest heaving while she clutched her knees. That's when she noticed three of the boats were in the water now, bobbing in the current, their hulls banging against the icy embankment. Surely this was a good sign. Now all she needed was Markus, and they could make their escape.

"Child!" Jon dropped his hammer and quickly bridged the distance between them. He grabbed her by the shoulders, the lines around his bright blue eyes crinkling. "What has happened?"

She wasn't prepared to tell him of her foiled theft, but she had no choice if they were to escape. "Dame Eryll caught me as I was stealing her clan stone," she said on a rush of air.

He stepped back. "What?" His blue face paled. "Why would you steal her stone?"

She searched her father's eyes with urgency, hoping to see a familiar kindness and understanding. "Markus needs it if he's to defeat Madhea. He demanded she not tell, but I'm afraid she will. He said we have to leave now. He went to round up the others." She looked over her father's shoulder, nervously chewing her lower lip. The builders appeared to be finishing up the last boat, which meant Markus had gone to the festival for nothing.

"The others are already here." Jon nodded at another man as he passed them with Ura's bags. He was loading the boats. Were they prepared to escape immediately? Had Odu seen something in the mists?

"Then he shouldn't be long." She looked over her shoulder, hoping to see Markus spring from the tunnel.

"I fear you're right. Dame Eryll will tell."

Her heart quickened. "What do we do?"

"Listen." He held a hand to his ear. "I hear a mob approaching. Where is the stone?"

Even though panic fought to rob her brain of reason, she had enough wits to pull the stone out of her pocket. "Here it is." She handed it to her father.

He dragged her toward Odu, who was sitting on a fur rug beside the embankment. Before Jon could speak, Odu lifted the rug, pointing to a hole in the ice. "In here," the old man said.

Jon shoved the stone into the hole. She watched with wonder as water filled the hole, then quickly turned to ice, completely obscuring the stone.

"Do not worry." Odu winked at Ura. "They won't find it." He smoothed the fur over the stone just as the lights from the mob's torches came into view.

Her heart fell into the pit of her stomach. Chieftain Ingred was at the helm with a scowling Dame Eryll by her side. Two burly guardians followed, dragging Ura's husband, whose face was so bloody and battered, he was barely recognizable, save for his wild mop of hair.

"Oh, Markus," she cried.

Ingred lifted a long arm, pointing a crooked finger at Ura's chest. "Arrest her!"

BORG LOOKED AT DIANNA and Zier with wide, innocent eyes when they returned to camp. "Where blue fwiend and doggie go?"

"Ryne was exhausted from the trip," Zier said, swinging the bush onto a flat slab of rock and pulling out a large blade. "He fell asleep. Don't you worry." He winked at Borg before chopping the heads off their stems in one blow. "His doggie is looking after him."

"Simeon, I need you to help me carry Ryne." Dianna struggled to keep eye contact with Simeon as she waved him over. Something about the accusation in his big golden eyes made her feel like she had a blade lodged in her chest, and Simeon could twist and turn it with one baleful look.

"Why?" He stood after tossing several sticks onto the fire. "What's the matter with him?"

"I will explain, if you'd just please do this for me." She spared a quick glance at Borg, then gave Simeon a knowing look.

Realization flashed in the sand dweller's eyes as he jumped to his feet and hurried after her.

"Fwiends no be gone wong," Borg said to her back. "Borg worry about fwiends."

As she side-stepped prickly plants and pushed leaves out of the way, she felt like ten shades of dirt for what they were about to do. He was such a kind, gentle giant. He deserved friends who treated him well. But it couldn't be helped. He was jeopardizing their lives by following them, and the weather was getting colder. She couldn't exactly lend her goddess stones to the giant and risk him losing them. For the last two nights, despite the roaring fire, Borg had shivered uncontrollably, making it hard for anyone to sleep with the ground shaking under them. Despite Simeon's heavy sighs and Ryne's swearing, she did nothing to ease the giant's misery. She'd been hoping he'd finally tire of the cold and turn back. After tomorrow, he'd have no choice, and everyone would be better off.

Despite the thick vegetation, it wasn't hard to locate Ryne. All she had to do was follow the sounds of Tar's low howls and frantic whimpers. The hound sitting by his master, on high alert as he shifted from paw to paw.

"What happened?" Simeon frowned at Ryne.

She leaned over him, swatting ants off his leg, grimacing as she lifted the hem of his breeches and saw large red welts on his calf. "Zier gave him Siren-song, a sleeping shade."

Simeon was close enough to make her aware of his broad chest. "Why?"

She was unable to hold back a smile. "To see if it works."

He laughed. "It obviously works." Simeon knelt beside the mutt, scratching behind his ears. "It's okay, boy. Your master will live."

"Zier's going to brew a tea tomorrow morning and give it to Borg," she said. "He says Borg should sleep for a day. We will mask our trail with fairy dust."

He stood. "So tomorrow we'll be rid of him?"

"Yes," she answered.

The faint lines around his drawn mouth made him look far more serious than she'd ever seen him. Come to think of it, he was looking more somber than ever, smiling and laughing far less. She wondered if it was because he was dreading the confrontation with Madhea or if something else was bothering him.

"I imagine Ryne won't wake up in a good mood," he said.

A bitter laugh escaped her throat. "When is he ever in a good mood?"

He arched a brow. "So you've noticed, too?"

She shrugged. "I'd be a fool not to."

"Does this mean you don't have feelings for the blue broot?"

She was taken aback. What had given Simeon the impression she cared for Ryne? "When did I ever say I had feelings for him?"

"I thought that since you...." His dark face turned a soft shade of crimson. "Never mind." He looked away, leaning over Ryne, swatting ants off his legs. "He'll be blaming us for his itchy shins."

A whirlwind of thoughts spun through her head. "Since I don't fancy you, I must fancy Ryne?"

He stiffened but didn't answer, swiping Ryne's legs though the ants had already scattered and Tar was licking his master's wounds clean.

"Simeon, listen." She knelt beside him, imploringly searching his golden gaze. "I don't fancy any man."

Liar, Sindri said.

Simeon's mouth fell open. "Then you prefer women?"

She refrained from rolling her eyes. Why must he insist she prefer anyone at all? Why couldn't he accept she'd rather be alone? "I prefer no one. I will outlive anyone I might love. Do you want us to be like Feira and Tumi in three hundred years? Do you want me to spoon-feed you while slobber drips down your chin?" She abruptly stood, ignoring Tar's protests, and turned her back to them, willing the tears to recede.

"I am a strong witch, too, Dianna. I should outlive any mere mortal man." Simeon stood behind her, his deep rumble a warm breath in her ear.

How badly she wanted to lean into him. How badly she wanted to love him and be loved in return.

Then do it, Neriphene admonished.

Please stay out of this, cousins. This is hard enough without your interference.

The stones' only response was a pair of indignant sighs.

"But can you say for certain you will outlive me?" she asked, then held her breath, dreading that she already knew the answer.

"My grandfather lived for two hundred years. So did my uncle and cousins."

She searched his eyes. "And I will live for thousands of years."

He flashed a sad smile, wiping her face with the pad of his thumb. "Is two hundred years of happiness not enough to make loving me worthwhile?"

How badly she relished the feel of his warm fingers on her skin. How she wanted to yield to him, like a reed bending toward a cool stream of water. "Not compared to centuries of depression and longing. I'm sorry, Simeon." She sniffled, then sucked in a sharp breath. "We need to carry Ryne back before those ants colonize his ears."

Simeon turned from her with a curse, then slung Ryne over his broad shoulders with barely any effort, draping him like a fur around his neck.

Did you think all those muscles were just for show? Sindri giggled.

"Oh, do shut up," Dianna hissed under her breath as she followed Simeon's stiff gait and Tar's wagging tail back to camp, feeling lower than she had in a long while. Two hundred years did seem like a long time, but not when compared to an eternity.

"TELL US WHERE THE STONE is." Chieftain Ingred's thin upper lip twitched.

Ura matched Ingred's look with one of her own. "I can't." She was not to be deterred by that giant, awful woman or her angry mob, no matter how much Ura's knees shook like runny soup.

The chieftain's lip curled back in a predatory snarl. "You can't or you won't? Because we have ways of making you talk." Smirking, Ingred cast a glance at Markus as he slumped against his captors.

His eyes were so swollen, they were practically sealed shut, his nose was bent to one side, and his lip was split open. Monsters. Her heart clenched as a low moan escaped his swollen lips. How could they have been so cruel to the one man who could save them from the ice witch? She feared she'd be next. The thought made her stomach churn, but if he could survive such a brutal beating, so could she.

Jon stepped forward, placing his hand on Ura's shoulder. "It's in a place of safe keeping."

"Jon Nordlund," Ingred said. "You are a part of this? I'm disappointed."

Jon's gaze swept the mob before settling on the chieftain. "I'm disappointed that you won't listen to my daughter's and son-in-law's warnings. When Madhea comes, do not ask for passage on our boats. We built them to escape her wrath."

"Don't expect to be going anywhere, Jon," Ingred said with a shrill laugh. "Neither will your children."

Rage boiled Ura's blood. That stupid bloated fish would be the death of them all! "On what grounds?" she demanded. "Trying to save our kingdom? What a terrible offense!"

"Come now." Ingred clucked her tongue and wagged a finger. "I'm sure by now everyone realizes you and your land-dwelling husband are lying about Madhea's attack simply to replace the stone he so foolishly gave his sister."

Ura wanted so badly to snap the chieftain's finger in two, but she knew one of her burly guardians would stop her, no doubt relishing a chance to make Ura's face match her husband's.

"I believe them."

Ura spun around as the crowd parted for the old prophet.

He slowly moved forward, pulling himself along with his cane, like a slog traversing a wall of ice.

"His sister will need all the stones if she's to defeat Madhea," Odu said between halting steps. "I have seen in the mists a great battle between them."

"Did Markus's sister win?" Ura asked, feeling hopeful.

The prophet frowned. "I did not see the outcome."

Ura's gaze shot back to Markus to gauge his response. His head hung limply, and she feared he had lost consciousness or worse.

"So you're part of this, you crazy old man?"

At that moment, Ura realized she loathed that woman more than anyone else on earth, even more than Madhea.

"You forget those were my stones once." Odu rested on his cane. "I gave them to your ancestors with the promise that should I ever need them, the Ice People would hand them over."

"Preposterous!" Ingred made a face, as if she'd just eaten spoiled serpents. "These stones belong to the Ice People now."

The prophet heaved a sigh. "Shall I show you the contracts signed by your ancestors? I still have them. It's time I reclaimed my stones. They should go to Markus, and from him to his sister, if the Ice People wish to survive the coming calamity."

"Here, here," Jon said, a confidence in his voice that Ura didn't feel.

"Guardians!" The chieftain pointed a long, crooked finger at Odu. "Arrest this old fool. Lock him up and take Jon and his children with him."

Ura grabbed the hilt of her blade as the guardians approached. They were no bigger than Markus, and her brother had taught her how to fight. She could take at least one of them down before they captured her.

"Daughter," Jon urged as he latched onto her wrist, shaking the blade from her grip, "do not fight them. There will be a trial, and we will plead our case. They have made a grave mistake in arresting Odu. The people will rally behind us."

Two guardians reached for Jon first, shoving his hands so hard against his back, Ura heard a snap, and he cried out.

"You can't do this!" Red hot anger blurred Ura's vision.

Ingred folded her arms, flashing a wicked grin. "I can and I will."

"On what grounds?" She fought her captors as the guardians latched onto her arms with brute force. There'd be bruising, but at least they'd spared her face, unlike what they'd done to her poor husband. "For reclaiming stones that are not rightfully yours?"

"For theft and deception," Ingred answered.

"Listen to me, people of Ice Kingdom," she yelled to the mob behind Markus. "There are only a few families who possess the stones. They seek to preserve their status. They don't care about protecting you. Madhea will come, and we will all perish."

The crowd broke into a rustle of whispers. She swore as her captors dragged her away. Her heart plummeted when her father and the old prophet were handled roughly by the guardians. She wasn't as optimistic as Jon about their trial, for the chieftain was determined to win no matter the cost.

Chapter Twelve

Dianna was amazed Borg was still awake, picking food out of his teeth after eating a hearty meal of flattened stag and drinking all of Zier's "euphoria" tea.

"It's not working," Simeon whispered in her ear.

"Just give it time," she answered. "It will." At least she hoped so.

She knelt beside Ryne, who was sitting on a tree stump, head in his hands, looking dazed. She handed him a cup of black tea. "You need to be on your feet soon." She nodded at the giant. "He's drunk all the tea, and you don't want to be flattened under him when he falls."

"Like any of you would care," Ryne grumbled, frowning into his mug as if he was waking from a hangover.

"Don't be silly," she said. "I mean it. You need to get up."

Ryne's mutt obviously agreed. He stuck by his master's side, his ears flat, eyeing the giant. Even the dog realized Borg was about to lose consciousness.

Zier was already out of shadow's reach of the giant, hanging back behind a copse of trees, peeking around a trunk and whistling to the others.

She wasn't about to leave the blue broot, no matter how much he annoyed her.

Borg knelt beside them, his big face looking no more droopy than usual, his hot breath no less rancid. He held out a hand. "Fwiends no want Borg to carry?"

"No, Borg. We're not ready to leave yet. Why don't you sit, so I can check your foot?"

He shook his head. "Foot all better."

"Still, I'd prefer you let me look at it, just in case."

He fell on his rump so hard, she stumbled into Simeon. She quickly pulled away and smoothed her vest, as if she was trying to rid her body of the feel of his hands around her waist. Ryne, who'd spilled hot tea down his trousers, swore mightily while Tar barked.

"You damn clumsy slog!" Ryne yelled.

"Sorry, fwiend." The giant pouted. "Borg tired." He yawned, then rubbed his eyes.

The giant fell over in slow motion.

"Look out, Ryne!" she hollered as Simeon hauled her out of the way.

Ryne scrambled to his feet and raced away, his dog at his heels, seconds before the giant's head hit the ground beside them.

Borg was flat on his back, his mouth hanging open. He let out several blubbery snorts before falling into a rhythmic snore, whistling through his nose and wheezing through his mouth, filling the clearing with the stench of his rotten breath.

Ryne backed up several steps, then broke into laughter, slapping his knees and wiping watery eyes.

"I don't see what's so funny," she said.

He looked her over with a sneer. "So none of you laughed when I fell over?"

She turned her back on him, refusing to answer, and shared a secret smile with Simeon.

Zier handed each of them several flower stems tied together with twine. "Attach these to your waists."

She recognized the flowers, smiling as the sparkling fairy dust fell on her boots.

Ryne made a face. "They smell disgusting."

"I think they smell quite nice." An odd thought struck her. She wondered why Simeon thought she'd favored Ryne over him. Though she knew Ryne had a lot on his mind, so did she, and she didn't complain half as much. He was perpetually brooding, as if a shadow had been cast over his heart. She wondered if he knew how bothersome he was to others. He wasn't like Simeon in the slightest, whose cheerful nature always boosted her spirits, even if she was loath to admit it.

Zier handed another bouquet to Ryne. "For the dog."

The ice dweller tied them around Tar's neck. "Sorry, boy." He scratched the pup behind the ears.

Ryne was kind to his dog. He deserved some respect for that. Not much, but some.

"Let's get a move on." Zier nodded to the sleeping giant. "Before he wakes and finds us."

"Elements save us if he does," she mumbled, casting one last glance at Borg. She felt bad for leaving him and hoped nothing happened to him in their absence. Then she tried again to reach the dragons through thought. *Tan'yi'na. Lydra. Are you there?* Again, she was met with silence.

AS URA WAS LED INTO a chamber, she took note of two things. First, this wasn't where the Council normally met. She recognized it as their private chamber. She'd seen it once when accompanying her father on an errand. It was small, with only room for about a dozen witnesses, none of them having friendly faces. None of Odu's followers and boat builders were there, though she had seen them lining the hall on the way to the chamber, their faces masks of worry.

She cast a worried glance at Markus, her father Jon, and Odu, who were roughly dragged in behind her. Why did their captors feel the need to be so abusive? Markus was hardly conscious, Odu didn't even appear to be alive, and Jon didn't put up a fight either.

Ingred was sitting on a makeshift throne, no other Council members by her side, which was odd and did not bode well for them. "Are you prepared to tell us where the stone is?"

Ura matched the chieftain's hard stare with one of her own.

She fought to keep her voice from trembling. "Only if you agree to free us and let Markus use the stone to defeat Madhea."

"Foolish child." Ingred snickered. "My guardians will find the stone without your help, and when they do, you shall regret your decision, for I was prepared to offer you leniency. Outing is too good for this land dweller." She turned her beady eyes on Markus. "He will be sentenced to a slow death, along with Jon and Odu."

Her knees weakened. Had it not been for the guardians gripping her arms, she would've fallen to the ground. She would survive the outing, for she was determined, but her husband and her father were to die a slow death!

"And should any of the crazy old fool's cult object," Ingred continued, "they shall be imprisoned beside him. Ura will be outed."

"This is not a proper trial!" Jon broke free of the guardians holding him. "We deserve a chance to speak."

Ingred's eyes narrowed to slits. "Your daughter was given a chance, and she failed to cooperate."

Jon's guardians reached for him, but he fought them off. "This is an outrage and goes against our rules of order," he hollered as his two burly captors pushed him, pressing his face against the ice. Jon cried out in pain as one of them twisted his arm behind his back.

"No!" Ura screamed, thrashing against her captors' grip even as they dug their claws into her arms. She turned to Ingred, tears streaming down her face. "How could you?"

Ingred glared at her. "I am chieftain. I make the rules."

"You are no chieftain." She spit at Ingred's feet. "You are a tyrant! No better than Madhea."

Odu loudly coughed, hacking and clearing his throat as if he was about to vomit. Rather than help him, his guardians released him.

The prophet looked at Ingred, clutching his chest. "I will speak, even if you won't listen. You are making a mistake." He waved feebly at Ura. "She is trying to save the Ice People from Madhea's wrath."

"Oh, really?" Ingred let out a cackling laugh. "I sent my guardians to find these contracts you said the Ice People signed, regarding the stones. They found nothing."

Odu shook his head, his long white beard nearly scraping the ground. "Or else you told them to destroy them."

"Now why would we do such a dishonest thing?" A wicked grin tugged at the corners of her mouth. "We are not thieves, like your land dweller." She leaned forward, eyeing him intently. "Tell me, have you seen Madhea's attack on our people in the mists as well?"

He gripped the ball of his cane with white knuckles. "I haven't, but I told you I saw her fighting Markus's sister."

She leaned back, her smug smile growing wider. "Then all we have to go by is the word of three thieves and one crazy old man."

Odu swayed like a reed in the breeze. "The mists don't need to show me. I know it in my heart to be true. Madhea will come, and we have no hope of defeating her without Markus and those stones."

"The ice witch doesn't know we are here." Ingred dismissed his concern with an indignant snort. "But should she attack, we have hunters."

"None with an aim like Markus," Ura said. "His arrows always strike true."

Ingred's serpentine stare focused on her. "Yet he was unable to defeat her when he scaled her mountain."

Markus lifted his head, spitting a wad of blood on the ground and moaning. He was trying to speak, but Ura knew it was impossible with a swollen face. Her heart clenched, for she feared her husband would die from his injuries.

"I vill stike her dis time," Markus mumbled. "Pwomise."

"Take the prisoners away." Ingred swatted the air as if she was shooing away a nest of buzzing mites. "Prepare Ura for her outing tomorrow morn."

"No!" she cried, feeling as if the very foundation was crumbling, and she was falling into an abyss. How had it come to this? They were trying to save the Ice People, and now the kingdom would perish, thanks to one ignorant tyrant. "Markus! Father!" she screamed as they were roughly carted away.

Her captors hauled her away, gripping her arms so tight, she feared her bones would snap. Markus cast a glance over his shoulder, blood dripping down his nose and into his mouth. "Vind Dianna."

"I will, husband," she cried. "I will!"

DIANNA WAS EXHAUSTED from running through the forest all day, but they were rewarded with a break in the trees opening onto a vast grassy field. Even though twilight was upon them, Madhea's mountain loomed in the distance. To the west was the Empire of Shadows. It appeared to have once been a vast city, though the wall surrounding it had crumbled in several places, and the great structures in the center of the town had toppled onto their sides. Even as she stared at the ruins from a distance, a shiver coursed through her. The place appeared haunted.

An icy wind blew from the north, smacking her exposed face. Though she was impervious to the Elements, she understood the ominous portent of such a shift in the weather. It was still early summer. It should not have been so cold.

Beside her, Simeon shivered.

"Is the stone not working?" she asked.

"It is, but it's not driving away my fear of demons." He gazed at the abandoned empire. A low howl echoed in the distance.

She turned to Zier. "I don't think we should camp close to that city."

He frowned. "There is no other option than for us to return to the forest."

"Just for one more night," she said, motioning to a copse of trees beneath an outcropping of rocks. "Or up there." She pointed to the rocks.

"Very well," Zier grumbled, warily eyeing the abandoned kingdom as if he expected his dead ancestors to rise and chase them.

AFTER DIANNA RELIEVED herself behind a thick band of bushes, she unrolled her furs and climbed under them. They'd decided to camp on the narrow ledge of rocks that overlooked both forest and empire. That way they could keep eyes on both menaces.

Ryne and Tar had first watch. They sat on a boulder, Ryne's crystal eyes standing out against the black night sky.

No sooner had Zier fallen into his bedroll than he was soundly snoring. They had made no fire, lest Borg or some other creature find them. Sleep eluded her. She was still hungry after eating only a handful of dried meats for supper. And then there was the matter of Simeon. The hurt in his eyes from yesternight still weighed heavily on her heart. She did not like causing him pain. Her friend had always been cheerful and lighthearted, finding ways to make her smile with the silliest of jokes, but he'd been all stony looks and frowns today, trudging through the forest as if his feet were made of bricks. It was all her fault. Curse her immortality! What she wouldn't give to live a normal life. She'd never asked to be born the daughter of a goddess, doomed to live out a lonely eternity.

"Why the long face, Dianna?" Simeon asked.

She leaned up on one elbow and looked over at him. She didn't know if she felt aggravated or thrilled at the way he stared so intently at her. "I don't know. Just thinking."

"Aletha was just telling me something interesting." He batted thick lashes and twirled a fairy dust petal between his fingers. "Something about how you were admiring my bare chest when we were traveling to Aloa-Shay." He flashed a grin so devilish, she expected pixie horns to sprout from his head. So much for his sulkiness.

Heat flushed her cheeks. "I-I didn't know she talked to you."

"They all do," Simeon answered.

Traitors, she thought.

We are not traitors, Sindri admonished. *We're just tired of listening to you pine over the sand dweller.*

"Then stay out of my head," she grumbled.

Where's the fun in that? Neriphene laughed.

She sat up, hoping the bedroll hadn't messed her hair up too much. Not that she should care if she looked pretty for him. "Don't listen to the stones." Unable to stand his scrutiny another moment, she broke eye contact after a few seconds. "They are only joking."

"Are they?" He arched a brow, then stretched, letting the flaps on his shirt fall open, exposing an expanse of dark, muscular chest. The relentless flirt!

"You don't give up, do you?"

"I admit I was feeling sorry for myself earlier today, but the stones have rallied my spirits." The sideways smile he flashed her turned her knees to butter. Curse the teasing sand dweller!

"Remind me to thank them later." She didn't bother masking her bitterness.

His smile faded, replaced with a look so severe, she feared he was about to impart some horrible news. "Do you remember your promise?"

She blinked at him. "What promise?"

"That you would let me kiss you after we defeat Madhea."

The impish smile returned, and she didn't know if she wanted to slap him senseless or kiss him silly. She turned her back on him, pounding the furs under her as if that would make the hard ground more forgiving. "We should get some rest."

"Don't tell me you're going to go back on your word." He sounded heartbroken, as if he'd watched her drown a sack of newborn kittens.

She blinked up at the stars, then heaved a sigh, fearing she'd get little sleep this night. "I didn't say that."

"Do you know how many girls I have kissed since I've met you?"

"No." She turned to face him. She couldn't help herself. Not that she wanted to know every juicy detail of Simeon's love life.

"None, unless you count the time I tried with you," he answered, his piercing golden gaze so unnerving, she had to squeeze her hands to repress a shudder. "Remember that day?"

"I do, and I remember how hard I slapped you." She slid beneath the furs and prayed he'd leave her be. "We really should go to sleep."

"Why?" He laughed. "Are you afraid I'll try to kiss you now?"

She wanted to say something wicked and clever, but a strange howl broke her concentration. She bolted upright. "Did you hear that?" It was like the wail of an injured child. Could it be a ghost? For she could have sworn the sound was coming from the Empire of Shadows.

Simeon's brows drew together. "It sounds like a baby crying."

She looked over at Zier, who'd scrambled out of his bedroll and was slipping into his boots.

"What is it, Zier?" she asked, stunned when he went straight for his pack and not his weapon.

"'Tis a sacrifice." He shrugged into the pack.

"A what?" She quickly slipped into her boots and rolled up her bed, aware of Simeon doing the same.

Zier's heavy pack pushed him forward as he made the slow descent down the cliffside with the dexterity of a goat. "They usually don't sacrifice babies until fall."

"Who?" She shoved the bedroll into her pack. Wherever Zier was going, she didn't want to be left behind.

"The giants," he said as he marched across the clearing toward the tall grasses.

"The giants? Wait up!"

She slipped down the rocks, almost twisting her ankle when it got stuck inside a crevice, grateful when Simeon lent her a hand. She raced up to Zier, chest heaving. She was surprised by the new worry lines creasing his eyes.

"Where do you think the dwarves get our adopted children?"

She shared a bewildered look with Simeon. "I-I don't understand."

Zier grimaced as the wailing grew louder. "We have to help that baby."

"That sound is coming from the Empire of Shadows." Ryne came barreling up to them. Tar followed, sounding stressed.

Zier nodded. "That's where they do the sacrifices, at an old dwarf temple."

"Hang on." Ryne threw up his hands. "We're not going to the Empire of Shadows."

"That child will die if we do nothing." Zier's stony glare would've melted any man except Ryne.

The ice dweller was either too bold or too pig-headed, or both, to back down from the trader. "How do we know the giants aren't still there?"

Zier trudged once more toward the cries. "They leave before nightfall."

Dianna and Simeon followed, but Ryne pushed ahead of them getting in front of Zier and blocking his path. "And what about the other creatures?"

"What about the other creatures?" Zier grumbled, plowing Ryne out of the way, nearly knocking him on his arse with the top end of his pack. "Do you not hear how loud that baby is crying?"

Ryne was not to be deterred; he dogged the dwarf's heels. "Yes, and I'm sure every predator in Werewood Forest has heard as well."

"Which is why we need to reach the baby before they do." Zier quickened his pace.

The dwarf had crossed the small clearing and was almost to the tall grasses, where Dianna feared she'd lose sight of him.

Ryne latched onto the dwarf's pack, stopping him before he disappeared into the field.

Zier turned around with a start, raising his hatchet to Ryne's throat. "Keep yer filthy blue hands off my pack."

Dianna stopped as if she'd struck a wall, her heart in her throat. She loathed fighting and didn't want to have to flatten them. When the baby's cries intensified, she instinctively grabbed Simeon's hand.

"We're wasting time," Simeon grumbled. "Step aside, Ryne."

Zier nodded his approval. "You took the words outta my mouth."

Ryne knocked Zier's blade aside with his bare hand. "We're not going to the Empire of Shadows."

"Speak for yourself, Ryne." Dianna gritted her teeth. "I'm going."

"So am I," Simeon agreed.

She smiled at him, grateful for his courage, and once more wondered why he thought she'd prefer Ryne over him.

"Siren's teeth!" Ryne stomped his foot like a toddler on the verge of a tantrum. "Are you all mad? And what are you going to do with the baby once you find it? We can't exactly carry it with us."

Zier straightened his shoulders, his heavy pack creaking with the movement. "I will stay with the child."

Dianna gulped. "And miss trading with the Ice People?"

Zier shrugged, then turned his back on them and marched into the field. His pack poked out the top of the grasses.

Simeon pulled Dianna along. "We need to go before we lose him."

She sucked in a sharp breath when they were engulfed by the grass, its dry, brittle stems breaking apart as Zier cleared the way, hacking them with his hatchet.

Simeon continued to pull her along. "Don't let go," she whispered.

"Never," he answered.

She didn't know whether to be relieved or unnerved by his answer, but decided to settle on relief—for now.

"Curse the Elements!" Ryne said behind them. "Wait up!" The ice dweller and his dog trailed behind them.

"I thought you weren't coming," she said.

Ryne's cold glare could have melted Madhea's ice caps. "And leave you stupid slogs to fight the monsters by yourselves?"

"Aw, and here I thought you had no heart." She laughed. "Are you sure it's not because you didn't want to be left alone?"

Ryne didn't need to answer. Tar's whimpers were answer enough.

MADHEA ADMIRED HER reflection in the looking glass, hardly believing the beautiful young face staring back at her. Her magic was so strong now, she could summon a powerful wind or thunderbolts with hardly any effort. Now that her beauty and strength had been restored, it was time for her to seduce the blue man. Her plan simply had to work. She had to reach the Ice People before Dianna reached her, for she needed leverage before waging a battle with her daughter.

She finished dragging a brush through her hair, which was as soft as a bird's wing, and then applied lavender oil to her already smooth and supple skin. With a confident smile, she fluttered out of her chamber to the blue man's door with only one plan in mind—earn his trust by seduction. It seemed simple enough, and from what she could tell, he was spineless and weak. She would prevail. Her life depended on it.

Chapter Thirteen

Dianna feared they'd never make it to the baby in time. The Shadow Empire looked small on the map and even from a distance, but it truly had been a great city, with a maze of brick roads and tall buildings. Though the place was in ruins, she respected the architectural details of the crumbling structures. Most appeared to have been made of smooth stone and mortar, many with fancy trim and smiling dwarf faces carved under the windows and eaves. She wondered why the dwarves had abandoned this place.

They hacked their way through overgrown weeds and climbed over the rubble of toppled buildings for what felt like hours. By the time they reached the old dwarf temple, she was out of breath and the babe's cries had stopped. She worried the child had already perished and sent a prayer to the Elements they weren't too late. The temple was a large structure, with seven-pointed star emblems carved into massive wooden doors that were triple Dianna's height. The walls stood at odd angles, and she wondered if the building had seven sides. If so, which goddess had they worshipped?

Simeon helped Zier push open the doors. They heaved and groaned until they opened them enough for everyone to squeeze through.

Zier set his pack against a wall on the inside, then waved everyone forward. "Follow me."

She was surprised to see the temple had no roof. Particles of dust shone like stars as the moonlight lit sections of the inside. The rest was cast in gloom and shadow.

Zier and Simeon pushed at another door, but this one was harder to move. Ryne stood by being useless, so she added her weight. Soon it creaked open, revealing a massive room sunk in the ground, with a platform at the bottom. The giant child was lying on the platform. Several rows of worn benches wound their way up the bowl. No doubt this temple had once been a great gathering place.

As they descended the crumbling stairs into the pit, she felt like a speck of gruel falling into a bowl. The babe—a girl, judging by her long, pretty lashes and tattered gown—sucked her fist and stared wide-eyed at them, her sweet face wet and splotchy from crying. Her legs were tied together at the ankles. Her hands must have been bound at one point, but a frayed rope hanging from her wrist indicated she'd broken free.

"There, there, wee mite." Zier waddled up to the child, patting her chubby leg and speaking in soothing tones. "No need to cry."

"Ha!" Ryne laughed, his hand on his sword while he walked a wide circle around her. "Wee mite!"

His dog barked agreement, ears flat against his skull while he skirted the child, sniffing the air, and then quickly backing up before sniffing again.

Zier turned to Ryne with a scowl. "She is wee for a giant."

Simeon said nothing, his usual smile replaced by a heavy frown.

The babe let out a pitiful whine as she kicked the air. Her flesh was covered in tiny bumps, no doubt from the frigid air. Had the giants truly left one of their own to starve and freeze to death?

Dianna didn't like the hollow shadows around her eyes and cheeks. "She looks malnourished."

"Aye, she is." Zier pulled a cloth out of his pocket, dabbing his wet eyes. "They don't usually sacrifice babes so small."

"Why do giants sacrifice their young at all?" Simeon asked, pulling the stone out of his pocket and placing it under the child's back.

The baby smiled at him, then cooed.

Dianna watched in relief as the stone pulsed red. Hopefully, it would bring her comfort.

"The giants sacrifice their young to appease Madhea in hopes for a mild winter." Zier turned to the babe. "They must have sacrificed early because of the unexpected drop in temperature."

"How barbaric," Dianna breathed, feeling as if pixies were tearing her heart to shreds every time the child whimpered.

"We need to find her food," Simeon said.

"Well, why don't we just go find a giant teet of mother's milk?" Ryne scoffed, waving his sword above his head. "I'm sure there's one nearby."

"Listen, you stupid blue broot." Zier slapped an open palm with the head of his hatchet, his bulbous nose turning bright crimson. "If ye can't be helpful, then shut yer blabbering mouth before I shut it for you."

Ryne had the decency to shut up, though his actions spoke for him when he stomped back up the steps and plopped down on a stone bench.

"How old do you think she is?" Dianna asked.

Zier thoughtfully rubbed his beard. "I'd say no more than eight months. She most likely can't walk yet." He turned to Simeon. "A hand up, lad."

Simeon gave Zier a boost to the platform. Zier walked down the length of her torso, winking at the baby. "Hold still, little mite. Uncle Zier will free you."

As if she could understand him, she became as motionless as stone while he waddled back down her body and cut the cords that bound her legs. No sooner had Zier slid down her leg than she rolled over on her tummy and scooted to her knees, smiling down at them, revealing a mouthful of gums except for two upper and two lower teeth. Dianna was struck by her bright blue eyes and how much her facial features resembled a human baby's. Her nose wasn't as wide or flat as most giants.

Simeon snatched the stone and backed up, staring at the child, who giggled and reached for him. He stumbled backward, nearly tumbling off the platform. "Easy, child," he cried.

The baby saw Ryne, whose blue skin shone like a beacon in a sliver of moonlight. She immediately lost interest in Simeon, cooing and reaching toward Ryne.

"Look out!" Ryne jumped from his bench as she tumbled down the platform and started crawling toward him.

The child giggled, crawling faster. Tar barked wildly, and Ryne gripped the hilt of his sword, racing backward up the steps.

"Have a care," Zier hollered. "She's just a babe."

"A baby who's as big as a gnull." He glared at the child after climbing out of reach. "She's looking at me like I'm her teething ring."

The child sat on her haunches, eagerly sucking her fist.

Simeon jumped down from the platform, walking a wide circle around the giant before coming to Dianna's side. "Do you think she's hungry?"

"Yes." Dianna recognized the look of hunger in the babe's eyes, especially the way she gnawed her hand. She remembered her brother acting this way when he was ready to nurse. "And we have nothing to feed her."

Zier spun a slow circle around the platform. "The giants usually leave a food sacrifice as well." He pointed his hatchet at a tall statue behind him. "Palma fruits!"

A stone shelf against the back wall was held up by the statue of a woman. Though her arms had fallen off, and one leg was beginning to crumble, she recognized the face.

My mother, Sindri echoed. *The dwarves worshipped her.*

"I thought she looked like you," she answered.

We were all created in her likeness. There was no mistaking the longing in Sindri's voice. *How I wish she could hold me once more.*

If she had Kyan on her side, Dianna knew she could defeat Madhea. "I wish she was here, too," she whispered. She looked at Zier. "Shall we give the babe some fruit?"

"Worth a try." He called to the child, pointing to the shelf.

As soon as the babe spotted the fruit, her eyes lit up, and she eagerly followed Zier to the offering. Dianna worried, because a bushel of palma pods weighed as much as three men. She breathed a sigh of relief when the child snatched the entire bushel off the shelf with ease and bit into the pod, swallowing leaves and all.

Dianna turned to Zier with a smile. "She likes them."

"Good," Ryne said. "Then you can volunteer to change her nappy later."

A sudden gust of wind ruffled Dianna's hair. *Beware, demons are coming,* a sibilant voice whispered in her ear.

Dianna spun around, looking for the source of the voice, realization sinking in her gut like a brick that the Elements had issued her a warning.

"Listen." Simeon held a hand to his ear. "Do you hear that?"

Dianna swallowed hard. She heard a faint buzzing. Could it be the demons the Elements had spoken of? "What is it?"

Simeon narrowed his eyes at the starry night sky. "It sounds like the flapping of birds' wings."

"They are not birds." Zier said. "'Tis what I feared. Arm yourselves. The gargoyles are coming!"

Dianna's hand flew to her throat. "Gargoyles!"

"Aye." Zier stood in front of the child, legs braced and holding his weapon at the ready. "They heard the babe's cries, too."

"Let us flee before they get here." Ryne raced toward them, wildly waving his arms for them to follow him back up the steps.

She cocked a hand on her hip. "And do what with the baby?"

"Leave her." His face turned from pale blue to deep crimson. "It's the baby they're after."

Zier shook his hatchet at Ryne. "You cowardly troll!"

"We're not on this mission to save giant babies." Ryne matched Zier's dark look with one of his own. "If we perish, the world perishes, or have you forgotten?"

Tar whined, anxiously looking from his master to Dianna.

"Go if you must." She waved him off. "I'm not leaving the baby." She turned her back on him. Zier was right. Ryne was a troll. Why had her brothers befriended such a man?

"I'm staying, too."

"Thank you," Dianna breathed, smiling up at Simeon as he stood beside her, spear in hand.

Simeon answered with a subtle nod before handing her his stone. "Just do what you did with the pixies," he said.

"Right." She was hardly aware of her actions as she pocketed the stone. "How big are gargoyles?" she asked Zier.

The dwarf held his arms wide. "The length of man with a wingspan to match."

She swallowed hard as the contents of her meager supper raced from her gut, threatening at the back of her throat. "I-I don't think I can...."

Yes you can, Dianna. We will help you, Sindri said.

Put us in your scarf and put the decoys in your pack. They are clever beasts, Neriphene warned.

She shrugged off her pack, inserted the stones in the scarf's pockets, then hurriedly wrapped it around her neck. She took the decoys out of her pack, slipping those inside a small satchel on her hip.

Fear pumped like raging torrents through her veins as the walls shook and crumbled from the rattle of the approaching monsters.

Dianna, you must have faith in yourself, Aletha said in a tone as soothing as warm broth.

"Thank you, Aletha." Dianna patted her neck. "I'll try."

Your lack of confidence could be your undoing, Neriphene chided.

"That's not helpful," she whispered.

The babe turned her chubby chin to the sky as a black cloud blotted out the moon and stars. She pointed and then began to wail, crawling behind Zier.

Remember, you have flattened Tan'yi'na before, Sindri said. *You have defeated a goddess. You can take on a few hundred gargoyles.*

Dianna gasped. "A few hundred?"

Or a few thousand, Neriphene answered.

"Oh, heavenly Elements!" What little moisture she had in her mouth dried up.

Never mind her. Just have faith, Aletha said.

Simeon swore as the black cloud descended.

Ryne raced to her other side. "You stupid stubborn slogs will be the death of us all!"

His dog bared his fangs, the fur on his back standing on end.

"You might want to get down!" Dianna screamed above the din of flapping wings as hundreds of red-eyed demons swarmed the temple. Magic pulsed through her veins as her spirit hovered between this world and the next, keeping one thread tethered to her body. "Be gone, demons!" she screamed as bolts shot out of her fingers.

The sky lit up like a cloudless summer day, and the monsters shrieked, spiraling through the air like spinning discs. Zier had fallen against the babe's leg, Simeon and Ryne had landed on their arses, and Tar was sprawled on his back. How Dianna was still standing was a wonder indeed, for her legs and arms wobbled like they were made of mud. Finally, her legs gave way and she fell to her knees, wiping her brow. The hot and heavy air was as thick as soup. Ryne and Simeon panted beside her. The eerie silence was splintered with ominous hissing and howls. She didn't know why she'd expected the gargoyles to splatter like the pixies, but they'd all but disappeared behind the temple walls.

Simeon stood, holding a hand down to her.

She latched on and was pulled to her feet, still unsteady on shaky legs. "I'm afraid I didn't kill them," she whispered.

He flashed a sideways smile. "But you were amazing."

"Amazing and victorious are two different things," Ryne grumbled as he raised his sword. "Zier," he called to the dwarf. "Do you see anything?"

Zier pulled himself up by clinging to the giant's grubby toe. "Nay, not a thing, but I hear them."

She heard them, too—a faint whisper at first, followed by rabid hissing and then menacing howls.

Ryne held up a silencing hand. "I think they're communicating."

Simeon laughed, a nervous sound that ended with a crack. "Hopefully they're deciding to retreat."

"Don't count on it." Ryne grimaced.

Tar turned to face the back wall.

An ear-piercing howl set Dianna's teeth on edge. She watched with a mixture of awe and terror as the walls around them began to crumble. Then a sea of red eyes, spindly legs, and dripping fangs crawled over the debris like giant winged spiders.

"Do something, Dianna!" Ryne screamed.

"Stop!" Dianna commanded. She'd had no time to travel to that space between two worlds, so the magic that flowed through her was less potent.

A strong wind blew out of her fingertips, sending the creatures tumbling back. They shrieked as they flipped spiky heads over long, barbed tails.

Simeon pointed his spear at something beyond her shoulder. "The other side, Dianna!"

She spun and sent those creatures away, too, though the magic that flowed out of her fingers was even less powerful than before.

"Sindri, help," she cried.

You're not focused, Sindri admonished. *You're letting fear rule you.*

"That's because I'm scared!" she cried.

A creature careened straight for her with an ear-splitting howl. Simeon struck the beast with his spear, and it faltered midair, tumbling at Dianna's feet. The thing let out a ghoulish yowl and shuddered as Simeon yanked his spear from its chest.

A shiver took hold of her, rattling her from the inside out as she gazed at the leathery, black creature with razor-sharp claws and fangs as long as daggers, reminding her of a human-sized blood-sucking bat.

Zier tried to hush the baby as she bawled, eyes wide with terror.

The hissing began anew. Elements save them all, for Dianna knew the monsters were formulating another attack.

She tried to send her spirit to that place between two worlds, but fear anchored her to her body like an invisible chain, weighing down her soul.

"Sindri," she cried. "What's happening?"

You are doing this to yourself, Sindri scolded. *Let go of your fear.*

"I can't!" She backed away from the creature Simeon had stabbed as it twitched at her feet. A spear to the chest, and it was still not dead! Were these beasts immortal?

Do it, Neriphene commanded, *or you will all perish, and we stones will be lost to those creatures!*

You are the daughter of a goddess! Sindri shrieked. *Act like one!*

A deep rumble shook the ground so hard, she fell into Simeon's arms. Tar spun in circles, barking wildly at something in the sky. Borg stomped up and down as if trying to put out a fire, swinging a massive tree trunk like a club, splattering those gargoyles who dared take to the air. He flung off the vicious creatures when they climbed up his body and bit into his flesh.

"Borg save fwiends!" he cried, eyes wide with panic. "Fwiends run!"

Her heart hit her ribcage with a dull thud. After the way they'd treated him, poor Borg was willing to sacrifice his life for them.

"Dianna!" Zier hollered. "Don't let him perish."

"I won't." She nodded, then shut her eyes, focusing on that space between worlds. The magic pulsed through her veins like rivers flowing from a bubbling volcano. Energy pooled in her palms, but she didn't strike. She let it flow until her hands felt weighted with bags of sand. Then she lifted her aching arms and flung her magic at the monsters, who had swarmed Borg like a nest of voracious pixies to a hapless mortal.

The force flew from her hands like giant thunderbolts, sending her careening through the air and smack into the baby's belly. She bounced off the child, landing on her side with a painful crack.

Grab hold of me, Aletha urged.

She placed a bloody hand on a stone in her scarf, clutching it though it pained her. She was weak, her eyelids heavy.

Simeon knelt beside her, stroking her back. "Are you okay?"

But she was too tired to answer. Her eyes fell shut as she sent a silent prayer to the Elements that the monsters had been destroyed.

DIANNA AWOKE BESIDE a campfire, nestled in Simeon's warm embrace. He was smiling.

"It's over." He stroked her cheek. "You saved us."

She breathed a sigh of relief. "The gargoyles?"

Simeon made a face. "Your magic cooked them all."

"She's awake." Ryne's grumble came from somewhere nearby. "You can let go of her now."

Simeon looked up with a scowl. "I'll let go when she's ready and not a moment before."

She struggled to sit up, momentarily mesmerized by the light from the hearth fire. They were sheltered inside a building that looked like it had once been a home. Like the temple, this place had no roof, just four stone walls and the starry sky above. Borg sat outside, looking down at them, debris flying from his lips as he loudly crunched his food. Was he eating tree bark? She looked over Simeon's shoulder at the sound of a loud giggle. Zier was with the baby in a room that may have once been a large family room. He was feeding her strips of what must have been the same tree bark Borg was eating. Giants ate trees?

She wrinkled her nose as a sickeningly sweet yet bitter odor accosted her senses. "What is that smell?"

Simeon frowned. "Borg's dinner. You may want to cover your nose."

Borg flashed a blackened grin, as if he'd devoured a mound of coal.

"Fwiend want some?" He reached over the wall and held down a charred gargoyle wing attached to part of a torso and a spindly arm. "They crunchy and good."

She turned away when the stench of burned gargoyle flesh hit her. Before she could stop herself, she vomited on Simeon's chest.

She coughed and gagged. "I'm sorry, Simeon." Wiping her mouth, she looked at him, mortified. His eyes were wide with horror and disgust.

He angled away from her with a grimace. "It's okay."

Ryne laughed so hard, he snorted like a wild hog. "You should've listened to me and let her go."

She rolled off Simeon, cringing when he stumbled to his feet and ripped off his tunic.

Well, at least you get another look at his muscular chest, Sindri teased.

It still looks good, even covered in vomit. Neriphene laughed.

"Shut up, you two," she groaned, clutching her burning gut and struggling to sit up. She fought the urge to vomit again when she noticed Tar sitting by the fire, chewing the end of a gargoyle tail.

"There's a bathing hut nearby," Simeon mumbled. "I'll be back soon." He grabbed his pack and stomped out of the room.

"I'm sorry, Simeon," she called to his back, trying to ignore the loud crunching sounds coming from the dog.

"No worries, lass. My ancestors had good wells and running water, and we've maintained that bathing hut for our pilgrimages." Zier raced to her side, holding out a metal flask. "Drink this."

"What is it?"

He pushed the flask under her nose. "It will settle the stomach, lass, and wash the taste of bile out of yer mouth."

She knew not what act of madness made her take a sip of Zier's brew. Mayhap it was that she was shamed by the look in Simeon's eyes and hoped she would indeed wash away the stench of vomit. She stifled a scream when the brew burned going down. Great goddess, it was if she'd swallowed dragon fire! She breathed through a wheeze as the fire raced back up her throat and out her nose.

"Well?" Zier corked the flask, nudging her side. "Is that better?"

She had to struggle for breath before she could answer. "I think you've turned me into Tan'yi'na." Surprisingly, though, she no longer had the urge to vomit. Her head swam and her eyes watered, but the fumes from the fiery brew had drowned out all stink of charred gargoyle. She pointed a shaky finger at Borg. "How can they eat that?"

"Giants have peculiar tastes." Zier slipped the flask inside his vest pocket. "At least the baby won't be hungry now."

"And I'll never be hungry again." She rubbed her churning gut.

"Come now, Dianna." Ryne laughed. "It's a shame to let good gargoyle go to waste."

"Shut up, Ryne." She wished she could shove a fistful of euphoria root down his throat.

The child peered over the wall with a sweet grin (despite the gargoyle meat that stuck to her few teeth like tar). Her eyes looked less hollow, her cheeks rounder. When Borg leaned over and scooped the babe into his arms, she giggled and bounced, waving her chubby fists.

Dianna didn't understand why the giants would sacrifice such a precious child. The people of Adolan would never give innocents to Madhea, unless, of course, the town suspected them to be witches. In that case, the parents would do everything in their power to hide their children's magical secrets, as Dianna's foster parents had.

"Couldn't the giants use goats or some other food for sacrifice?" Though she disagreed with all sacrifices, the people of Adolan and Kicelin had been using goats for centuries. Each week they also left fresh baked bread, vegetables, and wine on an altar. Never once had they heard a complaint from the goddess. Though it was forbidden to wait for Madhea after leaving the sacrifices, it was rumored the ice witch's pixies retrieved the food.

"What the giants don't know," Zier said, "is that we've been stealing their babes for the past fifteen years."

"And what about the children before that?" she asked, though she didn't want to know the answer.

The dwarf sat beside her and warmed his hands at the fire. "There was only one that we know of, and only because a cousin found the poor tot's remains, surrounded by gargoyle droppings, on his pilgrimage to pay homage to our dead kin. After that, King Furbald had the idea that we'd steal them from the altar and raise them as our own."

A dining table that had probably sat twenty dwarves was pushed up against a wall, along with a beautifully carved cabinet that housed dusty broken dishes and dented metal goblets. "How did this magnificent city come to be abandoned?"

He shook his head. "'Tis too sad a tale."

As if to emphasize Zier's point, Tar laid down, covering his snout with his paws.

"Please," she pressed. "I want to know." Though she regretted the pain in Zier's glossy eyes, knowing about their ancient city might help her understand the dwarves better, particularly their peculiar king.

"Very well." He heaved a groan, his shoulders falling inward. "It happened before my time, you see? About eighty years ago. King Furbald was a young prince, and Eris's army came from the sea to battle Madhea's army, which came from the mountain. That field we crossed was once the scene of a great battle."

Simeon reappeared, drying his braid with a towel, his dark, broad chest glistening in the firelight. She looked away before the stones caught her gawking.

Too late. Sindri giggled.

"Who won?" Simeon asked, taking a seat beside Dianna, his knee rubbing against hers.

She shifted away, still feeling self-conscious after vomiting on him.

"Eris's army," Zier said, the shadows from the fire lengthening his frown. "But not without great price. You see, Madhea's army had arrived the night before and demanded entrance into our city. The old king thought it best if the dwarves let them in, as they'd threatened to scale the walls and raze the city if the king did not. They pillaged the city anyway. They drank our whiskey, stole our gold, murdered our men, and used our women." He smiled up at Borg, who was crawling on all fours, letting the baby ride on his shoulders.

Dianna leaned toward Zier, eager to hear how the story ended, though she felt ten shades of selfish for wanting to put him through the torture of the retelling just to satisfy her curiosity.

"When morning came," he continued, "Eris's army attacked. Those dwarves who'd endured the ice witch's men fared even worse with the sea queen's army. They butchered Madhea's men and nearly wiped out our race. Those few who survived gathered their possessions and fled to the shore, rebuilding their lives on the cliffs of Aya-Shay."

"And that is why your king refuses to allow humans inside now? Because of what those soldiers did?"

She remembered the king saying that a giant's angry fist cuts a smaller path of destruction than the cunning of man, and now she understood his resentment toward humankind. She couldn't blame him for his bitterness or his unwillingness to allow humans into Aya-Shay. Given their past, it was actually generous of the dwarves to allow humans to stay in the hold.

"Aye." Zier stared into the fire. "I had not been born yet, but King Furbald remembers how our race was treated by men. His whole family perished, including his wife and young child."

"Oh, how tragic." Her heart ached from sadness.

"And that's why the dwarves adopted so many giants?" she asked. "For protection, should mankind try to breach your walls again?"

Zier nodded. "That might be why *he* wanted to adopt so many giants, but most dwarves who've taken in the orphans love those children as if they were their own."

"I've seen it with Grim and his giant daughter, Gorpat." She remembered the way Grim had wept with joy when she healed his daughter's deadly sea serpent bites and the many other times he doted on his child, referring to her as his pearl.

"King Furbald doesn't treat his adopted son so well, does he?" There was no mistaking the accusation in Ryne's voice. Though the ice dweller focused too often on the negative, she agreed with him on this.

Her gaze shot to Borg, who was too focused on playing with the baby to pay their conversation any heed.

"I do not like speaking ill of my king, but nay, he does not." Zier hung his head. "My parents told me he was once carefree and kind, but the great battle changed him."

"It's not Borg's fault," Ryne pressed, "though is it?"

Zier looked at Borg, who had the babe in his arms once more, tickling her chin while she cooed and clutched his vest. "Nay, it's not."

And that, she feared, was the crux of the problem. King Furbald might have had reason to mistrust humans, but his anger and rage had grown like an infected boil. Now he treated everyone with disdain, even his own people and his adopted son.

The cold had spread to the ancient dwarf kingdom, which meant Adolan was most likely frigid. Madhea's power was growing, and soon all the world would be ice. She'd rather have King Furbald on her side for the coming battle, though a nagging doubt told her his alliance would be hard won, mayhap not won at all.

MARKUS LEANED AGAINST the thin fur shielding his back from the frigid ice wall, welcoming the chill that seeped into his bones, for it helped numb the pain. Some of his ribs were certainly broken, for each breath was a painful wheeze. His jaw and nose felt cracked as well. His own pain he could bear, but the thought of Ura being outed, left alone to starve or be killed by snowbears, was an agony he couldn't endure. He silently wept for his lost love, praying to the Elements that if she were taken from this world, they'd be reunited soon.

"Do not lose hope, my boy. Your sister is coming."

Markus looked at Odu, who was sitting cross-legged beside Ura's sleeping father, Jon. The old prophet's spindly legs poked out from under his robe like sapling branches.

The hope that welled in Markus's chest was more like the dull stab of a blade. Even if Dianna were to come, would she be too late to save Ura?

"When?" he asked.

"Soon," the old man said and closed his eyes.

"How soon," he demanded, pain slicing through his torso when he raised his voice.

But the old prophet didn't answer. The man was more infuriating than helpful, planting a seed of hope yet refusing to water it. He prayed Dianna would arrive in time to save Ura, though he wasn't sure if the Elements would listen. They had failed his mother and father and so many others who'd perished under Madhea's wrath. Why would they wish to save him now?

Chapter Fourteen

Madhea scowled as she woke up in the scrawny arms of her lover. He'd been nothing like Rowlen, but a mouse of a man, lacking passion and stamina. She was glad last night was over, for now she could coax out of him the way to the Ice People. Once she gained entrance, she'd dispose of the blue fool and destroy the Ice People, but not before taking Rowlen's son as prisoner.

She heaved a sigh as she thought of the boy hunter with the strength and skill of a full-grown man. She wondered how it would feel to wake up in his arms, if he was as strong and capable as his father. If he wasn't too unpleasant a prisoner, she'd like to find out. She dared not use dark magic to trick him into her bed, for she'd no wish to sacrifice her power and beauty once more, no matter how alluring the temptation.

The blue man's beady eyes flew open, and he looked at her with a start, then down at his scrawny, bare body. "What happened? Did we?" He blushed and looked away.

Madhea fought the urge to snap his neck. "How could you forget our glorious night of passion?"

"Oh, yes," he mumbled, pulling the fur up to his chin.

"So," she drawled, yanking it down and tracing lazy circles across his collar bone, "are you ready to take your rightful place by my side and vanquish this boy hunter once and for all?"

The ice man's eyes lit with recognition. "Destroy the land dweller?" He eagerly nodded. "Yes, as long as you keep your word and don't harm the others."

"My darling," she cooed, nibbling his ear. "On my honor, I vow to keep my word." Too bad he hadn't thought to demand she make a blood oath, for Madhea knew nothing of honor. Only revenge. Sweet, bitter revenge.

URA STOOD ON THE PRECIPICE of fate, knowing her punishment could possibly be her salvation. They had gathered in the same chamber where she'd first found Markus unconscious on a wide spike the Ice People commonly referred to as a Dragon's Tooth, a column of ice that was ten men in height. They were surrounded by hundreds of such spikes, jutting up in to the air like a dragon's barbed tail. The only portion of the chamber devoid of them was the platform on which she stood.

She was amazed at how many ice dwellers had come to hate and mistrust her, yelling obscenities and throwing objects at her feet. She turned up her nose at their anger and dodged fish guts and chunks of ice. A few came to offer her their support. They didn't trust Ingred's tyranny and were mad at her for sentencing Odu to a slow death. If only their numbers were greater, they'd stand a chance at overthrowing the current ruler and saving her husband and father. Their chants of "Tyrant, tyrant!" were drowned out by the majority, calling for Ura's swift punishment.

Her only hope was to get down the unforgiving mountain, unseen by Madhea, and find Dianna in time to save Markus and her father. Her plan sounded impossible, but what other options did she have?

The ice climbers had scaled a spike and burned a hole through the ice ceiling with one of two remaining stones. They quickly came back down and prepared the harness for Ura.

Ingred sat behind her upon yet another throne carved of ice, clapping her hands. "It is time!"

Ura stepped back, shaking off the grip of a beefy guardian when the climbers came for her. "Wait!" she cried. "Where is my pack? Where are my bow and arrows?"

Ingred steepled long fingers beneath her pointed chin. "We're keeping your possessions in partial payment for the stone."

Ura had never heard of such an outing. The accused was allowed a pack and a weapon. "You can't do that! Our laws state that those outed are granted use of their weapons."

Ingred tapped the armrest of her chair. "We have given you another weapon." She nodded to a guardian, and he stepped forward with a rusty, dull blade.

"I can't fight with this!" She threw it at Ingred's feet, wishing she had the nerve to plunge it into her cold heart. "You are no chieftain. You are a tyrant. First a secret hearing, and now you break the laws again." She turned to the Ice People. Her bellow was so deep and powerful, it surprised even her. "Is this what you elected her to do? Is this the kind of ruler you want, deciding fates without the input of the Council? Outing people without giving them a chance at survival?"

A few people in the crowd yelled, "Give Ura her bow!" while others chanted "Tyrant! Tyrant!"

Ingred shifted in her chair, her mouth twisted in an uneasy grimace. "Very well," she snapped, then beckoned a guardian forward. "Bring her bow and pack." Then she flashed Ura a mocking smile. "I doubt your meager little weapon will stop a snowbear."

"I know it will, for my husband taught me how to shoot. You think this is over and that you've won, but you haven't. I will not die out there." She looked at the crowd, resolution hardening her voice. "I know how to survive, and I will be back with help, but not for those who have sided with the tyrant." She sneered at Ingred even as a guardian handed Ura her bow, quiver with arrows, and the soft doeskin pack Markus had made for her. "When Madhea comes, there will be no one here to save you."

"Foolish girl." Ingred snorted. "You will be snowbear bait before you make it halfway down the mountain."

"No, I will survive. I *have* to." Ura said to herself, even as two guardians jostled her into the harness. She was about to leave Ice Kingdom for the first time in her life, thrust into the unknown and beneath the vengeful eye of an evil goddess, her only hope of saving the people she loved.

DIANNA WOKE UP TO THE morning sun peeking through clouds. There was frost on the windows and ice hanging from the eaves. How had the temperature changed so drastically in a few hours? She knew without a doubt Borg and the babe would not survive the frigid air much longer. Borg's teeth rattled as he shifted from foot to foot, complaining of the frost on his toes. After using much of her energy to heal his gargoyle bites the night before, she couldn't imagine the strength it would take for her to continually heal frostbite. Twin frozen pendulums of snot trailed from each nostril to his upper lip. If Borg accompanied the group much longer he'd surely freeze to death.

Then there was the matter of the baby. The stone could only keep a child of that size slightly warm. She would perish before Borg, for they couldn't scrape together enough furs to cover her body.

She went outside, breathing in the crisp morning air and impatiently tapped her foot, waiting for Ryne to finish up in the bathing hut. She'd no idea what could take a grown man so long, but she was too distraught to stand around.

She'd tried to reach the dragons again, calling to them most of the morning, but neither answered. What if the giants had come across Lydra and Tan'yi'na on their way to the sacrifice? If they were heartless enough to sacrifice their young, they wouldn't think twice about butchering two dragons. The thought twisted her stomach in knots.

The babe's loud giggle pulled her from her worries. She couldn't help but smile as Borg played with the child, letting her ride on his back while he stomped through the city, heedless of the chafing on the frozen soles of his feet as he climbed over rubble.

"*Brrrrr!*"

She turned at the sound and looked through a broken window. Simeon shivered in front of the dying embers in the hearth. She was grateful to him for loaning his stone to the babe to keep warm, and though she wanted to make him comfortable, she couldn't risk parting with another stone, not after her trial with the gargoyles. The only option that made sense was for him to take back the stone he'd lent the babe, and Borg had to take the child to a warmer climate.

"The giants need to retreat to Aya-Shay," Dianna said to Zier as he joined her, back bent even though he had yet to shrug into his pack.

"Aye." He squinted, rubbing his bushy beard. "And I must volunteer to lead them."

"You, Zier? But you'll miss out on trading with the Ice People." Elements save her! He couldn't leave her alone with Simeon and Ryne!

"I know." He slipped his flask out of his vest, uncorked the cap, and took a hearty swallow. "But the babe's safety is more important. I cannot trust Borg to keep a steady eye on her."

She thought it ironic that Zier would accuse Borg of not being steady while drinking from a flask shortly after dawn had broken. Come to think of it, she'd seen him drink from that flask many times during their journey, yet he always appeared lucid. Perhaps there was something good to say about dwarf constitutions.

"Do you think Borg will agree to go back?" She'd be sad to see her friend go, but the baby needed someone with more experience to look after her. She didn't know Borg's age, but he acted as if he was still a child.

"He has to see he has no choice." Zier put away the flask. "Even if he cares nothing for his safety, the babe will perish if he doesn't turn back."

"Zier." Dianna knelt beside the dwarf, placing a hand on his shoulder. "Thank you for accompanying us this far."

When Zier turned his steady gaze on her, she thought she saw a sheen of tears in his eyes. "It was an honor, Dianna. I have faith in you. One day you will rightfully take your mother's place. The world will once again be ruled by a benevolent goddess like Kyan, and I can say I helped our deity on her way."

Emotion tightened her throat. "I hope you're right." She worried over her failure with the gargoyles. If Borg hadn't shown up to distract them, she wouldn't have had time to focus her magic. She doubted she'd have giants on hand to distract her mother when they faced each other in battle.

Zier surprised her by clutching her shoulder in a steady grip. "I know I am, lass. Mark my words, you will be victorious."

She swallowed. Zier put too much faith in her. She hoped she wouldn't disappoint him, for everyone's sake.

MADHEA'S WINGS BUZZED excitedly as she watched the ice on the ground beneath their ledge melt. The hole appeared on a sloping patch of Ice Mountain between Madhea's ledge and another one below. After an interminable wait, two blue men climbed through the opening, pulling with them a blue girl with a pale curtain of hair. They shoved her hard to the ground, laughing while she grunted and spit out snow. Then the men climbed back through the hole, and the ice magically sealed above their heads. No wonder Madhea couldn't find the way to their secret city. They had used their goddess stones to seal the entrance.

"So this is it?" she hissed in Bane's ear. "Who is that girl?" Madhea watched with fascination as the girl got to her feet, stomping the ground and cursing the Elements. Madhea knew the girl had been outed, just as the Ice People had done to Bane.

"Nobody important," Bane said rather too quickly, gawping at the girl.

"Why are they outing her?" she asked. If she were to conquer this disobedient race of people, she wanted to better understand them.

"I don't know." Bane turned to Madhea with a quivering lip. "Do you think we could help her?"

She narrowed her eyes as suspicion planted a seed in her gut. "Why?"

He turned back to the girl, his voice wistful. "She'll die out there."

That seed of suspicion sprouted, its long-barbed tendrils wrapping around Madhea's heart. How dare Bane pine for another! Never mind that she had already planned to discard the weakling ice dweller after she'd finished with him. He should've had eyes for Madhea and Madhea alone!

"Why should I care?" she asked accusingly, not bothering to hide the venom in her tone.

Bane's nostrils flared. "Because you told me you cared about the Ice People."

The girl threw a rope over the side of the mountain and rapidly descended out of view. Madhea wondered if that was the girl Ura whom Bane had mentioned was in love with Markus. She seemed in a hurry to leave the mountain.

"I didn't see Markus leave with her. Do you think Markus is still with the Ice People?"

Bane faced her with a stony expression. "You don't care about the Ice People, do you? You were only using me to enact your revenge."

She didn't know how to answer his defiance with anything other than mockery, so she laughed until her eyes watered. "Do you think I could love a scrawny bird like you when I've been wrapped in the strong arms of a real man?" She defiantly tossed her hair over her shoulder, flaunting her beauty. Let this be the last time the ice dweller looked upon her face. He didn't deserve her as a lover, and he certainly didn't deserve to live.

She saw the flash of steel in the ice dweller's hand, but her reflexes weren't fast enough. She buckled under the thrust of the blade when he drove it into her gut.

He stood above her as she clutched the hilt. She recognized the weapon as one of her own, a tool she'd given him when he'd complained the meat from his meal was too tough. The sneaky slog! How dare he deceive her!

"You are no goddess," he spat, his ugly, gaunt face contorting into a mask of malevolence. "You bleed just like a mortal."

Though her powers were weakening, she was able to summon a magic that blew in like the wind and knocked a shocked Bane right off the ledge, sending him careening though the air with a squeal before he hit the unforgiving ground below. Even from her perch high above the ground, she heard the sickening crack of his skull. Blood pooled around his head, darkening the ground around him.

Clutching her wound, she fluttered into the air, flapping as hard as she could. She had to reach her chamber before she bled out. Elements have mercy, only dark magic could save her now.

Chapter Fifteen

Dianna was grateful Ryne and Simeon were young and strong. A break in the weather meant they were able to make good time up the mountain. Another blessing: because they jogged most of the way, neither man had enough energy left to bicker. In fact, the most vocal member of their party was Tar, barking at every petrified tree as if he expected gargoyles to spring from them. He was so much on edge that he set the rest of the party on high alert, too, making for a very stressful journey.

She knew not what had happened, but the icicles on the trees began to melt, and the Danae River swelled once more. By the time they reached Adolan, the town appeared unchanged, other than the mud surrounding the huts from the sudden thaw. The town was devoid of life and eerily quiet. They heard not even the chirping of birds, but Tar's superior sniffing ability unearthed enough petrified nests and animal carcasses for her to know they hadn't survived the frost. She only hoped the people of Adolan had escaped in time.

"Why do you think winter has retreated?" Simeon asked as they trekked past the mighty lyme tree in the center of town. The tree's branches had wilted and sagged like a kneeling giant, bent over with fists planted on the ground.

"I'm not sure," she said. "My best guess is that Madhea has shown mercy or something has weakened her power."

"The ice witch is not capable of mercy," Ryne scoffed.

"No." Her heart plummeted, for Ryne was right. Her mother cared for no one but herself. But from what Markus had told her of the Elementals, they were kind and compassionate. What if her vision of them trapped in a heptacircle had been nothing more than a nightmare? What if they were finally able to rein in Madhea's power? Dianna prayed it was true and the Elementals were safe and well.

"Then let us hope she was dealt a blow," Ryne said, kicking a muddy doll out of his way. A trail of discarded pots and other household goods littered the path out of the town center. Tar sniffed them all, coming away with a crusty end of bread. She feared the discarded debris had become too burdensome for the fleeing people to carry, and that they'd left without enough provisions.

"Who would be powerful enough to take on the Sky Goddess?" Simeon asked.

She was about to mention the Elementals when Ryne answered, "Tan'yi'na."

She stopped as if she'd run into an invisible wall of ice. "Heavenly Elements, I hope not!" Mayhap that was why the dragons didn't answer when she called to them. They'd decided to take on Madhea themselves. She wouldn't put it past Tan'yi'na after carrying a grudge against the ice witch for over a thousand years. She hoped it wasn't true, for the dragons' silence could only mean they'd perished in the battle.

MADHEA TUMBLED INTO her chamber, clutching her stomach and frantically knocking potions off the dresser. They crashed on the hard floor in plumes of smoke until she found the one she needed, made from salamin oil and various medicinal herbs.

She uncorked the bottle with her teeth, grimacing while swallowing the bitter contents of the vial. She threw it to the floor and stumbled to her bed, lying down on the soft furs and closing her eyes, pressing a hand on the wound. She channeled healing magic into her fingers, though not enough poured out to stop the flow of blood. She was weakening, and so was her magic. She feared the herbs would do little to help, which meant she had only one other option if she wished to avoid certain death.

She called on the dark magic within her soul, the same poisonous seeds that had once caused her beauty to fade. It wrapped around her with sharp barbs, stitching her up until naught was left but a wicked black mark that circled her waist like a belt of thorns, a permanent and ugly reminder of her painful brush with death.

The ordeal exhausted her last bit of energy. As her heavy eyelids fell shut, she prayed to the Elements that the scar wouldn't spread to her beautiful face.

DIANNA HAD HOPED THEY could stop by her family's hut for one night, but she'd no time to reminisce. Instead, they trekked past the town, reaching Kicelin by nightfall. If Adolan was eerily barren, Kicelin was a graveyard beneath the shadow of the mountain's peak that loomed above it. Though some of the town had begun to thaw, frost still covered rows of brick huts with thatched roofs. They chose a lone hut on the edge of town and used a stone to melt the layer of ice coating the door. Inside was not much better. Tables and beds had splintered from the chill, but they hadn't found any petrified bodies.

There was a large pot of stew on the hearth, frozen in a block of ice. Dianna set to work melting it in hopes they'd have a nourishing meal for once, rather than rationed sticks of dried meats.

Simeon and Ryne tidied up the cottage, repairing what they could. The moon was rising by the time they gathered around the hearth to eat. They sat on their furs close to the fire, not trusting the wobbly dining chairs and table.

She moaned after her first bite. It was just as she had hoped, venison, cabbage, roots, and herbs preserved by the freeze, tasting freshly made when heated. 'Twas the most delicious meal she had ever eaten. Simeon and Ryne obviously agreed, because they wordlessly devoured bowl after bowl until the entire pot had been drained. Tar feasted on the discarded deer bones that had been left beside the fire.

Simeon dragged a hand across his full lips, letting out a satisfactory belch as he leaned back on his elbows. "That was delicious."

Ryne tossed his empty bowl on the ground with a *clank*. "It was tolerable at best."

"Tolerable?" Simeon eyed Ryne. "You devoured four bowls."

"I was famished after subsisting on nothing but dried meats and berries." Ryne picked a piece of meat out of his teeth. "I would've eaten a bowl of troll dung if it was edible."

"Honestly, Ryne." She was exasperated by the ice dweller's consistently negative outlook. "How did Alec put up with you without throwing you overboard?"

"Here, here." Simeon chuckled.

Even Ryne's dog appeared to agree. His tail heartily slapped the wooden floor, and he barked three times at Ryne before returning to his bones.

The blue man eyed Simeon through slits. "Alec and I got on fine. He knew when to shut up."

Simeon pointed an accusatory finger at Ryne. "Zier told me you broke Alec's nose."

She shot upright. "What? You broke my brother's nose?" Why was this the first she was hearing of it?

Ryne shrugged. "We had a disagreement."

She was so angry, magic crackled in her palms. Alec had been abused enough in his lifetime. He didn't need bullying from brooding blue beasts. "So you broke his nose?"

"I've apologized." Ryne picked more grime from his teeth, heedless of her simmering beside him like Eris's volcano, ready to explode.

Simeon smugly smiled. "You said you were sorry for breaking his nose *and* getting him caught in Eris's net?"

Ryne cocked a brow. "What else has Zier told you?"

"You were the reason he was captured," Simeon said without pause.

Ryne dismissed Simeon with a laugh. "There was a misunderstanding."

"In the short time I've known you, I can easily see it was not just a misunderstanding. You always seem to find a reason to be in a foul mood," Dianna said.

Ryne jerked back as if he'd been slapped. "I carry the weight of my people's fate on my shoulders, so forgive me for sometimes being in a mood."

A bitter laugh escaped her throat. "You think I don't carry a heavy burden? I'm tasked with the responsibility of killing my mother, lest the whole world perish. I don't use that as an excuse to be unpleasant to everyone."

Ryne looked away, staring blankly into the fire. "We each handle stress differently."

Simeon leaned against the wall, crossing his legs at the ankles. "Differently, as in you behaving like a troll with an infested boil on your bum."

Color flushed Ryne's cheeks. "Is it any wonder I'm in a mood, with you goading me all the time?"

Simeon tucked his chin into his chest, the merriment in his eyes belying his casual pose. "I can't help it you're an easy target."

"We're all easy targets when you have the magical ability to persuade, especially her." Ryne indicated Dianna with a sneer. "You have her fawning over you like starving kraehn set on a pile of rotten entrails."

She didn't fawn over Simeon, did she?

Need I remind you of his muscular chest? Neriphene teased.

Simeon uncrossed his legs. "You'd compare Dianna to some carnivorous ice-dwelling fish?"

An uncomfortable flush crept into her cheeks when Ryne looked her over with a sneer. "If the boot fits."

Before she could return the insult, Simeon launched himself at Ryne like a troll pouncing on its hapless prey.

"Stop it! Not here!" she scolded as they rolled around on the floor, pummeling each other's faces. "Are you trying to bring an avalanche down on our heads? You can pound each other to bits after we escape Ice Mountain."

They ignored her, rolling from one side of the hut to the other, fists and elbows flying. Bowls fell from the shelves, shattering on the floor when they banged into a cabinet.

Tar danced around them, barking for them to stop.

She didn't know what to do, for she could trigger an avalanche if she flattened them with magic. They'd beat each other senseless before they ascended Ice Mountain.

She jumped at the sound of a loud knock. "Someone's here!"

Tar growled at the door, hackles rising.

Simeon and Ryne stopped pummeling each other long enough to gape at the only door to the hut. Simeon bolted for his spear.

Ryne slid his sword from its sheath. "Who goes there?"

"Dafuar," a feeble voice answered.

"Dafuar!" She raced to the door, loosened the bolt, and threw it open, surprised to see the old man. Icicles coated his long beard in a frosty curtain. His bony knees poked through his thin fur robe. How had he survived such harsh weather?

Without waiting for an invitation, Dafuar stepped across the threshold. She shut the door behind him, still amazed to see the prophet.

He folded his arms, the creases around his eyes deepening. "I've come to warn you."

Her legs gave way, and she sank into a wobbly chair. "Of what?"

Her foster mother once said Dafuar had been the village prophet for centuries, mayhap longer. It wasn't until Dianna visited Feira in the Shifting Sands that she learned he was Kyan's son. He and his twin had been the original keepers of the stones until the Elements stole them, hiding them in the recesses of the earth. After that, Odu and Dafuar wandered the earth for hundreds of years, searching for something they'd lost but not remembering what. They were wise but unwise, old and frail, yet cursed with longevity. Their life was made all the worse after Madhea turned their mother and sisters to stone.

I do not know whose curse is worse, Aletha said. *Ours or our brothers'.*

'Tis true, agreed Neriphene. *Each time I see my brothers, they look worse than the time before, yet they do not die, cursed as they are to live an eternity in broken bodies.*

Dianna thought to ask how stones could see at all, but there were more pressing matters, namely hearing Dafuar's warning.

His bones creaked as he sat in an unsteady chair beside her, the pack strapped to his back pushing him forward at an odd angle. While Tar sniffed his hand and licked his fingertips, Dafuar's expression went blank. "Of what were we speaking?"

She placed a hand on his shriveled wrist. "You came to warn us of something."

"Oh, yes." He flashed a toothless grin, scratching Tar behind the ears. "I don't remember, but the warning was dire indeed."

Ryne eyed the prophet with suspicion. "You are Odu's brother, aren't you?"

"Odu?" He cupped Tar's chin, then rubbed the dog's furry neck. "Yes, that name sounds familiar." He tapped the table beside him. "I have a brother named Odu, you know?"

"Curse the Elements," Ryne spat. "That's what I said." He thumbed at Dafuar with a laugh. "This old fool is even more forgetful than his brother."

Tar shot Ryne a pleading look before laying his head in Dafuar's lap, turning sad eyes up at the old man.

Dianna was amused by how quickly the dog became attached to the prophet, though not surprised. He'd always had a way with animals.

"He is the son of the benevolent goddess, Kyan." She spoke through clenched teeth, hoping Dafuar was either too old or too slow to comprehend Ryne's insult. "Show some respect, Ryne."

Simeon dropped his spear and fell to his knees. "I was an idiot for not recognizing your name, Uncle. It is an honor to meet you."

Dafuar arched a brow, scratching his bushy beard. "You're my nephew?"

Simeon eagerly nodded. "I'm the grandson of Odu, many times removed."

"Odu?" The old man ran a hand over his patchy scalp. "That name sounds familiar."

"Siren's teeth!" Ryne threw up his hands. "Are we doomed to repeat the same conversation a hundred times?"

"Shut up, Ryne!" she snapped.

"Ah, snowbear!" Dafuar held up a finger, a broad, toothless smile splitting his face in two. "That was my warning. I spotted it circling the village."

"Thanks for the warning, old man," Ryne said.

Tar growled at the door once more, his back arched as if he planned on springing into action.

Ryne frowned at his dog. "What is it, boy?"

The wall to the hut caved in so fast, Dianna had scarcely any time to jump out of the way. Bricks scattered all over the wooden floor in a plume of dust. The snowbear's massive head filled the room, malice and hunger shining in his hollow eyes, drool dripping off his fangs and pooling on the floor.

Tar danced around the bear, jumping out of reach when the monster tried to catch him in its mighty maw. Dafuar stepped in front of the bear, facing Dianna as if a voracious monster wasn't behind him. "What seems to be the commotion?" the old man asked in a daze.

She yelped, "Dafuar, get back!"

The prophet made it too easy for the predator, whose massive jowls clamped down on his backpack. Before she could stop him, the beast jerked the old man backward. Dafuar actually had the common sense to scream as the bear took off at a run, dragging the prophet with him.

She grabbed her bow and arrows and led the chase, Simeon following with his spear, and Ryne and Tar not far behind. A blustery wind howled, pelting them with freezing chunks of ice and snow, making it hard to see, let alone run. They trudged across a frozen lake, guided only by the fading moonlight and the sound of Dafuar's pitiful cries.

Simeon hurled his spear, striking the beast's hindquarters. The bear let out an enraged cry, but he did not stop or release Dafuar. He did slow enough that their party was able to bridge the distance between them and see the bear more clearly. The pool of blood marring his white fur made it easier to spot him in the wintery haze.

She thought herself mad for chasing after an angry beast nearly as big as a broot. Even on all fours, he was several heads taller than her. She nocked an arrow as she advanced, pulled back her bow, and fired, hitting the bear in the other leg. The monster grunted, missed a step, then kept on running.

Just as they'd crossed the lake and had almost reached a line of pine trees, the bear surprised them by coming to a sudden halt. He dropped Dafuar into a snowdrift and spun around, baring large fangs.

Ryne waved his sword at the beast, as if he had any chance of defeating a monster who could devour him in one swallow. Tar ran circles around the bear, distracting him. Simeon crept toward the beast's rear, reaching for his spear. Dianna notched another arrow, but before she could fire, the bear charged her. She screamed, tripping as she scrambled away. The giant reared up on his two back legs, hovering over her like a dragon ready to devour its prey.

Stop him! Neriphene hollered.

"And bring an avalanche upon us all?" The shadow of Ice Mountain loomed above them. It was too great a risk.

Simeon grabbed the spear, crying out as he tried to yank it from the beast. The bear spun around with a roar so powerful, it rattled the marrow of her bones, and she feared an avalanche was imminent. Simeon held tight to the spear, even as the bear tried to swat him away. This was enough of a distraction for her to fire an arrow. Though she aimed for the beast's lungs, fear shook her limbs so hard, it missed its mark and lodged in its shoulder.

Tar nipped its paws when it bore down on Dianna. Ryne was able to cut open a leg with his sword, then ducked, jumping out of reach when the bear swiped at him. The monster advanced on Ryne, despite Simeon and Dianna yelling and chasing after it. She struck it again in the hind leg with another arrow, but the beast didn't flinch as it continued toward Ryne.

The ice dweller stumbled and fell, raising his sword. Out of the corner of her eye, Dianna spied a shadowy figure in the distance. She thought perhaps Dafuar had risen from the snowbank, but this person moved with alacrity while raising a bow. After the sound of six successive *thwacks*, the bear fell with a howl, its fanged jowls resting within a breath of Ryne's feet, two long arrows protruding from each eye.

She knew of only one person who could shoot an animal with such precision, yet as the figure came into view, she was shocked to see a waif of a girl holding a bow.

"Ryne, is that you?" the girl cried, falling on him and clutching his face.

"Ura!" He stumbled to his knees, gripping the girl's shoulders. "Sister, what in Elements' name are you doing here?"

"They've outed me." Ura trembled in his arms. "It's taken me days to get down the mountain."

"They outed you!" His features hardened. "Those bastards!"

"Oh, Ryne," she breathed. "You must save Markus and Father. We may already be too late." She fell against him, head lolling to one side.

He scooped his sister into his arms, his expression grim. "We've got to get her to shelter."

Dianna nodded, unable to speak over the knot of panic that lodged in her throat. What did she mean, they may be too late to save Markus? What had happened to her brother?

A deafening crack punctured the air, its echo reverberating off the mountain.

Her heart pounded against her ribs. "Avalanche! Run!"

She heard the rumble next, like a herd of a hundred dragons racing down the mountain. It looked like the entire bottom face of the mountain was sliding toward them.

"Great goddess!" she cried. "It will bury us!"

Her legs felt like they were weighted with bags of sand as she tried to plow through the dense snow. At this rate, she'd never outrun the avalanche. Ryne sprinted ahead of her, his sister bouncing over his shoulder, his dog at his heels. Dianna checked for Simeon, and then all of time seemed to stand still, her thudding heart coming to a sudden stop as she was overcome by a bone-crushing fear. He had stayed behind, grunting and swearing while trying to pull Dafuar out of the snowdrift as the white wall of destruction barreled toward him.

Simeon didn't stand a chance.

She was out of options. Though she doubted her strength after her encounter with the gargoyles, and she feared unleashing her magic would expose her to Madhea's eye, she had no choice. She refused to let Simeon die.

She sent her spirit soaring to that magical place, flinging it with a gasp, then snapping it back like a whip. "Freeze!" she cried, throwing out her arms.

The cascading snow halted, suspended in midair, hovering over Simeon's head like a frozen wave of water. He pulled Dafuar free, then glanced at the monolithic crest above him. He turned to Dianna, eyes wide with shock, before slinging the old man over his shoulders.

She raced to him, floating snow crystals coating her hair and face. When she reached him, she noted two things. One, his mahogany skin glowed like polished wood in the moonlight that shone through the curtain of snow. And two, it was hard, very hard, not to throw herself into his arms and kiss him senseless, knowing she'd nearly lost him to nature's fury. Elements save her! She'd fallen in love with Simeon.

"Come on!" Together they plowed through the snow and across the frozen lake until they were out of the avalanche's shadow.

MARKUS DRIFTED IN AND out of consciousness so often, he had no idea how many days had passed or if he was still alive. Each time he came to, he heard the old prophet mumbling something unintelligible.

He woke again, squinting as he tried to focus in the dark room, lit only with a few mite crystals. Jon slept beside him in a fetal position, shivering under a thin fur. Odu sat in front of him, mumbling and holding his hands over the floor.

Markus leaned up on his elbow, wincing as pain shot through him. His ribs hurt as much as ever, though he was growing accustomed to the pain. "What are you doing?" he asked Odu.

The prophet leaned over a hole carved in the ice, which was so deep, he couldn't see where it ended.

"Summoning the stones," Odu answered.

"What?"

"How do you think I found them the last time?" Odu chuckled.

"I-I don't know." Markus thought on it. He'd no idea where the stones had come from, just that Odu had brought them to Ice Mountain three hundred years ago.

"I called them from the recesses of the earth," Odu said.

Strange how the old prophet sounded so lucid when normally he made not a scrap of sense.

"Ah, there's one." The water in the hole bubbled and boiled as if a pod of kraehn were feeding and then a stone popped up, catapulting out of the water like a flying fish and landing in Odu's hands. "This was the chieftain's stone." Odu winked at Markus. "She will have a rude awakening."

"Where are the other two?" Markus looked through the small window into their cell. Luckily the guards had their backs to them.

Odu lifted the hem of his robe, revealing two stones. "Here."

He could hardly believe what he was seeing. "You have all three? Will the chieftain know to find them here?"

"Why would she? We've been locked away for days." He nodded to their cell door, an impenetrable block of ice the chieftain herself had sealed shut with a stone. "She will accuse others though."

"I hope no more are outed because of us," Markus breathed, sagging as he thought of Ura by herself. Had she survived alone on Ice Mountain, or had she perished? Between the snowbears, avalanches, and the vindictive ice witch, odds were not in her favor.

"You fear for your bride." Odu leaned back against the wall, tucking the stones under his bony legs. "Do not worry. Ura will not fail us."

He grimaced, laying gentle pressure on his sore ribs as he laid down on the fur. "For Ura's sake, I hope you're right."

DIANNA NUMBLY FOLLOWED Ryne, who carried Ura. Tar trotted at his heels. She held tight, mayhap too tight, to Simeon's hand as he wordlessly carried Dafuar over his shoulders. The old man looked to be unharmed, though his pack had been shredded.

She kept checking the avalanche behind them, but it appeared to be solidifying as the temperature dropped. There was no sign of Madhea flying down from her tower in the clouds. Mayhap she'd heard the avalanche but hadn't bothered to check its destruction. It would be like her not to care.

Ryne kicked down several doors until he found a hut to his liking, one that was larger than the last, with another cauldron of frozen food.

Simeon quickly set to warming the fire while Dianna ran her hands over Ura's bruised and battered body. Ura was thin and in need of nourishment, but other than a few frostbitten toes and fingers, and two busted shins, she was fine. It didn't take long for Dianna's healing magic to work, thanks to Aletha's help. She did encounter something odd, though. She thought she'd felt an unusual energy coming from Ura's abdomen. A seed had taken root. Had this simply been an illusion, or was Ura carrying a child? If so, was Markus the father? Dianna hoped so, for her brother had risked his neck and returned to Ice Kingdom because of the pretty ice girl.

Ryne wrapped his sister in thick furs, and Dianna eagerly waited for the girl to wake. What had happened to Markus? She'd get little sleep this night, worrying over her brother.

Dafuar was more difficult to heal. After removing his furs and robe, she was shocked to see he had a broken back and bleeding organs, where the beast had punctured both sides of his stomach. He hadn't complained of his wounds, or she would've healed him first. It was a wonder he'd survived at all.

Eventually the old prophet mended as well. The exertion of healing two people left her feeling spent and hungry. She ate a bowl of fish soup from the cauldron. It wasn't as tasty as the venison stew in the other hut, but it served its purpose.

Tar happily ate what Dianna couldn't eat. Rather than let the soup go to waste, she fed him a few more bowls and gave some to Dafuar, as well.

Ryne scooped the broth from the soup, holding it to Ura's lips and forcing her to drink as she drifted between a fitful dreamlike state and being awake. Eventually she sat up and appeared fully aware of her environment.

"I know you're tired, Ura, but could you please tell me what happened to Markus?" Dianna a sked.

Her eyes brimmed with tears. "They've imprisoned him and Father." She wiped her eyes. "They're going to starve them to death."

Ryne jumped to his feet and paced in front of the hearth. "They will come to regret this." He pounded the wall. "I will make sure of it."

"Flaming Elements!" Dianna slowly stood, clenching her hands so tight, her arms ached. "I will burn every one of them to the ground if they so much as harm my brother."

Easy, Dianna. Neriphene chided. *Remember your blood oath.*

Dianna swore under her breath. "I know." She'd never actually raze an entire city. She wasn't like her mother. But surely she wouldn't break her oath if she ensured those responsible paid for their crimes.

"Dianna? I thought it was you." Ura set down her cup of broth. "You are my husband's sister?"

"Husband?" Dianna and Ryne said in unison.

Her blue face turned a soft shade of pink as she focused on her hands. "We were only just wed."

Ryne reached his sister in a few long strides, falling beside her on his knees. "But you're both so young."

"He's almost seven and ten, and I'm almost eighteen winters." She toyed with the frayed end of her fur. "Our parents were our age when they wed."

"You couldn't have waited for me to return before marrying?" Ryne pouted. "I would've liked to have been there for the ceremony."

Great goddess! Did Ryne really need to make everything about him? She was happy Markus had wed Ura, for she remembered how much he'd pined for her.

"I'm sorry." Ura reached for her brother's hand. "The others were gossiping about Markus living with us. Besides, I love him." Her eyes watered with fresh tears. "I didn't want to wait."

She wondered if Markus and Ura had planned to have a child so soon. She hoped she was wrong, for the world was too volatile for an innocent babe as long as Madhea lived.

You're not wrong, Dianna, Aletha said. *I sensed the seed, too. She has a long way to go. Hopefully Madhea will be dead by then.*

"I hope so, too," Dianna whispered. Now she had one more reason to destroy her mother—the life of her unborn niece or nephew.

Ura tossed the fur off and threw her legs over the side of the cot, sucking in a sharp breath. "Ryne, Dianna, the mists revealed Madhea in Ice Kingdom."

Ryne jumped to his feet. "What?"

Dianna's heart came to a dull thudding stop. "Oh, heavenly Elements," she breathed, "save the Ice People if Madhea has found out where they're hiding."

"That's why we were trying to steal a stone," Ura said. "To protect Markus, so he could deflect her magic and shoot her."

"Let me guess." Ryne tapped a booted foot on the worn wooden planks, his mouth twisting in a snarl. "The Council didn't believe you, which is why you were outed."

Ura nodded as more tears cascaded down her face. "Ingred has taken over the Council. She thinks we're liars and thieves, and there's no convincing her otherwise."

"Don't worry," Dianna said, doing her best to keep her composure despite the rage that threatened to split her skull in two. "I'll convince her, and I'll make sure she regrets the way she's treated you and my brother." *And their unborn child..*

Chapter Sixteen

Dianna was frustrated they couldn't scale the mountain faster, but Dafuar had insisted he come along, that the Ice People would be more willing to listen to him, as the stones rightfully belonged to him and his brother.

She wasn't so sure the Ice People would care where the stones came from, as long as they were able to keep possession of them.

Ryne said he knew of a faster way to gain entrance to Ice Kingdom, and after two days, they found themselves at the very spot Ura claimed to have been outed. Unfortunately, they also found a corpse lying nearby, his face frozen in horror, blank eyes staring at the sky.

"Who is this?" Dianna knelt beside him, petting Tar's back while he sniffed the body.

"Bane Eryll." Ura knelt beside her. "He was outed weeks ago."

Odd that he would still be so close to Ice Kingdom's entrance instead of trying to find his way down the mountain. She gazed up the ledge above them. Bane had to have fallen from there. The ledge stretched at least five men in height from where he had fallen, its outer edges crumbling. Had he slipped, or had he decided to end his life?

Ura stood, frowning. "I thought he'd been eaten by a snowbear. Though I never cared for him, I hope the Elements are kind to him in the afterlife."

Dianna looked at Ura, surprised to see a lone tear slide down the girl's cheek. "I take it his body hasn't been here all this time?"

Ura wiped her tear, turning away. "I would've seen him when they outed me."

"Do you think it was an accident?" Simeon asked as he shivered beside Ryne, watching the ice dweller melt a hole in the ice with the stone Simeon had been carrying.

"I don't know." A strange shiver coursed down Dianna's spine, and she couldn't escape the feeling that she was being watched. She peered at the sky. Had Madhea seen them? "But I think it's a bad omen."

Tar's low growl was not reassuring. What did he see?

A frigid wind tickled the hair on Dianna's nape. *Hide,* the wind whispered.

Dianna! Nepherine's shrill scream was laced with urgency. *Get below! We sense Madhea is near!*

She turned to Ryne, who had melted a hole large enough for a person to squeeze through. "Madhea is coming! We need to get below now!"

MADHEA HAD NOT COME to do battle. She was there to ensure the fall had killed Bane. While she peered over the ledge, observing the small party near Bane's lifeless body, she was struck by the familiarity of the beautiful blonde witch—Dianna.

Her child.

Rowlen's child.

Her breath caught in her throat, and she clutched her sore stomach. How easy it would be for her to toss a deadly bolt at Dianna's chest. The girl wouldn't even see it coming. Then Madhea could spring into the air, flying out of bowshot from the others in her party.

If she killed her child, she'd rid herself of the threat for good. Magic pooled in Madhea's fingers as a dark voice within her soul urged her to strike.

But then Dianna looked up, her mouth falling open as she squinted at the sky. Madhea stepped back out of view, losing her courage. When she summoned the nerve to look over the ledge again. Dianna and her party had gone. They'd disappeared down a hole in the ice, leaving Bane's lifeless body behind.

Madhea cursed herself a fool for letting Dianna slip away. She feared the girl had come for Markus. If they escaped Ice Kingdom, Madhea's plan would fail. She needed the boy hunter. Though she was weak, she had no choice. She had to attack Ice Kingdom, but first she needed to collect reinforcements.

DIANNA FOLLOWED URA down the ice column while Simeon and Ryne helped Dafuar and Tar. She had thought her ice scaling skills were decent, but Ura put her to shame, deftly descending like a spider sliding down a thread. Mayhap it was because Dianna was distracted by the scenery. She was in awe of this place, which was like a crystal wonderland. Ice spikes thrust down from the iridescent ceiling like giant frozen teardrops while others, some as wide as mighty pines, shot up from the ground, reaching almost to the top of the cavern, which was at least ten men in height.

Two ice dwellers were waiting for Ura at the bottom of the massive cavern, spears aimed at her back. "Stop! Trespasser!" they yelled.

Dianna knocked them back just hard enough that their spears fell to the ground, and they landed on their arses with shocked grunts.

When they scrambled for their weapons, she threw them back again.

One of them shot to his feet and pointed at her, screaming, "Madhea!" Then they ran out of the cavern, sounding the alarm.

Dianna and Ura landed on solid ground just as a dozen armed men raced into the cavern. She knocked their spears out of their hands, wedging the tips into the wall. She drove the men back, and they slid across the ice like their arses were well oiled.

"Madhea! Madhea!" more men hollered as they charged her.

Again, she pushed them back. "I'm not Madhea!" she hollered. "I've come to speak to your chieftain."

Just as Simeon and the others jumped to the ground, a tall woman with a massive beak nose, who looked like a giant blue bird, marched into the cavern, armed men at her sides. "Calm yourselves, that's not Madhea." She pointed at Dianna. "This witch doesn't have wings." She turned a beady-eyed glare on Ura. "You have been outed. You're trespassing."

Ura jutted hands on her hips, bracing her legs. "Unjustly outed without a fair trial, Chieftain, but I will go as soon as you bring my husband and father to me."

The chieftain turned her iron-eyed glare on her brother. "Ryne? Where are the others?"

He stood beside his sister, arms crossed. "Bring me my father and brother-in-law, and I will tell you."

Ryne's loyal dog stood beside his master, lips pulled back in a fanged snarl.

The chieftain threw up her hands, her voice turning shrill. "What have you done with my son?"

More ice dwellers gathered around the bird woman, all various shades of blue, with hair that looked like ice crystals. Some grumbled and cast Dianna and her party accusatory glares while others shook their heads, scowling at their chieftain.

Ryne's voice echoed across the cavern. "You will not know where he is until I see that my family is safe and well."

The chieftain had the nerve to laugh. "They were thieves."

"They were trying to warn you Madhea is coming," Dianna said, "and you fools refused to listen." Even now Madhea could be upon them, if Nepherine was right.

I am right, Neriphene scoffed. *Madhea was watching you, and she could descend at any moment.*

Dianna backed up next to Simeon as the chieftain and Ryne argued. When she tapped him on the thigh, he slipped a stone into her hand. "Thank you," she whispered, her knees wobbly when she realized a battle with Madhea could be imminent. She didn't like standing under a ceiling of ice spikes. If Madhea were to collapse the roof on their heads, they would all perish.

"I demand you release my son!" the chieftain's voice ricocheted off the spikes, like hail striking a shield.

"What of the others who accompanied me, Chieftain?" Ryne smirked, clearly enjoying goading the woman, whose face had turned a deep purple. "Do you not care for their fates?"

"Them, too." The chieftain shrugged while others whispered behind her.

"Show me my family first," Ryne commanded. "This is the last time I tell you."

The chieftain laughed. "Or what?"

"Or this!" Dianna shot a bolt at a long spike hanging from the ceiling. It broke apart, shattering when it hit the ground by the chieftain's feet, sending people frantically scrambling.

Remember your blood oath, Sindri warned.

"I have not forgotten," she grumbled. But the Ice People didn't know about the oath not to use her magic to harm innocents. As far as they were concerned, she was a vindictive witch who would destroy their kingdom if they didn't release her brother. That's what she wanted them to believe, since they needed to make haste before Madhea arrived.

The chieftain stepped over the shattered ice, grinding a shard into the ground with her boot. "Well, if Madhea didn't know where we were before, your destruction will certainly alert her."

"Release the prisoners now!" Dianna aimed her magic at a spike above the woman's head.

"Very well." The chieftain heaved an overly-dramatic sigh. "Bring the prisoners here."

Dianna ground her teeth and watched the ceiling for any signs of Madhea. Her stones were getting restless. The wait was interminable. Finally, two large guards brought a battered, thin man toward her.

"We're sorry, Chieftain," one guard said. "Without a stone, we had to break the wall down with picks."

The Chieftain narrowed her eyes at Dianna. "I'm sure it's no coincidence our stones go missing and Ura shows up with this witch."

Dianna was less concerned with the chieftain's accusations and more worried about the thin man kneeling beside the guards. She hardly recognized her brother until Ura raced past her.

"Markus!" Ura fell to her knees before him, clutching his face, sobbing. She turned toward the chieftain with fire in her eyes. "What have you done to him? He was trying to save you!" She jumped to her feet. "Shame on you all!"

"Not all of them should be shamed." A man who looked like an older version of Ryne shook off the guards who held him. "We had a few families on our side."

Two other guards released an old man, reverently bowing to him. The man's spine was bent forward as if he carried a tremendous weight on his back. His wrinkled, wizened eyes looked much like Dafuar's, and Dianna knew he had to be Odu, Feira's father and grandfather of all the people of the Shifting Sands.

The crowd went silent when he cleared his throat. "Are the boats ready?"

A group of men and women pushed through the crowd, bowing before him. "They are."

"Good," Odu said. "We need to go. It's not safe here."

Simeon picked up Markus. A sobbing Ura followed at their heels. Dianna was alarmed at the ease with which Simeon carried her brother. He must have lost four stone since she'd last seen him.

"Lead the way," he said to Ryne.

"Wait!" The chieftain held out both hands when they tried to pass. "Where is my son?"

Ryne walked up to the woman, his back stiff. He looked her in the eyes, his expression unapologetic. "He and the others were killed by sirens and Eris's soldiers. I'm the only survivor."

"Guardians!" she shrieked, shoving a shaking finger in Ryne's face. "Arrest him at once!"

The crowd broke into a wave of murmurs and cries, but nobody made a move toward Ryne.

"Did you not hear me?" She snarled at a guard who'd let his weapon fall. "He murdered my son!"

The man stepped back, shaking his head. "That's not what he said."

"Do you believe that lying gnull?"

The guard blushed, glancing quickly at Dianna. "Does it matter? He has a powerful witch on his side."

"Oh, for Elements' sake!" the chieftain snapped, hefting the spear and aiming it at Ryne's chest.

Ryne sidestepped the chieftain, knocking it out of her hands. She fell, landing on her arse with an ear-shattering screech. She tried to stand, but Tar grabbed hold of her sleeve, keeping her from rising. A loud boom rent the air. The chieftain looked up as a massive spike detached from the ceiling and impaled her in the chest, pinning her to the floor. Tar raced away, yelping, while the Ice People scattered, screaming as a winged woman fell from the sky, shattering the ice floor when she landed and creating an avalanche of spikes to fall from the ceiling, striking hapless victims as they tried to flee. Then an angry, buzzing ball of pixies swarmed into the cavern, attacking those who were injured, ripping off fingers and ears with violent ferocity.

Elements save them all. Madhea had come!

"Stop!" Dianna yelled, shattering the spikes like glass while splattering pixie blood all over the walls.

But her magic wasn't strong enough, because several pixies had escaped, chasing after the ice dwellers as they ran down the hall.

Her mother turned to her, green eyes glowing with unnatural malice, her wings buzzing angrily. "Daughter."

Strike her now! Sindri cried.

Terror paralyzed Dianna's limbs. Her knees weakened as her mother stalked toward her. She backed up, collecting magic in her palms. "You are no mother to me!" she raged, hating how her trembling voice revealed her fear.

"I am your mother." Madhea held out a hand, a plea in her voice not masking the venom in her glare. "And this is your one chance to live. Join me or die."

Ura sobbed, bent over Markus. Simeon laid deathly still beside them, blood pooling around his head, shards of ice stuck in his hair. Elements, no! Simeon couldn't be dead!

Rage fueling her movements, Dianna leapt forward, throwing a ball of energy straight at her mother's heart. "I'd rather die than side with a vindictive bitch!"

Much to her dismay, Madhea caught the ball and threw it back. She ducked and the energy flew past her head, smashing the ice wall behind her. A thunderous crack rent the air. They were running out of time.

Focus, Sindri admonished. *You're letting anger and fear rule you.*

How could she focus when her world was falling to pieces? She flung another ball at her mother, then another. Madhea deflected them, laughing manically and taunting Dianna.

"You are half mortal," Madhea cackled. "What makes you think you can take on a goddess?"

"You won't be the first goddess I've brought down." She fired another ball at her mother's head.

"If you're referring to my dear sister, Eris, know this." Madhea threw her head back with a squeal, her arms lighting with magical fire. "I am far more powerful than she." As if to prove her point, she tossed a green bolt of lightning at Dianna.

She ducked, and an ice spike exploded into a million fragments. Madhea might be right. The ice witch was more powerful than Eris, but she didn't dare voice it aloud.

She's lying, Sindri said. *She's trying to get you to back down.*

Use us, Neriphene urged. *Let us channel through you. Together we can destroy her.*

She let herself be drawn to that space between two worlds. Energy raced down her arms and pooled in her palms, and she knew this blast would finish Madhea for good. Just as she was about to strike, her mother flew past her in a blur, Tar nipping at her heels.

Dianna spun around, prepared to fling her magic at her mother's back, but Madhea had Markus in her arms, using him as a shield.

"Markus, no!" Ura screamed, falling on her side, hands lifted toward them.

"Drop him!" Dianna commanded. "It's me you want."

"Is it?" Madhea laughed and launched into the air.

Tar jumped on his hind legs, catching the end of Madhea's robe, but the goddess jerked free, leaving the dog with a ripped piece of cloth between his teeth.

Dianna fell to her knees as Madhea flew away with her brother and several squealing pixies flew after her, clutching shreds of bloodied skin between their teeth. There was no telling what that evil witch and her little demons would to do him. If the woman was prepared to murder her own daughter, Markus didn't stand a chance.

Chapter Seventeen

A Mother's Curse

THERE WAS A CRACK, then, *boom*, the earth shook. Dianna had no time to mourn the loss of her brother. She had to get her friends to safety before the entire mountain fell on their heads.

She was relieved to see Ryne already had Simeon slung over his shoulders. He bent under his weight.

"Your lover weighs as much as a gnull," Ryne grumbled.

Simeon wasn't her lover but now wasn't the time to make that clear. "How do we get out of here?" she yelled over the din of the rumbling mountain.

"To the boats!" Ryne's father said, waving them on. Then he called to Ryne and Dianna. "Get Ura!"

Dianna tried to pull a sobbing Ura off the ground. "We need to go!"

"But Markus?" Ura cried.

"Siren's teeth, sister!" Ryne hissed. "There's nothing we can do for him now. Let's go, before we all perish."

As if to emphasize their peril, Tar wildly barked at Ura while dancing around in erratic circles.

Ura buried her face in her hands. "Leave me to die, then."

The wall beside them shook and rattled, pebbles of ice pelting their heads. "Do you want your unborn child to die as well?" Dianna jerked Ura's arm, trying to force her to stand. "Markus's child?"

Ura gaped up at her, clutching her stomach. "How do you know?"

"Never mind that." She finally managed to get Ura to her feet. Grasping her elbows, she looked deeply into Ura's silver, glossy eyes. "I will retrieve my brother, I swear to you. I will get him back from her if it kills me."

When Ura silently nodded, she pulled her out of the chamber seconds before the wall crashed down.

They followed the others, racing through a dark tunnel dimly lit with tiny glowing crystals on the ceiling that shone like starlight. The frigid air was so stifling, Dianna thought her lungs would burst. It soon became apparent she had no idea how to traverse the slick floor, and she was forced to lean on Ura for support. Even the old prophets had better footing than her, shaming her by gliding across the ice, though they were assisted by other ice dwellers.

"This way!" Ryne's father said when the tunnel came to a dead end, blocked with slabs of ice and snow.

They ran until her chest heaved and her leg muscles screamed in pain, finally emerging into a much larger tunnel of solid ice with a wide river flowing through it. Four boats nestled between two wooden platforms, banging against each other as the current threatened to snatch them from their cradle.

"They're taking our boats!" Ryne's father called. "Stop!"

Tar ran to the boats, biting a man's leg as he was about to climb aboard. Ryne unceremoniously dropped Simeon on the ground, unsheathed his sword, and brutally cut down the man as he was about to drive a sword through Tar's back.

"Out of the boat!" he yelled to the terrified woman already on board.

She obeyed, scrambling onto the slick embankment and falling beside her man, pressing her hands against his wound, trying in vain to stop the bleeding.

Dianna pitied the frantic woman, but she had to save Simeon before it was too late. She smoothed his hair, sucking in a hiss when she saw the deep gash that dented one side of his head. It was a mortal wound, to be sure, but she would not let him die.

"Aletha," she cried.

Press me against the wound, Aletha commanded.

Dianna pressed the stone against his bloody scalp, then shut her eyes, momentarily losing her soul as she flung herself to the other world.

"Dianna! We need to go," Ryne yelled, having loaded ice dwellers onto a boat.

Dianna's eyes snapped open. Several loud cracks sounded in the distance, and Dianna knew the mountain was buckling. She looked down at Simeon, who was blinking at her.

"Thank you, Aletha," she breathed.

It was my pleasure. You belong together, Aletha answered.

She held a hand down to Simeon. "Let's go."

Taking her hand, he struggled to his feet and staggered to a boat.

Ryne helped them both in, and they pushed off from the embankment as a swarm of ice dwellers burst from the tunnel, pleading for passage.

"Find another way out," Ryne called to them, clutching a mast.

"All the tunnels are blocked," a frenzied man called to him. "Please!" He fell to his knees, begging.

Each boat was already so full, some looked to be in danger of sinking.

Simeon wrapped his arms around her, pressing her face against his chest, shielding her from the horrors that ensued. Ice dwellers fought on the embankment, pushing each other into the river, and then the ceiling crashed down on their heads. The collapse knocked several large chunks of ice into the water, swelling the current and nearly capsizing the boats. The passengers sucked in collective gasps as they rode out each wave that pushed them quickly downriver. They emerged from the mouth of the tunnel moments before the tunnel collapsed and Ice Kingdom was lost.

Dianna looked up, expecting to see the sky but realized they were in another cavern, this one far larger than the last.

The waters finally slowed, and not a sound could be heard behind them, as if every remaining soul had been crushed. Dianna clutched the seven-pointed star that Sogred and Sofla had given her, recalling their mother's blessing and wondering if that spell had protected her and the others from her mother's curse.

MADHEA RAN HER HANDS down Markus's bruised arms. "What have they done to you?" she whispered, for he didn't appear to be the same mighty hunter as before.

Though his shoulders were still broad, like Rowlen's, he was far thinner. She pressed his broken ribs, feeling the bones fuse together in response to her touch. Then she held his cracked jaw until the disfigured bones fell back in place.

Healing him took far more strength than she'd imagined. Her fight with Dianna had weakened her, and she had still not recovered from Bane's attack. After she finished with the boy hunter, she poured a sleeping draught into his mouth, forcing him to swallow. Moaning, his head lolled to one side. Madhea was comforted with the soft sound of his snores. Knowing he'd be asleep for a while, she laid her head upon his hard chest and let her eyes fall shut, relishing the feel of his warm body under hers.

"So much like Rowlen," she breathed. Or he would be soon. She'd make sure of it. She'd been too long without a real man for a lover.

She thought of the sleeping potion she'd given him and recalled the amber liquid she used to pour into her soldiers' drinks. The herbal concoction increased their strength, but it also swelled their hearts with love for her. She smiled, vaguely remembering where to find the herbs to make the potion. Though it was tempting, she dared not risk using dark magic to make Markus hate his family. The risk to her beauty and strength was too great. But if she could make him love her, perhaps it would outweigh his feelings for everyone else.

THEY WERE PACKED IN the boat so tight, Dianna feared it would capsize if she made any sudden movements. The water carried them swiftly downstream, as if the Elements were adding momentum to the current. An odd thought struck her. Perhaps they were, just as they'd helped her reach Eris's island.

She sat down beside Simeon and looked at the other passengers. Ura was tucked away at the bow of the boat, wrapped in her father's arms, sobbing into his chest.

Dianna's heart ached at the sight, and she couldn't help feeling responsible for Markus's abduction. If only she'd attacked Madhea when the sky witch had first fallen into Ice Kingdom.

Odu sat beside Ura, looking angry. Dianna followed the direction of his gaze, shocked to see Dafuar sitting opposite him at the aft end, returning Odu's stony glare. Why would the two brothers stare at each other that way? Had they forgotten each other after three hundred years?

Dianna looked up at the translucent ice ceiling, stretching so far above their heads, she could see clouds rolling off it. "Where are we?"

"Beneath the glacier," Ryne grumbled, clutching the center mast.

She wondered why Ryne had refused to make eye contact with her. Was he distraught over the destruction of Ice Kingdom? Or was he angry with her for not destroying Madhea? A blade twisted in her chest at the thought. "How long does this go on?"

"About three more days," he answered tersely, still refusing to look at her. "Although at the rate we're moving, maybe sooner."

Simeon's jaw dropped. "I hope we're not stuck in these floating coffins for three days."

"Be careful what you wish for. This river ends at a large gnull colony."

Ryne's tone was far too even, though there was an underlying sense of smugness in his words. Was he happy they'd be forced to confront a nest of gnulls? Markus had told her about the gnulls, and she was none too excited to have to battle them, for she knew it was she who must be the one to drive them back.

"What are gnulls?" Simeon asked.

"Man-eating monsters as big as broots."

Aye, there was a smugness in his voice, as if he gleaned satisfaction in making their guts churn.

"Dragon balls! Why did we come this way?" Simeon jumped to his feet, making the boat rock. The ice dwellers gasped, giving him dirty looks.

"Have a care," one man grumbled.

Ryne cursed. "What other route did we have, Simeon?"

He drew back his shoulders, looking indignant. "Back down the mountain."

Dianna shook her head. "We'd be struck down by Madhea." Her vindictive mother had probably been waiting for them to emerge, prepared to throw deadly bolts at their retreating backs.

"You had her in your sights." Ryne shot her a look so deadly, a lesser woman would have cowered. "Why didn't you destroy her when she first fell into Ice Kingdom?"

She stared at Ryne a long moment, spine stiffening. She didn't know if she should feel shamed or angry at his accusation. "Because I was scared," she answered honestly, doing her best to stop her limbs from shaking at the mere mention of her mother's name.

"We were all scared. But only *you* had the power to take down your mother, unless you didn't want to."

Heat flamed her chest and face as she scrambled to her knees. He could have laced his words with barbed, poisonous darts, and they would've had the same effect. "How dare you! That woman is the reason my father is dead. She's taken my brother hostage." She took a shaky breath, wiping away angry tears. "And in case you didn't notice, I *did* fight Madhea. I was stunned at first, Ryne, though it wouldn't have done any good. When I did fight, she threw back all my magic."

"You were the Ice People's only hope. Thousands perished because of you."

The disgust in Ryne's eyes made Dianna feel lower than dirt.

"Do not dare blame Dianna for this!" Simeon leaned into Ryne, his words coming out on a hiss.

Tar whined, trying to nuzzle their legs in an effort to make peace between them.

Ryne backed up, still clutching the mast. "Shut up, Simeon."

"No, you shut up!" Simeon jerked forward, rocking the boat again and causing a wave of swearing to erupt around them. "Those same Ice People sentenced your family to die."

"Not all of them, just those few in power." Ryne pounded his chest, his blue skin turning crimson, then purple. "It has been my life's work to find safe haven for my people, and what have I to show for it?" He motioned to the boats behind them.

Simeon heaved a groan, turning his eyes skyward. "This isn't about you, Ryne."

Though Dianna could fight her own battles, she was relieved to have Simeon stand up for her. She'd been so overcome with guilt at failing to destroy her mother, at leaving the Ice People behind to perish, she couldn't go up against Ryne. And even though she had failed, Simeon was right. This wasn't about Ryne, yet the stubborn ice dweller made everything about him.

Ryne looked her over with a sneer. "Well, it's clearly not about the Ice People, because they're all dead, thanks to Dianna."

At that moment, she felt Ryne's hatred of her in the marrow of her bones, and instead of feeling shame or guilt, she was angry. Yes, he had a right to be upset, but his grudge was misplaced. She didn't deserve such treatment.

When Simeon raised his fists, she intervened.

"No fighting!" She jumped to her feet, then fell against Simeon as the boat tipped. "You'll capsize the boat and drown us all."

She looked down at the sound of Tar's pitiful whimper. "If you refuse to heed my advice, then heed the dog. He has more sense than both of you."

Simeon wrapped a possessive arm around Dianna's shoulder, helping her sit down. "When we get to shore, Ryne, your hide is mine." His threat was like the ominous rumble of a snowbear seconds before attack.

Ryne tossed back his head, laughing. "I'm quivering with fear."

Though Dianna secretly wouldn't mind seeing Simeon smash Ryne's face, all of this strife was not good for morale. The others on-board were getting anxious, nervously watching the two and murmuring to each other. She thought a peace offering was in order, something to pacify Ryne so they could finish their voyage without any added strife.

"What can I say, Ryne?" she said, her voice shaking with regret and sorrow. "I'm sorry your people are dead. I didn't mean for this to happen. I will fight harder next time."

Both of his pale brows rose. "Next time? She will use your brother as a barrier next time! Maybe she's even poisoned his mind against us. Are you prepared to kill Markus, too?"

She felt like she'd buckle from the weight of his words. She couldn't kill her brother. How could he even ask her such a question? A thought struck her. What if Madhea poisoned Markus against his loved ones, as she'd done with Rowlen? What if she was left with no choice but to fight her brother?

Simeon's right, Dianna, Sindri said. *You did your best.*

"But my best wasn't good enough," she mumbled.

"Ignore him," Simeon whispered. He cleared his throat. "You're a heartless bastard, Ryne."

The ice dweller snorted before turning away.

Dianna chanced a look at Ura, dismayed to see she was crying harder. Stupid Ryne! Didn't he realize his callous words had hurt his sister, too? Or maybe he didn't care.

She inwardly smiled when Tar barked at his master several times, sounding like a father scolding his wayward child.

"Quiet, mutt." Ryne shook a finger at the dog. "Before you alert every gnull in this river we're here."

Simeon was right. Ryne *was* heartless. Unfortunately, he might also be correct in his prediction. If that cursed witch turned Markus's heart against his family, her beloved brother might turn his bow on them, and his aim always struck true. Then what would she do? Kill her brother, as Alec had been forced to kill their father? The thought was too painful to consider.

Chapter Eighteen

Dianna had a restless night, trying to find comfort in Simeon's arms. By the time dawn broke, her neck was sore and her bones ached. She'd drifted to sleep a few times, waking at the slightest sound. She'd jerked awake, screaming, when a fish flew into her lap, then bounced around on the floor of the boat until Ura and Ryne's father, who'd introduced himself as Jon, smashed it with an oar.

"Soaring perch," Jon said with a wink, bagging the fish. "We shall dine on him when we dock."

Dianna failed to sleep after that, jumping every time another fish flew into their boat. Tar seemed to have fun with the fish, his tail madly wagging while he swatted them with his paws. Jon let the dog keep one, and he happily devoured it in a few swallows. More surprising than flying fish was that Simeon slept through the whole thing, his neck bent at an awkward angle as he rested against a sack of vegetables. By the time the morning sun's rays peeked through their ice dome, they'd netted several dozen perch between the four boats.

Dianna was fatigued beyond comprehension but refused to feel sorry for herself, as Ryne hadn't slept at all, choosing to keep watch. Though he was an angry boil on a boar's butt, she did admire his dedication to his people, perhaps his only redeeming quality.

"Son," Jon said as he stretched with a groan, "why don't you get some rest?" He patted an empty spot beside him.

Ryne glanced at his father. "I can't. This river is moving too swiftly. We'll reach the gnulls soon."

The ice dwellers in the other boats were worried, too. Men and women clutched spears and watched the water.

The riverbank in their narrow tunnel was widening, and she wasn't sure, but she thought she felt pockets of warm air blasting her from somewhere downriver. Change was coming, of that she was certain. She just wasn't sure she'd welcome the change.

She froze at the sound of Tar's low growl.

A loud splash beside the boat made her look over the side. She nearly fainted from fright. A slick, splotchy brown beast swam alongside the boat, its massive body curving like a snake disappearing into a hole. She never saw its face, and she didn't want to. Its low, dark sounds rattled the boat so hard, she feared it would capsize.

Ryne held a finger to his lips when the others nervously shifted in their seats. Surprisingly, nobody screamed, though their trembling limbs and wide eyes revealed their terror. Even Tar had gone quiet. There was another splash and a second monster swam on the other side of the boat, his slick body rubbing against the hull and tipping it to one side.

The ice dwellers remained silent. Mothers held their hands over their children's mouths while others watched the water, their spears aimed at the beasts.

When Simeon shifted and stretched, his eyes opening, she held a finger to his lips and pointed. He peered over the side, his jaw dropping when he saw the slick beast.

Ryne pointed to something in the distance, then slid down the mast, clinging to his dog's neck while the others on-board ducked their heads.

"Stay down. Their hearing is better than their eyesight," Ryne whispered.

As if they wouldn't see four ships sailing downriver, she thought.

Four ships made from gnull hide, Sindri answered. *They might think the ships are gnulls, too.*

The first thing she noticed was a pungent smell so strong and foul, she had to cover her nose and breathe through her mouth. The beasts bleated and grunted and made all kinds of low rumbles. When more splashes sounded around them, she worried her pounding heart would give them away. She looked at the other frightened people in the boat, their blue hues turning a sickly shade of white. Some were crying, some praying, though they all did so in silence. Simeon held tightly to her hand, perhaps her only source of comfort while her veins solidified with fear.

The boat behind theirs was struck with such violence, a loud crack was followed by terrified screams shattering the frigid air.

Two men in Dianna's boat shot upright and hurled spears into the water.

I may need your help, Dianna said to the stones as she sat up.

We know you will, Sindri answered.

The sight before her stole the breath from her lungs. Resting along the shore were at least fifty giant blubbery beasts, some the size of Lydra, with tusks as long as spears protruding from their mouths. Many of the monsters had heaved themselves to the riverbank, which was a mixture of ice and mud. They slid in with a massive splash, disappearing beneath the boats. Ryne had to pull back Tar, who nearly fell out of the boat as he scrambled up the side to bark at the beasts.

In the distance the icy tunnel ended, opening onto a vast, dark lake. If they could just propel past the nest of gnulls. The boats behind her seemed stable except for one, which had been pushed into a pocket of water beside shore. Ice dwellers frantically scooped buckets of water out of their hull, but it was sinking at an alarming rate. At least ten gnulls circled the boat, isolating them from the others. Though the ice dwellers threw spears at them, they were no match for the monsters' numbers. Their only other option was to jump onshore, where dozens of gnulls lay in wait.

"Oarsmen!" Ryne hollered. "Back!"

She lurched when six men grabbed oars and rowed back to the disabled boat.

Dianna didn't dare risk fighting the gnulls in the water and toppling the other boats, but she could clear a path to shore for an escape.

"Sindri," she cried.

We're here, Sindri answered.

Screaming mothers held crying children when the water-logged boat slowly began to tip.

No, no, no! She couldn't let them become gnull bait.

"Tar!" Ryne cried, but it was too late.

The dog sprang from the boat, surprising everyone when he landed onshore and faced down the beasts. The monsters bleated, backing up as Tar advanced. The dog wouldn't hold them off for long.

She stood, holding onto the mast beside Ryne.

"Do not sink us all," he grumbled.

She ignored him, pushing all other thoughts out of her mind as she flung her soul to that space between two worlds, reeling in her magic like she was winding a rope, knowing she'd need far more strength than ever before if she was to knock back a nest of giant predators.

Hurry, Dianna, Neriphene cried.

She launched her magic, flinging it at the monsters onshore. "Get back!" she boomed, throwing her arms wide.

The beasts fell over with such violence, they shattered the wall of the ice tunnel behind them, their necks snapping from the blow. They landed on their sides, shards of ice pinning their blubbery flesh to the ground.

The gnulls in the water let out low, ominous wails as they popped their heads above the current and stared at the dead gnulls onshore. 'Twas then she noticed the gnulls in the water were considerably bigger.

Her hand flew to her throat. "I killed their babies."

The ice dwellers scurried from their sinking boat onto the embankment, gawking at the bloodied monsters and then back at the voracious beasts that circled their boat. Just as the last ice dweller disembarked, the boat sank, devoured by several hungry gnulls like a pack of wild dogs on a deer carcass.

The three remaining boats helped the displaced ice dwellers on board, somehow making room where there was none. Tar was the last to jump onboard. Dianna sucked in a hiss when their boat sank lower in the water, the waves coming dangerously close to spilling over the sides.

They couldn't afford to lose another boat, but she expected the beasts would retaliate for the deaths of their young.

Elements save them!

MADHEA HOVERED OVER the young hunter, poised to give him the potion the moment he awoke. She'd already healed his wounds, restoring the pink to his flesh and erasing the dark circles from under his eyes. She was pleased to see the blue tint to his skin had faded, and he resembled his father once more.

She traced the side of his square jaw, which was dotted with dark stubble. He looked less like the boy hunter she'd last seen and so much like Rowlen. She touched his broad chest, solid like Rowlen's. He had no trace of his thin, sickly mother in him. No, this boy, this man, was exactly as his father had been, brave and strong, and very soon he'd be hers.

She clutched the potion like a lifeline, thanking the Elements she'd found the herbs she needed in her reserve stores. After using all she had to make the brew, she'd sent her pixies in search of more. Hopefully, they'd return soon, but she had enough potion to last several days. She'd made it twice as strong as the brews she'd given to her soldiers, for she didn't simply want Markus to fall in love with her. She wanted him to fall *madly* in love with her, so much so that he'd never want to leave. If only she'd thought to use such a potion on Rowlen, he'd still be with her. But now was not a time for regrets. It was a time for celebration. In Markus she'd been given a second chance, and she was determined to make the most of it.

She jumped when he suddenly thrashed about the bed, his eyelids moving.

"Ura! Ura!" he cried.

Madhea's temper soared. How did this Ura shrew have such a hold on him that he'd call her name in his sleep? 'Twas Madhea's name he should've been uttering.

She fluttered over him, landing ungracefully on his chest and sloshing drops of precious liquid onto the bed when he swiped her elbow.

"Be still!" she shrieked. Then she held his mouth open, accidentally spilling the entire contents of the bottle down his throat while he struggled against her.

Curse the Elements! That potion was supposed to last several days!

She leaned over him, breathing against his mouth. "You don't love Ura. You love Madhea."

"Madhea?" He thrashed about, knocking her off him, tangling her in the furs.

"You love Madhea!"

He jerked up, glaring, his eyes still foggy from sleep. "Madhea? No." He groaned. "She's evil."

Did Markus not recognize her after her transformation, or was he still half asleep?

"Not evil," she rasped. "Misunderstood."

She reached for the vial of sleeping potion beside the bed, then lurched forward, forcing him to drink. "Sleep, my darling," she soothed. He fell on his side, slipping back into a dream state. "When you wake, you will be in love with Madhea."

"Madhea?" he mumbled.

"Yes, Madhea," she breathed into his ear, "your true love."

"Madhea, my love," he murmured.

A wide smile split Madhea's face in two, and her heart soared. She flew out of his chamber in high spirits, her laughter echoing off the walls. Markus was hers.

THE OARSMEN PADDLED swiftly, though not fast enough. The gnulls swam alongside them, grunting and groaning while lifting their massive heads and spraying their boats with water. The beasts were toying with them, waiting for the right moment to sink every boat at once.

The walls of the tunnel were thinning, completely melted in some spots, warm pockets of air bursting through the holes. Ahead lay a smooth lake surrounded by pines. If only they could make it to the shore. Dianna stood a better chance fighting the gnulls with the ice dwellers out of the water.

"Hold on!" Ryne called when the water got rougher.

Her head felt full of rocks, rattling around when the boat bounced through the rapids toward the wide mouth of the lake. She shut her eyes after a final, sharp dip. The river spit them out with great force, and they careened across the water, ending up almost in the center of the lake.

She opened her eyes, pleased to see the other boats floating nearby. She looked back at the long tube that looked like the mountain's icy lung. Behind the tube loomed Madhea's mountain, its top obscured by a thick bank of clouds. Her stomach twisted in knots when she saw gnull after gnull slide into the lake like slugs dripping out of a pail.

They were coming for the boats.

She had never used her magic underwater. How would she fight them?

"Row! Row!" Ryne hollered as the gnulls swam toward them.

The oarsmen rowed until their foreheads ran with sweat, yet it wasn't fast enough. The gnull pod quickly closed the distance between them. The largest gnull had his big, dark gaze pinned on Dianna. He let out a primal roar that vibrated the floorboards of the boat.

Tar answered with several angry barks, but the dog was no match for the beasts.

The other passengers looked at Dianna. Were they apprehensive to have Madhea's daughter in their company or waiting for her to help?

A familiar roar was heard in the distance. A giant shadow flew past, followed by another. It took her a moment to register what she was seeing.

When her fellow passengers screamed and gasped, Ryne held out a silencing hand. "Don't fear, everyone. They are our friends. They obey Dianna."

Dianna wasn't so sure Tan'yi'na would appreciate being told to obey anyone, but she wasn't about to argue.

She cupped her hands around her mouth. "Lydra! Tan'yi'na! We're glad to see you."

Lydra answered with another roar.

Tan'yi'na turned up his snout as he flew above her head. *I didn't think you'd miss us.*

She gazed the proud golden dragon. *Not fair. I've been worried something happened to you. As you can see, we're about to be eaten. A little help would be appreciated.*

Of course. We're hungry anyway, and these creatures look filling. The dragon flew swiftly past her, rocking the boat and ruffling her hair with a warm wind. He swooped down like a hawk diving for fish, making such a splash, all three boats took on water.

"Row!" Ryne bellowed.

Tan'yi'na came up with a gnull almost his size in his talons. The beast cried and flopped, blood bubbling out of its mouth and punctured sides. Tan'yi'na tossed the creature in the air. It spiraled and dove toward the water, right through a burst of the golden dragon's flame. It was cooked by the time it landed with a hard splash. Luckily, the boats were far enough away that the ripples only aided in pushing them along.

Tan'yi'na did this to several more gnulls before the pod retreated into the icy lung of the glacier. Lydra helped him pull five charred gnulls to shore. By the time the boats had sailed to the continuation of the Danae River on the other side of the lake, the dragons were nearly finished feasting on charred flesh.

They sailed past a smaller colony of gnulls, but the beasts scattered when Tan'yi'na flew above them with a roar. They continued their journey.

Tan'yi'na, thank you for saving us. Please don't leave, Dianna pleaded.

I won't, little witch.

She slid into Simeon's arms, shoulders falling as the weight of her worry slipped away. Knowing the dragons were close by not only eased her mind, but she was finally able to find a small amount of peace. Markus was still in Madhea's clutches, and she still had to face down the evil bitch, but the dragons and her fellow passengers were safe—for now.

She was able to shut her eyes and succumb to an overwhelming fatigue. What she needed was rest. After that, she'd regroup and plan her next attack.

Chapter Nineteen

Madhea rested her head on Markus's shoulder, relishing his warmth and manly scent, a mixture of leather and herbs, herbs from the love-potion she'd force-fed him, but a pleasing smell nonetheless.

When she felt him stir beneath her, she sat up, pinching her cheeks and rubbing her lips together to add a touch of youthful color to her flawless face. She pulled her pale hair forward, letting the tips fall across his bare chest, knowing he wouldn't be able to resist her beauty.

When his eyes flew open, she batted her lashes, coyly biting her lower lip. "You're awake."

He blinked up at her with cloudy eyes, his full lips stretched into a thin line. Madhea didn't like the look. It reminded her of Rowlen, moments before he'd walked out on her.

He flipped her over so fast, the air whooshed from her lungs. He circled her throat with meaty hands, his dark eyes alight with fire. "What have you done to me, you wicked bitch? I should kill you right now."

He clutched her neck so tight, she could hardly breathe. The predatory gleam in his eyes should've frightened her, but it only made her lust for him rise. He was a magnificent beast! She relished the task of taming him.

"But you won't," she choked out. She could've thrown him off with a bolt, but she enjoyed the game too much. Besides, she hoped to appeal to his masculine chivalry by pretending to be a weak female.

To her surprise, he tightened his hold. "Name one reason why I shouldn't."

She tried to pry his fingers off her neck, but 'twas no use. She grabbed his wrists, zapping his arms with just enough magic to shock him.

He released her with a hiss, tumbling off her and cradling his hands to his chest. He turned from her when she reached for him, but she was not to be deterred.

"Because you love me," she whispered at his back, resting a hand on his arm.

He curled into a ball, burying his face in his hands. "What curse have you put on my heart?"

"Curse you?" She draped herself over him, running her fingers over his broad chest. "Why would I curse the man I love?"

He spun toward her, growling like a bear caught in a trap. "You deceptive shrew! I'm a married man."

She refused to give up. She placed a gentle hand over his pounding heart, forcing her eyes to water. "But you love me more than her."

He looked away. "You're too sure of yourself." The hollowness in his voice was belied by the flush that flamed his face like wildfire.

"Don't deny our love, Markus." She leaned into him, resting a hand on his heart once more. "I can feel it here."

His eyes filled with unshed tears as he trembled beneath her touch. Good. He was breaking. "What do you want from me?"

"Oh, Markus." She took a chance, planting a soft kiss on his lips, inwardly smiling when he didn't push her away. She buried her fingers in his coarse, thick hair, so much like Rowlen's. "I want everything."

THEY STOPPED FOR THE night along a shoreline that was shrouded in shadows from a canopy of pines. The air was warmer, and the distant mountain was barely visible behind its blanket of clouds, which meant they were getting closer to Aloa-Shay. Ryne had said the river would take them straight into the part of the ocean near the seaside town.

Tar chased a cluster of fowl who'd been resting on the shore, disappearing into the forest with eager barks. Dianna sensed the dog was happier to be on land than to have discovered dinner waiting nearby. The dragons soared above them, wingtip to wingtip, before landing downriver. The ice dwellers warily watched the pair while setting up primitive tents and preparing a fire.

Dianna and Simeon helped Ura get comfortable in the shade of a pine. The ice girl had hardly spoken on the journey, preferring to bury her face against her father's chest rather than look at anyone. Dianna didn't know if 'twas from grief or the sickness that accompanied expectant mothers. Either way, she worried for the girl. She pressed her hand against Ura's forehead to ensure she wasn't feverish before leaving her with a bladder of fresh water, promising to return with food after the campfire was lit.

She was getting used to Simeon shadowing her as she marched up to the dragons. Though the warmer weather didn't bother her, her heavy clothes were too restrictive, so she slipped off her fur vest. "Where have you been?" she demanded of them.

In the Werewood Forest, Tan'yi'na answered with a raised brow, *waiting as you commanded.*

When she leaned into Lydra, wrapping her arms around her neck, she was stunned and a little hurt when her dragon arched away. Lydra refused to look her in the eye.

"Why didn't you answer when I called to you?"

Lydra's answer was a grunt. She nuzzled Dianna's neck and then scooted back, pressing her hindquarters against Tan'yi'na.

How odd. What was going on with these dragons?

Dianna's glare shot to Tan'yi'na. "Well?" she asked impatiently.

We were preoccupied, Tan'yi'na answered, looking away. His behavior was surprising for such a proud monster.

The stones giggled, rattling her collarbone. What was so funny?

She should've shrugged off Simeon when he settled a possessive hand on her shoulder, but he'd been a source of comfort to her. She didn't want to drive him away. She turned back to Tan'yi'na. "Preoccupied doing what?"

Lydra turned her head into the golden dragon, nuzzling his neck, which was surprising considering it hadn't been too long ago that Tan'yi'na had tried to kill her. Even more shocking was that Tan'yi'na returned Lydra's affection, purring against her like a cat. A giant love-struck cat.

Simeon let out a hearty laugh. "Tan'yi'na, you wicked monster."

His response was a low growl that reverberated in the marrow of Dianna's bones. *Mind your brazen tongue, sand dweller.*

Dianna's chest and cheeks flamed with heat when Simeon flashed her a devious grin. Oh, heavenly Elements! How could she have been so blind? "You know what?" Dianna kicked up dirt. "Never mind. I don't want to know."

She left Simeon behind and went to the edge of the river, assisting with chopping off perch heads while trying to push images of little baby fire- and ice-breathing hatchlings out of her mind. Then she wondered how a dragon could breathe fire and ice at once. She supposed it didn't matter, but she made a mental note to have a talk with Tan'yi'na. That would be one terribly awkward conversation.

She straightened at the sound of a commotion in the center of camp. Tar was racing around a cluster of people. Simeon was already there, shaking his head and waving her over. She wasn't Simeon's obedient puppy, but she was curious, so she washed her hands in the river and joined the gathering crowd, ignoring Simeon's outstretched hand. She peered over a few heads, surprised when she saw Ryne and Jon pulling two men apart, but not just any two men: the old prophets Dafuar and Odu.

The brothers released each other with feeble groans, trying to claw each other's faces like cats. Their canes were lying in the mud, and their robes and faces were covered with grime.

Not this again. Sindri groaned.

I was hoping they'd forgotten their rivalry by now. Neriphene clucked her tongue.

Apparently not, Aletha answered.

"What is going on?" Jon stood between them, wincing as he pushed them apart. "You're brothers! You're not supposed to fight."

"Brothers!" Dafuar raised a crooked finger. "He's no brother of mine. He stole my woman!"

Odu tossed up his hands with a feeble shrug. "I didn't steal her."

"She was my soulmate," Dafuar cried, tears streaming down his leathery face, "and you took her away with your persuasive magic."

"She was *my* soulmate." Odu nearly fell over backward as he pounded his chest. "And she preferred me to you. You were too hardheaded to see it. She's waiting for me now beyond the Elements. If these old bones are ever granted rest, we'll be reunited again."

Ryne stepped forward, observing the two men with disdain. "Who are you talking about?"

Both men looked at him and then at each other with blank expressions.

Finally, Odu rubbed his bearded chin. "I don't remember her name."

Ryne laughed. "She was your soulmate, and you don't remember her name?"

"Yes, my soulmate." Odu's bottom lip quivered. "Large golden eyes, beautiful ebony skin. She looked like my mother."

Dafuar waved him away. "You don't remember our mother, you senile old fool."

Odu thrust a fist in the air. "I remember her from paintings!"

Dafuar shook his head. "Don't get your twig and berries in a twist, you ugly old crow!"

Odu lurched for his brother so slowly, he looked like a slog stretching for a nest of mites. He nearly fell face-first into the mud when his brother stumbled back. "You impotent cross-eyed kraehn!" Odu snarled.

Simeon whispered in Dianna's ear, "Do they realize they're twins?"

Dianna shrugged, turning back to the fight, which was so awkward, it was painful to watch.

"You always had control of all the women." Dafuar shook a fist at his brother. "Just as you had control over all the stones."

Odu pulled back his shoulders, flashing a toothless grin. "I can't help it if women prefer me over you."

All three stones heaved audible sighs.

"Brothers, stop, please," Jon begged, trying once again to step between them. "Can't you see your fighting is upsetting everyone?"

She wasn't sure whether people were upset or amused, but the latter seemed likely, as the crowd of onlookers smirked at the quarreling prophets. Even the dragons hung close by, watching the epic battle with fanged smiles.

Time seemed to stall as the brothers lurched for one another, their limbs tangling like mangled tree roots. They toppled over into the mud so slowly that Ryne and Jon had time to ease them to the ground.

Tar sniffed the old men, then gazed at Ryne, his ears turning in confusion.

Ryne scratched his head. "It's like watching two slogs trying to mate."

It was the most awkward and painful thing Dianna had ever had the misfortune of witnessing. The brothers twisted in each other's arms with a groan, and three smooth stones rolled from Odu's robe pocket.

"The goddess stones!" She pushed through the crowd, scooping them up before the brothers rolled onto them.

My sisters! Neriphene cried. *I hadn't sensed their presence.*

They must have gone silent, fearing Madhea would steal them, Sindri answered.

Dianna glared at Odu, who stared up at her with a frozen expression, like a petrified corpse. "You had them all this time?" She didn't bother masking her anger. "I thought these had been buried with the Ice People."

"Oh, I forgot about them." He sat up, flinging mud from his hands and sharing a baffled look with his brother. "Did you know I had them?"

Dafuar blinked as Jon helped him to his feet. "Had what?"

Ryne stepped behind Odu, helping him up with a curse. "She could've used them when she was fighting Madhea or the gnulls."

Odu craned his neck at Ryne. "Used what?"

Ryne swatted mud off his trews. "Some days, Odu, I swear you fake senility just to test my patience."

For once Dianna was in agreement with Ryne, but she bit her tongue, lest she say something she'd regret. Not that the prophets would remember anyway.

Bored or distracted, Tar left the old men, running back into the forest. The others scattered as well, shaking their heads and casting wary glances at the two prophets, who gawped at each other as if they'd forgotten their fight.

Dianna and Simeon sat on a log beside the riverbank and cleaned the stones. She removed the decoys from her satchel, slipping them into a pack. Then she placed all six goddess stones inside her satchel, blanketing them with the scarf.

The stones warmed and vibrated on her hip. No doubt the sisters were having a tender reunion. She didn't dare interrupt, though she hoped to meet the new stones soon, even if that meant she'd have six nosy sisters teasing her about Simeon's muscular chest.

"Only one stone left to find," Simeon said. "Kyan."

"If I had all seven, I would defeat Madhea for sure."

Jon walked over, then bowed before her as if he was addressing a queen. "My lady...."

She emitted a very unladylike snort. "I'm simply Dianna."

"Very well."

She noticed how he favored one arm, cradling it as if he were carrying a newborn babe.

She held out a hand. "Let me see."

When he placed his hand in hers, she was shocked at the way his arm curved at an unnatural angle.

"What happened?"

Jon hung his head. "The guardians."

"Oh," she breathed. She wondered how long the poor man had suffered with a broken arm. The stones were still buzzing in her pocket, and she didn't want to bother Aletha, so she decided to heal him herself. She shut her eyes, drawing on her healing magic. In her mind's eye, she saw a split in the bone going from his wrist to his elbow. She threw her spirit out, roped her magic in, and felt the bone fuse.

When she was done, she smiled at Jon, who turned his hand. "Thank you, my lady."

"Call me Dianna," she said with a wink. "We are in-laws, after all."

He answered her with a wide smile. "Thank you, Dianna."

Behind him, Ryne cleared his throat, looking sheepish, with his hands thrust in his pockets.

Simeon stood, hands clenched. "You're not going to blame Odu, like you did Dianna? Tell him he's the reason the Ice People are dead, since he kept the stones from her?"

Ryne glared at Simeon. Then his gaze softened as he turned to Dianna. "I was upset, and I acted like a fool. It was wrong of me to blame you."

"Damn right it was," Simeon grumbled.

"Look, I apologized." Ryne's face turned a deep purple. "So you can get off my back."

Jon placed a hand on Ryne's shoulder. "Easy, Son. We've had enough battles for one day."

Simeon jumped to his feet, raising his fists. "If you were truly sorry, you wouldn't have said it at all."

"Let it go." Dianna stood, squeezing his arm.

The two men stared each other down before Jon pulled away his son.

"I still owe him a punch to the face," Simeon grumbled.

Though Dianna wanted to be frustrated with Simeon for nearly causing yet another fight, she only felt admiration and gratification toward her defender. Simeon had been loyal to her through every battle, staying by her side and risking his life to help her. She'd never forget his kindness. She thought of Odu and Dafuar, and how they'd forgotten the name of their soulmate. She prayed to the Elements she'd never get so old and decrepit she forgot Simeon, for she was starting to realize he was quite possibly her soulmate.

"THIS IS ALL YOU GOT?" Madhea shrieked, throwing the flimsy bushel of herbs at her pixies.

They dodged the object with squeals, flying to the top of the ice ceiling in a frenzied swarm, communicating in their primitive telepathic language.

Madhea understood enough to decipher that the freeze had destroyed most of the bushes or buried them deep under the snow.

"Then fly farther south. Go deeper into the forest," she commanded.

They buzzed again, speaking so fast Madhea could only make out one word—trolls.

"I don't care if a voracious troll army is on your tails!" She jumped into the air, waving an angry fist at the little demons. "Come back with more herbs or don't come back at all!" She snatched the flimsy bushel off the ground. It wasn't much, but it would make enough to last a few more days, enough time for the pixies to hopefully find more. She prayed they would, for now that she had Markus's love, she couldn't imagine life without it.

Chapter Twenty

They'd come so close. Just as their kisses became more passionate, and Madhea knew Markus was on the verge of proclaiming his love for her, the potion began to wear off. She found herself on her back with Markus's meaty hands wrapped around her throat again. Like before, she'd been forced to knock him back, this time with a stronger jolt, for he seemed determined to squeeze the life out of her. After that, while he twitched and sputtered beneath her, Madhea poured sleeping potion down his throat. After she fell on the furs beside the sleeping hunter, she touched her tender throat and winced, knowing there'd be bruises come morning. She could've healed the bruises, but she chose to keep them as a brutal reminder she needed to fight harder for his love.

The pixies had not returned with the herbs. Madhea feared they would never return, for she recalled her stupidly telling them to come back with the herbs or not come back at all. In doing so, she'd inadvertently released them from their bonds. Curse them! Speaking of curses, Madhea had been sorely tempted to curse Markus's heart against that idiot ice girl, but she couldn't risk the dark magic destroying her newfound beauty and power. If only she had someone else to curse him for her. An idea took root in her mind.

The Elementals!

She flung off her furs and jumped out of bed. After gathering supplies from the food stores, she flew quickly toward the heptacircle. It had been so long since she'd last fed her daughters, she hoped they weren't yet dead, for she still had need of them.

After leaving the basket of food nearby, she grabbed a palma fruit and flew to the ceiling. Their emaciated forms huddled around a listless Ariette, softly sobbing while stroking their sister's hair.

"Mother!" Kia looked up at her with a scowl. "She is dying because of you! What kind of a monster would kill her own children?"

She tossed the fruit down to them. It crackled when it passed through the invisible shield but landed safely at Kia's feet. "I'm willing to feed you all on one condition."

Kia eyed the fruit, an anxious hunger in her eyes. "What condition?"

Madhea jutted hands on her hips, smiling down at her daughter. "That you sign a blood oath to obey me, Kia."

"No, Kia, no." Ariette lifted her head, waving a skeletal hand at her sister. "Let me die."

"Hush." Kia leaned over her sister, smoothing back her hair. "Save your strength." Kia turned to Madhea, determination in bloodshot and frightened eyes that screamed of desperation. "If I sign this blood oath, I want you to free my sisters."

"I will." Madhea inwardly smiled. How easily Kia was breaking. "Once you have completed your service to me."

Kia wrung her hands. "What will you force me to do?"

If she couldn't have their love, she'd settle for their fear. She tapped her chin, pretending to be lost in contemplation. "I haven't decided yet." In truth, she'd thought of a few wicked chores for her daughter, starting with turning Markus's heart against that stupid ice girl and the rest of his worthless family.

The dark shadows beneath Kia's eyes were even more pronounced as she turned up her chin. "I'm not fighting Dianna for you."

Madhea shrugged. "If you wish."

"Sister, don't do this," the other girls cried, tugging on Kia's robe as she slowly stood.

"That will be included in the blood oath." Kia yanked the hem of her robe out of their clutches and kicked the palma fruit toward her sisters. "I will not harm Dianna."

Madhea smiled. "Of course."

When Kia stepped forward, her sisters lurched for her ankles. She jumped into the air, her shoulders sagging with the effort while they tried to drag her back down. "Sister, no," they pleaded. "It's a trap."

Kia shook them off with a hiss. "I cannot not let Ariette die."

"You must," they begged.

"Come, Kia." Madhea leaned forward, holding out a hand. "I will release you from the heptacircle."

Kia flew to the top of her prison, eyeing Madhea with disdain. "Drop the food first."

Madhea quickly flew down and back, not wishing to give Kia time to change her mind. "There." She dumped a basket of fruit, breads, cheeses, and bladders of drink onto the floor beneath. Also included was a blade which clanked against the hard stone. "I have honored my word." She pointed at the blade. "Now you must honor yours. This is your final chance."

Kia flew down and swiped the blade before her sisters could reach it. She sliced open her thumb, swaying when blood trickled down her hand.

"No!" Ariette feebly cried.

"I must." Kia turned pleading eyes upon her sister. "I will not let you die." She placed her bloodied hand upon her heart and pledged her loyalty to Madhea while also vowing not to harm Dianna.

Madhea held out a hand to her daughter. "Good girl." She did her best to channel her sweet motherly voice, one that she'd practiced for years. "Come with me. I will nourish you and let you sleep in your soft bed tonight."

Madhea winced when she placed her hand through the barrier, and it sent a jolt up her arm, but she was able to pull Kia through it to freedom.

Madhea narrowed her eyes. "My first command to you is that you shall not return here to free your sisters without my blessing."

Kia landed with a wobble, needing to lean against the tunnel wall for support. "You're just going to leave them trapped?"

"Don't worry, daughter." Madhea patted Kia on the back, trying not to be offended when her daughter jerked away. "I'll feed them as long as you obey me."

"Of course I'll obey you, Mother." She glared at Madhea with a look of pure malice. "You've left me with no choice."

Madhea smiled. Too bad she couldn't make Kia destroy Dianna, but her traitorous daughter wouldn't have agreed to the blood oath without that provision. Madhea shrugged, tossing back her silky mane of hair. It made no difference who killed Dianna. If Kia refused to do it, Madhea would persuade the boy hunter to kill his sister. His arrows always struck true.

DIANNA HAD NEVER BEEN happier than when they finally landed in Aloa-Shay. A journey that would've taken a few days by dragon had taken over a week. How badly she wanted to steal away with Simeon and leave the ice dwellers to fend for themselves, so she could retrieve the final stone and save Markus. But she knew he would've wanted her to ensure Ura's safe arrival in Aloa-Shay, so she confined herself to that crowded boat. Lydra was too preoccupied with Tan'yi'na to offer her a ride anyway, which filled Dianna with a mixture of joy that her friend had found love and sadness that her bond with the dragon would no longer be as strong.

She was eager to stretch her cramped legs as Simeon helped her onto the dock. It was warmer here, though not as hot as she remembered. A breeze from the north tickled the nape of her neck and sent chills down her spine, for she understood the ominous portent of the cooler weather. The air was pungent with the smells of the ocean and rife with the sounds of waves, crashing on the shore. She admired the vast evening sky lit in myriad colors of fire, while the sun dipped into the ocean as if quenching its thirst. 'Twas at that moment she realized how much she enjoyed being by the sea.

A crowd of curious onlookers, eager to catch a glimpse of the blue people, swarmed the docks. Simeon pulled her through the throng until they reached a cobblestone road dotted with several thatched cottages and various shops. The news of the ice dwellers' arrival spread fast enough that Alec and Des were racing to greet them by the time they'd finished unloading the last boat.

She was vaguely aware of Simeon saying he needed to help the ice dwellers as she fiercely hugged her brothers. She planted so many kisses on Des's face that he finally pushed her away with a grimy hand.

Alec's brow furrowed as he scanned the throng of people on the docks. "Where's Markus?"

Her heart sank, for Alec was close to Markus, and she feared he wouldn't take the news well. "I-I had a fight with Madhea, and she took him."

The color drained from his face, and he slumped onto a wooden bench beside a thatched cottage.

She sat beside him while he cried, placing a gentle hand on his knee, though she felt unworthy to touch him. She'd failed Markus. She'd failed everyone.

She swallowed the rising tide of emotion that welled in her throat. "Ryne thinks she means to use him as leverage in the coming battle."

Alec swayed, hand over his heart while his skin turned deathly pale.

"Alec?"

When he didn't answer, she took his clammy hand, rubbing warmth into his skin. "Brother, I swear to you I will do everything in my power to get him back."

He silently nodded, then sniffled as the tears slowed.

She cursed herself for failing to save her brother. Throughout her quest, she'd struggled to stay strong, but seeing Alec cry was too much burden to bear. "Brother, I'm sorry. I'm so sorry." She ended on a sob.

He wiped her cheek, his eyes softening. "Don't blame yourself, sister. None of this is your fault."

"Yeah." Des sat beside her, resting his head against her shoulder.

She didn't deserve such kindness. If only she'd struck Madhea when she'd first fallen into Ice Kingdom. If only she hadn't been ruled by fear. When her brothers wrapped their arms around her, she sank into their embrace, crying so hard, she feared her remaining two brothers would be washed away by her tears.

"Dianna?"

Markus's sweet wife looked from Dianna to Alec while biting her lip.

Dianna wiped her face, then gestured to Ura. "Alec," she said to her brother, "this is Ura, Markus's wife."

Alec's knees wobbled as he rose. "I've heard so much about you." He pulled her against him for a hug.

"And I you. I have wanted so badly to meet my husband's brother." She dropped her gaze. "But not under these circumstances." She swayed in his arms. Alec lowered her to the bench. "Are you unwell, Ura?"

"Just tired. I need rest."

He knelt beside her, clasping her hands in his. "Are you with child?"

Ura looked up at Dianna. "I believe so."

She nodded to Alec. "She is. I felt a quickening in her womb."

"You can feel it, sister?" He flashed a watery smile. "Indeed your magic is strengthening."

Alec patted Ura's hands. "Let me take you home. My wife can attend you."

"Your wife?" She recalled how Alec and Mari had had eyes only for each other on their journey back from Eris's island. Was it any wonder they'd marry soon after? "Why am I not surprised?"

Alec stood, dusting off his breeches. "Tung and I are nearly finished building a bigger barn. We'll have room for at least two dozen ice dwellers to sleep there. The rest are welcome to set up camp around the field."

"All of them?" Dianna asked.

"Aye." Alec nodded to the throng of ice dwellers as they exchanged greetings with the people of Aloa-Shay. "They sheltered my brother when the ice dragon pursued him. It's time I returned the favor."

Ura looked up at Alec with an appreciative smile. "Markus didn't exaggerate your kindness."

Dianna had to agree. Of all her brothers, Alec had the gentlest heart. The smell of fresh, warm bread accosted her senses. She realized they were sitting in front of a bakery, for there were myriad pies and cakes in the window, some with fresh fruit and others with thick icing. What a welcome reprieve from salted perch and dried meat. The sight made her mouth water.

"Let's get you something to eat," she said to Ura, mayhap a little too eagerly, for she had her eye on a berry tart.

Ura place a hand over her belly. "I'm not sure I could hold any food down right now."

"Let's get something anyway." The rumble in Dianna's stomach rivaled a snowbear's roar.

Des jumped from his seat. "I agree." He rubbed his hands together, licking his lips.

"Oh, how I've missed you, brother." She ruffled his hair, which had sprouted considerably and was starting to resemble the wild mop of curls she had always adored. She took his hand and fumbled for a few coins in her satchel, wishing she had enough gold to buy out the entire shop.

"YOU WANT ME TO WHAT?" Kia could hardly believe what her mother was asking. She'd always known her mother to be selfish and unkind, but this act of cruelty was beyond belief.

Madhea eyed her daughter with a look of pure hatred, one that made Kia's heart weep with sadness. Though she'd never known love from her mother, she wasn't prepared for this level of contempt.

The Sky Goddess fluttered over to Kia's bed, plopping beside her and examining her painted fingernails as if she had not a care in the world. "You heard me."

Kia crawled out from under the furs, praying that beneath Madhea's façade of ice, her cold, dead heart would beat once more. "But, Mother, that kind of curse requires dark magic. Do you not remember what it did to your beauty when you cursed Rowlen?"

Madhea flashed a devious grin. "Of course I remember, which is why I'm having you curse Markus for me."

Kia's hands flew to her face, her smooth, youthful face that would soon be a bag of cracked leather. "Oh, Mother. Your cruelty and selfishness knows no bounds."

Shadows darkened Madhea's eyes, revealing the cold, fathomless depths beneath. "You knew this, and yet you accepted my blood oath."

"I did it to save my beloved sister."

Madhea patted Kia's knee, her smile not enough to mask the coldness in her serpentine stare. "And now you shall save your beloved mother."

She jerked away as if she'd been scalded by Madhea's touch. "You are no mother to me!"

"Silence!" Madhea slapped her so hard, her face throbbed and her ears rang. She jutted a finger toward the door. "Go to Markus!"

Now Kia understood why Ariette had begged her not to accept the oath, for in saving Ariette, Kia might have damned the world.

Chapter Twenty-One

Dianna rested against the trunk of a tree along the bank of the stream that ran beside Mari's farm. She enjoyed the cool water lapping at her heels while her brother chased fish downstream with a few of the ice children. Though her heart was heavy from worry and grief, listening to the children's laughter gave her a momentary reprieve from the ugliness of the world.

The stones in her pocket buzzed with activity, reuniting after some of them had spent hundreds of years apart. During their voyage Sindri had introduced her to Metis, Dalia, and Thesan, who'd been living with the ice dwellers, warming their baths and ovens. Dalia had spent most of her time with Odu, silently watching her brother's mind decay. Dianna could tell she was kind and patient, though she would have to be to live with the senile prophet. Metis had warmed an oven for the Eryll clan. She'd been neglected and mistreated, and as a result, was the quietest of the three. Thesan had been with Chieftain Ingred. Dianna didn't know if the chieftain's abrasive personality had rubbed off on Thesan, but the only time she spoke to Dianna was to chide her for not defeating Madhea. Sindri had to repeatedly intervene, begging her sister to show kindness and understanding, which resulted in quarrels between the sisters.

Dianna had finally given up and handed Thesan to Simeon. He quickly smooth-talked the stone into submission. The cold wind from the north was getting stronger, so Dianna generously allowed Simeon to keep the stone. He'd thanked her with a smile that made her knees go weak and then he'd returned to Alec to help him finish the barn.

About half of the ice dwellers accepted Alec's gracious offer, which meant the small farm was bustling with activity. The other half made camp along the river, preferring to be close to easy fishing and to keep an eye on the boats should they need them again.

The split also enabled her to separate Odu and Dafuar. She had taken Dafuar to the farm to keep an eye on him. After listening to him prattle on about how a belt of thorns would soon serve justice, she decided to leave him in Mari's capable hands. She had wanted to help with the barn building, but Alec and Simeon both insisted she rest. She couldn't be useless, so she'd agreed to supervise the children, which was how she ended up at the creek. She wasn't needed, though, for several of the children were old enough to take care of themselves and the others.

"You never said if you accepted my apology."

She looked over her shoulder, surprised to see Ryne standing behind her, looking sheepish.

She turned back to the children. "I kept Simeon from punching you. That should be acceptance enough."

"You didn't need to." He sat beside her, pressing his shoulder against hers without so much as asking. "I'm not afraid of him."

"Why must there always be a competition between you two?" She scowled at the ice dweller. Gone was her fleeting moment of rest, for now she had to put up with Ryne's complaints.

"Because of this."

Before she could stop him, he leaned in and brushed his lips against hers.

She jerked back as if his mouth was a scalding poker. Then she slapped him so hard, she sucked in a hiss at the venomous throbbing in her hand. She rose on shaky legs, clutching the tree for support. "How dare you think you can kiss me! You have annoyed and berated me this entire journey. You don't get the privilege of winning my heart after treating me so poorly."

He rubbed his face, which swelled with the imprint of her hand. "I know I can behave like a slog at times, and I'm sorry."

She tried to shake the pain out of her hand, wishing she hadn't struck him so hard. She recalled the time she'd slapped Simeon, the only differences being she hadn't hit Simeon quite so hard and she'd actually enjoyed Simeon's near-kiss, whereas she'd been repulsed by the feel of Ryne's lips on hers.

"I accept your apology." She pressed her back into the tree, watching him with mistrust as he stood beside her, looking down at her with doe eyes. "But that doesn't mean I'm obligated to give you any affection."

"So is it to be Simeon then?" Ryne leaned against the tree once again, filling up far too much of her personal space. "Because you know he won't be faithful."

She was so angry, she saw red. How dare this cocky broot drag Simeon into this! "You know what, Ryne?" She jabbed a finger in his chest. "You can take back your apology. I hope you choke on it." She stormed off before she slapped him again.

MARKUS WAS TIED TO the bed, the ropes having cut deep welts into his wrists and ankles, no doubt because he'd been thrashing. That would explain why the furs had fallen to the floor and the bed frame tilted to one side.

"You can't do this, Kia," she whispered to herself. "You will be a monster if you do."

When white-hot pain lanced through her chest, she hunched over, crying out. The stab was so sharp, she thought she'd die from it. This was just a glimpse of the pain she'd endure should she go back on her blood oath.

She sucked in a harsh breath and hesitantly fluttered toward the boy hunter. He looked much the same as before, only his face was more angular, and there was a haunted look in his dark eyes that hadn't been there before.

He fought his restraints. "Stay away from me, you cursed witch!"

She took a chance and sat beside hm. "I'm not Madhea. I'm an Elemental. My name is Kia."

"Kia?" He froze, eyes widening. "You helped me once. It was after Madhea killed Jae."

She nodded. "I did."

The shadows lifted from his eyes. "Will you help me now?"

Her heart was so heavy with sorrow and regret, she feared it might detach from her ribs and spatter at her feet. "No. I'm so sorry. My mother has cursed my heart, and I'm bound to obey her."

His eyes shone with fear. "You must resist. Fight the curse!"

She didn't know if the loud pounding in her ears was coming from her own heart or Markus's. "I can't." She hung her head, shame washing over her like a tidal wave. "No more than your father could have fought his curse or you could fight the hunter's mark. I'm sorry, Markus." She placed a hand on his arm, feeling the dark magic pulse through her veins like venom. "I'm so, so sorry."

DIANNA MARCHED INTO Mari's small hut, cracked open a palma fruit, and drank the sweet liquid. Not only was the drink cool and refreshing, but it washed away the taste and feel of Ryne's lips on hers. Bleh!

"You're in quite a predicament, having two men fighting for your favor."

Alec was in the doorway, flashing a teasing grin. "I'm in no predicament," she spat. "They're in predicaments if they think I'd return their affection." *Especially Ryne*, she thought, still unable to believe he'd kissed her without so much as asking permission. The more she thought of it, the more her indignation caused her internal temperature to soar.

Alec folded his arms, casually leaning against the doorframe. "You don't love either of them?"

"Immortals can't enjoy the luxury of love." Though Dianna wished she could.

"Kyan loved." Alec shrugged. "Feira loved."

She rolled her eyes. "And look where that got them." Kyan turned to stone, and Feira was overcome by evil mages because she let love for her husband weaken her magic.

"Having experienced love firsthand," Alec said as he closed the distance between them, "I can tell you it is worth dying for."

She gritted her teeth. Alec, being mortal, could never understand her position. He and Mari would live mortal lives, most likely passing to the Elements within a few years, not a few thousand years, of each other.

"I understand love is worth dying for, brother," she said through a groan, "but is it worth *living* for?"

He tilted his head, reminding her of Des's dog Brendle when he passed loud gas and looked for the source of the sound. "I don't understand what you mean."

Of course he didn't. That was exactly her point. "Any man I should give my heart to will not live as long as me, the daughter of a goddess, and I shall be left a widow before my first gray hair."

His mouth fell open. "So you are to never love a man at all?"

"I love three men." She paused, expelling a shaky breath. "My brothers. The devastation of losing you will tear my heart to shreds. I will not torture myself with yet another man to grieve."

She couldn't imagine being the last of her family. She would most likely have nephews and nieces after her brothers died, but those children would die, too. Was she to give her love to each new generation, only to suffer the heartache of loss time and again?

"But think of the years you could spend together," he pleaded. "Any children you may have."

"Children I will most likely outlive, given their father is mortal."

"So Ryne would've been your choice?"

"What?" She shrank back, memories of his lips on hers causing an uncomfortable shiver to steal up her spine. "I didn't say that."

"You said their father would've been mortal, and Simeon isn't mortal."

"He has the magical ability to charm. That's it," she answered. "To me, he's a mortal."

His brows vanished beneath his pale bangs. "So Simeon's your choice?"

She turned her back on him. His tedious questions were making her head hurt. "It doesn't matter."

"Of course it matters," he said. "Please tell me, if Simeon and Ryne were both gifted with eternal life, which one would you choose?"

She spun around, tossing up her hands. "Alec, this is foolish."

He grasped her shoulders, searching her eyes as if all of life's happiness hinged on her answer. "Tell me, sister."

"Simeon." She silently cursed her brother for forcing her to speak the sand dweller's name.

I knew it, Sindri squealed!

We all knew, Neriphene answered flatly. *It's so obvious by the way your heart quickens wherever he's near.*

Or whenever he takes off his shirt, Aletha teased.

Dianna stomped a foot. "Now look at what you made me do!" She wagged a finger in her brother's face. "These nosy stones will be teasing me for weeks!"

"Why Simeon?" Alec asked, ignoring her outburst.

She sighed, sliding down the wall and landing on her rear with a grunt. "Because he makes me laugh, he loves his sisters, he defends my honor, and if you must know, his smile makes my knees go weak."

He knelt beside her, taking her hand in his. "You should tell him how you feel."

She swore again. "Have you been listening to a word I've been saying?"

"I've been listening to your heart," he said with a wink. "You should, too."

THE ELEMENTS MUST HAVE been smiling on Madhea this day. The weapons storeroom had been closed for almost a century, ever since all her soldiers had been killed in that humiliating defeat against Eris's army. Madhea had never wanted to visit the depressing room again, until now.

She'd gone merely to retrieve a bow, arrows, and armor that would fit the broad-shouldered boy hunter. What she found was a miracle. Not only were there several magnificent cuts of armor and weapons ready to fire, but there were dozens of barrels of love potion, enough to quench the thirst of thousands of men, or in Madhea's case, enough to feed one man for thousands of days. How had Madhea forgotten about her precious stores? She tapped a solid wooden barrel, tasting just a drop, and was pleased the brew hadn't gone sour.

She placed a hand on her stomach, which burned slightly as she sampled another barrel. She need not worry about potency, for each sample was as strong as the first. But why was it upsetting her gut? Her stomach burned again, the sensation wrapping around her waist and spreading up her ribs. She pulled back her robe, looking at her reflection in the underside of a reflective silver shield, shocked to see the belt of thorns that wrapped around her waist had now spread upward, twisting and turning like an ugly, mangled vine.

What was happening? How had the dark magic gotten loose? And when would it stop? Elements forbid if the hideous tattoo were to spread to her beautiful face! Perhaps the potion would convince Markus to fall in love with her, despite her scars. But she wanted more than love. How would she convince Markus to desire her if her beauty was marred by an ugly curse?

"SIMEON!" DIANNA HOLLERED as she stormed to the barn.

He climbed down the ladder, hammer in hand, sweat beaded on his brow, down his neck, and across his glistening chest. Great goddess! He was the epitome of masculine beauty, and fool that she was, she admired him like a love-struck pup.

He set the hammer down, closing the distance between them in a few long strides. "Are you okay?"

At the risk of acting like a complete dung-faced troll, she rose on her toes and feathered a soft kiss across his lips.

When she pulled back, he clutched her shoulders, his body as rigid as the planks he'd been hammering. "W-What was that for?"

"I've decided not to wait until after we defeat Madhea." She paused to clear her throat, the realization of her brazen action pounding her skull like a mallet. "Just in case," she added.

His full lips pulled back in a wicked grin. He cupped her chin and kissed her back, this one a lot longer than the timid peck she'd given him. "You're going to defeat her," he breathed against her lips. "I know you will."

His kiss turned her knees to porridge, so she threw her arms around his neck, leaning against him for support. "I'm going to live a lot longer than you."

"My Oaňa. My destiny," he murmured, gently stroking her jaw. "I'll make sure to cherish every moment we have together, and I'll wait for you when I pass to the Elements."

The thought of him waiting for her, of having to wait for him, made a knot of regret well in her throat. But it was too late now. She'd committed to this man, and she was not letting go. There was only one thing that could come between them now. She desperately searched his golden eyes, wishing he could reassure her, even if 'twas a lie. "I'm frightened Madhea will kill us before we even get a chance."

He ran his hands down her arms. "What can I do to soothe your fears?"

"Kiss me again," she pleaded.

And so he did, right there in front of her brothers and the ice dwellers and even the barking dogs. He kissed her until her legs gave way and then he carried her to the shade of a palma tree and kissed her again. Somewhere in the recesses of her mind, she thought she heard Ryne swearing and stomping past them, but she didn't care. Her heart belonged to Simeon now. It had always belonged to him. She'd just been too stubborn to admit it.

Chapter Twenty-Two

"Markus, my love." Madhea buzzed into her chamber, doing her best not to drag the heavy weapon across the ice. She was pleased to see him smiling at her and sitting up in bed. "I have a gift for you."

She had already removed his bonds. After she'd forced him to drink an ample amount of the potion, he was no longer combative. He had such a doe-eyed look of admiration whenever he gazed at her, she felt it was now safe to present him with his new bow.

She heaved it into his arms and dropped the quiver beside him.

He turned the bow over in his hand as if it weighed no more than a few stone. "Thank you. It's beautiful."

She pulled her robe tightly around her neck, concealing the ugly scars which had wrapped around her, choking her beauty like a noose. "What else here do you see that's beautiful?" She coyly batted her eyes. Thank the Elements, her fair face was still preserved.

He brushed a hand across the soft fur of the quiver. "The arrows and quiver are beautiful as well. Such fine workmanship."

Why didn't he think her beautiful? Had he seen her hideous scars when she wasn't looking? She hadn't let him see her without her robe. Had he looked under the folds of her collar during the few times they'd shared kisses? She hoped not. It was becoming clear he didn't find her attractive, and it had to be the scars.

This left her with only one option—she needed to free Ariette, for her daughter had talented healing powers. If anyone could remove the scars, she could. But how would Madhea force Ariette to do her bidding? Her daughter was selfish and cruel. She wouldn't want to help her mother unless Madhea agreed to some sort of bothersome pact.

"Mother," Kia rasped, her cane making an ear-piercing grating sound as she scraped it across the floor.

Madhea sneered at Kia's hideous face. Her once youthful daughter looked centuries old now, just as Madhea had once looked after cursing Rowlen. Kia looked even worse though, bent over, her eyes milky with degeneration. No longer able to fly, she was forced to rely on a cane, moving as slow as a slog lest she slip on the ice and break her neck. Kia's powers had faded as well, rendering her quite useless.

After the girl had finally dragged herself to the center of Madhea's chamber, she cleared her throat, a hacking sound filled with phlegm. "May I have a word with you?"

"Of course," Madhea said, turning up her chin and forcing herself to play the role of the doting mother. "Darling," she said to Markus, "would you please excuse us?" Without waiting for his reply, she latched onto Kia's arm, dragging the feeble girl out of the chamber. "Why do you look at me that way?" she snapped, hating the revulsion she saw in her daughter's eyes.

"He's just a boy." Kia slumped against the gnarled cane she used to hold her bent frame upright.

"He *was* a boy." She flashed her daughter a wicked smile, hoping to shock her into silence. "He's a man now." Though she still hadn't spent the night in Markus's arms, she hoped it wouldn't be long. As soon as she found a way to erase the scars.

Kia's red-rimmed eyes widened and then she shuddered.

"I will have no more of your judgment, daughter." She jutted a finger in Kia's bony chest. "Do you understand?"

Kia hung her head, a lone tear slipping down her leathery face. "Yes, Mother."

"Well," she snapped, "what was so important you had to interrupt a tender moment with my true love?"

"Mother, when will you free my sisters?" Kia looked at her with a trembling lip.

She heaved a weary sigh. "In due time."

"But I did as you asked." Her voice splintered like brittle ice. "As you can see, his heart is cursed." Kia touched her hideous face.

She turned up her nose. "Not cursed enough, daughter, for he still will not tell me he loves me or share my bed."

"Look at me." Kia struck the floor with her cane, the sound ricocheting down the cavernous halls. "My beauty is gone. I cursed him, I swear."

Madhea was so aggravated with her pestering child, it took all her willpower not to smack her to the ground. The only thing preventing her from tossing her daughter over the side of her mountain was that she had one more task for her to complete. One more final act of revenge against the children who'd so cruelly betrayed her.

"So you say, but since the curse didn't work properly, you will need to do me another favor before I set your sisters free."

Kia clutched her cane with whitened knuckles. "What?"

She eagerly rubbed her hands together, licking her lips. "You shall learn soon enough."

DIANNA WOKE WITH A scream.

Simeon tossed his furs aside and scrambled to her side. "Dianna, my love. What is it?"

She sat up, trying to make sense of her surroundings. Her memories slowly filtered in like sediment from a cool stream trickling between her fingers. She'd fallen asleep in the hearth room of Alec and Mari's hut. The dying embers of the fire flickered beside the cot she shared with Des. Simeon had made a bed of furs beside them.

She looked at Des, who, surprisingly, was still sleeping soundly. She slid off the cot and into Simeon's arms, needing the reassurance of his strength to chase away her nightmares. They snuggled together.

He kissed her forehead, murmuring in her ear. "Was it a nightmare?"

She silently nodded, tears slipping down her cheeks. "It felt so real. There was this old woman. I believe she was my sister. She was begging me to save her. She said Markus's heart has been cursed against me." She ended on a sob, covering her face with her hands.

Simeon smoothed his hands down her arms. "Do you think the dream was real?"

"It felt real," she breathed.

It was real, Sindri said, her voice a hollow, dark echo in Dianna's skull.

She shot up. "Sindri says it's real."

Simeon leaned up on his elbow, his forehead marred by lines of worry. "Does she know what we should do?"

Speak to Dafuar, Sindri answered.

With a groan, she staggered to her feet. "We have to go see Dafuar."

Simeon's face fell. "And he's supposed to have the answers?"

She shrugged. "Sometimes he makes sense."

He jumped to his feet and put a hand on her back. "Let us hope we understand him tonight."

THE MOON WAS FULL AND heavy, like a giant glowing thumb pressing upon the sky. Simeon held Dianna's hand, leading her down the path from Mari's field of vegetables and grains to the jungle forest behind it. Not a creature made a sound, though that wasn't surprising. They'd all gone eerily silent after the dragons arrived. They tiptoed past Lydra and Tan'yi'na. The ice dragon slept in a stream, slowing the flow of water as it turned to icy mush. The entire stream would have most likely frozen if it hadn't been for the heat radiating off the fire dragon sleeping on the bank beside her. His tail was entwined with hers in such a sweet display of affection, her heart expanded with joy.

Dafuar had formed a makeshift tent of animal skins in a clearing in the woods. Where he'd gotten the hides, she had no idea, but the prophet had always been resourceful. A fire burned brightly within the tent, casting his crooked shadow eerily across the hide.

When Simeon pulled back the tent flap and she ducked inside, she was surprised to see 'twas not a fire burning at all, but a glow from a raised pool of swirling mists.

"Come." He waved her forward. "I've been waiting."

She sat beside him on a low stool, staring into the mists. How odd that they flowed out of a raised pool of water, as if there was a source of clouds somewhere under her feet. She didn't know what magic the prophet had used to create the mists, though 'twould be good to know. One day she may find her own swirling mists useful. She looked at Simeon, disappointed he still stood on the threshold. There was little room inside, so she could understand his reluctance to pack in like they'd done in the boats.

Dafuar took a long pull from a pipe, his eyes nearly crossing before he set it on the ground beside his feet. "Look." He nodded to the mists.

She stared into them, puzzled by a black pattern of circular thorns that marred the white clouds. "Simeon." She waved him over. "What do you think that's supposed to be?"

He knelt beside her, squinting into the mist. "It looks like ivy. Dead ivy."

Dafuar blew out a long puff of smoke. "It's a belt of thorns."

They looked at Dafuar as if he'd grown a second head.

"The barbs have pierced Madhea's heart," Dafuar continued, "leaking poison into her veins."

"How?" she asked.

"When a witch forces her child to use dark magic, the curse will also poison the mother."

She had many questions, but if she asked too many, the old prophet would become confused. "Will these thorns kill Madhea?"

"Possibly, but it will take time." He took another long draw of his pipe, the pungent odor making the room smell like rotten cabbage. "It will weaken her magic, which may give you an advantage in the coming battle."

Her heart thudded. "You have seen me battling Madhea?"

He grimaced. "I have."

Simeon silently squeezed her hand, offering her a steady source of comfort when she was so frightened, she wanted to jump out of her skin.

"Have you seen the outcome?" she begged. Namely, would Markus live? Would she? Elements forbid Madhea had cursed his heart, for she didn't know if she could strike down her own brother.

Dafuar's eyes glazed over. "What outcome?"

Dianna clenched her teeth. "The outcome of the battle."

He tilted his head. "What battle?"

"Oh, Dafuar!" she groaned.

"His moment of lucidity has passed," Simeon whispered.

She bit her lip, lest she take out her frustration on the senile prophet. "I'm afraid so," she grumbled.

The prophet straightened, and he looked around the hut like a hungry fox who'd caught the scent of a rabbit. "If you have any hope of defeating Madhea, you will need to retrieve my mother's stone."

She straightened. "Do you know where to find it?"

"Yes." He leaned forward, tapping her forehead with the tip of his pipe. "And so do you."

DIANNA FOUND URA ON the path when they returned. She had something to say to Dianna, of that she was certain. She just didn't think she'd want to hear it, for she feared Ura would ask to come with her to fight Madhea, and she refused to risk the life of her brother's unborn child.

"I'll leave you two to talk," Simeon whispered in her ear before kissing her on the cheek and setting off toward Mari's hut.

Out of the corner of her eye, she noticed Ryne by the barn, doing a poor job of feigning interest in his dog while looking sideways at Simeon, his dark scowl following the sand dweller. Ryne had to have seen that she had made her choice. Hopefully, he'd leave her be and wouldn't pick a fight with Simeon.

Ura cleared her throat. "Dianna?"

"Yes?" Dianna turned a smile on the pretty ice girl.

She twisted her fingers, biting down on her lip. "I want to go with—"

She held out a silencing hand. "You are *not* going with us to battle Madhea."

Ura's bottom lip quivered. "But she has my husband."

"Aye," she agreed. "The father of the baby you carry in your womb. The battlefield is no place for an unborn child, especially not when you risk Madhea capturing you and doing harm to the baby."

"I won't let her capture me. I'm good with the bow. You've seen me."

"No, Ura." She vehemently shook her head, her heart sinking at the look of pain in Ura's eyes.

Ura swiped tears, her face twisted with emotion. "I can't do nothing while others fight for my husband."

"Listen to me, Ura. You're not doing nothing. You're taking care of my brother and Mari. She's not as strong as you. They will need to be fed and protected." She reached for Ura's hands, pleased when the ice girl didn't pull away. "I can't fight Madhea and rescue Markus if I'm not sure of Des's safety. I need you here."

Tears streamed down Ura's face as she silently nodded.

Dianna wiped Ura's tears away. "I know you love my brother, and I thank you for it. You're a wonderful wife, and I'm proud to call you my sister."

With that, they alternated between crying and hugging, infusing each other with strength for the days to come.

Chapter Twenty-Three

After an emotional goodbye with Des, Dianna set out with Simeon, Alec, Ryne, and Tar toward Aya-Shay. Though they didn't have a giant to carry them, they reached the dwarf city in a few days.

Dianna had reluctantly agreed to let Alec accompany her, thinking she'd need him to help her negotiate with the dwarves. After all, she was about to ask them to surrender their food source.

The hold had now swelled into the size of a veritable city, as most of the villagers from Kicelin and Adolan had gathered there, pitching tents outside the crowded shelter. Dianna noted how much warmer and greener it was here than Aloa-Shay, more proof that her assumption was correct.

Ryne had planted the seed in her mind when they'd first visited Aya-Shay when he'd suggested the true reason Furbald wouldn't allow humans into the dwarf fortress was because he was hiding Kyan's stone. She understood the king's fear after Eris and Madhea's armies had pillaged the Shadow Kingdom, but that didn't justify his treatment of Zier's family. No, the king had to be hiding something, and that something had to be the stone.

"How are you going to get the goddess stone from Furbald, if it's even here?" Ryne grumbled, bringing up the rear of their party.

Ironic how Ryne had first suggested King Furbald was hiding the stone, yet now he was casting doubts on that theory. Ever the thorn in Dianna's side, she didn't dare admit that she'd become accustomed to his grumbling, most likely in the same way her father had learned to tolerate the bunions on his toes.

"It's here." She remembered the way Simeon's little sister, Kyani, named after the benevolent goddess Kyan, was able to grow plants at will, making them spring to life in a matter of moments. No wonder the dwarves were able to keep over a dozen giants well fed. Their goddess stone must have been growing food for them.

And now dwarves had come to the hold handing out fresh vegetables, no doubt, without Furbald's blessing. This abundance of food further proved Dianna's suspicion.

She thanked the dwarves for their generosity, then greeted old friends, wishing them well, saddened, but not surprised, when many gave her a wide berth. Whispers of "Madhea's daughter" had already reached them. No doubt the dwarves had told them, but if not, then the dragons circling overhead would've given her away.

Alec narrowed his eyes at Rolf Leifson, the town barkeep, after he backed away from her when she tried to say hello.

"You'd show her more respect if you realized she is the only thing between you and Madhea's wrath." Alec wagged a finger in the barkeep's face. Then he spun a slow circle, eying their former neighbors with a look of contempt. "One day you will all owe her an apology."

Matron Thisben, the old baker, stepped forward, handing Dianna a basket of bread. "For your journey." She bowed low. "May the Elements keep you safe."

Dianna cupped Matron Thisben's shoulder. "Please do not bow to me. I remember how your back bothers you." She bent beside the old woman, rubbed her lower back, and used her magic to douse the fire of her inflamed bones.

Matron Thisben stomped the dirt and kicked her legs. "Praise the Elements! My back no longer pains me!" She clasped her hands together. "Thank you, Dianna. Thank you!"

Dianna held up her basket with a grin. "You've thanked me enough." Then she turned to the other villagers, who'd gathered to gawk and whisper. "If any of you have children with fevers, please do not hesitate to ask for help."

"It's true, then?" Rolf stepped forward, crossing his arms over his distended belly with a look of defiance. "That you're a witch?"

"Aye." She held her ground. She'd battled mages, an earth speaker, and two goddesses. She wasn't about to be intimidated by the man who kept half of the village men addicted to his stale brew and indebted to him due to his outrageous prices. "I'm a witch and not ashamed of it."

Rolf frowned, stroking his grimy, graying beard. "Law states we must burn you at the stake."

She laughed. "Whose law? Madhea's? You would continue to uphold her laws and honor a goddess whose freeze has driven you out of your homes?" She marched up to Rolf, jabbing his distended gut with an accusatory finger. "Madhea's reign is almost over. I will bring her down, and when I do, I vow that anyone who burns a witch will be tried for murder."

Rolf backed up, scowling. "What makes you think you can take on a goddess?"

"She has already brought down Eris." Simeon stepped between them, his voice cutting through the crowd like the sound of a sledgehammer striking stone. "She will defeat Madhea as well. Now, unless you want to invoke the ire of Dianna's dragons, you all need to stand down."

The crowd of onlookers collectively stepped back, gaping at Simeon as if they were in a trance. Indeed, they had to have been, for Dianna was certainly mesmerized by him, too.

MADHEA LET OUT A HORRIFIED wail when she saw her reflection in the looking glass. Her face! Her beautiful face had been marred by the vine of thorns. The ugly thorns had snaked their way up her neck overnight, swirling across her left cheekbone, like her pigment had been dyed with black ink.

Curse the Elements! Why had this happened to her? 'Twas Kia who'd used the dark magic to curse Markus's heart, not her. She frantically added powder to her face to no avail. The vines absorbed it like a sponge. Stifling a sob, she pulled her thick curtain of hair down over the scars, completely obscuring one eye. She looked a fool, but she couldn't allow Markus to see the thorns, which also meant she dared not get too close to him.

How would she erase the vine of thorns when her healing magic had failed with the other scars? She realized she'd have no choice but to use Ariette, for she had strong healing magic. She was the one her sisters turned to when they caught a fever or broke a wing. If anyone could cure Madhea's ugly face, 'twould be Ariette.

Madhea flung her powders to the floor, flying swiftly to the heptacircle. When she looked down upon her daughters, she was shocked to see Ariette still gaunt and listless, despite the food and drink she'd thrown down to them.

"Losna!" She called to the daughter hovering over Ariette. "Why is she still unwell?"

Losna looked up at her with hatred in her emerald eyes. "She refuses to eat food bought with the sacrifice of Kia's soul."

This was no good. If Ariette died, Madhea would have no one to restore her beauty. 'Twas then she knew what she had to do.

"ARE YOU GOING TO PUT your hands on every kid with a runny nose?"

Dianna looked up at the scowling Ryne, who clutched a loaf of Matron Thisben's bread. She had already given most of the bread to her friends, but she'd been saving that last loaf for strength after she finished healing the children.

"Runny noses turn to fever, and fever leads to death," she said through clenched teeth.

He took a bite of the bread, swallowing it without savoring it. "You should be more concerned with getting that stone, for the ice witch leads to death, too."

"Relax." She turned back to the black-haired toddler, tickling his chin as he smiled at her. "Furbald will come to me."

"How can you be sure?" he asked.

She bit back a curse. This blue bunion of hers was becoming more uncomfortable than she could bear.

Simeon walked into the tent, frowning at a gaggle of giggling girls who lapped at his heels like a pack of loyal mutts. "Please return to your families." He waved them away. "I already told you I'm taken." When he closed the tent flap on them, collective sighs ensued.

She wanted to be aggravated, but she could tell by the look in his eyes that he hadn't meant for them to follow him. Besides, she couldn't fault the girls for falling for him, when she'd fallen hard, too. He had already told her he only had eyes for her, which was what mattered most. Those girls would just have to drool from a distance.

"I imagine it's going to be hard to be faithful to Dianna with so many girls throwing themselves at you." Ryne sneered.

"That's where you're wrong, Ryne, because Dianna isn't like 'so many girls.' It's like comparing the sun to a cluster of buzzing light mites."

Dianna thought she felt her heart do a somersault. If she'd been aggravated by the girls before, she certainly wasn't now. Her sand dweller certainly knew how to charm, and she ate it up like a starving girl with a rack of roasted mutton.

"I told you to save the last loaf for Dianna." Simeon snatched the bread out of Ryne's hands.

"Hey!" Ryne snapped. "There's no shortage of food around here. I'm sure she can find more."

"No," Simeon growled. "*You* can find more." He tossed the bread to Dianna with a wink.

When Ryne raised his fists, Tar jumped between them, barking at the ice dweller. Even the dog knew his master was a broot.

Simeon turned his back on Ryne with a laugh. Ryne's face turned a bright fuchsia before he stormed out of the tent.

"Thanks, Simeon." She leaned up and kissed him on the cheek. She couldn't help herself. She was falling more in love with Simeon by the moment. He made her so happy. She was determined to cherish every day they had together, no matter how short that time may be.

She tore off a piece of bread and handed it to the toddler when he held out chubby hands with a squeal. Then she kissed the mite on the forehead and left him with his mother, who graciously gave her some dried venison to add to her modest meal.

She held Simeon's hand, eating her food while they strolled around the camp, receiving warm smiles from everyone. She finished off her meal with a cup of palma juice given to her by another appreciative mother.

The ground beneath them rattled. Though she had grown accustomed to the booms, for the giants traveled from Aya-Shay to the hold quite often, bringing food and supplies with them, she had an unpleasant feeling in her gut this giant approaching would bring with him bad omens.

Sure enough, Borg broke through the trees, carrying a scowling King Furbald on his shoulder.

"Borg!" She waved up at him, purposely avoiding King Furbald. "I'm glad to see you well. I hope the babe is in good health, too."

"She good." Borg was about to say more, but when the king loudly cleared his throat, the giant focused on his grimy toes.

King Furbald pointed his scepter at Dianna, his eyes nearly crossing beneath his furrowed brow. "Your dragons take great risk in flying over my city."

"Why?" She feigned innocence. "They mean you no harm."

Truthfully, she'd sent the dragons over the city to spy for any signs of Kyan's stone. Tan'yi'na had already messaged back that he sensed his goddess was near. It had taken much convincing for the golden dragon to agree not to swoop down and dig up the dwarves' garden, for she didn't wish to provoke a war.

The king thrust a fist in the air. "They have no business poking their snouts in our sacred space!"

"Tan'yi'na has told me something interesting." She did her best to keep her tone neutral. "That there's a vast garden in the center of town in which grow vegetables as large as a giant's hand."

The king looked away. "The dragon lies."

Simeon squeezed Dianna's hand, whispering in her ear. "No, the king lies."

She leaned into Simeon, relying on his strength for courage. "He also senses the spirit of the Goddess Kyan deep within the garden."

The king's face went from moonlight pale to bright crimson. "More lies!"

"Why would he lie about something like that?" Simeon asked, humor in his tone and a slight smile tugging at his lips. "And why would you be so quick to call a dragon whom you admire a liar?"

If 'twere at all possible, the king's face turned even redder. "I never said I admired him."

Simeon shook his head, snickering. "You showed him great reverence at our first meeting."

Dianna hid a smile behind her hand, though she knew it was wrong. King Furbald's stubbornness would lead them to war.

"I-I was wrong," the king stammered. "He is clearly a deceitful monster. Tell him to stay away from my city, or my soldiers will fill his belly full of cannon fire."

"No hurt dwagons," Borg mumbled.

"Silence!"

Dianna flinched when the king thwacked Borg's ear with his scepter. Borg covered the ear with his hand, a tear slipping down his wide nose.

The stones gasped, then grumbled.

That man is not fit to be a father, much less a king, Sindri said.

Dianna silently agreed. Clearly the only deceitful monster here was the king. "Have a care with Borg, King Furbald," Dianna admonished. "He is a gentle giant and deserves kindness."

He shook the staff at her. "Do not tell me how to raise my son!"

"You'd have better results convincing Lydra to spit fire," Simeon whispered.

She heaved a frustrated groan. "I must have the stone, King Furbald, if I'm to defeat Madhea and save the world."

"There is no stone." The king shook his staff at the gathering crowd. "If you continue to press me on this, you and all of these pesky humans will be banished from the hold. I don't want them here, anyway."

That elicited gasps and cries from the refugees. Curse the king's selfishness. She might have no choice but to take the stone by force, which could lead to a bloody war. She didn't want that for the dwarves. Other than the king, they all had been kind to her and her family and friends.

After releasing a deep and steadying breath, Dianna said, "And where would they go, when the rest of the world is turning to ice?"

"The plight of humans is not my problem," the king said with a sneer. "I've said my piece. Keep your dragons away."

"Let me handle this," Simeon said to her. "I will convince him to relinquish the stone."

She nodded. She needed his persuasive skills now more than ever. Simeon cleared his throat to speak, but Zier pushed in front of them.

"So this is why our gardens grow in abundance and why you denied my family entrance into Aya-Shay?" Zier shook his fist at the king.

Oh, no! She didn't wish to encourage the dwarves to turn on their king. "Zier, wait."

"Zier Wanderson!" the king boomed, his eyes darkening to coal. "You will show your king reverence, and you will not speak unless directed, or you and your family can find shelter elsewhere!"

Zier rolled up his sleeves, baring his fists at the king. "As a village elder and a council member, I should've been told about the stone. You've no right to keep such secrets from us."

"That's it!" The king's skin flushed purple. "Zier, your family is no longer welcome at Aya-Shay's hold." He waved his staff at the crowd. "None of you worthless humans are either."

"You can't send them away," Dianna cried. "They will freeze to death."

King Furbald shook his head. "Your fire-breathing nuisance can keep them warm. Go now, all of you, before I unleash the arrows and cannons."

Borg made a startling sound before pressing his lips together. His limbs shook and his eyes glossed over, until finally the dam of tears broke and he started bawling. King Furbald struck him on the ear, the *thwack* sounding twice as loud as the last time.

"Owie!" the giant cried, trying to angle his head away from the king.

The king rolled his eyes to the heavens. "Calm yourself, you big, stupid broot."

Her heart fell. King Furbald didn't deserve such a sweet son.

"Borg no want fwiends to die." Borg stomped a foot so hard that Dianna stumbled into Simeon.

"Shut up!" The king smacked his son a third time. "We're finished here. Take me back inside."

Borg frowned. "Da not nice." He plucked the king off his shoulder and set him on the ground beside his feet. Leaning over, he wagged a finger in Furbald's face. "Da no hit Borg no more." He wiped his eyes and moved over to Dianna.

Simeon pushed her to the ground when the giant's dirty foot soared over them.

"You worthless piece of troll dung." The king stomped up and down like a toddler, crying for a sweet. "Get back here!"

The throng of onlookers stepped back when Borg sat down on his rear, crossing his legs. "No!" He pounded the ground with a fist. "Borg stay wif fwiends."

The giant Gorpat stomped up to Borg with her father riding on her shoulder. The girl giant leaned over and laid a hand on Borg's shoulder. "Borg okay?"

"Gorpat!" the king demanded. "Leave that broot and carry me inside."

Grim crossed his arms, frowning down at his king. "You will not give commands to my child."

"Fine!" Furbald threw up his hands. "Then the lot of you traitors can perish. You are all hereby banished." He stormed off, only to trip over a root and land face-first in the dirt. He pulled himself up, cursing his "stupid broot of an ungrateful son" and marched back to the fortress of Aya-Shay.

Simeon jutted a foot forward. "I should go after him. I can make him change his mind."

"For how long?" Zier asked. "He will only change his mind later and declare war after realizing he'd been tricked."

Dianna felt as if the weight of the world was pressing down on her as she watched Furbald go. If the king refused to relinquish the stone, a bloody and brutal war with the dwarves was inevitable. How many of them would side with Zier and Grim, and how many would side with the mad king? The last thing she wanted to do was divide the dwarves, but what other options did she have? She needed that stone.

Chapter Twenty-Four

After the dwarves sent several warning arrows into the hold, the refugees fled south. They ended up on a beach between Aya-Shay and Siren's Cove. It made many of the refugees nervous to be so near the demon fish. Dianna wouldn't put it past the voracious vixens to try an attack, so she gathered volunteers with ear muffs and spears to keep watch along the shore. Tan'yi'na and Lydra flew up and down the shoreline to scare off any lingering sirens.

They built three large bonfires and roasted fish Gorpat harvested with her net. Dianna preferred the ocean breeze and the fresh smell of the sea to the hold anyway. She especially loved the feel of the wet sand between her toes. She saw to it that no one went hungry that night, but she couldn't take care of them all forever. She had to leave soon to save her brother and defeat her mother.

Dianna, Simeon, Zier, Grim, Ryne, and Alec gathered around a smaller fire and debated the best means for retrieving the stone. Ryne wanted to attack with brute force, using Tan'yi'na and Lydra to burn and tear down the walls of Aya-Shay. Alec and Simeon suggested using Simeon's persuasion to convince Furbald to stand down while they took the stone. Grim and Zier thought they could rally their cousins to turn on the king, saying there had been dissention among the dwarves for a while. Apparently, as the king's second cousin, Grim was next in line to the throne. Law stated that giants couldn't hold royal titles, so Borg could not be king. Dianna thought it best, as Borg didn't seem mature enough to rule a city.

She thought Grim would make a fine king, especially as he'd agreed to let Dianna have the stone. Apparently the dwarves already had hundreds of years of canned fruits and vegetables and would not starve anytime soon.

Kyan's stone had indeed been a blessing, but it was time she reunited with her daughters and helped Dianna defeat the witch who'd reduced her to a rock.

"I don't think your persuasion will work," Grim said to Simeon. "We dwarves are a stubborn lot."

"I see." Simeon looked solemnly at Grim. "Cluck like a chicken."

Simeon's command was so strong and deep, Dianna fought the urge to start clucking and pecking the dirt.

Grim, however, jerked his head back and forth while kicking up his heels and clucking.

Simeon flashed a broad smile. "Now brood like a broot."

Grim let out a low, dark wail, flapping his arms and walking around the campfire.

She had to bite back her laughter, grateful that Des wasn't there, for he'd tease the dwarf for sure.

"Okay, you may return to normal," Simeon said and sipped from his palma fruit shell.

Grim returned to his position by the fire, his cheeks as bright as the fire's flames. "Very well, sand dweller," he grumbled. "Methinks your plan may work."

Ryne made a snorting sound. "Of course he's persuasive." He waved at Dianna with a scowl. "Look what he did to her."

Simeon shot him a glare. "What's that supposed to mean?"

Ryne pouted. "You've tricked her into loving you with your persuasive magic."

"No, I didn't." Simeon threw the empty shell into the fire, then rolled up his sleeves. "I care too much for her to trick her. I wanted her to decide on her own."

Ryne laughed. "Yeah, right."

Not again. She had hoped the two would form some sort of truce after she picked Simeon. "It's true, Ryne." She laced her arm through Simeon's, not just because she wanted to be near him, but she was afraid he'd race around the fire and start pummeling the obnoxious ice man. "I want to be with him."

Ryne shook his head, snickering. "You only think you do because he tricked you."

Simeon slipped away from her so fast, she'd no time to catch him.

"You know what, Ryne?" he hollered. "I still owe you a punch to the face."

Ryne was prepared for Simeon when the sand dweller plowed face-first into his chest.

She screamed when they fell to the ground in a tangled heap, rolling dangerously close to the fire. Simeon quickly got the upper hand, getting in a few bone-cracking punches before Borg pulled them apart.

"Friends no fight." Borg frowned at them as they each punched the air.

"Fine!" Simeon yelled. "I won't hit him."

Then he flashed a smile so wicked, she held her breath, dreading what was to come.

Cupping his hands around his mouth, Simeon hollered to Ryne. "Punch yourself in the face."

Ryne let out a roar before banging his fists against his head.

"Simeon, stop!" she cried.

"Very well." He heaved an overly-dramatic sigh. "Stop punching yourself, Ryne."

When Borg set them both down, Dianna turned away from Simeon when he tried to comfort her. She hadn't even realized she was shaking until she raised her palm in an effort to push him away.

"Why are you angry with me? Was I not to defend our honor?"

"You took it too far, Simeon," she said. "How do we stand a chance against Madhea when we're fighting each other?"

"You're right. I'm sorry." His shoulders fell, and he looked at her with big, sad eyes. "Do you forgive me?"

His pout was so adorable, she almost felt compelled to forgive him. Almost.

"No, I don't." She crossed her arms and held her ground. "And you can stop using your persuasion on me. I know when you're doing it."

"Hush!" Zier hissed, cupping an ear. "Do you hear that?"

Grim frowned, then knelt beside his cousin, placing an ear to the ground. He abruptly shot up. "Sounds like giants."

She dug her bare toes into the sand and felt the grains vibrate. "Could the king have sent them after us?"

"I doubt it." Zier shook his head. "He needs them to protect the stone."

Grim held up a silencing hand, still listening. "This doesn't sound like just a few giants."

"Brace yourselves!" Zier stepped back, reaching for his hatchet. "A giant army approaches!"

The contents of Dianna's meager fish dinner threatened to make a reappearance. If a giant army was indeed approaching, a dwarf and his hatchet would be no match for them.

"The fires!" Grim raced down the beach, wildly waving his arms. "Put out the fires!"

Fear iced her limbs, and she watched with a feeling of detached dread as Borg and Gorpat poured sand over the flames. Grim held a finger to his lips and led the refugees into the shadows of the forest. The ground shook with such violent tremors, she could scarcely walk.

Lydra! Tan'yi'na! she called. *I need you!*

The dragons circled overhead, then landed none too gracefully, kicking up a plume of sand.

Dianna gagged as she ran to the dragons. "Giants are coming!"

We know, little witch. Tan'yi'na's jowls hung down in a deep frown. *We were coming to warn you.*

Simeon climbed on Tan'yi'na's back and Dianna mounted Lydra. The dragons leapt into the sky, soaring into the clouds. Lydra flew northeast, just past Siren's Cove.

That's when she saw them, dozens of giants flattening trees with massive clubs, and they were all headed to Aya-Shay.

Elements save the dwarves.

AFTER USING TOO MUCH time and energy feeding Ariette broth and healing her emaciated body, Madhea then forced her to drink a sleeping potion while she designed a crude heptacircle around her daughter's bed. Madhea threw a spark at the seven-pointed star, instantly igniting it, then she fluttered to a chair and impatiently tapped her foot, waiting for Ariette to waken.

After an interminable amount of time, Ariette shot up in bed. "My sisters!" she cried. "Kia!"

Madhea stood, wings drooping. "Your sisters are well," she said, careful not to step past the burning edge of the star. "Kia is resting in her chamber."

Ariette blinked at her mother. "Why is there a heptacircle around my bed?"

"You know why," she scoffed. "I can't trust you not to attack me."

"What happened to your face?" Ariette pointed at her mother with a shaky finger.

She broke eye contact with Ariette, staring at the intricately carved headboard behind her. She had had it crafted for her once-favorite daughter over a hundred years ago, back when her army numbered several thousand soldiers and riches poured into her ice palace on a daily basis. "I don't know."

"Liar."

She had to bite her tongue to keep from swearing. "You are the Elemental with the most powerful healing magic. If you erase the scars, I'll set all of your sisters free." She'd set them free by killing them, but they'd be free.

Ariette frowned, throwing out her arms in a gesture of surrender. "I cannot heal you from inside this circle."

"I know." She moved closer, until her toe was nearly touching the point's searing flame. "Swear a blood oath that you won't harm me, and I'll remove it."

Ariette crossed her arms, smiling smugly at her mother. "I'm not swearing to anything. You swear a blood oath that you will free my sisters, and then you will step down and let us rule in your stead. Only then will I try to heal your scars."

"I knew it!" She thrust a fist into the air, then screamed when the fire singed her toe. "You've planned to overthrow me all along."

Madhea was not prepared for Ariette's humiliating look of pity. "You've become mad with power. You have imprisoned and starved your own children. You need to step down."

"So you can steal my throne from me! So you can take Markus as your lover!" Now that the boy hunter had finally fallen in love with her, she refused to relinquish her position. Those power-hungry traitors wouldn't think twice about taking him for themselves.

"The boy hunter is here? Oh, Mother. What have you done?"

The judgment in her daughter's eyes was more than she could bear. She turned her back on her child, her spine rigid. "I will not abide your censure. He loves me, and I love him."

"What dark magic did you use to force him to love you? 'Tis probably why your face is scarred. All the healing magic in the world will not erase the ugliness from your soul."

Her hands flew to her face. That couldn't be why. She hadn't used dark magic to secure Markus's love. 'Twas a simple potion she'd used thousands of times with no ill effects. Kia had woven the dark spell to turn Markus against his family. It was Kia who'd been cursed. Her youthful beauty was no more. No, these vines had been caused by a more sinister magic. Dianna had cast a spell on her. 'Twas the only explanation.

Madhea spun around with a curse. "So you can't help me then? Fine. I will find another way." She buzzed angrily to the door.

"Mother, if there is any chance of halting this blackening of your soul," Ariette said to her back, "you must reverse the dark magic you used on the boy hunter and free your daughters. Stop this madness."

After she slammed the door to her child's room, she decided the next time she looked upon her traitorous daughter, Ariette's face would be twisted from the agonizing throes of a brutal death.

WHERE TO NOW, LITTLE witch?

"We need to warn the dwarves," Dianna said to Tan'yi'na, the icy wind deflecting off Lydra's wings whipping her hair into a tangle.

Why not let the giants take care of Furbald for us? Tan'yi'na asked.

"Because," she said, "innocent dwarves will suffer."

She beckoned Lydra to turn, and they headed west toward Aya-Shay. The massive wall came into view. As they flew over the city, she was shocked to see it was larger than she'd imagined. The garden in the center of town took up far more space than the narrow rows of stone cottages lining the inside of the wall. There was so much foliage, she could imagine Lydra getting lost there.

As she peered down at the cobblestone streets, a horn sounded and the lights suddenly went dark, as if a giant had blown out all flames that lit the city. The kingdom became eerily quiet. Did they already know the giants were coming? Mayhap they'd felt the vibrations, too, even though the giants still had to pass Siren's Cove.

They must be preparing for battle, Sindri said. *The question is, which one? It's not safe here, Dianna.*

Her sisters voiced their agreement.

She hadn't thought of that. Mayhap the king was preparing for the dragons to attack in order for her to steal the stone.

Her priority was the safety of her people. She remembered the giants' superior sense of smell. What if they detoured to the beach and decided on a snack?

"Turn, girl," she called to Lydra. "We need to return to the refugees."

Lydra grunted her understanding and spun a slow and graceful circle. Dianna heard a sharp *thwack.*

Her dragon shuddered and cried out, dipping to one side.

"Lydra!" Dianna cried.

The ice dragon faltered, then tumbled head over tail. Dianna's head spun as she clung to a spiky scale, the wind tossing her about like a leaf in a wind storm.

Lydra! Tan'yi'na boomed. *Straighten your wings!*

The ice dragon grunted, then straightened, but it was too late. They were barreling straight toward the dwarves' garden. Lydra landed with a crash, and Dianna flew off her back, careening through the air with a terrified scream.

Use your magic, Sindri commanded.

She threw out her hands, flinging ropes of magic at a giant pod hanging from a leafy plant. The ropes caught, and she swung from the pod like a troll hanging from a vine. After the rope slowly lowered her to the ground, she hurried to her dragon, praying she wasn't too late.

We sense our mother is near! Sindri squealed. *She is buried in the soil.*

"I will search for her, Sindri," she answered. "After we heal Lydra."

She found Lydra with her snout planted in the dirt. Tan'yi'na was beside her, nudging her wing and making worried sounds. *Over here, little witch.*

Simeon jumped from Tan'yi'na's back. "Dianna!" He rushed toward her, grasping her in a fierce hug. "I thought I'd lost you."

She had no time for his affection. She broke the hug, took his hand, and climbed though a field of pea pods as big as melons. She stepped cautiously up to Lydra, gasping at the giant spear sticking out of her dragon's wing. Had the dwarves done this? The thought made her blood boil, though she knew they were probably following Furbald's orders.

Tan'yi'na looked at Dianna through hooded eyes. *I'll pull it, you heal it.*

She nodded, releasing Simeon's hand and climbing up Lydra's side.

The golden dragon grasped the spear between his teeth, then yanked it out with a growl. Lydra roared in pain, nearly knocking Dianna off her.

"Easy girl," she soothed, placing her hands across the bloody membranes. "Aletha," she begged.

I'm here.

She closed her eyes and pulled in powerful ropes of magic, throwing them across Lydra's wing like a net. When she opened her eyes, the wing was marked with dry splatters of blood but otherwise healed.

Tan'yi'na let out a deafening roar, blowing a curtain of fire around them in a wide circle, setting the nearby vegetation on fire.

She scrambled down Lydra into Simeon's arms.

"What's happening?" she asked.

He frowned, looking at the ring of fire surrounding them. "The dwarves are advancing with spears and arrows."

"Those fools!" she spat.

Tan'yi'na stood near her, chest heaving, wings spread, while he growled at the approaching army.

She turned to Simeon, the knot of panic that welled in her throat threatening to block her words. "Stop them," she pleaded.

Simeon nodded, then climbed up on Tan'yi'na's back. "Stand down, dwarves!" he boomed. "We've not come to battle you. We're here to warn you a giant army approaches."

Though she could barely see the dwarves through the ring of fire, she was relieved to hear the clanking sounds of weapons dropping.

A loud horn echoed from somewhere beyond the wall. She wondered if Simeon's warning had come too late.

Chapter Twenty-Five

Markus shot upright when the door creaked open, heaving a sigh of relief when 'twas Madhea who entered into the room.

He flung off his furs and jumped out of bed, racing to her side. "Why have you been avoiding me?" He clutched her narrow shoulders, desperately searching her eyes, distraught to see the moisture there. "Why are you crying, my love?"

"Oh, Markus." She let out a strangled sob, biting down on her knuckles. "I didn't want you to see me like this."

Panic burst through his veins, filling them with icy sludge that slowed his movements. He needed to know what ailed her yet was terrified he wouldn't be able to help. The thought of his true love suffering in any way filled him with sorrow and dread. "What has happened?"

"Dianna has cursed me." She rolled back her sleeves, and he was horrified to see the ugly black marks marring her beautiful skin.

His sister had done this? That witch would pay!

"These poisonous vines are eating me alive," she cried.

He gently pulled back her hood, treating her with the same tender care he would a newborn babe. His heart broke at the sight of the vines twisting and turning up her neck and across one side of her face. "Great goddess! How can we stop this?"

She sniffled, daintily wiping her eyes with the hem of one sleeve. "There is only one way to stop a witch's curse."

"How?" He'd do anything to cure the woman he loved. Anything.

Her eyes widened, then narrowed. "Kill the witch who laid the curse."

He sucked in a sharp breath. He hated his sister for many reasons, though they all eluded him at the moment. Still, did he hate her enough to let Madhea kill her? Aye, he did, for he loved Madhea more than his own soul. He couldn't take another breath if she was no longer a part of his world. If killing Dianna was the only way to save Madhea, then it must be done. "If you kill her, these vines will stop poisoning you?"

"I can't kill her." She stepped back, a hand splayed across her heart. "She's too powerful now, and she has poisoned my dragon against me." Sighing, she turned her gaze to the ground. "I fear it will only be a matter of days before I succumb to her curse."

Markus's blood began to boil. "Not if I can help it."

THE WALLS TO AYA-SHAY shook with such force, Dianna thought the entire dwarf town might be razed in a matter of moments.

The lights flickered on, revealing an army of dwarves with crossbows the size of cannons, loaded with arrows the size of spears. So this was what they'd used on Lydra. The crossbows faced the wall the giants were trying to breach. Behind the army of dwarves, their giant children nervously huddled together, gnawing on their nails and crying. Oh, the poor dears. Would they be expected to help the dwarves fight off the kin who'd abandoned them?

"What are you standing there for?" King Furbald marched up to Dianna. "Help us!"

The nerve of him. First he was shooting at them, and then he was demanding they fight his battle. She turned away. "I must heal my dragon." Something was still wrong. Dianna had healed her wing, yet Lydra still groaned, unable to lift her head.

She ignored the king's litany of swearing and placed her hand on Lydra's belly. She was shocked to sense a quickening within. In her mind's eye she saw a small purple dragon blowing blue rings of smoke.

"Lydra, my love," she said, rubbing her giant armored belly, "can you hear me?"

"I know what's wrong with her." Simeon patted Lydra's scales. "I've seen my mother in labor enough times."

Dianna worried her bottom lip. "I'm not sure what's normal for a dragon. Is she supposed to be so sick so soon? Do you think the fall harmed her baby?"

He frowned. "I'm not sure."

"Sindri, Aletha," she whispered.

We're not sure, either, they answered in unison. *We've never seen a dragon give birth.*

She prayed to the Elements the dragon mother and child would be all right.

She started at the sound of a deep, reverberating snap, followed by a crash so loud, it filled her ears with a cacophony of noise.

The giants had breached the fortress walls. They burst through with swinging clubs, deflecting arrows and roaring at the dwarves.

Tan'yi'na hovered above Lydra. The ice dragon's tail slapped the ground, and she groaned aloud. There was nothing more she could do for Lydra, but she couldn't let the dwarves and their adopted children perish.

"Simeon, help me!" she implored, scrambling up a tall vine that was twisted around a lattice fence almost as tall as a giant.

He aided her ascent up the vine until they both found a sturdy leaf the size of a small boat to stand on.

She flung her spirit into that between world, feeling the stones' magic infuse with hers. She gathered armfuls and returned to the mortal plane, releasing bands of magic in strong pulses.

The giants fell back, landing hard on their rears, causing the remainder of the wall to collapse and the dwarves to topple over.

One of the largest giants, who wore a primitive crown of branches on his head, sat up and pointed his club at Dianna. "Madhea!"

The other giants rubbed sore backs and gawped at her. Before she knew what was happening, they were all on their knees.

"Great Goddess, me King Munluc," the giant with the crown said bowing so low, his wide, flat nose scraped the ground. "Me not know why dwarves took giant sacrifices from goddess, but me sorry. Please stop cold. Most giants die already."

"I'm not Madhea. I'm Dianna, her daughter." She scanned the giants standing in the smoke and rubble. They couldn't have numbered more than fifty grimy, gaunt faces. They wore pieced together animal hides, most of which didn't shield their arms and legs from the night air. Many of them had blackened fingers and toes, which Dianna thought was due to frostbite. They were totally unfazed by the dwarf army pointing cannons and crossbows at their backs.

She tensed, searching the crowd for King Furbald. She hoped he wouldn't order an attack. She'd much rather get the giants to leave without any more violence. "The dwarves saved your children from the altar because the gargoyles were eating them," she said, hoping to appeal to their forgiving sides. If they had any.

The giants grumbled. A few Dianna thought were women began to cry.

"I'm not sure Madhea was aware of the sacrifices," she continued, "but if she had discovered the babies, they wouldn't have fared well in her care either. They have thrived with the dwarves. You should be thanking them, not tearing down their walls."

"Giants had no choice." King Munluc wrapped saggy arms around his waist. "We cold and hungry."

Dianna and Simeon shared a look. "I'm so sorry."

The giant's forehead folds drew down over his eyes. "So Madhea no send cold because dwarves took sacrifices?"

"No." She splayed her hands in an apologetic gesture. "Madhea sent the cold because she means to destroy the world."

King Munluc dropped his club on the ground, scratching the back of his head. "Why goddess do that?"

"Because she's heartless and cruel, and I intend to stop her."

He picked up his club and aimed it at her, a wide grin revealing a mouthful of rotten teeth. "You fight mother, and you become new goddess?"

She wasn't keen on becoming a goddess, but she decided not to bother the giants with small details, especially not while they were still on their knees bowing to her, and most importantly, not hurting anyone. "I intend to put an end to my mother's reign and restore peace to the planet, as in the days of Kyan."

King Munluc's jaw dropped. "Kyan, the benevolent goddess?"

"Aye." She smiled. "Kyan, my aunt and the one true goddess."

A rumbling beneath her almost caused her to topple from her perch. The ground shook with earthquake force before it began to split apart.

The giants hurriedly scooted back.

"Sindri," Dianna cried. "What's happening?"

I think my mother has heard you.

A mound of dirt rose from the split in the ground, rumbling and spewing like a volcano. When the ground finally stopped heaving, a polished white stone appeared at the top of the mound, gleaming in the moonlight.

Tan'yi'na bowed low before it with a fanged smile. *My Deity, it has been too long.*

The stone pulsed a vivid gold.

Oh, benevolent goddess, Tan'yi'na continued, *may I present you to Dianna, daughter of Madhea, a half-mortal witch who means to overthrow her mother.*

The stone pulsed red.

She is a good witch, My Deity. I give you my word. The Elementals switched her at birth, and she was raised by mortals. I have witnessed her many acts of compassion and kindness. She has collected all your daughters' stones as well.

Dianna was taken aback by the golden dragon's praise, hardly believing he had once tried to kill her.

The stone flashed a brilliant white, so bright she was forced to look away.

Tan'yi'na tenderly picked up the stone in his mouth, turned to Dianna, and dropped it at her feet.

She cradled it in her hands. "It's an honor to meet you, My Deity."

The stone flashed a soft blue. *You may call me Aunt Kyan. Now please re-unite me with my daughters.*

"Of course." She set the stone in her satchel, smiling when it warmed her hip.

"No!!!" King Furbald ran between the giants' kneecaps, waving his scepter like a victory flag. "Thief! Thief!" He jutted his scepter toward Dianna. "Drop that stone!"

Simeon chuckled, gripping a spear in one hand. "Come and take it, dwarf."

"That stone has belonged to my family for centuries, passed down from king to king," the king bellowed. "I am its keeper."

She wanted to tell the king that her Aunt Kyan belonged to no one, but she doubted it would do any good, so she tried one last time to reason with him. "That stone could mean the difference between me defeating Madhea or losing to her."

A familiar-looking giant made his way through the crowd, staring warily at the other giants on their knees.

King Furbald spun around. "Borg! Get that stone! Do you hear me, you big, stupid broot?" He jumped up and down. "Get my stone!"

The giant king slowly stood, scowling at King Furbald. "Me had son named Borg. Me put him on altar when he was three winters old."

Borg's similarities to King Munluc were uncanny. Both had the same cleft lips and flat noses. They could have passed for twins except for the king's graying hair and the lines around his eyes and mouth.

Borg scratched the back of his head. "Da?"

"Borg." The giant king's eyes watered. "Me thought you were with goddess."

"No, Da." He vehemently shook his head. "Dwarves took me. All dwarves kind except king. King not nice to Borg."

King Furbald shook his fist at his adopted son. "Why you ungrateful heap of troll dung!"

King Munluc raised his grimy foot so suddenly, Dianna didn't have time to react. The terrified dwarf king squealed like a stuck pig and then she heard the distinctive splatter and crunch of organs and bones.

"Now dwarf king not mean to anyone," King Munluc said.

Dianna didn't know how to react to Furbald's gruesome death. She and Simeon shared shocked glances before she turned back to King Munluc. Her breath stilled as she watched the dwarves, waiting for them to sound the alarm and advance on the giants, but with the exception of Lydra grunting and panting behind her, their war-torn garden was in a hush.

Borg looked at the splattered remains of his adoptive father with a heavy frown. He placed a hand on his heart, mumbling something so softly, she had to strain to hear what he was saying.

When the rest of the dwarves joined in, she recognized the souls' prayer. "In life these dreams we make. In death our spirits wake. To the Elements we ask our souls to take. Amen."

She hung her head and quickly mouthed "amen" while dwarves and giants did the same. Then Borg scooped up a handful of dirt and dumped it over his adoptive father's remains.

She waited again for a call to arms, but the dwarves remained stoic, looking to her. Mayhap Grim was right, that there were many dwarves who had wanted to overthrow Furbald. She suspected his sour mood had affected more than just Borg.

The giant king once again knelt in front of Dianna. "Young goddess, King Munluc no want to give any more sacrifice to Madhea and no want Madhea to destroy world."

Simeon stepped forward, clasping her hand in his. "Then join with her, King Munluc. Help Dianna defeat her mother and take her rightful place as your new goddess."

The king looked at Simeon as if in a trance. "King Munluc and giants will follow Dianna," he said in a monotone.

So much for Simeon's magic not working on giants. It had clearly worked on Munluc. Then again, she didn't think he'd been trying that day Ryne had asked him to use his persuasion on Borg. He'd been sulking over her rejection, after all.

"Thank you, King Munluc." She heaved a sigh of relief. "Now that I have the final stone, I believe I will be victorious."

Lydra let out a low dark wail that sounded like a brooding broot, only far more heartbreaking. She rushed to her dragon's side. Lydra sat up, heaving and sputtering as water dripped from her fangs.

She let out a primal roar, then slumped back down, raising a hind leg and rolling onto her side. A purple egg about the size of a full-grown human, tucked into a ball, rolled out of Lydra and onto the soft soil.

Tan'yi'na sniffed the egg before turning to Dianna with a fanged smile. *I'm going to be a father, little witch. We must kill the ice shrew before my hatchling enters this world.*

She clasped her hands, smiling at Simeon as he wrapped an arm around her shoulder. "Oh, Tan'yi'na," she said to the golden dragon, "I swear on the Elements I will do everything in my power to make the world a safe place for your child."

Tan'yi'na was right about you, niece, Kyan's soothing voice echoed in Dianna's skull. *You are indeed a good witch.*

TAN'YI'NA REFUSED TO leave Lydra's side, growling at any giant who walked too close to his mate and the egg. Grim showed up with Gorpat as Dianna and Simeon were leaving. She had the pleasure of informing Grim that he was the new king of Aya-Shay. With Grim eager to take on his new duties as king, she and Simeon were left alone outside the remains of the gate.

As they walked back to the refugees, he squeezed her hand while they went over the night's events. She was still too stunned to process all that had happened, but it appeared she'd have a giant army to assist her in bringing down Madhea. She believed she had a very good chance of overthrowing the ice witch, especially now that she had all seven stones. They had been buzzing with activity since mother had been reunited with her daughters. It warmed Dianna's heart that they were together once more. If only they could be restored to their true forms.

She assured Alec, Ryne, and several elders the giants had vowed not to harm them. She was surprised to find the rest of the refugees gathered around the two prophets. Knowing they'd slow their party down, and not wanting to have to break up any more awkward fights, Dianna had left the old men in Aloa-Shay. How had they gotten here so fast?

"Dafuar, Odu?" She walked over to the brothers. "How did you get here and *what* are you doing here?"

We were carried by two brawny young men." Odu nodded to ice men hunched over under a palma tree, rubbing their lower backs.

"And we've come to warn you," Dafuar added, worry lines marring his wrinkled brow.

Her legs weakened, nearly buckling beneath her. She'd have fallen if Simeon hadn't been there to catch her. He helped her sink onto the soft sand, then sat beside her, wrapping a comforting arm around her.

The look in the prophets' eyes told her their warning was dire. She hadn't realized until that moment how weakened she'd become over the day's stressful events, but she was feeling it now. If only she had some of Zier's strong brew to recharge her. "W-warn me of what?"

Odu tugged his scraggly beard, sharing a look of confusion with his brother. "We don't remember, but we're hoping it will come to us in the mists."

Oh, my poor sons, Kyan cried. *Their minds are more decayed than their bones.*

Dianna realized Kyan hadn't seen her sons in hundreds of years. She reminded herself to be more patient around the prophets. If not for their sake, then for their mother's.

Two other ice dwellers were stacking rocks in a circular pattern. So that was how the mists were built. The prophets must have to infuse the stones with Elemental magic after completion. But how long would that take? She and the giants were to set off at daybreak, which was in just a few more hours, leaving her little time for rest before her journey.

"I don't have time to wait, prophets," she said, then mentally berated herself for showing impatience so easily. "I have to prepare for war with my mother before I'm too late to save my brother."

"Ah, your brother, yes!" Dafuar held up a finger. "I believe that was the warning."

"There is a dark curse on his heart," Odu added.

A lump of sorrow welled in her throat. She knew the ice witch would have most likely cursed Markus, but she still wasn't prepared for the bleak emotions that threatened to shatter her already broken heart. "Knowing my mother," she spat, "I'm not surprised."

"Before you strike down your mother," Dafuar said, calmly, "you must kill the boy hunter."

Dianna swore her heart did shatter then. Kill her brother? Never! If it wasn't for Simeon grounding her, she would've flown from her seat and kicked sand in Dafuar's face for even suggesting such a thing.

"Are you mad?"

"Perhaps." Odu flashed a toothless grin.

Why in Elements name was he smiling? What was so amusing about killing Markus? She decided to discard all notion of showing the prophets more patience. Her head throbbed, and her hands shook so hard, she fought to keep them steady.

"I'm not doing it," she said, challenging him to contradict her.

Odu shrugged, picking a piece of food out of his gums. "Then have a dragon kill him for you."

She turned on him, imagining her rebuke was laced with venom. "No, Odu. I intend on *saving* him."

Dafuar's shoulders fell. "Then I fear you shall die."

She stomped over to the prophets, hovering over them like an angry bear defending her cubs. "Then. Let. Me. Die."

"Dianna," Simeon begged. "You don't mean that."

She jabbed him hard, angry and hurt that he'd side with them. "I do. I will not blacken my soul with my brother's death. Shame on all of you for expecting me to kill Markus."

She stalked off to find Alec, knowing he'd take her side in this. She cursed Madhea and the mad prophets. Then she cursed Simeon for not wanting her to die. In hindsight, she understood why he wanted to save her, but she refused to consider sacrificing the life of her innocent, bewitched brother. There had to be another way to defeat Madhea without harming Markus.

Chapter Twenty-Six

Aﬁter the dwarves performed a quick coronation of King Grim Hogbot-tom, Gorpat and her father had an emotional parting. The giant princess sobbed so hard, long pendulums of snot hung from her nose, breaking off and splattering the ground. Dianna hated to separate them, but as King, Grim was obligated to lead his army, and Gorpat was too young to accompany her father. No matter how big she was, she still had the heart of a little girl.

The dwarf king led a troop of dwarves and giants northeast to the Danae. Their plan was to travel upstream to the icy tunnel, letting the giants snack on gnulls along the way. They'd track Madhea and Markus, should they flee down the east side of the mountain. The giants had suggested they tear down the mountain, as they'd done with the walls of Aya-Shay, but Dianna had to explain more than once that banging on the mountain with clubs could cause deadly avalanches.

Lydra and Tan'yi'na shared an emotional goodbye as well. Dianna thought she heard her heart hit the ground when Tan'yi'na nuzzled the egg Lydra kept tucked under her belly.

Dianna and Simeon finally climbed on Tan'yi'na and flew after King Munluc and the other half of the giant and dwarf armies as they traveled northwest toward Adolan and Kicelin. The giants carried the dwarves, as well as Alec, Ryne, the prophets, and an assembly of human volunteers, enabling them to cut through the forest in a matter of days.

By the time they reached a clearing at the edge of the Werewood Forest, and within sight of Shadow Kingdom, Tan'yi'na had finished sniffling and pretending not to cry for his mate and hatchling. The air wasn't as cool as she expected, making her wonder if the belt of thorns Dafuar had seen in the mists had compromised Madhea's power. She hoped so, for the giants' tattered furs didn't look warm enough to shield them from the cold. The trees at the edge of the forest were covered in a light frost, but most of it had melted, creating pools of mud mixed with pine needles.

As they set up camp, she had no fear of the dark sounds, with a mighty dragon and a few dozen giants on her side. Let the gargoyles and trolls do their worst. They'd probably take one look at their army and fly the other direction.

Dianna, Simeon, and Alec had just tucked in for the night when Borg stomped up to them.

The giant jutted a thumb in his chest. "Borg find blue people. Borg smell them. They hiding."

King Munluc patted him on the back. "Good nose, Borg." When the king trudged back to the bonfire in the center of camp, Borg gazed at his birth father's retreating back with longing in his eyes.

Borg flashed a triumphant grin. "I show fwiends where they hiding."

Dianna and Ryne slipped on their boots, and Borg wandered into a copse of trees, disappearing quickly.

"Damn him," Ryne grumbled, holding a hand down to Dianna. "Does he think we can catch up?"

She reluctantly took Ryne's hand, hating how close he pulled her against him when she was on her feet. "He'll come back if he loses us," she said, not bothering to mask her displeasure at his nearness. "Remember his good sense of smell."

She cast her gaze at Simeon, who was sleeping so soundly, he made cute little snorting sounds while his nostrils flared.

Ryne rolled his eyes. "Just leave him. They're my people. We don't need Simeon."

She wasn't so sure about that, but she left Simeon behind, not wanting to leave Alec alone. "You never know when his persuasive powers will come in handy," she said to Ryne and then cringed.

"Yeah, like when he's manipulating you." Ryne snorted as he strode after Borg with long steps.

'Twas Dianna's fault. She'd left Simeon wide open for insult. "For the last time, Ryne," she said, running to keep up with him. "He's *not* manipulating me. I choose to be with him of my own free will."

He stepped over a vine as thick as his leg, then ducked under a leafy branch. "Even though he won't be faithful?"

"What do *you* know?" she scoffed, her irritation with the ice dweller rising.

"I know women are always throwing themselves at his feet, and they will continue to do so even after you marry."

He jumped into a deep, empty ravine, holding his hand up to her. She looked across the gully, hoping Borg would lend a hand, but he'd run off. With a grumble, she took his hand, because she was in no mood to dirty her last clean pair of trews.

"Those girls don't matter." She pushed away from him as soon as she found solid footing. "What matters is that I love Simeon, and he loves me."

"Until you tire of each other." She spun on him so fast, she nearly tripped over her own feet, but she was so tired of this game. "Why must you do this? Why must you look for the negative in everything? Your attitude made it so easy for me, even if I hadn't been in love with Simeon."

When his face fell, she almost regretted her choice of wording. Almost. The ice dweller needed to be taught a lesson.

He pushed past her, jarring her shoulder and not even having the decency to apologize. She decided to let the man baby go. She trailed after him as best she could, dirtying her trews when he refused to help her out of the ravine.

She followed him through thick vegetation before emerging in a clearing. What she saw simply amazed her. Though Borg was no longer in sight, she and Ryne had stumbled on a bustling camp with hundreds, mayhap thousands of ice dwellers. They'd survived!

"Liam! Great goddess!" Ryne and another blue man hugged like long-lost brothers. "I thought you'd all perished." Ryne clapped his friend on the back. "How many of you are there?"

Liam, who appeared to be around Ryne's age and about a head shorter, rocked back on his heels. "Well over a thousand." Liam looked past Ryne, his eyes widening when he spotted Dianna. "We must be quiet." He held a finger to his lips. "Giants have been spotted in the area."

"We know," Ryne said a little too casually. "We're traveling with them."

Liam's mouth fell open. "You're what?"

"They will not harm the Ice People," Dianna said. "You have my word."

She heard a rustling in the bushes and suspected Borg was nearby. She was grateful the giant hadn't made an appearance and frightened the Ice People.

"How did you escape the mountain?" Ryne asked Liam, still not bothering to introduce or even acknowledge Dianna.

"We dug a tunnel and climbed through a section of shattered ice shield." Liam used exaggerated hand gestures. "We were buried under the mountain for three days before we escaped."

"You don't know how glad I am to see you all alive and well." Ryne chuckled, one of the few times Dianna had ever heard him laugh.

"Most of us are well." Liam frowned. "But some of our children are sick with fever."

"Bring them to me," she said, growing tired of being ignored. "I will heal them."

Liam blinked at her. "You'd do that for us?"

"Of course," Ryne answered, though Dianna didn't need a man to speak for her.

"Thank you," Liam said to her before turning back to Ryne. "Many of us protested when Ingred outed your sister and locked away your father and the land dweller, but we were overruled. She was mad with power."

"I know, Liam." Ryne clasped the man's shoulder. "I'm not blaming you."

Wow. So not like Ryne to drop a grudge. Either he was showing off for her, or he only had a soft spot for his own kind.

"And how about your family and Odu and his followers?" Liam asked. "Did they escape as well?"

"All but my brother-in-law." Ryne frowned. "The ice witch has him."

"I was not there, but I was told she took him." Liam pulled off his leather cap and hung his head. "I'm sorry for your loss, my friend."

Ryne nodded, scrunching his face so tightly, she suspected he was holding back tears. Was this just a show, or did he truly care for her brother?

Liam cast another wary glance at Dianna. "Where are you fleeing to?"

"Fleeing?" Ryne chuckled, rocking on his heels. "We're not fleeing. We've assembled an army of giants and dwarves to defeat Madhea once and for all."

"Truly?" Liam gasped. "What a sight that must be. Do you need more volunteers?"

"We could always use more support," Dianna interjected again.

Liam nodded to her, then gave an awkward, low bow. "I will assemble a team."

SHE FOLLOWED RYNE AND Liam back to camp, the two old friends laughing and elbowing each other. She was amazed by Ryne's transformation in mood. Mayhap that's all he needed to be happy—assurances that his people were alive and well.

They located Zier in the center of camp, plotting routes with his cousins. Grim, the new dwarf king, had knighted Zier, giving him command of the northwest army.

Ryne pushed forward, not waiting for Dianna. "Sir Zier," he said. "A team of almost a hundred ice dwellers will join our ranks."

Liam held his cap in his hands, bowing to Zier. "I know we're a weary crew, but we're tired of hiding from the ice witch."

"We welcome you and your kin." Zier flashed a broad grin. "The glow of a thousand tiny mites burns brighter than any light."

She prayed to the Elements that was true, because she'd need a whole lot of mites to conquer her mother.

THOUGH DIANNA WASN'T ready for sleep, she climbed under her furs, nestled between Alec and Simeon. Dawn would be breaking soon, and she needed her rest for the battle. At the rate the giants moved, they'd be at the base of Madhea's mountain by tomorrow afternoon. Then what? Nervous energy coursed through her. Tomorrow she was going to have to face down her mother, and this time she couldn't lose. But what of Markus? How would she avoid hurting him?

Sindri told me Dafuar had seen Madhea with a belt of thorns in his mists, Kyan said, her stone warming Dianna's vest pocket.

"Yes," she whispered, absently rubbing the stone. "He did."

Do you understand the significance of the belt of thorns? Kyan asked.

She blinked up at the starry sky, partially obscured by the branches of a lone pine. "Not really."

Only a dark, evil magic can unleash such a curse. She had to have gravely mistreated her children.

She choked back a sob when she remembered the dream where Madhea locked her Elemental daughters in a heptacircle. Just as Eris had done with her daughters. And yet Eris had no thorns that Dianna was aware of. "You've seen such a belt?" she asked Kyan.

No, but the Elements spoke of it in the scrolls. It goes against a mother's nature to willfully harm her children. This is nature fighting back.

"But Eris had no such scars," Dianna said.

Maybe not on the outside, but on her soul for sure. It was why you were able to overcome her with only a few stones.

"How are Madhea's scars visible?"

A deep wound could have released them.

She considered Kyan's words. Mayhap Markus had stabbed her when he'd first been captured. "Dafuar said it will weaken her power."

It will, Kyan answered. *Look at how the frost is melting. You need not fear your mother tomorrow. You could defeat her now without the stones.*

The other stones voiced their agreement.

"But what of Markus?" she asked, her chest tightening with fear and sorrow as she recalled the prophets telling her she must kill her brother.

"Leave him to me."

She looked over at Simeon, who was leaning up on one elbow, staring intently at her. "You, Simeon? I don't want you to hurt Markus, and I don't want him hurting you." Just the thought of her brother engaged in battle with the man she loved filled her heart with dread.

"We won't hurt each other." He flashed a confident grin. "I will keep him occupied until you kill Madhea. Once the Sky Goddess is dead, the curse on his heart will be broken."

"It will?"

Kill the witch, break the curse, the stones echoed.

"Oh." All she had to do to save her brother and the world was kill her mother. Sounded simple enough, though it was anything but.

"Dianna, you will be victorious. I know you will." Alec was blinking up at her from his makeshift bed.

"You have a lot of faith in me, but if something were to happen to Markus—" She had to bite down on her knuckles to keep from saying anymore. Alec and Simeon made it sound so easy, but what if it wasn't? What if she panicked and didn't strike her mother in time?

Alec tossed the furs off and sat up, crossing his legs. "Zier taught me a dwarf limerick today. Want to hear it?"

What did limericks have to do with preparing her for battle with the Sky Goddess? "Okay."

Alec straightened his spine, clearing his throat.

"Thinking just to think
Can cause the brain to blink
And fart and bleed and juice and stink,
And yet we think and think and think
Until nothing is left but naught.
Our brains begin to rot
From thinking how we thought."

She shook her head, unable to hide a smile. Farting brains? "That is the silliest thing I've ever heard."

"It means you're thinking too hard, sister." Alec leaned forward and tapped her head. "We all have faith in you. It's time you had faith in yourself."

She wanted to argue with him, but she couldn't get the image of farting brains out of her head, no matter how hard she tried. "Thank you, brother." She kissed his cheek. "Goodnight."

Turning to Simeon, she blew him a kiss. "Goodnight."

"An air kiss? Surely you can do better than that," he whispered, his mouth hitched up in a wicked grin.

She heaved a weary sigh. "A quick one. My brother is watching."

She was determined to give him a quick peck on the cheek, but the tricky pixie quickly turned his cheek, capturing a kiss on the lips.

She shoved him hard while Alec swore. "Behave yourself, sand dweller."

"I'm sorry, but mouth kisses bring better luck."

He has inherited my late husband's charms, Kyan chuckled. *Now you see why I was never able to resist him.*

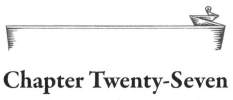

Chapter Twenty-Seven

Madhea buzzed into Kia's chamber, scowling at the ugly old woman curled up in her bed, sobbing and clutching a tattered doll. "I'm leaving."

Kia looked up at her through a mess of scraggly, gray hair. "Where are you going?"

She fought the urge to scratch her scars. They itched and burned, as if the curse had set fire to her veins. "Your bitch sister is approaching with an army of giants." The traitorous swirling mists had finally revealed Dianna to her, and Madhea was none too happy.

"Mother," Kia said, "you can't destroy her. She's grown too powerful."

Madhea looked at Kia with smug disdain. "She has, but I have a secret weapon, and his arrows always strike true."

Kia shot up, clutching the doll to her chest. "Does your cruelty know no bounds?"

"No." Madhea tossed her head. "It doesn't." She caressed the sharp blade in her robe pocket. "I need you to do something for me while I'm away."

"No, Mother!" Kia cried out as soon as the words were spoken, hunching over and sobbing into her doll's hair.

Good. The blood oath still held strong. Kia would not be able to disobey her.

"What was that?" she taunted.

Kia slowly raised smoldering eyes. "What do you wish of me, Mother?"

"Ariette is in her chamber, resting inside a heptacircle." Madhea snatched the doll from Kia, and in one fluid movement, whipped out her blade and stabbed the doll in the heart. Then she tossed it and the blade on Kia's bed. "I need you to kill her."

"Mother, please don't ask that of me." Kia's straggly hair was plastered to her wet face. "Please."

"I'm not asking." She turned up her chin. "I'm commanding."

She left the room, ignoring Kia's ear-piercing wails. Kia would do it. The blood oath left her with no alternative. And Ariette, the soft-hearted fool, wouldn't fight back.

She smiled at the boy hunter who was waiting for her, a fine specimen in armor that accentuated his broad shoulders and muscular chest. "Are you ready to kill your deceitful sister?"

"Yes, my love." The hunter's eyes were devoid of expression. "I'm ready to kill Dianna."

THE MOUNTAIN HAD NEVER appeared so daunting as the morning Dianna looked upon it, sitting on the back of a mighty golden dragon. She sucked in a deep breath, but the air was so thick and frigid, 'twas almost like trying to breathe underwater. She was unable to see the peak, where Madhea ruled, through the thick haze of clouds shrouding it.

There was only one way she would be able to reach her mother. She'd have to cut through the clouds, flying blind.

"I can't see the top." Simeon's voice shook as he held tightly to her waist.

You should stay behind, Simeon, Tan'yi'na growled.

"No. Dianna needs me." He clung so tightly to her, her ribs ached.

"You no need to go to mother." King Munluc stomped up to them, raising his club with a hungry gleam in his eyes. "We giants bring mother down to daughter."

"King Munluc." Dianna stifled a curse. "I've already told you an avalanche would kill everyone below. Besides, do you know what would happen to the snow once it melted? It would flood every town downriver."

The king's lip hung down. "Then why we come?"

"Because, should Madhea send her pixies, I will need your clubs, and if one of us should fall down the mountain, I will need you to catch us."

"And what if ice witch kills daughter and dragon?"

She cringed at the thought. "Elements forbid she kills us, but if she does, then, and only then, you must tear down the mountain." She didn't want to put any of them in harm's way, but if Madhea succeeded in killing Dianna and Tan'yi'na, her ice mountain must come down or her cruel reign would destroy the world.

King Munluc scratched his head. "But we no club mountain now?"

"No, King Munluc," Dianna said. "Please don't club the mountain now."

When the giant king averted his eyes, she feared he'd do something stupid Why had she thought bringing along giants was a good idea?

Before she had time to give the signal, Tan'yi'na jumped into the clouds, displacing the thick air and making it harder for Dianna to breathe.

Finally, the day of revenge I've been waiting for. The dragon's deep, dark rumble reverberated in her skull.

Remember to let reason rule you, Tan'yi'na, Kyan admonished. *Not anger, or my sister will use that anger against you.*

Dianna bit her tongue, praying to the Elements both the giants and Tan'yi'na wouldn't be ruled by anger.

"CAN YOU SEE ANYTHING?" Simeon called.

Dianna squinted into the clouds. "No, nothing."

"How long does this go?" he asked.

"For a very long time," she answered. Having grown up in the shadow of the mountain, she'd known it was vast, so big that Rowlen and Markus had been the only mortals to reach the top, and that was only because of help from the pixies.

"D-do y-you think s-she k-knows we're here?"

Simeon shook so hard, she suspected 'twas the drop in temperature, for the higher they climbed, the more frigid the air became.

She knows, Tan'yi'na answered with a feeble grunt.

"Tan'yi'na, are you okay?" She leaned over the golden dragon, stroking his neck, alarmed to see frost forming on his scales and icicles on his wingtips. "Tan'yi'na?"

I suddenly recalled why I was unable to chase Madhea back to her mountain and burn her to a crisp, Tan'yi'na said, his wings flapping slower. *This air is too cold for a fire dragon.*

"Kyan?" Dianna whispered, stroking the stones in the thick scarf that hung around her neck. "What do I do?"

Her scarf lit in a red, fiery glow and warmth radiated from her, spreading across Tan'yi'na's wings in pulses.

The dragon heaved a thankful sigh and flew faster. Soon he broke through the clouds, flapping toward an icy cavern carved into the mountain's peak.

They were almost to the ledge when a familiar cloaked figure stepped into view, clutching a bow in his grip and aiming an arrow right at Tan'yi'na's heart.

Dianna threw out her magic. Her brother fell over backward, losing his grip on the bow.

Madhea flew to Markus's side with a screech. "My love!"

Dianna roped in her magic, jumped off Tan'yi'na's back, and flung a bolt at her mother, knocking her off Markus. "My brother is not your love, you sick, twisted bitch."

She inwardly smiled when Madhea slid across the smooth ice floor, bumping into a wall with a groan. Now was not the time for second guesses and lack of confidence. Now was the time to stand up to her mother. Too many lives depended on it. She threw another bolt at Madhea when the ice witch tried to get to her feet.

She was vaguely aware of Simeon jumping off Tan'yi'na and standing behind her as she threw her mother down again, knocking back the hood of Madhea's robe and revealing the thick, black scars that curved up her face like a vine of thorns. The Sky Goddess tried to sit up, then crumbled to the ground. 'Twas true, then. The thorns had weakened her.

Tan'yi'na let out a victory roar. *Finish the witch, Dianna.*

She nodded and flung her soul between worlds, feeling the stones infuse her with boundless strength as she roped in her magic. She faltered when Tan'yi'na's agonizing howl ricocheted in her skull. She fell back to the mortal plane so fast, she lost hold of her magic.

The dragon's piercing golden eyes faded as he tipped off the ledge, an arrow stuck in his chest.

"Tan'yi'na!" she screamed, racing to the ledge, her heart pounding a painful thud in her ears as he fell down the mountain, disappearing through the clouds.

Markus turned an arrow on her.

"Don't shoot her, Markus!" Simeon's command was a thunderous boom in her ears.

Markus looked at Simeon with wide-eyed shock and slowly lowered his bow.

"Don't listen to him," Madhea rasped, stretching a hand toward Markus. "Shoot her, my love, before she kills me."

Markus shook his head as if waking from a dream before raising his bow once again.

"Lower your weapon, Markus." Simeon stepped toward him, holding out a hand.

"Brother," Dianna pleaded, taking a cautious step toward him. "Have you forgotten Ura?"

"I have not forgotten her." He dropped the bow to the ground, then drew a long blade out of his belt. "She manipulated me into marrying her when Madhea was my true love all along."

"No," Dianna said, backing away from her brother. "You're being tricked."

He vehemently shook his head. "She loves me. She wouldn't trick me."

"Oh, Markus." She heaved a weary sigh. Keeping one eye trained on him, she roped in her magic, prepared to knock the blade out of his hand so she could finish off her mother for good.

A bolt flew past her, and Simeon cried out, falling to his knees and clutching his gut.

"Simeon! No!" She hurried to his side, pressing her hands against his stomach to stop the bleeding.

Look out! Sindri cried.

She looked up to see Markus standing over her with a blade in his hand. Madhea hovered behind him, cackling in his ear. "What are you waiting for? Kill her!"

"Brother," she pleaded. "Please."

The mountain shook so hard, Markus fell over and Madhea was flung against the wall. It shook another time and another. A loud crack sounded under Dianna's feet.

Elements save them! The giants were attacking the mountain.

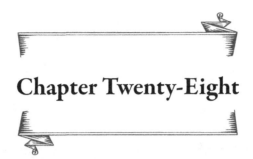

Chapter Twenty-Eight

Kia stumbled into Ariette's chamber, clutching the knife beneath her robe. A flaming heptacircle surrounded the bed, which had been moved to the center of the room. The flames rose to Kia's calves. She'd had to burn her legs to pass through, as she was too tired to fly. It made no difference to her. 'Twould all be over soon enough anyway, for she knew Madhea wouldn't let her live. Once she passed through the flame and killed her sister, she'd be stuck there, just as her four sisters were stuck in the stone heptacircle. Mother planned to kill them all. Kia had been dumb enough to fall for her tricks.

Ariette was sitting cross-legged in the center of the bed, staring at Kia with a mixture of shock and horror. "Kia, is that you?"

"It is," Kia said as she passed through the flames. The hem of her robe caught fire and pain lanced through her feet.

Ariette jumped from her bed and pushed Kia to the floor, burning her own feet as she trampled the flames. When the fire went out, Ariette fell on top of her sister, smoothing healing hands across her blistered feet. "What has happened to you?"

Kia fingered the blade in her pocket. "Mother forced me to use dark magic."

"Oh, dear sister." Ariette stroked Kia's legs. "I will try to heal you."

"You can't." A tear slipped down Kia's face. Ariette was so kind, so good. She didn't deserve to die. She'd warned Kia not to swear the blood oath. Why hadn't she listened? She shook her sister off. "Stop. It's too late for me."

"Don't say that. I refuse to give up on you!" Ariette sobbed, running her healing hands down Kia's legs. Though the burns had eased, her legs were still wrinkled and covered in bulging veins.

"Forgive me." Kia looked away from her sweet sister, unable to bear the look of pity in her eyes. "Mother sent me to kill you."

"Kia, no!" Ariette cupped Kia's face, desperately searching her eyes. "Fight the blood oath that binds you."

Just the thought of fighting the oath made her writhe in pain so dark and fowl, 'twas like poison permeating not just her veins but her very soul. The pain would've been bearable if it hadn't been accompanied by a madness that made her want to scratch her eyes out.

"I've tried to fight it." She bucked against her sister, rolling her off her chest. "I can't."

Ariette refused to give up, climbing back on Kia and pinning her shoulders. "You must try. Please. I love you, sister. I love you."

"And I love you. That is why I swore the blood oath. To save you. Look at the mess I've made." She ended on a strangled sob. She saw no way out of her present fate. The blood oath had too strong a hold on her.

"Oh, dearest." Ariette dried Kia's tears with her fingertips. "Let me help you."

"Nobody can help me. Nobody." She slipped her hand back into her pocket, withdrawing the knife. With one fluid stroke, she sliced open Ariette's arm.

Ariette shrieked, flying off Kia and falling on her back.

Kia rolled to her knees, clutching the bloody knife. "I'm sorry I hurt you. I had to get you off me."

"Please don't, sister." Ariette shielded her face with her hands, not even trying to put up a fight. "Please."

Kia held the knife poised over Ariette's heart, cursing her fate, cursing herself, but mostly cursing her heartless mother. Then she turned the blade on herself and plunged it deep into her chest. With a gasp and a shudder, she fell into her sister's arms, her heartbeat skipping and then slowing to a dull thud.

"No, sister! No!" Ariette screamed, trying to wrench the blade from her hands.

Kia pulled away, driving the blade deeper.

Ariette jerked out the knife and buried her hands in Kia's bloody cavity. Kia wanted to tell her sister to let her die. 'Twas the only way to break the curse she'd placed on Markus's heart, but when she opened her mouth to speak, blood poured out. Her heart beat one final, painful time and then she soared above her sister, looking down at her own lifeless eyes staring back at her. For the first time in many days, she smiled. Her soul had been set free.

DIANNA PULLED HERSELF to her feet, struggling to stand while the quakes continued beneath her. Those giants were going to topple the mountain and everyone in it! Why had they attacked? Then she remembered Tan'yi'na falling though the sky with an arrow in his chest. Her heart ached for the golden dragon. The giants probably thought Madhea had won. She needed to defeat the Sky Goddess once and for all, before the mountain crumbled.

She cast a quick glance at Simeon, relieved to see the shallow rise and fall of his chest. Her magic had saved him, but she hadn't enough time to completely heal him. One more reason she had to destroy the ice witch now.

Markus stood in the center of the icy cavern, legs braced while the ceiling rained crystallized debris on his head. He clutched his bow and arrow, looking at her through hooded eyes and panting like a wounded animal.

"Markus, please listen to reason," she pleaded, clutching a wall for support while the mountain continued to tremble. "You'd abandon your wife and unborn child for a heartless goddess who has caused so much death and destruction?"

Realization slowly dawned in his eyes. "Ura's with child?"

"She is." She held out a staying hand. "Please lower your weapon."

"Don't listen to her." Madhea shot to her feet, clutching the scarred side of her face, a look of pain contorting her features. "She's lying. She's jealous of our love."

Dianna heard the crack behind her, but jumped out of the way too late. When something solid struck the back of her head, she fell to the ground with a scream, a cyclone spinning in her skull.

Dianna, get up! Sindri hollered.

Touch the scarf, Aletha said. *I will heal you.*

Her hand flew to her neck. She blacked out for a moment, feeling the healing warmth pulse through her. When she opened her eyes, Markus hovered over her, tears streaming down his face, an arrow pointed at her chest.

The dizziness in her head slowly subsided. "You don't love Madhea. She's poisoned your heart."

Madhea angrily buzzed above Markus, pointing a shaky finger at Dianna's chest. "Shoot her now!"

"No." Markus turned to Madhea, lowering his bow. "I love my sister."

The witch who poisoned his soul must be dead, Kyan said, her voice a somber echo in Dianna's ears.

Her head must have still been in a fog, for Kyan didn't make any sense. If the witch who'd poisoned Markus's soul was dead, then Madhea wouldn't still be here, screaming in his face.

"You don't love Dianna." Madhea's ear-piercing screech echoed off the crumbling walls before she slapped him hard across the face. "You hate your family."

Markus stumbled back from the force of the slap, then rubbed his cheek, scowling at her. "I don't hate them. You tricked me. Why? I thought you loved me."

She fluttered down to him, clutching his shoulders. "I do love you, Markus, just as you love me."

"But you expect me to turn my back on my bride? Kill my sister?" He unstrung his bow. "If you loved me, you wouldn't ask that of me."

"Something's wrong." Madhea chewed her bottom lip, casting a worried glance from Markus to Dianna. "Ariette must have turned the blade on Kia."

That didn't make sense to her, but she struggled to her feet, determined to finish off her mother for good.

"I will end her then." Madhea buzzed past Dianna, ripping the satchel of decoy stones off her hip and tossing it over the cliff. "Not so strong without your stones, are you?"

Strike now, Dianna! Kyan commanded.

But Dianna was still dizzy, because she stumbled for a moment before reaching for her magic. That was all the time Madhea needed to hit Dianna with a bolt. She was thrown against the wall with brute force. The magic hit her chest hard, like a wave of electrified water, before bouncing off her and hitting Madhea.

The ice witch was flung back, hitting the opposite wall with a shriek and crumpling to the floor.

"What happened?" Dianna asked the stones as she struggled to stand.

We deflected her magic, Sindri said. *Good thing, too, because it was as rotten as her heart.*

"She hit me with dark magic?" Dianna whispered. "Wouldn't she know that would curse her too?"

I don't think she realized the magic was foul. When a mother curses her daughter, it's a vile thing, releasing a darkness that's like breaking a blood oath, Kyan explained. *It's especially bad if the daughter has had the Mother's Blessing.*

She looked at the seven-pointed star hanging around her neck, given to her by Sofia and Sogred when they'd blessed her. "Thank you," she breathed.

Madhea was on her knees, leaning against the opposite wall, precariously close to the ledge. The black vines on Madhea's cheek snaked across her entire face like slithering serpents, crawling up her nose and over her eyes. Markus stood over the Sky Goddess, an arrow ready to fly.

The goddess's wings drooped while she tried in vain to swat the black thorns off her face. "I love you, Markus."

He released the arrow with a *thwack*, flinching when it pierced Madhea's heart.

The goddess gaped at him, blood appearing on her lips.

"You love no one but yourself." He leaned down and shoved the arrow deeper into her chest, then drove her over the ledge.

Dianna stumbled to her feet, watching her mother fall without a sound, black smoke trailing from her fingers as she disappeared into the clouds.

Markus fell to his knees, sobbing into his hands. "What have I done?"

No doubt the effects of Madhea's love spell still hadn't worn off, and yet Markus had killed her anyway.

"Thank you, brother," she breathed.

The mountain trembled again. She heard a snap above her.

Move! Sindri screamed.

But she didn't move fast enough, and debris rained down on her head. Shielding her eyes, she fell to her knees. A sharp spike of ice drove into her back and through her heart. She coughed up blood, looking at the thick nail of ice sticking out of her chest. She thought she heard Markus scream, but she could only focus on the pain. Her heart ached so bad, she knew it had been cleaved in two. She slid to the ground, blood spurting from her mouth. Her eyes closed as her heart slowed.

Chapter Twenty-Nine

Dianna awoke to a familiar face. She recognized her large golden eyes and smooth ebony skin. She'd seen her a few times when she'd crossed over the barrier into the Elemental world.

"Sindri," she breathed. "Am I dead?"

"No, cousin." Sindri stroked Dianna's brow. "You are resting."

A woman knelt beside Sindri. Though she was just as beautiful, and had a youthful glow to her skin, there was a look of sagacity in her eyes that told Dianna she was looking at the benevolent goddess, Kyan.

"Aunt Kyan?" She reached for her, brushing her fingers across a face that felt like real flesh and bone. "You are no longer stones?"

Kyan flashed a soft smile, one that made her eyes glow with warmth. "The witch who cursed us is dead. We have returned to our true selves."

She released a pent-up breath of relief. Her mother was finally dead. She could no longer inflict pain and suffering on the mortal world.

"Dear niece, that spike mortally wounded your heart." She grasped her hand. "I'm afraid we were only able to bring you back for a short while."

Her heart leapt into her throat, and it felt like her world was crashing around her. She searched Kyan's face through a sheen of tears. "How long do I have?"

"However long I have." Simeon knelt beside her, taking her hand in his and brushing a kiss across her knuckles. "Our souls have been tethered, like Feira and Tumi. It was the only way I could save you."

She blinked at Simeon. "So when you die, I die?"

His mouth hitched up in a devilish grin. "Yes. Now you have no choice but to marry me."

"I would've tethered your soul to mine, cousin, even at the risk of using dark magic." Sindri said. "But not after listening to you mourn the thought

273

of living an eternity without Simeon and your brothers." Her shoulders fell. "We thought you'd prefer to have your soul tethered to Simeon's."

"Oh, cousin." She sat up, her chest expanding as if her heart had grown thrice in size. "If you only knew how happy I am." She leaned into Simeon, planting a kiss on his lips. "I think I said I owed you one after we defeated Madhea."

"You do," he whispered in her ear. "But not here. I'll collect a proper one later."

The walls shook, and Kyan fell beside her. Dianna clutched Simeon's hand, looking at the alarmed faces of her six cousins and Markus. With Tan'yi'na gone, how would they get down the mountain?

Kyan sat up, whistling so loudly, she had to shield her ears. A giant, buzzing ball floated into the cavern.

Pixies!

Markus rolled his eyes. "Not these demons again."

But she didn't mind. She'd gladly accept the winged creatures' help, as long as she got off the mountain.

DIANNA AND SIMEON LAY in the crook of Tan'yi'na's wing, massaging the dragon's thick membranes while he grunted his approval. The dwarves had taken them to a comfortable clearing in the shade of the mighty lyme tree in the heart of Adolan. The tree's branches perked under the warmth of the midday sun, and the birds nesting there happily sang to their neighbors. 'Twas as if Madhea's death had lifted the shade of doom that had befallen the village.

When Tan'yi'na rolled over on his side, Dianna couldn't help but laugh. *Scratch my belly next, little witches.*

Simeon stood, puffing up his chest. "Who are you calling little?"

Tan'yi'na arched a brow, flashing a fanged smile. *I can swallow you whole. You are little to me.*

He sat back down, scratching the dragon's belly. "Point taken."

Dianna laughed and rubbed up and down Tan'yi'na's smooth scales. She didn't mind the intensive labor. Not long ago she'd thought him dead. After he'd fallen from the mountain and landed in a snowdrift, the giants had carried him to camp, giving him to the old prophets, who set aside their animosity for one another and worked together to help him. Fortunately, the layer of ice that had accumulated across the dragon's chest scales was thick enough that only the tip of the arrow had pierced his heart. The brothers had applied poultices, keeping him alive until Kyan and Aletha laid their hands on his chest, healing him completely. Tan'yi'na said he bore no hard feelings toward Markus for shooting him, for he understood the strength of Madhea's spell.

Markus slept beside them after taking a draught that Aletha said would rid him of all tender feelings for Madhea. Dianna feared her brother would have a brutal awakening when he fully realized he'd been tricked into loving the ice witch.

A familiar bark heralded Ryne's arrival. He came into the clearing, his loyal companion trotting beside him, tail in full wag. Ryne grimaced at Markus before turning his scowl on Dianna and Simeon. "King Hogbottom has sent me with updates."

"Well?" She gave the sour ice dweller an expectant look.

"The glacier broke off and flattened the gnull colony downriver. The goddesses were able to push it back before it went any farther. The mountain has stopped shaking, and the goddesses have freed the Elementals."

"My sisters!" She jumped to her feet, her heart filling with so much joy, she felt like bursting. "They're alive!" She'd thought Madhea had killed them.

When Markus groaned, she knelt beside him until his eyes opened.

"Sister?" Wincing, he leaned against the wide tree trunk and rubbed his head. "What happened?"

Dianna took his large hands in hers. "You don't remember?" She fought back a grimace, doing her best to infuse cheer into her voice. "Madhea cursed your heart, but you fought back and killed her. You saved us." She squeezed hard, waiting for the memories to hit.

"Boar's blood!" He released her and fell on his side, flinging an arm across his eyes. "That cursed witch!" He pulled back his arm, looking up at her with watery eyes. "I'm so sorry."

She kissed his cheek. "It wasn't your fault."

"She tricked me." He turned away again, curling into a fetal position. "I betrayed my family, my wife."

Tar sat beside Markus, placing a comforting paw on his arm.

Her heart broke for him. "We're not angry with you."

"I am!" Ryne pounded his chest. "Did you betray my sister and bed that heartless shrew?"

"No, but I kissed her." He buried his face in the dirt as a sob wracked him. "And I held her and told her I loved her."

She crawled over to him and wrapped an arm around his wide shoulders. "Don't listen to Ryne. Ura will understand you were bewitched. Trust me. She only cares about your safe return."

He looked at her with a grimy, wet face. "Is she truly with child?"

"Aye." She smiled. "She is."

"If the curse hadn't been broken, I would've hated that child like my father loathed Alec."

"But the curse was broken." She rubbed his back, refusing to let him suffer for something that had been out of his control. "The evil witch is dead, the goddesses have been restored, and we're safe. Now is a time for celebration, not tears."

As if to emphasize her point, Tar licked Markus's tears away, eliciting a chuckle from him.

"Not everyone is safe, cousin." Sindri stood beneath one of the low branches, twisting the hem of her belt. "One of the Elementals sacrificed her life in order to save us. We must prepare a funeral pyre."

THE ELEMENTALS LAID their sister to rest on an altar made of pine, clinging to each other while Tan'yi'na lit the pyre. Dianna's heart broke when she saw her sister's wrinkled, shriveled body melt like a ball of wax. The flames spread, consuming the entire altar and lighting up the night sky.

Dianna turned to Simeon, wrapping her arms around his neck, sobbing into his chest while Kyan and her daughters recited the prayer.

"Through life these dreams we make. With magic, these blessings we partake. In death our spirits wake. To the Elements we ask our souls to take. Amen."

After the funeral, Dianna sat beside her sisters while they stared at the dying embers in stony silence.

"Will you join us, sister?" Ariette reached for Dianna's hand, giving her a watery smile. "Take Kia's place in our coven?"

She shook her head, feeling bad for letting them down. "I'm sorry, no." She sought Simeon, who was standing under the lyme tree, helping Alec comfort Markus. "My soul has chosen a different destiny."

Ariette laid a hand on her knee, solemnly nodding before turning her gaze back to the pyre. "We wish you and Simeon much joy and happiness for as long as you both shall live and well into the afterlife."

"Aye, for as long as we both shall live," she agreed, the break in her heart slowly starting to fuse back together. "For we will pass to the Elements together."

AFTER RETURNING TO Aya-Shay, Markus, Dianna, the Goddess Kyan and her daughters received a hero's welcome, though Markus felt anything but. King Hogbottom allowed everyone into the beautiful town of Aya-Shay. Markus was hardly aware of the flowers and coins that were thrown on the street as he stood stoically on Borg's shoulder, the goddesses flying above them on Tan'yi'na's back.

Cheers rolled through the crowd when Kyan and her daughters circled the village, repairing rubble with simple sweeps of their hands. By night's end, Aya-Shay had been restored to a mystical village with ivy-covered cottages, bright cobblestone paths, and a clear stream running through town, jumping with colorful trout.

After Borg set Markus, Dianna, and Simeon down, they were presented with chests of gold and silver. Kyan promised them more jewels from the Shifting Sands. Markus cared nothing for treasure, but he knew he could trade the jewels for provisions to make a new life for Ura and his family.

"Now all I have to do is convince Ura to take me back," he whispered to Dianna.

She placed a hand on his back. "She will take you. Of that I'm sure." She nodded at something behind his shoulder.

Ura stood beneath the soft glow of an overhead lamp, wringing her hands and looking at him with a longing in her eyes that nearly shattered his heart.

"Ura," he breathed, taking a hesitant step forward. He'd not expected to see her here.

"Markus!" she cried, running to him.

He stood there like a deer in a hunter's crosshairs, too stunned to make a move when she wrapped her arms around his neck.

"Oh, Markus." She looked at him with tears in her silver eyes. "Do you still love me?"

"Of course, I love you, Ura." He barely choked out the words. "More than anything. I'm just stunned you're here."

"King Hogbottom and the giants brought us. They passed through Aloa-Shay on their return home. They told us the ice witch had been killed and Kyan and her daughters had returned." She touched his face, frowning. "You look like a land dweller again."

Too ashamed to look into her eyes a moment longer, he cast his gaze to his feet. "The ice witch changed me."

"Oh." She released him, taking a step back. "I was afraid she would."

He felt as if Ura had ripped out his heart and taken it with her when she pulled away. "My heart is still yours."

"She hasn't poisoned you against me?"

He splayed his hands in surrender, wishing there was some way he could erase the memory of his adultery. "I will admit she blackened my heart with dark magic for a time, but the curse has been lifted."

Ura's hand flew to her throat. "Words cannot describe my relief."

"Forgive me. I was not myself. I kissed her—" He hung his head as a new wave of shame washed over him. "And told her I loved her."

"I don't care." Her shoulders fell as she released a long sigh. "You're safe and returned to me, and that's all that matters."

Emotion tightened his chest. "So you forgive me?"

"Oh, husband." She launched herself into his arms again. "There's nothing to forgive. You cannot blame yourself for falling under the witch's spell."

"I fought it—so hard." He coursed his hands through her fine hair, knowing he didn't deserve her.

She placed a finger on his lips. "Let us not speak of the past again when we have so much to look forward to in the future."

He clutched his bride, searching her eyes. How in Elements did he deserve such a loving wife? "I love you, Ura, and only you."

"I love you, Markus." She looked up at him with heartfelt eyes. "I'll always love you."

LATER THAT NIGHT ALEC, Markus, and Des were with Dianna when she married Simeon. Kyan officiated. After blessing their union, Kyan threw sparks of magic into the air, lighting the sky with myriad colors. Everyone laughed when the sparks dissipated and flower petals fell on their heads. The dwarves picked up their instruments, and Dianna danced the rest of the night with her husband and brothers while passing around goblets of wine and platters of food.

She had wished the Elementals had joined in their revelry, but they refused to leave their home in Ice Mountain, insisting on a year of mourning for Kia. Though she was sad at the loss of the sister she never knew, she also had much to be thankful for. The celebration in Aya-Shay lasted two straight days and nights before the benevolent goddesses decided it was time to fly back to the Shifting Sands.

Before leaving, Kyan negotiated a pact between the dwarves and giants, allowing the giant children the option of staying or returning home with their biological kin. All giants save for Borg decided to remain with the dwarves, and Kyan promised them she'd return every spring to fertilize their soil, so they could continue to feed their adopted children. As their deity, Kyan said it was her duty to ensure the dwarves lived in comfort and safety. Besides, she'd need to check on her sons, who'd both disappeared sometime during the festivities, no doubt in search of the stones, not remembering they had been found and restored.

Before Lydra followed her mate to the Shifting Sands, Dianna said goodbye to the ice dragon, wrapping her arms around her cold scales and trying not to cry. Though Kyan promised she'd provide cool sanctuary for Lydra, she couldn't help but worry for her friend. It was short-lived, though, when Tan'yi'na nuzzled Lydra's scales while hovering over their egg.

Dianna and Sindri shared emotional goodbyes as well, both promising to write to one another. Kyan assured them she'd reopen trade routes between the Shifting Sands and Aloa-Shay.

She watched her aunt and cousins fly away with joy in her heart, for she knew the goddesses would ensure safety and happiness for generations to come. Should she and Simeon be blessed with children, they'd grow up without fear of being persecuted for their magic.

Walking hand-in-hand, she and Simeon strolled through the town, squinting at the brilliant morning sky while smiling and waving to passersby. They found her brothers at Zier's spacious cottage, sitting by the hearth, breaking their fast. Luckily, Ryne wasn't with them. He'd disappeared before the wedding, and she hadn't seen him since. Not that she missed his scowling face.

She leaned over Des, who was sleeping soundly on his cot, and kissed his cheek, sticky with sugar and berries. Then she and Simeon took a seat beside her brothers, gladly accepting offerings of palma juice, and fresh meat and berry pies.

"Now what?" Alec asked, leaning against a bench, his sleeping wife in his arms.

"Ura and I are returning to Adolan." Markus smiled at his wife, who was licking her fingers after greedily eating a pie. "We're bringing her brother and father with us. Won't you come, too? We can all build homes on Father's land."

Dianna shared a look with Simeon, knowing already what the answer would be, for they'd discussed the future on their honeymoon night—a future that Simeon insisted be without Ryne. Dianna had agreed, as long as she wasn't too far from her brothers.

"Simeon prefers a warmer climate," she said, "and I love the ocean. We were thinking of making our home in Aloa-Shay. We've sent a letter with Sindri to Simeon's sister, Jae, asking her and her betrothed to join us."

Alec sat up, beaming. "You can build a home near us."

Markus looked from Dianna to Alec as if they'd shot him in the heart with poisoned arrows. "You're leaving Adolan, too, brother?"

"I'm able to breathe by the sea." Alec nodded at his sleeping wife. "And I do not wish to take Mari from her home."

Markus's shoulders fell. "Then I suppose this is goodbye."

"Not forever," Alec said. "You and Ura's family can visit us during Adolan's harsh winters."

Dianna elbowed Simeon when he grumbled. "They'll stay with Alec," she whispered.

"And we will visit you during the summer," Alec added, "so make sure the home you build is a big one."

She would visit her brother in Adolan, even if Ryne lived with him. Simeon would have to put up with the blue broot for a few days every year.

Markus grinned. "Do you plan on having big families?"

Alec eagerly nodded. "Absolutely."

Dianna and Simeon shared covert glances as heat crept into her cheeks. "I pray to the Elements we do."

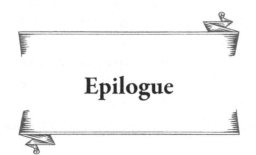

Epilogue

"Mommy! Mommy! Look what I grew."

Kyana skipped into the hearth room, holding up a fresh bouquet of flowers, and Dianna took her daughter in her arms, kissing her smooth cheek.

"Beautiful, Kyana. It's just what I needed." She took the flowers and slipped a pink one behind her ear, then wove a vine of orange bells into Kyana's thick hair. The flowers were a stunning compliment to her blonde curls, golden eyes, and olive skin. "Kyana, darling?" She tapped her daughter's button nose. "Could you grow us some of those delicious green beans? Uncle Zier is coming for supper. Aunt Jae and Uncle Kerr will be joining us, too."

Simeon strode into the room, carrying baby Rowlena while a gaggle of giggling little girls ran circles around his legs.

"Girls, go help your sister pick them," he said. "Ask Uncle Des to help."

"Yes, Daddy," the girls said in unison, obediently obeying their father with cheery smiles. The warm Aloa-Shay sea breeze and the pungent smells of the ocean carried into the room when they flung open the door and ran out.

Even though when Simeon had used dark magic to tether their souls, it should've weakened his magical ability to charm, he still turned heads wherever he went, and he had sway with his five daughters. Had she been a jealous mother, Dianna would've been bothered by the way they doted on him, but having experienced her own mother's vindictive jealousy, she wanted her daughters to know only love and compassion from her. And she did love her family so. They put so much happiness in her heart, washing away painful memories and creating joyful ones.

"How's Mari?" Simeon asked, handing Rowlena to her.

"Fine." She balanced Rowlena on her hip, not surprised when the baby reached for the flower in her hair. "She's not in labor. The baby was just stretching." She handed the flower to her daughter, then planted a gentle kiss on her forehead before digging two letters out of her vest pocket.

"What are those?" Simeon asked.

"Zier delivered them." She held up the parchment with a smile. She was anxious to hear the latest news from Markus and Sindri.

Simeon arched a brow and bit into a piece of palma fruit. "Where is the trader?"

She leaned into her husband, wiping a trickle of juice off his chin. "He's still visiting Alec's family, but I invited him to stay the night when he's finished."

Simeon nodded to the letters. "Well, are you going to read them?"

"Of course!" She eagerly tore into Markus's letter first. It wasn't often her brother found the time to write, with the responsibility of teaching three young sons how to hunt and fish the wilds of Adolan while also preserving the forest creatures for future generations.

She scanned the letter, then frowned, a feeling of dread racing through her veins like liquid sludge. "Oh, no," she groaned, slumping into a nearby chair while Rowlena tried to tear the parchment from her hands.

Simeon sat beside her. "What is it?"

"Markus's family is coming for a visit next month."

A quizzical smile tugged at his mouth. "But you enjoy his visits, and the girls love playing with their cousins."

She eyed him with a smirk. "They're also bringing Ryne."

Simeon blinked hard, as if he was waiting for her to pinch his leg and tell him she was only jesting. "Good time for the girls and me to visit my family in the Shifting Sands."

"Don't you dare." She waved the letter in his face. "Ryne's got a new wife, and it's your turn to break up their marital fights."

He swore. "Wife number three?"

"Or four." Dianna shifted Rowlena, gently rubbing the baby's back when she rested a chubby cheek on her shoulder. "I can't keep up. Hopefully this wife doesn't run off with a sand dweller, too."

He rolled his eyes. "Maybe if he was nicer."

She couldn't help laughing. "That's like asking Tan'yi'na to breathe ice."

He nodded at the other piece of parchment in her hand. "What does Sindri say?"

She popped the seal. "Kyan and her daughters will be visiting my sisters this fall." She quickly read the news from The Shifting Sands. "Kyan's garden is bigger than ever. Oh," she squealed. "Little Amar is breathing blue fire." She loved getting updates on Lydra and Tan'yi'na's hatchling. When she got to the last line, she threw down the letter. "They want me to act as liaison when they visit Ice Mountain." Even though Kyan and her daughters appeared to get along well with the Elementals, there was tension between them. Mayhap a lingering thread of animosity left behind by Madhea. Meetings between the Land and Sky Goddesses had always been awkward, and they relied on Dianna to bridge any gaps left behind by Madhea's taint.

He shook his head. "One of these days, they will have to conduct their meetings without you."

"I think this little mite is ready for a nap." She smiled at her baby, who was struggling to keep her large green eyes open.

Simeon followed her as she carried the baby into the nursery. She stepped over wooden toy dragons Zier had whittled for the girls and pushed aside a golden-eyed, dark-skinned doll with her foot. Then she laid little Rowlena in her crib. She shut her eyes and snuggled with the quilt Mari had stitched for her.

He leaned over the crib, kissing his daughter on the cheek. "She's been sleeping more soundly since the Mother's Blessing."

"It's worked wonders for all our daughters." She brushed her hip against his, winking at him. "Hopefully, it will work for the next one."

He took her hand in his. "The next one?"

"Aye." She smiled. "Another girl." She still didn't understand how her intuition worked, but she'd accurately guessed the sex, eye color, and magical gifts of each of her children. Elements save them all, daughter number six would be born with Simeon's golden eyes and persuasive charms. She suspected this child would wrap mother, father, and the rest of the family around her little finger.

"Daughter number six. He laughed, pulling her out of the room. "We're creating our own family coven."

"I know." She wrapped her arms around his neck and leaned up on her tiptoes for a kiss. "And I couldn't be happier."

The End

For more books by Tara West visit www.tarawest.com

GLOSSARY

A dolan – A village below the glacier, and far below the peak of Ice Mountain.

Alec – Brother to Markus and Dianna.

Aletha – One of Kyan's daughters turned to stone.

Aloa-Shay – A seaside village, several weeks' journey from Adolan.

Ariette – An Elemental, she is Madhea's daughter and Kia's sister.

Aya-Shay – The dwarf village by the sea.

Bane Eryll – Oldest son of Elof Eryll. Outed for cowardice.

Borg – Adopted Giant son of King Hogbottom.

Brendle – Desryn's little dog.

Broot – A large horned whale

Carnivus – Man-eating plants created by Eris that grow beneath the ocean.

Cotulla Blossoms – Common flowers to the region of Adolan and Werewood Forest.

Dafuar – Ancient prophet and son of the fallen Goddess, Kyan. He dwells in Adolan and his twin brother is Odu.

Dalia – One of Kyan's daughters turned to stone.

The Danae – A stream beside Adolan. It branches off from The Danae River, which flows beneath the glacier.

Desryn (Des) – Younger brother to Dianna, the witch huntress.

Dianna – A young witch, secret daughter of Madhea and half-sister to Markus and Alec. Dianna is a foster sister to Desryn, whom she has cared for since their parents died.

Dragon's Tooth – A large 'spiked' tower of ice.

The Elementals – Daughters of the Elements and of the goddesses. Six Elementals serve Madhea and six served Eris.

The Elements – The creators of Tehra, and the source of magic for the witches and Goddesses.

Eris – Goddess of the Sea. Also known as the sea witch, she was Madhea's sister.

Feira – Granddaughter to Kyan and daughter of Odu. She ruled the Shifting Sands in her grandmother's absence.

Gargoyles – Flying demon creatures as large as humans.

Gnull – Large predatory ice creatures (think prehistoric walrus) that are very dangerous and a threat to the Ice People. However, they are prized for their blubbery oil, which is used as candle tallow. Gnull fur is used for clothing, and their bones are used for weapons and crafting boats.

Gorpat – The dwarf Grim's giant daughter.

Grimley (Grim) – Gorpat's dwarf father.

Ice Kingdom – City within the glacier.

Ice Mites – Light bugs that dwell in frozen crystals, giving the ice formations a glowing appearance.

Ice Mountain – A towering column of ice that stretches beyond the Heavens, built by Madhea as a shrine to herself. She dwells at the top of Ice Mountain with her daughters, the Elementals.

Ice Shield – A thin layer of ice shielding Ice Kingdom from the outside world.

Ingred Johan – Council chieftain. Her son was Ven Jonan.

Jon Nordlund – Kind ice dweller, and father to Ura and Ryne.

Jae (Ghost) – Simeon's non-magical twin.

Jae – The girl the Elementals had switched Dianna with at birth. She was killed by Madhea in book one.

Jon Nordlund – Kind ice dweller, and father to Ura and Ryne.

Khashka – Mari's father who died in book two.

Kia – An Elemental, she is Madhea's daughter and Ariette's sister.

Kicelin – Village at the base of Ice Mountain.

King Furbald – The unpleasant dwarf king.

King Munluc – King of the giants.

Kraehn – Fanged fish that dwell beneath the icy river. They devour just about anything, even people, in a matter of moments.

Lazy Eyed Serpents – Ugly, long eel-like fish. Though their meat is soft and slimy, serpents are the main food source for the ice dwellers.

Liam – An ice dweller. Ryne's friend.

Losna – One of Madhea's Elemental daughters.

Lydra – Madhea's (now Dianna's) dragon, which breathes impenetrable ice.

Lyme tree – A tree large enough for a gathering hall to be built within its branches. Found at the base of the mountain and surrounding the village of Adolan.

Madhea – The Ice Witch. An evil goddess sometimes referred to as the Sky Goddess.

Mari- The young spirit girl whose body was taken by Eris. Alec's love interest.

Markus – The hunter who brought on The Hunter's Curse. He is the son of Rowlen and brother of Alec and husband to Ura.

Matron Thisben – The baker from Adolan.

Metis – One of Kyan's daughters turned to stone.

Neriphene – One of Kyan's daughters turned to stone.

Odu – Ancient prophet and son of the fallen Goddess, Kyan. Twin brother to

Orhan (O-Ran) – Kyan's mortal husband, and father to Odu, Dafuar, and their six daughters.

Palma fruit – Delicious fruit that grows in Aloa-Shay. Think of a cross between a mango and a coconut.

Pixies – Small, flying, fanged creatures with razor-sharp teeth, long claws and red eyes. With a penchant for creating mischief and an appetite for blood, they answer to the bidding of Madhea or her daughters.

Rení the Wise – An ancient and wise earth speaker who lives in the mines of the Shifting Sands.

Riverweed – A source of sustenance for the people of Aloa-Shay.

Rolf Leifson – The barkeep of Adolan.

Rowlen Jägerrson – Alec, Markus's, and Dianna's deceased father.

Ryne – Ice dweller who tries to convince his people that the ice is melting.

Jon's son and Ura's brother.

The Sacred Stones (Goddess Stones) – Seven stones, each one possessing the spirit of the fallen goddess, Kyan, and her six daughters.

Salamin – Fish that swim up river near Aloa-Shay.

Shadow Kingdom – Abandoned dwarf empire, razed by Madhea and Eris's armies nearly a century ago.

The Shifting Sands – A land with a hostile, dry climate, which serves as a sanctuary from the goddesses.

Simeon – A handsome Shifting Sands witch who has the magical power of persuasion.

Sindrí – One of Kyan's daughters turned to stone by Madhea.

Sirens – Man-eating mermaids.

Slog- A creature who eats mites. Think of a sloth.

Soaring Perch – Fat, winged fish that swim in The Danae River, beneath the glacier.

Sofla – One of the dwarf Zier's grown twin daughters.

Sogred - One of the dwarf Zier's grown twin daughters.

Snowbear – Similar to a Polar Bear. These bears can be found all along the glacier, Ice Mountain and, occasionally, south of Adolan.

Tan'yi'na – Magnificent golden dragon and guardian to the fallen Goddess Kyan.

Tar – Ryne's loyal dog companion. Think of an Alaskan Husky.

Tehra – Their world.

Thesan – One of Kyan's daughters turned to stone.

Trolls – Ugly, strong creatures that feast off human flesh.

Tryads – The three goddesses.

Tumi- Feira's corpse-like husband.

Tung – Mari's disabled cousin and Khashka's nephew.

Ura – Ice dweller. Jon's daughter and Ryne's sister. Also, Markus's wife.

Ven Johan – Ingred's son who travels with Ryne.

Werewood Forest – An enchanted forest, halfway between Adolan and Aloa-Shay.

Zephyra – Head mage of The Seven.

Zelda – The dwarf trader's wife and mother to Sofla and Sogred.

Zier – The dwarf trader and father to Sofla and Sogred.

For more books by Tara West visit www.tarawest.com

Books by Tara West

Eternally Yours
Divine and Dateless
Damned and Desirable
Damned and Desperate
Demonic and Deserted
Dead and Delicious
Something More Series
Say When
Say Yes
Say Forever
Say Please
Say You Want Me
Say You Love Me
Say You Need Me
Dawn of the Dragon Queen Saga
Dragon Song
Dragon Storm
Whispers Series
Sophie's Secret
Don't Tell Mother
Krysta's Curse
Visions of the Witch
Sophie's Secret Crush
Witch Blood
Witch Hunt
Keepers of the Stones
Witch Flame, Prelude

Curse of the Ice Dragon, Book One
Spirit of the Sea Witch, Book Two
Scorn of the Sky Goddess, Book Three

About Tara West

TARA WEST WRITES BOOKS about dragons, witches, and handsome heroes while eating chocolate, lots and lots of chocolate. She's willing to share her dragons, witches, and heroes. Keep your hands off her chocolate. A former high school English teacher, Tara is now a full-time writer and graphic artist. She enjoys spending time with her family, interacting with her fans, and fishing the Texas coast.

Awards include: Dragon Song, Grave Ellis 2015 Readers Choice Award, Favorite Fantasy Romance

Divine and Dateless, 2015 eFestival of Words, Best Romance

Damned and Desirable, 2014 Coffee Time Romance Book of the Year

Sophie's Secret, selected by The Duff and Paranormal V Activity movies and Wattpad recommended reading lists

Curse of the Ice Dragon, Best Action/Adventure 2013 eFestival of Words

Hang out with her on her Facebook fan page at: https://www.facebook.com/tarawestauthor

Or check out her website: www.tarawest.com
She loves to hear from her readers at: tara@tarawest.com

Made in the USA
Las Vegas, NV
22 January 2021

16374809R00173